SOUL OBSESSION

KALISTA NEITH

<u>**Of Chaos and Darkness Series**</u>

Invoking the Blood
A Trial of Lace and Bone
Whispers in the Dark Vol. 1
(twelve short stories best savored after devouring Invoking the Blood and
A Trial of Lace and Bone)

<u>**Stand Alone**</u>

Soul Obsession

Dedication

For the girlies who would slit Prince Charming's throat before they
ever settled for a life with him.

First published in the United States of America in April 2025 by Ammewnition Studios LLC
www.KalistaNeith.com

ISBN 978-1-957303-24-6 (ebook)
ISBN 978-1-957303-28-4 (hardback)
ISBN 978-1-957303-27-7 (paperback)

Book cover art by Zoe Holland, and Lulybot
Character art by Tonyviento, Lulybot, and Zoe Holland
Russian translations by J.R.Hermes

Keep up with all of Kalista's dark realms by visiting www.kalistaneith.com and signing up for our newsletter.

Trigger Warnings of Soul Obsession

- Attempted Murder
- Biting
- Blood
- Branding
- Breath Play
- Choking
- Dubious Consent between the main characters
- Exhibitionism
- FMC is grouped and attempted SA (not by the MMC)
- Forced Proximity
- If you're afraid of heights, I'm sorry.
- Improper use of a sword handle
- Involuntary body modification
- Involuntary marriage
- Involuntary waxing
- Manipulation
- Mutilation (not of the main characters)
- Non-Con between the main characters
- Sexual Themes Throughout
- Sexually Explicit Scenes
- Violence
- Wing Play

KALISTA NEITH

Soul Obsession

AMMEWNITION STUDIOS

CLOREA - LEDIVION

Chapter One

Astrid bowed her head and slowly lowered to her knees, surrounded by the scaled rasp of serpentine bodies coiling against stone. She flattened her hands against the chilled tiles beneath the altar. The sunlight was warm on her skin, filtering in through paneless, elegant windows cascading down the east and west walls. It bathed the Serpents' Temple in golden hues, intensifying the shadows of the retreating day.

Mothers, hear me. My fate cannot lie beneath yet another male. Open my path. Guide my hand to where I truly belong. Liberate me from my father's grasp and show me how I might live in your service.

A tepid breeze tossed her long dark hair, and Astrid took a slow breath. The sweet floral scent of the gardens filled the space making Astrid clench her teeth. Fates, she would miss it here.

Years of meticulous planning, wasted, because she anticipated every outcome… except the one that entrapped her now.

For all the pairings her father could have made, for every path he could have taken, she never expected her hand would be sold to the very kingdom she planned to raze. Indignation and temper infested her mind. If she were a male, her father and Clorea's nobility would listen to her. She would be conquering new territories with her cousins, expanding the reach of her kingdom.

Astrid slicked the torrent of emotions down—smoothing them into silence with cold calculations. She must adjust her strategy to her new circumstances.

Her future husband and king would view her as an extraordinary asset, while she orchestrated the fall of his kingdom from within.

Astrid opened her eyes to the Three-Faced Mother, beseeching the marble statues. The Mothers were silent. Three motionless females, shrouded in long, flowing cloaks that obscured their faces. Each cradled a portion of life—the egg, the serpent, and the shed—in an outstretched hand.

Birth, life, and death.

The endless cycle with fate its vanguard.

A gray python lowered from the center statue onto the white marble altar and hissed before it surged past her. A choir of hisses arose at the disruption when the cadenced click of boots echoed through the cathedral. Astrid dug her nails into her palm, burying her turmoil. Her father regularly interrupted her prayers, deeming her faith inconsequential while ironically insisting her place was in the healers' ward.

Or on her back to placate the beastly king and his grotesque wings.

A silenced rage festered within her chest as she donned a cold mask of neutrality and turned. Her father had sold her and leaving her a final night of prayer inconvenienced his transaction.

Astrid's barbed words fell mute at the sight of her only male ally.

Sterling carefully stepped around the plethora of dark, serpentine bodies slithering across the temple and pews. Fates, she would miss him most of all. He'd accepted the position of executioner in court, overseeing the dungeon and game houses of the city when she was sixteen. She would never admit it, but she shared in the young females' infatuation when he first arrived. The court ladies fawned over him. He was tall with thick black hair and clear, luminous eyes the color of the finest jade.

The top two buttons of Sterling's shirt were undone. A habitual practice she noticed he performed when prisoners refused to answer his questions. Astrid had asked him about it when she began her transition from the healers' ward to the dungeons. He'd tugged on his collar and admitted, "I need more room to breathe when I extract their secrets."

Sterling lifted his stubbled chin in greeting. His sleeves were rolled, exposing his toned forearms. The metal bowl in his hands caught Astrid's attention and her expression softened.

"The Mothers appreciate your diligent offerings," she teased, rising to her feet.

"Someone needs to dirty their hands since our sole princess is…" his bright green eyes lifted to the Three-Faced Mother, "*occupied* this evening."

"Trust me," Astrid sighed, "I would much rather be in the dungeons with you." She took the pristine silver dish filled with slices of raw meat and skin and jostled it, revealing a male's finger.

Someone's been busy.

Sterling leaned against the altar and crossed his arms. "Shouldn't you be in the Royal Hall right now? You're already dressed." Sterling gestured at her ensemble.

Astrid glanced down at herself. Wide strips of peacock-teal silk draped over her high breasts. The fabric connected to an elaborate gold lotus belt cinching her waist and tied into a small, golden pauldron harness with elegant scrollwork across her back. The royal dress of her people left most of her torso exposed.

"I'd rather show it to our caged friends," Astrid said as she poured the offering of fresh meat over the altar.

"If you go into the dungeon now, your father will have my head," he hissed, as though he were her older brother and she was asking him to lie while she snuck away.

Astrid spared him a glance and strolled toward the darkened corner behind the statues—her serpent's favorite place to doze. Foxglove was an albino cobra with gleaming white scales and blush-tinted plates covering his belly. He coiled around her hand and lifted his head as she brought him to eye level. Her snake flared his hood and swayed, watching her as his forked tongue flicked the air.

"Were you sleeping?" Astrid asked affectionately, stroking his throat. She kissed the side of his head and gently placed him on the altar before grasping Sterling's wrist. "Come. He doesn't eat in front of heretics."

Sterling exhaled heavily and Astrid laughed, glancing back at him. Her dearest friend didn't worship the Three-Faced Mother. He didn't revere anything. She didn't feel sorry for him, but she couldn't imagine a life outside of her service. How lost she would feel.

"Your celebration is starting," he insisted.

Astrid dropped his wrist. Celebration wasn't a word she would use to describe the nobles gathering in the Royal Hall.

"You can show me where my talents might be useful or I'll just pick one," Astrid stated dryly. She didn't need his permission to enter the dungeon, but his input would determine how she spent her last night in her kingdom.

He could let her break a spy, or she would take the first soul who didn't begin sobbing the moment her shadow crossed their rancid cell.

Sterling pursed his lips as he looked down at her. A moment passed and he looked away, stepping into the corridor.

Wise choice.

Astrid followed him through several halls. Her skirt rustled across the stone steps as they descended a spiral staircase. Torchlight illuminated her fine silks. Soon enough, she was greeted by an ill-tuned symphony of screams and desperate wails.

Anguish she was responsible for.

Astrid was a soul weaver, blessed with the innate magic to stitch souls into bodies and keep death from claiming her charge. The Fae were immortal but laughably fragile—existing only as long as the flesh and bones which housed them drew breath. Astrid's divine abilities bought the precious time needed for their immortal bodies to heal and regenerate.

Astrid grinned to herself; her gifts surpassed any soul weaver before her. The E'lan Vital served in the healers' ward, but Astrid preferred to utilize her gifts in other ways.

"We have a tight-lipped scout." Sterling's jade eyes lowered to her ornamental gown. "You'll get blood on your dress playing with him."

Astrid lifted her head higher. For all her power, her father only saw her worth within the constraints of a marital bed.

"My father expects me to spread my legs and bleed for the beastly king." Bitterness coated her tongue. "A little blood now will make no difference."

Sterling's expression fell and he glanced away. "I…I advised him against the match."

Astrid knew he had. When she turned twenty, her abilities brought suitors from every kingdom and her father dragged the negotiations out for years. They fell into a bidding war, and the winged, war-mongering king purchased her hand with the promise of a third of his army instead of riches.

Her father immediately accepted the bride price, expecting her to bring her would-be husband into the fold. She would align his interests with her family's dynasty along with the rest of his army for her cousins to command.

Astrid's temper churned like spikes digging into her ribcage. She was far more capable than any of her cousins, who routinely sought her judgment regarding battle tactics and strategies. Her name was conveniently forgotten after each victory. If she were born with a cock, she would have been her father's shining son. But her king dismissed her for one simple fact.

She was a female.

A royal daughter was expected to serve the family on her back and if her adoring husband could not be brought to heel… she'd been trained to kill him and maneuver his court to serve their mourning queen.

Astrid had no intention of letting the disgusting male touch her. Ledivion was a kingdom which worshiped conquest. They were shortsighted and rash, living for the thrill of battle. Worse than their disposition were their additional appendages. While some admired their wings, Astrid hated them. They were beastly attributes. Animal parts; never meant to sprout from a Fae's back.

Ledivion's customs demanded their king to collect her and bring her back to his kingdom where she would suffer in his marital bed. She was expected to flee her future husband, and he would chase her, like she was a common hind on a royal hunt.

Astrid would not be participating in their archaic ritual. His bed would be inevitable, and her wedding sheets *would* stain crimson. Only it wouldn't be her virgin blood darkening the fine silk she imagined adorned his bed.

She splayed her fingers and made a momentary fist before relaxing her hand. "I'd like to slit their throats," Astrid said absently as they passed the cells lining either end of the hallway. Sterling arched a brow. "Father insists I have nothing to offer and should bend to the will of a male. Why must I pay for his army? He can lie beneath King Ambrose and buy the army he covets himself."

Sterling shook his head and ran a hand through his thick black hair. "You shouldn't say such things, Princess." Astrid glared up at him, and he returned her stare. "Can I *please* escort you to your engagement dinner?"

"No."

The elaborate meal was a veneer of wealth and sophistication obscuring the evening's true purpose. It was a cattle auction, and her buyer had come to collect. She couldn't turn her fate but would serve her kingdom in the manner she preferred, down to the final moment.

King Ambrose Morana might soon sequester her to his frozen domain, but he would never control her.

Sterling turned and she followed him into a dimly lit cell. Damp moss crept from the corners, stretching to a single barred window no bigger than a brick. It offered a narrow view of the armory's courtyard above them.

A dirt-streaked male hung, shackled to a pillar in the center of the room. His wrists were bound above his head and Astrid narrowed her eyes at the spiked chains binding his rust-colored wings.

Prisoners tended to arrive stubborn, believing their bravery would somehow win out. Slicing into the leathery membrane of their prized, yet most sensitive, features proved particularly effective. She reveled in the way they cried as she maimed them.

The way they always died weak.

Astrid scrutinized the spy. Her honored guests gathering in the Royal Hall were from northern Ledivion, a region recognized for wings that ranged in color from gray to black. Those with wings of reds and oranges dwelled in the southern territories, and while it was uncommon for them to travel together, it wasn't impossible.

She stepped closer to the bound male. His clothing was adequate but torn. A series of cuts, burns, and dried blood decorated his large frame. Astrid stopped in front of her newest plaything and glanced at Sterling.

"Are you sure he's not with our *esteemed* guests?" she asked, returning her attention to the chained male, who grimaced and lifted his head. Astrid held his gaze and continued, "I'd hate to torture one of my future husband's males."

"He's not, though your king will take custody of him when you depart tomorrow," Sterling informed her.

The male grinned and licked his bloody teeth. "Are you another one of his whores coming to stab me?" he asked, shifting his broad shoulders. "You can suck my cock instead of his if you want a go at me."

In the span of a moment, Sterling's hand closed over the male's throat and his head cracked against the stone pillar. The captive glared at his tormentor, completely unconcerned with her.

Astrid couldn't decide if she should be offended or laugh. The tied fool didn't recognize her. For the last three years her reputation had preceded her, and most males lamented the sight of her.

A flush of excitement spread across Astrid's cheeks. *He's a real plaything.*

"You will address the princess with respect," Sterling rasped, deathly quiet.

"He doesn't have to bow to me," Astrid purred.

She knew Sterling entertained company in the dungeons from time to time, but he must be catching the eye of some high-ranking ladies. Their winged companion was mistaking her for one of Sterling's moonlight trysts.

Astrid toyed with the prisoner's belt and unfastened it, meeting his stare. The foolish male's eyes skimmed across the silk bands draped over her breasts and lingered.

Males, too often, saw beauty and dismissed the threat beneath the allure. A lustful mistake she happily exploited.

The prisoner rattled his shackles as he leaned into her. "Untie me," he groaned, "and I'll show you what a real cock feels like."

"Will you?" Astrid asked coyly. She pulled his dick free and reached lower, cupping his balls. They were heavy, and a shuddered moan slipped from him as she gently squeezed.

"Fates, darling, are you a palace whore?" He leaned his head back and stared at Sterling beneath heavy lids. "Is she my complimentary fuck before you execute me?"

Astrid laughed, drawing his attention. Males were so protective of this relatively small sack of flesh, but they let anyone with a pretty face handle it. She reached up, twisting the large ruby at the end of her hair stick. A subtle click she felt more than heard freed her weapon as the smaller rubies dangled from chains gathered in her palm.

Astrid extracted her stiletto dagger, and the male stiffened. His pupils dilated as his gaze followed the point. Astrid tapped it to the center of his lips.

"The blade isn't what you should be afraid of," she murmured sweetly. "I have much darker gifts."

Astrid exhaled and tilted her head back as her magic engulfed her. Keeping it at bay took concentration, but as soon as she relaxed her hold, the power came in a furious rush. Her vision blurred, then refocused as flickering lights danced in her vision.

Souls were bright and golden, glittering through the bodies housing them. The sparkling aura was malleable to the E'lan Vital. They felt like water and reminded Astrid of painting with alcohol inks. The shining mass was weightless, and eagerly obeyed her slightest whim.

Her hands were necessary to manipulate a soul, and Astrid had this male by the balls.

She drew his soul from his legs and the prisoner screamed as he collapsed. He struggled, scuffing his feet against the dirt-covered floor like a broken puppet. The poor thing was suspended both by the iron shackles cutting into his wrists and Astrid's tight hold on his reddening testicles.

Panic lit his amber eyes anew, incited by a sudden understanding. "You're the Carnifex! The Anima Carnifex!"

Astrid batted her lashes at him and leaned back to glance down at his useless legs before tsking. Only the E'lan Vital could see the soul shining through the flesh, and her plaything's legs no longer held luster. How she wanted to impart her sight to him. Let him know what exactly she planned on taking.

The male screamed in earnest, looking past her to Sterling as she lowered the blade.

"He won't help you," Astrid sighed against his cheek.

She drew the blade over the taut skin of his sack, allowing the razor-sharp edge to do the work. A clean pull, as though she were slicing a prized cut of beef.

A second swipe of her stiletto freed the male's testicles and his sweat-drenched body fell heavy against the chains.

"Kill me," he whispered.

His voice was hollow and broken. A beautiful melody to her ears.

Astrid lifted her dagger to his chest and gently traced her index and middle fingers down his sternum. Hundreds of brilliant golden threads arced from the male's body and curled back, reentering his flesh before pulling tight. Astrid envisioned it as stitching two fabrics together, only her needlework was the soul and the flesh. A single stitch lasted a day or two among the E'lan Vital, but Astrid's bindings lasted more than a week.

She barred the male's soul from his balls and lifted the flesh she'd parted from him to his mouth. He recoiled, quaking as he pressed his back into the pillar. The spiked chains trapping his wings sliced through the membrane with every quiver, but her newest toy continued to struggle.

"What I've taken from you is lost. You won't regenerate. It will heal as though they were never there. If you don't want me returning to do the same to your cock, tell Sterling exactly what he wants to know, hm?" Astrid hummed, patting the side of his face.

A single tear tracked from the corner of his eye before vanishing into the blood and sweat smeared over his stubble. He stared at the ground and muttered, "I will die with honor."

"You will die," she said sweetly, before whispering the remainder of her promise, "*when I allow it.*"

His mouth slacked and his sun-streaked eyes dulled like so many others before him—in stark realization.

The power thrilled her, racing through her veins and making her wet. She stepped away from the broken male and turned to Sterling.

"Will you see Foxglove gets these? They're his favorite," she said, containing her power once more.

The glimmering soul stars faded, and Astrid glanced down at herself. Red dots splattered across her thighs and skirt. It was too subtle. Astrid wiped her bloodied hand over her throat and dragged her hand lower, between her breasts.

"What are you doing?" Sterling snapped, turning to retrieve a cleansing towel.

Astrid ignored her friend and started toward the Royal Hall.

Her father used her to secure an army. If blood was to be his currency… he shouldn't be squeamish seeing it.

Chapter Two

Astrid stalked toward the Royal Hall's imposing entryway. Double-beamed oak doors towered above her. Metal inlaid snakes with jeweled eyes decorated the panels. A bitter sense of loss cracked her resolve. This might be the last time she entered through these doors. She straightened her back and took a slow breath. Tonight, they would meet the queen they bartered for, and Astrid would make a lasting impression.

An orange haze glowed beneath the doors. She spared the footmen a withering glance, her face draped in shadows. They remained frozen, staring at the smear of crimson coating her throat and sternum.

"Open it," Astrid ordered.

One of the males stepped toward her. "Princess, your—"

"Open it!"

The footmen scurried to do as she commanded. Astrid stepped into the Royal Hall as the doors parted.

"Your princess, Astrid Noctis," the footman announced as her heeled boots strode across the polished floor.

By her second step, the collective chatter abruptly ceased.

On her fourth, every head turned to their king.

Her father's eyes, however, remained fixed on her. He was dressed in ceremonial robes. The same dark, flowing material he would wear when she married in a few short weeks. She would never inherit the Serpents' Crown that rested atop his long black hair.

Clorea's crown was a gold circlet closed by twin snake heads. An amethyst glittered in one serpent's eye; a rose quartz embedded in the other. Between their biting jaws, a quartz crystal reflected the candlelight, affixed by their mirrored fangs. She coveted the golden crown woven with intricate silver threads, but it would never be hers.

Daughters were passed over entirely.

Clorean succession passed to the oldest male in each generation. The best she could hope for was to produce a male heir to take her father's throne… and murder her male cousins preceding his succession.

Astrid buried the idea. Her future husband would expect her to spread her legs like a dutiful wife until he cursed her with his winged heir. But to Astrid, his wants and expectations were meaningless. He would be dead long before he could force his expected wifely duties on her.

She lifted her chin higher and prowled down the walkway created by the ornate tables rowed along either side of the vast space. The tall, narrow windows lining the east wall were open, and their gauzy white curtains swayed gently. The garden's sweet fragrance that floated in on the warm evening breeze added an air of sophistication to the room.

A raised dais divided the eastern wall, backlit by twin pointed arch windows. Two tables with formal settings occupied the space. One table remained empty and her parents occupied the other.

Her father folded his napkin in his fist and drew it onto his lap, the only indication of his displeasure. The table to their right was reserved for their guests of honor—who were barred on the opposite side of the Royal Hall until she was seated.

Astrid unhurriedly took her seat between her parents, dismissing her father's glare and her mother's pleading gaze.

Let the winged brutes wait.

King Ambrose would do well to realize this arrangement would be conducted on her terms.

Her father inclined his head as he reached for his drink. "Clean your fucking neck," he whispered through an otherwise beaming smile, lifting his wine glass to address the crowd. "Let our kingdom of Clorea welcome the kingdom of Ledivion."

A footman placed a small silver tray between Astrid and her mother. Curls of steam rose from the folded napkin.

"Asti, where have you been?" her mother asked, and Astrid bristled at the pet name. Asti was the young female who thought she was as important as her male relatives, more so because she was of her father's blood. Asti believed a female heir held as much weight as a male.

Astrid knew better.

"We've been waiting more than thirty minutes," her mother continued, dabbing the heated, wet cloth against her throat.

Astrid snatched the reddened rag and threw it behind her. "I made an offering to the Three-Faced Mother asking them to guide my path."

"Your *path* is what I name it," her father snarled, but remained poised for the masses.

She made eye contact with a footman holding a pitcher of wine. Her night-streaked nails clinked against her empty glass, and he immediately started toward her.

"The serpent guides me," Astrid answered simply as sparkling, honeyed wine filled her champagne flute.

"You will sit beside your new king and bring Ledivion under our control. If Ambrose deigns you to suck his cock…" Her father turned toward her and tapped his glass to hers. "…by the Fates, daughter, you will do so."

Astrid didn't bother masking her discontent behind a smile as her father did. "There are more effective ways to steer a kingdom than spreading my legs," she bit out, before sipping her drink.

"You are not a son. Know your place."

Astrid's temper flared as the footman announced, "His Majesty, the King of Ledivion, Ambrose Morana."

"He's quite handsome," her mother said in a low tone as he entered the Royal Hall. "This is a good match, Asti."

It most certainly was not. Astrid steeled her expression. Ambrose's grotesque wings swayed with each of his steps as he proudly strolled to his table with his equally-deformed entourage. Their complexions were a bronze-kissed brown, despite coming from a harsh and sprawling wintery kingdom. Their lands nearly eclipsed her own.

He moved like a king, confident with his head held high. The light from the glittering chandeliers overhead reflected against his crown of daggers. The blades cast shadows over his face, emphasizing his sharp cheekbones and the strong cut of his jaw. If she could manage to cut off his wings, she might find his appearance pleasing.

He peered at her as a stray lock of dark hair fell across his eyes. His gaze didn't soften at the sight of her. Kindness and affection were absent from his expression.

Astrid gave nothing, offering Ambrose the same pleasantry he'd extended. Her future husband narrowed his honey-colored eyes, and a thin line of muscle ticked in his jaw. She smirked. If this male thought the Anima Carnifex was a simpering female eager to get on her knees, she would rectify his misjudgment.

Immediately.

Astrid studied the rest of his entourage and paused on the females. Swords, hatchets, and what Astrid could only infer were metal sticks were strapped to their backs and hips. *Did Ambrose allow females on the battlefield?* Astrid inspected him again and her opinion of the male rose a notch in her mind.

A female caught Astrid's attention. The bones framing her wings were white and the coloring spread in patches through her leathery membrane. They looked like snow scattered across obsidian. The others avoided meeting her gaze as the winged guests took their seats among Astrid's people.

Ambrose stepped onto the dais, followed by a taller male. His night-gray wings were larger, the tops menacingly curved behind him to halo his sharp features. Ambrose's eyes were the color of honey in sunlight, but this male, his irises gleamed like polished gold.

The male bared his teeth in a smile. His heated gaze lowered to the crimson smear down her throat and followed it between her breasts. A flicker of amusement lit his molten eyes before they rose to hers. He popped a small piece of bread into his mouth before silently turning toward his king's table as Ambrose stepped in front of her.

Her betrothed stabbed two fingers onto the table and spoke in a rough accent. "You've kept us waiting, Princess."

Astrid leaned back in her chair and craned her neck to meet the towering male's gaze. "I was praying," she clipped.

He leaned closer and Astrid grinned up at his futile attempt at intimidation.

"I've had males beaten for less. I'm looking forward to teaching you manners," Ambrose said in a hushed whisper.

Her mother gasped but Astrid knew his kind well. The male before her was no king. He was a frightened youth who'd grown into a weak adult. She stood and leaned closer as she glided a nail over the lip of her champagne flute in a slow, controlled stroke. The onlookers quieted, impatient for the inevitable meeting of their lips. Her breath fanned the corner of his mouth, and she turned her head, so they were cheek to cheek.

"How frightening will you be if I cut off your arms and legs?" she asked.

King Ambrose stiffened, and Astrid laughed softly as she pulled away. She returned to her seat and offered an innocent smile. Maroon tinged his cheeks, but he swallowed it, recovering quickly.

Oh, does no one talk back to the King? Astrid wondered.

He stood before her for another moment then turned, taking his seat.

Astrid's mother clutched her wrist in a bruising grip, and discreetly whispered, "Asti, you cannot speak to your husband that way. You must make yourself more agreeable."

She ripped her hand away as a servant stepped in front of her. He placed a gleaming silver pitcher where her plate setting should have been. Clorean ritual dictated she take the pitcher to her future king and fill his cup, signifying her subservience to him and his kingdom.

Astrid contemplated knocking the pitcher from the table before she noticed a small spear of vegetation covered in tiny red flowers. It was placed beside the pitcher on its tray. She would have thought it was decorative if she hadn't seen Sterling collecting them. The unusual flower was a snow plant and allowed Sterling's network of spies to identify each other.

She stared at the red blooms and a hint of her tension subsided. She wouldn't be alone in Ledivion. Her betrothal had been sudden; Sterling wouldn't have had time to install spies this quickly. Did he have existing spies in place within her new kingdom?

Astrid fixated on the possibilities and her father's voice called her attention back to the present. "Pour your king his drink."

Astrid stood and moved to the other table as expected. Ambrose would never be her king, and neither would her father. She lifted the pitcher, trudging to the male she'd been condemned to.

Cruelty glinted in Ambrose's honey-colored eyes as he stared at her. He took pleasure in her subservience, and she felt certain he would attempt to injure her during their Grand Chase tomorrow. His plans meant nothing—she would never lower herself to their idiotic customs.

He could chase her father if he wished.

Astrid smiled to herself and glanced at the male seated to Ambrose's right. His features were elegant but far colder than his sovereign's. The anger simmering beneath her composed surface reflected in him. Bright golden eyes framed with thick black lashes met hers and she swallowed.

He drummed his fingers and Astrid's gaze lowered to the white gold jewelry adorning his middle finger. The signet ring didn't represent her future kingdom. Ledivion's crest displayed three blades intersected, but this male's ring was engraved with a single sword flanked by wings.

"Does your ring mark your position?" Astrid asked.

A few regions in the far West wore symbols to indicate their positions and ranks within their courts. He remained silent and propped his elbows on the table.

Astrid's rage licked the surface. "What is your name?"

He ripped a chunk out of his baked roll filled with dark meat, arrogantly eating while every other plate remained empty. The feast was withheld until Astrid poured Ambrose his drink.

The rude male held her stare and seductively licked a bit of filling off his thumb. "Dimitri. Ja ub'ju vas vseh," he said, flashing his teeth in what could be construed as a smile.

Astrid narrowed her eyes at his foreign words. "I don't understand you."

"He said pour my drink," Ambrose snapped, flicking his glass toward her. The champagne flute rattled as it slid to her but settled without breaking.

Astrid shifted her weight to one hip, focusing the scope of her attention on the arrogant king before her. With his parents assassinated, Ambrose was the last of his royal bloodline and Astrid would make sure the Morana name died with him.

Becoming a eunuch would certainly adjust his attitude.

She poured his wine as was expected, lifting the pitcher high and allowing the thin stream of dark liquid to cascade into the thin flute. Ambrose smiled, easy in his imagined victory.

Astrid sharpened the angle of her pour, and the stream thickened. Wine overflowed, sloshing over the rim with the rough pour. It reddened the table, racing toward her future king.

Ambrose struck his boney, membranous appendage against the oak edge, shielding himself from the brunt of her deluge. He rose and snapped his wing, flicking the dark liquid in an arch, staining the stone floor.

Astrid lifted her chin and splayed her fingers, letting the pitcher fall. It fractured the glass beneath it, tumbling shards and dark liquid across the dinner settings.

"Your cup is far too shallow for my divine gifts."

Astrid turned on her heel and made a show of her exit.

Chapter Three

Dimitri licked the pad of his thumb and leaned forward, staring after the female promised to his king. The princess who Ambrose promised a third of his army for.

Which meant Dimitri would have her... if for no reason other than to deny his king the pleasure of her cunt. He scrutinized her feline movements as she stalked away. She reminded him of a hunting neva, the long-haired domestic cat native to Ledivion.

Dimitri smiled darkly. The Clorean Princess would never know his king's touch... but she would know his.

Her paneled skirt parted with each step and his gaze followed the blue-green material as it revealed a delectable view of her toned legs.

Killing her would be such a waste. Dimitri exhaled slowly. He could play with her before he extinguished the royal family. Bind her wrists behind her back and have her on her knees. She would look so beautiful stripped of her pretty silk. He would spread her legs wide and shove her shoulders to the ground.

Astrid's dress tightened over the perfect curve of her ass as she climbed the steps to the double doors. Dimitri wondered if she would moan or whimper when he fucked her; if her gold belt would hold while he trained her to take his cock.

She stalked out of sight, and he finished the last piece of his stuffed roll. He wasn't particularly hungry. Hunger didn't visit him as it did others. Souls were his sustenance—he could do without food entirely.

Dimitri ate for pleasure. The pleasure of warm bread and the succulent taste of swan. The pleasure of knowing every other mouth in the hall sat hungry before their empty plates.

The pleasure of reminding each of them, especially his so-called king, he was beyond their rules.

Servants swarmed his table like ants. They gathered the settings and tablecloth, replacing it in moments. His king took his seat once more and threw him a disapproving glare. A dark laugh slipped past Dimitri's lips, and he outstretched his wing, catching the attention of the male who poured Astrid Noctis's drink.

When the thin male's eyes met his, he tapped two fingers beside his glass. The cupbearer hurriedly poured his drink and returned to his station.

Dimitri lifted the flute and took a slow inhalation before tasting the effervescent liquid. The taste prickled over his tongue. The sweet sparkling wine would pair better with a dessert than their meal.

He lowered the glass and wondered where his princess had scurried off to. The pretty thing was clearly used to having her way. Like drinking a dessert wine because she enjoyed the taste. A robust red would better complement the roasted deer he scented when he passed the kitchens.

Astrid was a spoiled E'lan Vital who developed a predilection for toying with souls who couldn't fight back.

He would be the only one making kills during this excursion and each victor was owed a war prize. The little neva would be his. He'd swallow the remnants of her soul after she was sufficiently broken, choking on his cock.

He would make a gift of her cold, desiccated corpse. Tuck her into his king's bed when he was done with her. Ambrose didn't have the stomach for his dark gifts, and Dimitri relished every moment of his monarch's pitiful squirming.

"Gather their officers," Dimitri said flatly. A muscle ticked in Ambrose's jaw, and Dimitri bared his teeth in a cavalier grin. "I'll fetch my future queen. If we are not *discussing* where to assign our troops along their borders within the hour, I am heading home."

There was a plan to adhere to and Dimitri impatiently accelerated Ledivion's timeline.

"Sit down," the King bit out in Luska.

"Nyet," Dimitri answered.

Ambrose casually leaned toward him and hissed in their native tongue, "My grace affords you your position in court. Sit."

Dimitri stood and bowed in a flourish before starting toward the hall down which Princess Noctis ventured.

Two Clorean male guards, armed with ornate spears, stepped before the doorway and crossed their weapons. Dimitri chuckled. When he'd cared to, he'd single-handedly turned the tides of war, and these two males sought to keep him from his curiosity.

Dimitri dusted his embroidered vest under his tailored coat and shot the leading edge of his wing forward without warning. The clawed tip pierced the footman's shoulder, annihilating their formation.

He withdrew his wing, and the remaining guard leveled his spear against the dip beneath Dimitri's Adam's apple. The rush of battle sang through him, giving him a heady feeling. His blood heated and an errant thought danced through his mind: a vision of Astrid panting against the wall, wearing nothing but the blood he painted the corridor in while he fucked her.

Dimitri lifted his chin and leaned into the razored edge. "Do it and I promise you'll be unhappy with the outcome."

The guard wavered and Dimitri smiled, stepping past him into the hall. He spared a look to the bleeding male sprawled at his feet in a growing pool of crimson.

"Go see an E'lan Vital. Your court is littered with them," Dimitri said, ignoring the rising voices and clamor behind him.

The halls were quiet as Dimitri searched for the female who'd whet his appetite. His thoughts fixated on her. Teaching her obedience would be a pleasure but her blatant disdain for his king kindled his obsession. She might even rival his own hatred toward his monarch, which made her worth keeping. The hall forked and Dimitri paused, scenting the air. He hadn't been able to isolate her scent in the crowded dining hall. The first thing he needed to do was fist her hair and breathe in her scent at the nape of her neck. She'd never escape him once he could track her.

He followed the left hall through firelit archways and down a flight of stairs. The princess turned the corner and paused, seemingly surprised to see him. Dimitri instinctively flared his wings, and she drew a quiet breath as her gaze lifted to the taloned points. She hid her reaction beneath a mask of indifference and Dimitri nearly grinned.

Her scornful gaze returned to his face, and she snapped, "Are you lost?"

Dimitri contemplated her disdain and permitted her little outburst.

She'll be dead soon.

Chapter Four

Astrid held her ground as Dimitri stepped into her space. He stood more than a foot taller than her—an advantage she could more than equalize by tearing his soul from his legs.

The corners of his mouth lifted in what could be construed as a smile. He reminded her of a wolf who'd cornered a rabbit, certain of its impending kill. Only she wasn't a harmless woodland creature. If he wanted trembling prey, he would not find it in her.

"Your presence is requested in the War Room," he said with a slight bow.

Astrid blinked and her heart raced in a sudden rush. Her cousins regularly requested her council during times of war. Her insight and plotting produced victory after victory, yet her name was never hailed when they returned triumphant. They sought her out in her temples, libraries, and gardens, but never invited her to their War Room.

Astrid thought of the females who accompanied her winged betrothed, the weapons on their hips. Astrid's rank and station were the only reason she learned to handle a blade. To kill discreetly before donning the mask of a stricken queen who happened upon her husband's assassinated corpse.

Perhaps the serpent was guiding her to a better life. One where she would be respected for her insight and intelligence—not discarded for the simple fact she didn't have a cock.

Astrid curtsied. "Thank you, Lord Dimitri."

Excitement quickened her steps as she rushed to the War Room. She thanked the Three-Faced Mother she decided against returning to Sterling. If she worked out her aggression on the winged spy, she would still be washing the blood off herself. She must get to the War Room before her father had her attendance revoked.

Astrid turned down a corridor. The sound of heavy boots echoed her steps. She slowed and glanced over her shoulder to find Dimitri following. His grey wings crowded the width of the hall like an ominous shadow. She eased her pace, and her winged escort adjusted his to remain a half-step behind. She didn't want his wings near her and wondered if perhaps it was considered rude to have a female beneath his additional appendages. She'd never bothered to learn the customs of Ledivion—the kingdom she planned for years to raze and prove her worth to her father and misogynistic kingdom.

Two guards stood at the doors. Astrid stopped before them and lifted her head higher as they crossed their spears.

"Open the doors," she ordered.

The males didn't budge. Their expressions wilted into sympathy. "Princess, you know—"

Astrid jumped as the leading edge of Dimitri's wing whipped past her, flinging her dark hair in a rush of momentum. His talon crashed into the oak, splintering the wood beside the guard's face.

They jerked back and trained their weapons on her winged escort.

"Don't disrespect my future queen," he threatened. A portion of the door tore free with a flick of his wing and the twin doors creaked open. His large night-grey wing waved in a flourish before her. The movement reminded Astrid of a gentleman welcoming a female.

"After you, Princess," he said. Dimitri glared at the guards, daring them to interfere.

Astrid wasn't sure what to make of him. She was grateful he forced the guards to step down, but his methods were unorthodox.

Did Ledivites not bother with pleasantries?

She'd snuck into the War Room more times than she could count. The large room with arched ceilings and stone pillars were familiar to her. She'd come here as a child with her cousins, dreaming of the day they would see battle and expand the borders of Clorea. She approached the ornate table dominating the center of the room. It had been her sole companion among her stolen moments in this room, but today, it felt like a stranger.

Her father's hateful gaze caught hers and fury coursed through her blood. Astrid lifted her chin, holding his stare. His opinion no longer mattered. He'd sold her to Ledivion, and her new kingdom would accept her vicious nature and sharp mind.

If he was lucky, she wouldn't steer her new king to conquer her homeland and offer her the Serpents' Crown as a wedding gift.

The seats on either side of her future husband were occupied. Her family and the nobility making up Clorea's council lined one side of the table and the winged Ledivites crowded the other. She took the only available seat, beside Dimitri. She'd never been invited here as the Princess of Clorea, but she would force their acceptance as the future Queen of Ledivion.

The clattering of armor and the clink of metal drew Astrid's attention. Her mother stared at her father through the crossed spearheads at the War Room's entry, ringing her hands.

"Let her enter and shut the doors," Dimitri demanded.

His king didn't chastise him, and her father meticulously folded his hands. Astrid stole a glance at Dimitri's signet ring: a sword flanked by a pair of membranous wings.

Who was he to speak commands so freely? And for his king…

Astrid expected her father to clear a space beside him for her mother. He didn't acknowledge her presence when she stood beside him. Astrid's ire only grew as her mother slinked to the empty seat across her and Dimitri at the end of the table.

Her father stood. "A hundred thousand soldiers will be added to the garrison defending our western border." He placed markers along the map depicting Clorea. "Fifty thousand to the South and Southeast."

Astrid clicked her night-streaked nails against the carved walnut edge as she examined her mother. The Queen of Clorea should be proud, but her mother sat in silence with her head downturned. Astrid wondered if her father would blame her for her forced attendance. Surely it was King Ambrose who demanded her presence. Her father couldn't possibly place the blame on her mother's shoulders.

Astrid suddenly felt sorry for her and wondered if she'd been more spirited in her youth. If her father's constant dismissal and exclusion eroded her into the quiet female she was now.

Astrid dismissed her musings. Her mother allowed this life to befall her; accepted the collar her father strangled her with. She stole a glance at King Ambrose. He ignored her entirely and studied the map. His blatant disregard stung.

But I am here, Astrid reminded herself.

She scrutinized the map between them. Her father foolishly left the northern border thin. He thought of Ledivion as an ally who would protect their shared border. She would convince Ambrose to crush Clorea and gift it to her. It would be a simple task with a third of his troops bolstering her kingdom's weak points. He could wear his crown of daggers, and she would wear the Serpents' Cro—

Pain suddenly seized her, and Astrid's scream locked in her throat. Her focus left her as her own soul's brilliance shone through the flesh which housed it. Through blurry vision, a haze of tiny golden stars stirred as though caught in a current.

Astrid clenched her teeth and flattened her hand to her sternum. She restitched her soul to her body, replacing each snapped thread as what felt like serrated teeth dragged over every inch of her. It tore bits of her soul free, but Astrid was able to withstand the onslaught.

Agony blinded her as her muscles spasmed. Her father choked as the glimmering aura of his soul tore from his body in a wild rush. Blackened veins surfaced over his skin as his body shriveled like a corpse left in the desert. His dark eyes grew cloudy before they sunk into his death mask framed in now thin, gray hair.

Her father's desiccated body fell onto the table. The Serpents' Crown tumbled from his once-proud head, clattering across the map of Clorea.

This can't be. Astrid struggled to breathe as the other members of Clorea's court withered before her eyes. She was well-acquainted with poisons, but she'd never seen anything kill in this manner. Astrid turned, following the ribbons of stolen souls as they condensed into a single stream.

Dimitri stood and the souls spiraled around him, tossing his dark hair until the glimmering haze vanished between his lips. Astrid scarcely recognized their flickering presence; all she could see was the vortex of shadows raging in the center of his chest.

There was no star-lit haze of a soul present.

His shadows lashed at the misted light, extinguishing the stolen souls of her court. Astrid could only stare.

What was he?

"Asti," her mother cried, leaning over the table. Her arm outstretched toward her as her warm brown skin withered and black veins forked up her arm like the roots of a noxious plant.

Astrid lurched for her mother, clawing at the table. A single touch was all she needed. The Queen was weak and a coward for swallowing the life her father saddled her with, but she didn't deserve to die.

Not like this.

Their fingertips touched and Astrid's magic surged over her mother. Dozens of golden threads stitched and restitched her soul to her body. A healthy flush returned to her mother's still face.

She's unconscious, not dead. Astrid shoved her panic down.

She threw herself into Dimitri next, catching him by the throat and flattening her hand over the side of his face. His soul was a wild current beneath her touch as charged and fathomless as a raging sea. Their magic collided and his soul writhed beneath her touch. She concentrated on the feel of him. Her nails dug into his throat as she tore his soul from his body.

Dimitri's back bowed, and his wings snapped open, shoving the heavy table several inches with an angry groan. He fell to his knees staring deep into her eyes as his sharp features contorted in pain.

Astrid smiled. Once she was done with him, she was going to collect the rest of her betrothed's court.

The pain glazing Dimitri's molten gold eyes evaporated, and Astrid faltered. He caught the back of her knee and stood, taking her with him. Her back slammed onto the table the next moment, knocking the breath from her lungs. His fingers now cruelly circled her throat in a crushing grip.

Astrid held his hate-filled gaze and clutched his wrist. She focused her power as he wedged his hips between her legs. She ignored the burning pinpricks in her lungs. *He must be an E'lan Vital.* Once she tore his soul free this would be over—the others would be easy prey.

She tore at his soul again and again. In her desperation, she wrapped her legs over his ribs and dragged him closer. She slammed her hand to the center of his muscular chest, focusing on the vortex of shadows twisting within him.

Her magic viciously lashed and struck, but it was Astrid who was caught. Freezing cold encased her limbs as what felt like serrated teeth raked over her body. It cut chunks of her soul free, and a chill fell over Astrid as the starred-haze of her soul extinguished between his lips.

Dimitri chuckled darkly and the harrowing attack ended as suddenly as it began. Astrid fell limp against the table. His crushing grip relented, and she choked, sucking in wet coughs. Astrid struggled to keep her eyes open. She was the strongest E'lan Vital in history and this male commanded her soul like she was a common novice.

Dimitri smiled as though he was pleased with her. Too weak to rein in her power, she could only stare at the shadows curling in his chest. They seemed calmer, *satisfied*, with the souls it consumed. She winced as pain erupted over her scalp. He lifted her by a fistful of hair and leaned so close the warmth of his breath feathered across her mouth.

She wanted to scream. To snap her teeth at his arrogant smile. His soul would be hers. She would tear it from his flesh. He wouldn't look so smug after she bound his soul to his skin and gave him to a leather worker to fashion into a throw pillow.

He drew on her soul once more and Astrid tensed. But this wasn't the desperate tearing that assaulted her moments before, the serrated teeth gentled. The sensation danced over her nerve endings.

Her pain evaporated, replaced by ecstasy. Euphoria stole her breath as her nipples tightened and heat pooled between her thighs. The edges of her vision blackened.

This wasn't over. She could kill him…

She desperately clawed at consciousness.

Astrid's arms remained useless at her sides, indifferent to her struggle. Dimitri dragged his thumb across her bottom lip, and she didn't have the strength to fight him.

His callused hand smoothed down the back of her thigh before trailing beneath her skirt. He squeezed her ass, and her vision blurred. Inky black splotches marred her sight as her consciousness slipped.

His deep, accented voice followed her into the shrouded oblivion.

"Take this one to my carriage. She's mine."

Chapter Five

A strid woke to the rhythmic cadence of trotting hooves and carriage wheels over gravel. Pink gleamed through her eyelids, announcing daybreak—but Fates, she was cold. The chill in the air numbed her hands and Astrid pressed her tongue to her teeth to keep them from chattering.

She remained still as images of her father's gaunt face lined with dark veins flooded her memory. His council had been massacred. And her mother… had she survived their ambush? Every noble would have traveled to her father's palace to witness her betrothal and garner the Clorean King's favor.

Were the walls washed in their blood?

Rage fueled her heart until its beat outpaced the horses' gait. The memory of Dimitri's crushing grip on her throat, pinning her against the table resurfaced. His callused hand skimming beneath her skirt and palming her ass. She'd mistaken the vortex of shadows for his soul.

An error she wouldn't repeat.

Astrid kept her breathing even and feigned sleep between two much larger travel companions. Her abilities were known, yet they left her unbound. The hard body beside her shifted and the rough scales covering the boning of his massive wings abraded her side.

A bump jarred her spine, and she leaned onto the male, letting her hand fall onto his lap. A sharp elbow shoved her off and Astrid opened her eyes, snatching the dagger at his waist. She swung hard at the other male, burying several inches of blade into his chest. The plates of steel over his leather armor deflected the blow and the tip slipped lower, embedding between his ribs but missing his heart.

The brute she'd stolen the dagger from stood and backhanded her. Astrid's head snapped to one side as pain exploded over her cheek. Her knees cracked against the freezing wood as she struck the floor. The rush of battle consumed her.

The male she stabbed crumpled beside her, howling as he yanked the blade free.

Astrid gripped his face as she righted herself. The golden aura of his soul gleamed past his flesh. Astrid twisted it, stripping him of the use of his arms and weapon before focusing on the soldier who'd struck her.

Blood trickled from her nose, flowing over her lips and falling onto the wooden floor. Neither of these males would best her again. After she incapacitated her immediate aggressor, she would tie Dimitri's soul to his head and decapitate him. He would be a ball she kicked around her palace for the rest of eternity.

The male's wings lifted behind him as he stepped toward her. Astrid gripped the leather strap across his chest and flattened her hand over his sternum.

Before she could rend his soul from his body, the male arched his back and screamed. Wet snapping echoed through the small space, and he was torn from her grasp.

Dimitri effortlessly dragged him away, then kicked the carriage door open. The cliffside raced by and Astrid glimpsed the tops of pines far below them.

"My Lord, no. I'm sorry," her assailant wailed.

Snapped bones jutted from his back and his useless wings looked more like a wrinkled cape fisted in Dimitri's hand. He threw the male from the carriage and his anguished screams faded as he plummeted.

Astrid's mouth went dry. Dimitri murdered one of his own soldiers. Her mind raced as she assessed the enigma before her. He wore his own crest. Killed with no concern of consequence. His clothing rivaled that of any noble-born, but his hands were as callused as a battle-worn soldier.

He opened his embroidered suit jacket and withdrew a black handkerchief. He glanced down at the male she stabbed as though he'd forgotten there were others in the carriage with him.

"Leave us," he grated as he meticulously wiped the blood from his hand.

To Astrid's surprise, the wounded male didn't object. His voice cracked as he quickly muttered, "Thank you, Lord Dimitri."

The male awkwardly crawled without the use of his arms to the swaying cab door. He hurled himself from their moving carriage and Astrid was struck mute. There were no shouts. No halting of the caravan.

Is this commonplace? Astrid's eyes shot back to her captor. Who was he and how was she going to get away from him?

Dimitri closed the door and turned toward her. "Sit with me."

The order lingered between them as an unspoken threat.

Astrid hesitated and scrutinized him through her magic. His soul didn't gleam like the others. There were no stars, no golden aura. He emitted no light. The shadowed vortex churning in his chest was the sole occupant of his vessel.

Her power had proven useless against his ominous energy, so she shifted her strategy—quietly curling her fingers around her remaining weapon.

His interest.

Apprehension stiffened Astrid's movements as she neared him. "Did you murder my mother?" she asked.

His lashes lowered as she approached, and Astrid's pulse quickened beneath his gaze. *A normal reaction in anticipation of a kill,* she assured herself. The heat in his molten gold stare didn't affect her.

His mouth curved into a smirk and Astrid blanked her mind.

"Not yet," he teased.

Hope and relief swelled in her chest. "Where is she?" Astrid demanded.

Was she being held in another one of these carriages? Astrid stepped past Dimitri to the window and peered out. The narrow road ran along a cliffside. A dozen black carriages rode before and after theirs, but she didn't see the garrison Ambrose traveled with.

Did her betrothed even travel with his promised soldiers? *A third of Ledivion's army he would never forfeit as her bride price since he murdered every high-ranking official in her father's council.*

Dimitri's callused hand circled her wrist and firmly guided her to his side as he took his seat. "If you want her life, you'll have to bargain with me." He smoothed his fingertips down her wrist and over her palm.

Astrid swallowed the urge to recoil and sweetly twined her fingers with his. "What do you want?"

Bargains were regularly struck among the Fae. While they weren't magically binding, it was believed to be an agreement stitched in fate.

Breaking such a promise reaped dire consequences.

Astrid considered the marked gentleness in his touch. She needed information to devise an escape. Their location, the size of the entourage they traveled with, her mother's location, all were plots and points required to contrive her gambit.

Killing a handful of males would have been a simple task, but a battalion? Her betrothed supposedly traveled with a full garrison. Even if half the soldiers had been left to defend the palace they'd stolen, she couldn't fight them all.

Astrid swallowed. Dimitri's desire was the only weapon in her arsenal. She would play her part…

Until she extracted his secrets and secured his death.

Astrid lowered herself on his thigh, sitting on his knee, as far from him as possible.

Dimitri's lips parted in an arrogant smile as he leaned closer. She nearly moaned at the heat of his hand on the small of her back. His touch glided over her side as his arm circled her waist. There was no hesitation in his movements. No gauging her response.

The winged brute simply took.

His fingertips moved higher, lightly caressing the underside of her breast. "What are you offering?" he asked, dabbing his handkerchief under her nose.

His warmth and scent surrounded her, an offer of comfort Astrid knew was a lie. He was a winter night—crisp, clean, and deadly. An unforgiving beauty with notes of warmth meant to lure the unsuspecting to their demise.

If she could manage to hack off his wings, he would be the most stunning male she'd ever seen. His eyes drew her in as he methodically kept to task, cleaning the blood from her face. This close his eyes were like molten gold streaked in sunlight. His dark lashes raised, and Astrid averted her gaze to stare out the window.

His chuckle reignited her resolve. She was the Anima Carnifex. Males cowered before her. Her anger cooled only with her plans. She would keep his head for eternity, leave him a voice. The corners of her lips lifted into a sweet smile as she envisioned kicking his gagged head down her palace halls. It was a strange thing, when she confined a soul to the head it didn't need lungs to speak. She'd look forward to removing his gag and listening to his broken cries as he begged for death.

A death she would never grant.

Astrid dismissed her daydreams of their future and focused on the present. If he was entertaining a trade, her mother would be safe for the time being.

She studied the passing scenery. The snowy forest far below them and the sheer face of a towering mountain blurred with the motion of the carriage. All she could ascertain was they traveled north for so much snow to remain piled on the trees.

Astrid rubbed her arm and exhaled a calculated breath, letting it fog. She turned a pleading gaze to her captor. "It's cold. Where are we?"

"We're heading to the southern palace," he answered.

Their southern palace was less than a mile from the edge of her northern borders.

Astrid embraced the winter chill and let her teeth chatter. "Will we be there soon? I'm not dressed for your weather."

"We'll arrive within the hour," he purred. "You can bundle under the furs on my bed."

Astrid instantly bristled but masked her expression. The only thing she would be bundling in his bed was his cold, lifeless body.

Ledivion's southern palace was the first conquest she planned in her subjugation of the war-mongering kingdom. She would reduce the sprawling estate along the trade route between their kingdoms to ashes in the snow. The cliffside road confirmed her location. There were game trails that branched through the forest. She could escape him and reach her cousin Sorin in two days.

Dimitri pinched her chin and tilted her head to one side, inspecting her injury. She endured his caress and prodding gaze. With her father dead, she would retake her birthright. If her cousins argued a female couldn't wear the Serpents' Crown… she would bind them to their bodies and leave them spiked outside her palace as a warning to any who dared to oppose her.

My reign begins now, she assured herself. Dispatch Dimitri. Kill the coachman. Steer the carriage to the game trail and block her pursuers. Unhitch a horse and escape.

Confident in her plan, Astrid glided her night-streaked nails up the side of Dimitri's throat. The corners of his mouth tilted up as she trailed her thumb over the strong cut of his jaw. Her fingers tangled in his short dark hair and Astrid's power flowed through him.

His energy was a wild current, centered in the vortex of shadows within his chest. Astrid focused her magic, engulfing his. His soul's natural ebb and flow didn't bend to her will. It pulsed beneath her hold like a purring cat.

His muscular arms encircled her, and Astrid gasped as he dragged her closer, up his thigh. Panic seized her and her mind blanked. He was too close. Too strong. Her breasts molded to his unyielding body…

And his lips met hers.

Chapter Six

Dimitri groaned at the feel of Astrid's soft lips. Her magic curled around his, stroking him delicately. Learning him. Making his cock hard.

Her scent of honey and wildflowers engulfed his senses. Her affection was a pleasant surprise. The E'lan Vital worshiped fate, a fatal flaw that would make his task remarkably easier. He squeezed her closer, possessive and intent. Astrid Noctis accepted she was his, but his mercy would depend on her willingness to take direction. He could be kind, Dimitri mused, for a sweet, purring neva. He broke their kiss, grazing his lips across her cheek to her ear.

"Spread your legs and I'll let you ride my—"

His little neva caught him by the throat and shoved away from him. Aggravated, Dimitri knocked her hand away and his fearless captive followed his movement. The point of her elbow caught the corner of his mouth, and a stinging pain shot through him.

Astrid broke out of his hold and scurried backward, sprawled on the carriage floor.

He'd been gentle, and his vicious neva repaid his mercy by splitting his lip.

She retreated until her back collided with the opposite bench. Pain flickered through her dark gaze, and she lifted her palm, breathing heavily. "I'm sorry."

Her *apology* was as fleeting as her gaze, darting around the carriage. She'd struck him with her elbow. Not a slap. Not the rake of nails so many other princesses used. He'd wager her labored breathing was meant to disarm him. To lure him closer. She played a damsel well, but there was technique in her aggression.

Dimitri licked his lip. The metallic taste of blood spread over his tongue, and he grinned, stepping closer. "You're sorry?"

"I'm not used to males being so forward."

"Do you need sweet words before giving a male the warmth of your cunt?"

"I'm a princess."

Dimitri raised his brows. "Jewels, then?"

His vicious neva's eyes narrowed to slits and Dimitri welcomed the unfettered rage burning within them. If she had wielded an element, he would certainly be at the center of an inferno.

Dimitri lowered to his knees before her, amused by the way she folded her legs to the side. She turned away from him and he chuckled. "Isn't it beneath the Anima Carnifex to pout?"

Her gaze snapped to his and he grinned. "I always research my targets, princess. Which is why," he said, smoothing the backs of his fingers down her calf, "I know you prefer your males bound and screaming."

Astrid squared her shoulders but didn't deny his words. "I demand the respect of my station," she announced. She moved to rise to her feet.

Dimitri caught her ankle and yanked her beneath him. His fingers wrapped around her slender throat, and he moved over her, looming above her delicate frame. Her erratic pulse thrummed against his palm, and he leaned closer, spreading his wings. His weight choked her as she struggled against his grasp, uselessly kicking her legs.

She opened her mouth, gasping for breath as she fought to break his grip. Their eyes met in the struggle, and he paused. Terror didn't permeate her midnight gaze. Fury, violence, and a glimmer of hatred sneered at him as her cheeks pinkened.

Such a beautifully vicious thing.

Stunningly defiant.

He licked the blood from his lip and spit into her mouth. "You belong to me."

Astrid was shocked still for the space of a heartbeat. Two. Then her eyes hardened. She bucked her hips and drove her fist down on the bend of his arm. Dimitri pitched forward, catching himself mere inches before crashing into her. Pain erupted over his scalp as she fisted a handful of hair and yanked him closer. He scarcely had time to close his eyes before a mixture of her spit and his blood struck his face.

Malice kissed Dimitri's heart. Astrid afforded him no choking sound, or whimper of defeat. His spirited princess lifted her chin, positioning her fingers beneath his grip around her neck. Her nails sank into his skin as she pried open his hold. His neva, caged yet free. She knew he couldn't cut her air off entirely. A stalemate.

Dimitri's dark smile widened.

He bent lower, cleaning his cheek with the silk across her breasts.

"Get off me, you disgusting beast," Astrid shouted.

He ignored her, enjoying the way she squirmed and writhed beneath him. He brushed his lips over her sternum and trailed kisses over the swell of her breast. His magic unraveled, reaching for her.

He was a soul drinker, consuming the living to sustain himself. He'd swallowed souls hastily, draining them in moments… not out of hunger, but because fear rotted the soul. Every soul decayed as he drank. He'd taken thousands, each ending the same.

All except hers.

There was no hint of fear in her soul. No taint of rot to turn his stomach. Dimitri drew against her soul slowly, savoring her essence. Her soul was rich and sweet with notes of heat, he believed to be her temper.

Astrid stilled and pursed her lips, unable to hide a muffled moan. *Curious.* Dimitri watched her and lapped at her soul again. She kept her breathing even, but a flush crept over her cheeks.

"You like when I drink you slow," Dimitri mused.

She struggled with his grip on her throat but relented after a few moments, hissing, "I hate it."

Liar. He took a deep inhalation and leaned over her. "I can scent how wet you're getting. Should I spread your legs and prove I'm right?"

Her heel stabbed into the wooden floor, uncomfortably close to his leg. Dimitri made a show of turning to glance behind him before returning to her. "Such a vicious neva. Don't the E'lan Vital worship fate?"

"What's your point?" Astrid bit out.

"You're mine. Your precious Fate delivered you to me. Shouldn't you accept it?"

"I am not yours," Astrid answered on the heels of his question.

Dimitri brought his wings down on either side of them and leaned closer. "You'll learn to take my cock in your throat, cunt, and ass, neva… And you'll beg me to drink you slow while I'm fucking you."

Astrid raised her elbow in a swift motion, but he deflected her blow with the leading edge of his wing. Dimitri chuckled. *Taming her will be exquisite.* He captured both her wrists in one hand and positioned them above her head.

"I want you to hold on to this viciousness," he said, while holding her still and replacing his hand with the curved talon of his wing, "as the days turn into months and you realize—you'll never escape me."

"Fuck you."

"Keep that, too." Dimitri smirked. "I think your temper adds a bit of something to your soul."

He held her stare and smoothed his hand up her side before slipping beneath her peacock silk. She raised her chin as he palmed her breast. By the blood, her soft curves fit his hand perfectly.

He fisted her lotus belt, holding her down while he guided her legs over his lean waist and caressed the back of her thigh with the tip of his wing.

His fiery princess kicked but it did little to stop his claw from trailing to the curve of her ass.

Vicious anger swirled in her midnight gaze. "Don't touch me

with those grotesque wings you use on your whores."

"Are you jealous? Would you prefer I fuck you with something I've never used on a female?" Dimitri asked as he removed his weapon from the scabbard on his hip.

Her silence answered him.

"My sword will remind me of you when I'm in battle," he whispered, inching the chilled pommel up her inner thigh. He leaned closer and his princess turned from him. He nipped under her jaw and fanned his breath over her throat before moving to her ear. "And I'll hurry back to you."

Chapter Seven

Astrid understood her virginity would be bought and traded like a gambling marker. She was a princess. A symbol of Clorea. A commodity to be exploited for the success and longevity of her kingdom. She'd always believed she would control the grounds of her inevitable surrender. If an overly enthusiastic male overstepped her boundaries, she would cripple him for a month or two with a mere touch.

Every comfort and certainty she'd once held cracked as the chilled metal trailed up her thigh.

Rage kindled and blazed beneath her skin as her mind raced. She wasn't going to bleed for this monstrosity, and he wouldn't be fucking her with a filthy piece of metal.

"I am betrothed to your king." Astrid had seen the golden stars illuminating King Ambrose's soul. Her magic would work on him.

Dimitri's expression hardened at the mention of his monarch and the tip of the sword handle stilled on the edge of her narrow skirt.

Relief stole her breath and Astrid shoved it down. She was far from safe. Astrid clung to her rage and let the cruelty in her convictions drip from her words. "I will ask my king for your head as a wedding gift."

A flash of teeth gave her hope, then the ground fell away as the corners of his mouth pulled into a dark smile.

"He's your sovereign, Princess," Dimitri replied, casually admiring the panel of silk between her legs.

The snow-chilled planks rattled against her back and Astrid hissed. She'd raised the stakes, and he called her bluff. Astrid took a deep breath and centered her mind. Fear wouldn't take her. Her dignity and temper were her armor. He might spill her blood, but she would trap his soul. Her pain would be fleeting and his would stretch for centuries.

He lifted his sword into her view and the fine material of her skirt slid across the leather-wrapped handle. "I have no king, neva." His tone grated her temper as the length of her peacock silk slipped from his weapon and pooled beside her hip. His molten gold stare lowered to the junction of her thighs and her cheeks heated as he took in the lace embroidery covering her.

"Ambrose made no kills," Dimitri crooned as his gaze lifted, pinning her. "I killed dozens within your palace walls, and you are mine by right of conquest."

Astrid swallowed her revulsion as his fingertips caressed her hip and hooked under the strap of her thong. She concentrated on her breathing. If she couldn't maneuver his soul, she would break his body.

His touch skimmed lower, and Astrid used the wing trapping her arms as leverage. She rotated onto her hip and snapped her leg to her chest before kicking out her heel, aiming for his throat.

Dimitri's wing intercepted her blow. The leading edge of his wing scraped down the length of her leg as clashing sword edges would. Their limbs crashed and the talon at the top of his wing splintered the wooden floor, inches from her face.

He cruelly shifted his knee over her remaining thigh. His weight cut into her muscle and Astrid clenched her jaw. She twisted her hands, sliding her nails along the claw trapping her wrists. Her magic swept into her vision. The vortex of shadows pulsed in his chest, completely unaffected by her will.

"Relax. I'll make sure you enjoy it," Dimitri said, sweeping the peacock silk away from her breasts. The pad of his thumb circled her tightening nipple and Astrid thrashed. He laughed, continuing his exploration. "You'll beg for my touch before long."

"Serpents devour you," Astrid hissed. She stared past him at the intersecting trim holding the dark tapestry in place above them. Her face heated each time he roughly pinched or tugged on her sensitive peaks. The pain woven in pleasure burned her. Shame warred with her temper. Her resolve teetered on the edge of fear's abyss.

No. Astrid exhaled. She would lay waste to Ledivion; this was the first battle in a long war.

This is nothing. He is nothing, Astrid chanted in her mind like a mantra.

Dimitri squeezed her breast, and the heat of his mouth closed over her nipple. Astrid's breaths grew short as he licked and sucked, teasing her with his tongue and a hint of teeth.

Another sensation flickered within her. Serrated teeth meant to rip and tear at her soul, held her gently, sensually caressing her—body and soul.

Her lids fluttered in ecstasy as glimmers of her soul swept into the current of his shadows. Pleasure blanketed her mind. Each teasing lick heightened her euphoria and intensified the dull ache between her legs.

She didn't care when the rounded pommel nudged her thong aside. The smooth metal pressed to her clit and Astrid rocked against it, desperate to come.

Dimitri's lips trailed along her throat. The embroidery stitched into his vest scraped over her nipples and Astrid arched her back for more contact. He was winter descended upon her. His scent was clean and ruthless, trapping her with notes of warmth.

"You taste divine," he groaned into her hair.

Dimitri moved his sword handle lower. The blunt tip pressed into her cunt, stretching her.

Astrid's eyes snapped open at the cold pressure. Her mind was clouded, and she blinked at the cloth swaying above her. Gray panels streaked in pinks and oranges as the sunlight permeated them. The material had the oddest pattern of intersecting lines.

Veins, Astrid realized. The panels were Dimitri's membranous wings unfurled above her.

Wings pinning her to the floor of a carriage.

Wings she hated.

"Stop," she breathed, fighting the haze.

Astrid had the palace apothecary make her the aphrodisiac she would take on her wedding night. She'd wanted to know what to expect before taking it in front of a male she didn't know. It had made her wet and heightened every touch, but it paled in comparison to this.

The sensation of his magic enveloped her, and pleasure saturated her mind. A moan slipped past her lips as the hilt of his sword pressed deeper. She came hard, her cunt squeezing the leather and metal as he fucked her with long, forceful strokes. The stinging discomfort she'd objected to was long forgotten in the rain of bliss.

Dimitri chuckled. "I can taste you coming."

His words tore the fog from Astrid's mind. Her captor crouched over her. She couldn't see his face while he kissed her throat, but she had a view of his shoulder. His muscles rhythmically rippled back and forth as the handle of his sword stroked in and out of her.

Astrid twisted beneath him, unable to escape. "Get off me."

"Come for me again and I'll let you up," Dimitri groaned.

Astrid couldn't move and her deranged captor outweighed her. His disgusting wings gave him a steep advantage. He'd effectively restrained her and still had both hands to torment her with.

He couldn't fuck her if he was bleeding out.

She spread her legs and rocked her hips in time with his strokes, swallowing a moan.

"Kiss me," she whispered breathlessly.

Astrid struggled to remain clearheaded as Dimitri lifted his head. His molten gold stare met hers, then lowered to her mouth.

"Please," Astrid whimpered.

His lips met hers. A quiet, untrusting, chaste kiss.

Frustrated, Astrid lifted her face to his, sweeping her tongue across his lips and into his mouth. She deepened the kiss and fell back onto the carriage floor. Her pleasure-addled mind threatened to usurp her plans. She arched her back while the hilt of his sword was thrusted inside her. Astrid clung to her plan with feral desperation.

The fool took her bait. He slanted his mouth over hers and she submitted for him, opening wider. His tongue slid over hers once. Twice.

On the third stroke, she snapped her teeth together and bit down hard. A pained growl answered her but the trickle of blood flowing over her tongue was hardly the torrent she'd hoped for. Tongues came out so easily with tools, she'd imagined biting them off would be the same.

His hand closed over her jaw, crushing her cheeks into her teeth until the pain forced her to relent.

Dimitri pulled away and a pair of fingers invaded her mouth before she could close her lips. Dimitri's golden stare caught hers, daring her.

Astrid left his fingers on her tongue and stared up at him. His thumb hooked under her chin, and he withdrew his fingers before pressing them back into her mouth.

"Show me how well you'll suck my cock, neva," Dimitri commanded. When she remained still, he withdrew his sword to its pommel and pressed the length of the handle into her. She winced. "Do it or I'll fuck your needy cunt with the sharp end."

Astrid swallowed her pride and sealed her lips around his fingers.

"Good girl," Dimitri murmured. "Now suck and use your tongue."

Humiliation abraded her soul each time his index and middle finger slid past her lips. It was uncomfortable but he didn't press far enough to make her gag and choke.

The sword remained buried deep within her while the rhythmic pace of his fingers gently coaxed her mouth. He'd stopped thrusting into her, but Astrid was still at a loss. His thumb glided along her pussy. Astrid tossed her head, protesting as he teased her clit. The sensation was overwhelming, and she grew taut beneath the onslaught.

"Are you always this sensitive, Princess? Or just after you come?"

Her heart pounded as the tension within her pulled tighter. Dimitri's magic was affecting her. She'd touched herself, had even used toys, but it'd never been like this.

"Come for me, neva," he purred, stroking slower. "Rock your hips and fuck yourself on my sword."

Serpents, devour him. She would dedicate the rest of her life to his suffering. She would peel the skin from his body and use it for a gown.

Astrid lifted her chin, tilting her head back. Dimitri's fingers slipped from her lips, and she cried, "Slower."

She panted as he relented. When he reinserted his fingers, she sucked on them, twirling her tongue over the tips. He wanted a plaything, and she needed him close to deliver a killing blow. Astrid closed her eyes and rolled her hips, concentrating on the feel of the handle inside her, the friction on her clit. These were toys and she was in her bed.

A lie she couldn't force herself to believe with the scent of a winter night surrounding her. His molten gold eyes invaded her thoughts. The feel of his mouth haunted her. She rocked harder, taking the leather wrapped metal deeper. The pressure built to a knife's edge and snapped as she came.

She gasped as Dimitri suddenly released her, withdrawing his hand and sword while her traitorous cunt mourned the loss. Hatred and shame burned deep within her as he adjusted her thong to cover her once more.

Astrid knocked his hand away and rose to her feet. She'd expected him to rush her, to grab her by the throat. She'd braced for a fight and the bastard gave her his back. He nonchalantly returned to his seat, and she wanted to shriek. She was the Anima Carnifex. Males sobbed when she approached their cells.

Astrid's mood turned somber as she adjusted the peacock silk over her breasts. A myriad of red marks covered her, depicting the desecration she'd suffered at his hands and teeth. Tension straightened her spine.

Had he desecrated the temple as well? Butcher the serpents? Foxglove?

"You bled on my sword."

Astrid's hateful gaze snapped to her captor. Dimitri held his weapon by the scabbard and turned it. The setting sun reflected over the sword hilt. The pommel and leather glistened in a mixture of streaked crimson and her arousal.

"My virgin blood stains your…"

She couldn't name it. Saying it aloud would embed it in truth. Vicious fury rushed through her with no outlet. It thrummed just beneath her skin.

"Sit with me."

The same threat they'd begun with. The same arrogance.

When she didn't immediately acquiesce, Dimitri stood in a sharp motion and caught her wrist. Astrid nearly lost her footing as he yanked her to his side. His arm snaked around her waist, and he took a seat, forcing her to sit across his lap. She hated the delectable heat of his body. The way it permeated his suit and warmed her, even though she wished to freeze. Her demented jailor pulled her into him. His firm lips brushed the side of her throat, and she stiffened as the length of his cock pressed against her thigh.

"Don't look so disappointed, neva," Dimitri crooned. His breath fanned over her clavicle as he smoothed her hair behind her shoulder. "My sword hasn't stolen your virginity. You'll bleed on my cock, too."

Chapter Eight

Astrid leaned away from Dimitri. His arm rested on her hip and the infuriating male idly traced circles where his fingertips dropped to her thigh. The raw ache between her thighs anchored her hatred and she clung to it, covering her shame.

It would've been less complicated if he'd just used her, but he'd forced orgasms on her just as he forced her to take the hilt of his sword.

The tops of snowy pines rushed past the large coach window. She would bide her time. His soul might not obey her, but it didn't feel stitched to his body. He might be immune to her gifts but a dagger between the ribs would kill him all the same.

A towering gatehouse crept above the tree line. Wind-kissed turrets and gables rose beyond the stone walls and stretched into the darkening sky. The southern palace was built on a cliff, and the forest had been cleared for miles. Her hopes of escape soared as they rode through the grand entry. There were no gates. A massive archway welcomed them into the palace grounds. A residence more than a fortress built for defense.

The carriage slowed to a stop at the center of the courtyard and Dimitri's lips warmed her shoulder. "This will be our home for a time," he rasped.

Astrid recoiled. "This is not my home, nor *ours.*"

It would be his grave before she escaped.

His hand tightened over her hip and Astrid lifted her chin as he leaned into her. "You're mine, neva," he said, tracing the bridge of his nose along the curve of her tapered ear. "And I keep my belongings *very* close."

Astrid shoved against him and stood. She'd expected her captor to drag her back down. Instead, she eyed him warily as Dimitri rose to his full height. He fastened his sword belt and smirked at her before stepping out of the carriage. Astrid stood her ground as he turned to offer his hand.

He couldn't possibly try to be a gentleman while her virgin blood stained the sword at his waist.

"Come here, or I'll drag you out."

Astrid weighed her options. Her gaze fell to his upturned hand, and she gripped the vertical bars on either side of the carriage door, exiting without his assistance. Her breath fogged and Astrid cursed, willing herself not to shiver.

A muscle ticked in Dimitri's sharp jaw, and he snatched her hand, yanking her closer. Astrid's heels stabbed into the loose gravel as she reclaimed her balance.

"You'll learn to appreciate my kindness," he said in a low rumble. He caressed her side as gently as a lover before tracing the curve of her breast. "Though I'll appreciate every time I have to punish you."

"The only thing you could grant me, that I would *appreciate,*" Astrid purred, smoothing her fingers down the center of his chest, "is your death."

He smiled down at her as his index slipped beneath her silk. The back of his finger circled her nipple, and he whispered, "I look forward to your attempts."

Astrid met his stare, reminding herself her nipples were hard because she was freezing, not because of this winged asshole's touch.

Dimitri stepped back and led her to the stone stairway at the edge of a massive, raised platform within the grounds. It rose two stories and acted as a courtyard connecting the elegant palace to its adjacent guard house.

Astrid made note of the stable near the gate house and committed the layout to memory. The caravan they traveled with was much smaller than she'd expected. King Ambrose would have had to leave most of his army to defend against her cousins.

If they killed everyone within the walls, she figured word wouldn't travel to her family's neighboring kingdoms for days. King Ambrose had time to fortify her palace, and he likely had another garrison in wait. Ledivion was a nation that worshiped war and battle. What they lacked in strategic planning, they made up for with steadfast determination.

Dimitri led Astrid through the sprawling estate, and she wondered if he was purposefully leading her in circles. They'd strolled through halls and climbed stairways she was certain they'd passed previously.

The gray stone walls opened into a hall with vaulted ceilings. His heavy, booted steps muffled the sound of hers and echoed through the candlelit passage.

The door at the end of the hall opened into a grand space. The walls and furnishings were satin-black trimmed with bronze accents. It was both a large study and bedroom rolled into one. Arched floor to ceiling windows offered a view of a beautiful private garden. Frost iced the edges of the panes and, despite the flames roaring in the fireplace, the entire palace was too cold for her liking.

Dimitri dropped her hand to shut the door. Astrid took the opportunity to create distance between them. The massive bed dominating one side of the room made her stomach knot. She moved past the armoire near the door and took a few steps toward his desk. His gaze slid over her, but he said nothing. He crossed the room to a smaller door on the side of his bed opposite her.

"Come. You'll need to bathe before you can sleep," he said simply.

Sleep? If her jailor thought she would willingly crawl into his bed, he was more demented—

"Now, neva," he called again. Firmer.

Astrid's temper coiled and flared. "My name is Princess Astrid, and you will address me as—"

He stalked toward her, closing the distance between them in moments. His hand crushed her throat and Astrid's head snapped back as he dragged her closer.

"You will answer to anything I call you because you are mine, *neva*," he rasped, so close his breath fanned over her lips.

Rage embodied her temper, and she squeezed two words past his suffocating grip. "Fuck. You."

Dimitri smiled and leaned into her, whispering, "I intend to, after you're clean and fed."

Astrid forced out a laugh and his fingers loosened. "Why not now? Do you have a problem getting it up?"

He cut off her air and affectionately brought the side of his face to hers. "When I mark you as mine, I'm going to take my time branding my name on your soul," he promised. His lips warmed her temple. A gentle touch in complete opposition to the crushing grip on her throat. "You'll cry, and moan, and come for me, neva. For hours."

"I'm going to make you beg for your life before I kill you," Astrid hissed.

"And I'm going to make you beg me to ride you harder," Dimitri murmured, brushing her dark hair from her neck. His lips warmed the space behind her ear, and he smiled. "But we can start here."

Dimitri cruelly fisted her hair at the base of her skull and hoisted her up, so she stood on her toes. Pain radiated over her scalp and Astrid threw her elbow into his ribs. It was like hitting a stone wall and Dimitri's grip never faltered.

A new pain, sharp and cold burned her. Dimitri held his fist behind her ear and white-hot pain blinded her. It intensified and Astrid's breaths became labored. She clenched her jaw, refusing to scream. She wouldn't show weakness.

It persisted another moment then eased. Dimitri meticulously rolled his fist off her throat. A thin film of perspiration covered her, and Dimitri tilted his head to inspect the space behind her ear.

Astrid tugged her hair from his grasp and stepped away from him. His molten gold eyes gleamed with perverse humor.

"What did you do to me?" she demanded. Her hand lifted to her neck and Astrid's fingertips met chilled, raised flesh. It burned and she immediately covered the wound with her palm. Her gaze fell to the signet ring on his index. "Did you brand me?"

She didn't wait for an answer. Astrid's magic answered her in a rush, and she began repairing the injury. Dimitri tore her hand from her wound and stepped into her, maneuvering her until her back met the wall.

"Let it scar, or we'll do it again," Dimitri purred.

Astrid's temper rattled. She squared her shoulders and stood tall. "I won't allow you to maim me," she said, lifting her other hand.

He trapped both of her wrists and leaned down. "You'll wear my mark because I own you," he said against her lips. "Just like you'll scream my name while I fuck your pretty cunt."

Astrid remained still. She knew war—knew he would hurt her. Use her. If she acknowledged the fear clawing at the edges of her mind, her situation would dramatically worsen. Healing his brand now or after her cousins rescued her made no difference. The outcome of the first few battles rarely dictated the war's victor.

"Is hurting females the only way you can get your dick hard?" Astrid asked.

"Should I be kind to you?" Dimitri dragged his thumb down the center of her lip. Astrid didn't answer and he leaned into her. His lips met hers and Astrid wanted to bite him until her teeth drew blood but rejected the impulse. He would retaliate and injure her.

When she delivered her blow, it would be fatal.

He pulled back and immediately shoved her into the wall, face first. Pain exploded over her temple as she collided with the blackened stone. The edge of his wing punched the center of her back, trapping her. Before she could react, Dimitri yanked her hands behind her, holding her wrists.

"Sorin and my cousins will come for me, and when they do, I'm going to tie your soul to your body and have you drawn and quartered every day during my first meal," Astrid hissed, kicking backward.

She broke one hand free and used it to grab his wrist. On contact, she willed his soul to move, to obey her, but he chuckled at her efforts.

"For someone who spews such hatred…" His condescending tone grated her temper but the sound of him unbuckling his belt cooled her rancor. "…you're always holding on to me," he finished before kicking her legs further apart.

"I'm an E'lan Vital. Release me or I'll rip your soul from your body," she lied.

His dark laughter answered her as his leather belt circled her wrists. He turned her to face him and caged her throat in his grasp, forcing her to look up at him.

"You saw the bodies. Do you know what I am?" Dimitri asked, leaning his unyielding body into hers.

She'd diligently researched his kingdom while she'd trained at the temples with the E'lan Vital. She knew every war, every battle, and siege. There were no formal reports in Ledivion but the people of the regions and kingdoms they'd conquered had claimed a Death Spirit fought among them.

A soul drinker.

The immortal creature was a fable of Ledivion's design, said to consume souls and leave a trail of withered, black-veined husks in their wake. A dozen years ago, there had been a battle beyond Clorea's borders, and it was one of the few times Ledivion lost. The victors claimed to have killed the Death Spirit and Ledivion answered in force, annihilating them.

"Soul drinkers don't exist," Astrid insisted, even as the memory of her parents in the War Room saturated her mind.

It must have been a poison, combined with their own E'lan Vital, meant to cause hysteria. It had to be.

"I do," Dimitri promised. He parted his lips and drew against her soul.

A silken caress licked across her senses as euphoria and pleasure clouded her mind. It was like overindulging in aphrodisiacs and liquor. A blinding combination that left her desperate to grind against the closest body for relief.

Astrid clenched her jaw to keep the moan from her lips. Her focus wavered and the bright aura of her soul gleamed past her skin. Dimitri's gentle current lifted the glimmering sparks of her soul. They fed the night-spun vortex at his core, emitting tiny blue embers each time a glimmer of her essence met his shadows.

His pull slowed and he groaned against her. Astrid's mind cleared and he bent low as though he would kiss her.

"By the blood, your taste." His lips brushed her as he spoke. "You'll be mine for an eternity."

Astrid turned away from him, as far as Dimitri's grip would allow. He chuckled and ran the tip of his nose through her hairline above her ear.

"When I drink slowly, you like it," he purred, basking in the intimacy she didn't invite.

"There is nothing pleasing about you," Astrid snapped.

His amusement burned her pride. His fingertips traced up her inner thigh and he rasped, "I can scent your arousal. Should I prove you're wet for me, Princess?"

Astrid bit her tongue as her heart raced.

He lightly brushed the lace covering her pussy and Astrid tensed.

"Obey me and you'll know my kindness, but I find myself hoping you'll fight. I thoroughly enjoy punishing you," he teased before pulling away and hauling her to his ensuite.

Chapter Nine

Dimitri opened the faucets to the oversized soaking tub designed to accommodate his wings. The rooms they'd occupied in Clorea had been cramped. He would've had to cocoon himself in his wings to fit into their shower stalls, rendering bathing ineffective. Thankfully, they had no intention of spending the night. His wings, even folded, would have hung off their beds.

He grinned to himself. His little ground-born neva would look like she was in a small pool. Dimitri reached for his newest acquisition, and she pulled away from him.

"I can bathe myself. Get out," Astrid snapped, with all the entitlement of her station.

Dimitri gripped her throat and dragged her closer. "No," he whispered, before inspecting the intricate scrollwork making up her pauldron. Their clothing was pretty to look at but completely impractical. Bits of decorative armor to hold silk to their bodies.

He unfastened a hinge, and the gold fell from her shoulders. It crashed against the tiles, denting upon impact. Astrid whirled to gape at her ill-designed armor.

"Untie me if you're too stupid to remove my garments without breaking them!" she screamed.

Her silk slipped to her waist, but she didn't shrink away or try to give him her back. Dimitri pulled her toward him by her lotus belt and she tensed. Her back arched to lean her shoulders away.

She was brave… until she was within reach.

He allowed her insolence and shifted his attention to the ornate combs and jeweled sticks in her black hair. Curls were meticulously pinned and arranged while the length of it tumbled down her back. He wanted to tangle his fingers through her silken waves and thrust his cock down her throat.

Dimitri smiled. He would have to ease her into that.

His gaze lowered to her belt. The locking mechanism had to be in the front. He'd studied the solid bands that laid across her hips when he bound her hands. He traced his fingers along the inside of her belt. Dimitri lifted his gaze when it pulled tighter. Prideful anger smoldered behind her midnight eyes, and it gave him a sense of satisfaction. She was his belonging; it was only right she would be fierce.

"Afraid I'll drop your belt?" he asked before continuing his exploration.

"When I'm free, I'm going to repurpose the top you ruined and use it to skewer your organs," Astrid said dryly.

"By the blood, I'm going to enjoy fucking that attitude out of you, my sweet, vicious neva," he purred.

He found the locking mechanism disguised as a petal and unfastened it. The belt fell open on hinges at her waist, but she continued to hold the golden contraption to her back with straight arms.

She seemed unbothered, standing before him in nothing but an embroidered lace thong. His princess backed into his counter and stood on her toes. She twisted to look over her shoulder and carefully placed her belt on the marble edge. Once satisfied it wouldn't fall, she moved to her discarded pauldron next and kneeled.

Dimitri was already hard, but his cock pulsed at the sight of her on her knees before him.

Astrid placed her gold ensemble beside her belt then stepped carefully into the bath. Dimitri waited as she bent forward to toss her hair over one shoulder. She managed to lower herself into the steaming water and toss her dark waves over the edge of the oversized tub.

She closed her eyes and sighed, seemingly content to ignore him. Dimitri stripped and arranged his clothing in a neatly folded pile beside her things, before bundling the yards of silk she'd abandoned on the floor. He gathered a collection of soaps and oils from the shower enclosure and stepped into the bath.

Astrid's eyes shot open. "What do you think you're doing?"

She lurched away from him, but Dimitri caught her before she could put any meaningful distance between them. He positioned her legs around his waist and took his usual seat.

"I need you clean before you touch my bed."

The leading edge of his wing stroked her waist. Astrid recoiled, futilely struggling against his hold. He brushed her hair behind her shoulder.

"Why are you so perturbed by my wings?" he asked as he sliced her thong off her body with the talon on his wingtip.

Dimitri yanked her forward until the warmth of her spread pussy pressed against the base of his cock. A flush spread over her cheeks and bloomed down her throat before settling between her high breasts. He shifted his hips, wanting nothing more than to bury himself in the warmth of her cunt.

"Did one of our ambassadors catch your eye and leave you jilted?"

"Your animal deformities should never grace a Fae back." Vicious anger gleamed in her midnight gaze. "Fuck me and get it over with."

"Impatient neva," Dimitri murmured. He leaned back and reached for the vile of cleansing oil, pleased she remained still. He poured it over her breasts and rubbed it into her skin. "You can have my cock once you're cleaned and fed."

She said nothing as he leisurely traced her nipples, smiling at the little jumps of breath she was so desperate to hide. Her apathy vanished when his fingers met the junction of her thighs. He toyed with her clit, and she squirmed against him.

"You said after I was cleaned and fed," she said, glaring down at him accusingly.

"This is foreplay." He drove a finger into her.

Astrid's lashes lowered and he pressed deeper, swearing when she rolled her hips.

"And I need to wash your hair," he groaned, reaching for the black curl plastered against her wet body.

"No," Astrid snapped, the spell between them broken.

Dimitri peered up at her curiously and asked, "I can finger your little cunt, pinch your nipples, but your hair is where you draw the line?"

She looked away. "Leave me this."

"A bargain?" he asked.

Her midnight stare met his and contempt swirled in their depths. "What do you want that you haven't already taken?"

A feral grin curled his lips. "A kiss."

She regarded him skeptically.

As she should, he mused.

Her eyes narrowed. "Define your terms."

"Kiss me, like you mean it, until I come," he purred the last.

Chapter Ten

Astrid pulled away and Dimitri's fingertips dug into her hip, keeping her close.

"I didn't say you could leave," he rasped.

She leaned in and the arrogant male lifted his chin as though she were going to kiss him. Rancor consumed Astrid. Landing a fatal blow while he was awake would be a messy victory at best. She couldn't surrender her hair ornaments, or the daggers concealed within them.

Not before he fell asleep. Then, she would stab the thin blade through his heart.

"If I make you come in the water, I'll need another bath to get your wretched stench off me," Astrid said at his lips. She pulled away again and this time Dimitri's fingers trailed down her leg, letting her go. The image of him catching her ankle and dragging her beneath him in the carriage flashed through her mind. She regarded him suspiciously as she exited, and he followed her out of the tub with the grace of a predator.

Water droplets cascaded over the side of his throat and down the chiseled dips between the muscles of his broad chest. Her gaze followed the beaded path as it fell over his abs to the base of his hard cock. He was veined and far thicker than the handle of his sword.

"Like what you see, Princess?"

Astrid raised a brow. Did he expect her to be frightened? To beg him to be gentle? This wasn't the first cock she'd seen, but they tended to shrivel when her prisoners realized the Anima Carnifex stood before them.

Astrid kept her expression bored and met his molten stare, then shifted her attention to his unsightly wings. "Hardly," Astrid quibbled. He huffed a laugh and turned to retrieve a pair of black towels from the nearest shelf. Astrid shrugged at his reflection and added, "They're not as big when I cut them off."

Dimitri prowled toward her, closing the space between them until the small of her back pressed against the obsidian vanity. The head of his cock prodded her waist, but his attention remained on her face. He reached behind her and Astrid stiffened, trapped in his embrace.

"Relax, neva," he murmured.

The leather trapping her wrists loosened and fell into the sink. Astrid pulled her hands in front of her and immediately began healing the red indentions he'd left.

Dimitri dabbed the fluffy towel on the side of her throat and smoothed the material lower, where her neck met her shoulder.

"I can dry myself," Astrid said, snatching the fabric from him. His grip tightened and their eyes met. She yanked, unable to free it, then exhaled sharply and turned to leave. His wings shot open, and Astrid froze. The membranous cage closed in around her. He bent the leading edge of his wing at the first joint, resting the heavy bones on the obsidian vanity on either side of her.

Astrid squared her shoulders as he lowered his face to hers. The clean scent of a winter night surrounded her. Dimitri was snowfall in a forest with a hint of pine. Notes of ambered warmth accompanied the temptation of heat radiating from his unyielding body.

"I'd prefer you bent over," he murmured, tracing his index across the curve of her hip, "but if you spread your legs for me, neva, I'll let you lie on your back."

Astrid's face warmed with the rising hatred in her chest. Her captor might be the latest on the list of males who thoughtlessly stripped away her autonomy, but he would be the first she killed for the insult.

She traced the vein running along the underside of his cock with her night-streaked nails. His wings shifted, curving behind her as she circled the tip. He groaned and the low rumble cooled Astrid's flush. She'd allow him to lower his guard without consequence. She would invite him closer.

He'd never see the Clorean steel she planned to slip between his ribs coming.

"And if I want to be on top?" Astrid asked, innocently stroking him once more. Dimitri lifted his head a fraction and she angled toward him. Her lips brushed his stubbled cheek, the sharp cut of his jaw. Her gaze swept over the opulent space, and she whispered, "Have a seat in your shower, my Lord."

Astrid gasped when he picked her up roughly, forcing her legs around his waist. Her nerves frayed with each jarring step and he stilled, taking a seat in the spacious shower.

He was too big, too close, and she was too vulnerable with her legs spread like this. Her captor would force her down, impaling her on his monstrous cock and relish her suffering. She clamped her mouth shut and tensed, waiting for the sharp agony.

But none came.

Dimitri's hold loosened and his callused hands found the small of her back. She eased down his body and the length of his cock tightened underneath everything she wanted to keep away from him.

Heat flushed Astrid's face, and she shot to her knees. A dry breath of laughter brushed her collarbone and Astrid held still while he palmed her ass.

He was better behaved than she expected, and his hands were a welcomed alternative to his cock. His bargain had been vague. *Kiss him until he comes.* She had no intention of bleeding on his cock—as he so eloquently phrased it. She knew he would fight her if she tried to reposition herself from where he'd placed her.

Astrid stalled, brushing her lips over his temple and tangled a hand in his dark hair. She systematically ran scenario after scenario through her mind. A shiver snaked up her spine as the warmth she'd found in the bath abated and she paused.

"Your weather is too cold for me. I'm going to turn the shower on," she whispered.

Dimitri's callused hands left her waist, and Astrid suppressed a victorious smile. Her captor leaned back as she stood, bracing himself up on the edge of the black marble bench. Amusement flickered in his amber eyes and Astrid's temper resurfaced.

Serpents, devour this smug bastard.

A quick death was too good for him. She wanted to draw out his pain for lifetimes or until she got bored of his screams.

Astrid sauntered toward the faucets. His shower was much larger than anything she'd been accustomed to. She supposed he needed the space to properly wash his insidious wings.

She turned on the spray and picked up a vile of cleansing oil. Tendrils of steam curled around her steps as she made her way back to Dimitri and her unpleasant task.

He silently observed her when she stood between his legs, remained still as she crawled onto his lap and set her smooth thighs over either side of his lean waist. She opened the vile and poured the slippery contents over his cock. The clear oil spilled over the crown and followed the veins down his thick shaft. Mothers' willing, she'd never have to take it into her body.

Her fingers circled his cock, and Dimitri tipped his head back. He sat forward the next moment. The gold in his irises seemed to glow, illuminated amidst the curls of steam and black marble like polished amber. Astrid swallowed the urge to lean away.

A kiss and an orgasm would be his demise, Astrid reminded herself.

His forthcoming death gave her comfort. Astrid let the steam warm her. The steady spray of water on tiles quieted her mind. This was the cost of her freedom. She leaned in. Her lips met his and Astrid closed her eyes. It wasn't like the kiss they shared in the carriage. The strokes of his tongue had been as rough and possessive as the sword he used on her. No, this was quieter. Savoring.

His tongue smoothed over hers, coaxing her closer, deepening their kiss as his rough hands slid up her thighs at an agonizing pace.

Astrid stroked his cock, adjusting her pressure and speed by the approving sounds he groaned into her mouth. He dragged her closer, spreading her legs over his waist so her pussy pressed into the base of his oiled cock. She tensed and he rocked forward, sliding his inches against her clit. Astrid broke the kiss with a gasp. He pinned her there, legs spread wide, unable to escape him nor shield herself from the unrelenting onslaught of sensations. From the heat pooling between her legs.

Dimitri dipped his head. His mouth met her throat, hotter than the waves of steam engulfing them. Astrid blinked, working her fist over his cock in time with his thrusts. She could withstand this. He would come quickly and—

His mouth closed over the tight peak of her nipple, and he sucked, teasing the tip with a roll of his tongue.

She stifled a moan. "Our bargain was to kiss you until you come."

His hands moved to her ass, and he continued licking and sucking, teasing the tender bud.

"Dimitri," Astrid hissed.

He lifted his head then, slowing his rocking thrusts against her clit. "I said, 'kiss me, like you mean it, until I come,'" Dimitri said, knocking the vial of cleansing oil onto its side. The contents poured onto the bench and Dimitri coated his index and middle finger. "I didn't say I wouldn't touch you."

"No," she breathed. Astrid softened her voice the next instant. "I want to see to your pleasure, my lord."

The corners of his mouth widened into a smirk. "You are. Now kiss me until I come."

His oiled fingers circled her entrance, but he didn't penetrate her.

Yet, Astrid thought bitterly.

Her lips met his as she stroked his cock at a feverish pace. She wouldn't draw this out, he would come now, and she would be done with this.

He smiled against her lips and one of his fingers left her cunt and moved to her ass. Astrid's eyes snapped open, and he chuckled darkly as she squirmed against him.

She gasped when he applied more pressure. "Bargain with me. Take something else."

"There's nothing you can offer me," he murmured at her lips.

The tips of his fingers pressed into her, and he withdrew them, whispering, "There is nothing I want more than your cunt, ass, and throat stretched around my cock, neva."

A scream circled Astrid's chest like a caged animal. She silenced it. If she relented now, her depraved captor would take the jeweled combs and sticks adorning her hair. He would use her, torment her—and she would be weaponless.

Dimitri's fingers pressed deeper, and a mixture of shame and hatred simmered beneath her somewhat composed surface. Astrid donned her temper as armor and moved her fist up and down his cock in measured strokes. She yanked on the thick dark strands at the base of his skull and upturned his face. A dark hunger lit in his molten gold eyes, and he grinned.

"Your touch disgusts me," Astrid said. This was an exchange. A bargain that would end in his death.

"I'll teach you to like it. You'll crave me, neva. Beg me to fuck you in whatever way I'll have you," Dimitri replied. Then, his insatiable death magic enveloped her soul.

Chapter Eleven

The serrated teeth of Dimitri's magic confined Astrid in ecstasy. It devoured her, cascading across her senses. Every place their skin met, each invading stroke of his fingers, his touch heightened into a maddening bliss she couldn't fight. Serpents save her, she wanted to push her hips back and take more of him.

Astrid struggled to focus as Dimitri trailed kisses down the side of her throat. She couldn't think through the graze of his teeth. The flicks of his tongue. The feel of his fingers pressing in and out of her in a steady rhythm.

Her lashes fluttered and the golden haze of her soul glittered across her field of vision. Arcs of Dimitri's death magic stretched outward from within the dark vortex churning at the center of his chest. It surrounded her, mingling with the steam, like splashes of paint suspended around them.

Pinpoints of light speckled the billowing shadows, tiny golden soul stars drawn away from her. How many times had he fed on her? How much of her soul remained?

"How long can you feast on my soul before it kills me?" Astrid breathed.

His dark chuckle answered, and she closed her eyes, silently whimpering. Even his voice seemed to touch her, gliding over her skin in dark, shimmering notes.

"I'm tasting you, neva," he purred. "The same way I'd lick your aching cunt if you asked me nicely."

The image of him between her legs surfaced in her mind. She could nearly feel the gold hoops and cuffs that adorned his ears brushing her thighs as he licked and worked her to frenzy with his mouth.

"Ask me," he rasped.

Astrid's temper cleared a corner of her mind and she clasped his throat. Her thumb and forefinger dug into the hinge of his jaw. She forced his head up and hissed, "Fuck you."

His cock twitched as she stroked him harder. This male wouldn't control her. No male would. Astrid clung to her hatred as his lips parted and his breaths turned ragged.

His eyes dilated. The black swallowed the gold of his irises until all that remained was an amber ring. His thick lashes lowered, and a heady rush of power intertwined with her lust-drenched thoughts. She might be in the grip of his intoxicating death magic, but he was just as affected.

His shadows enveloped them completely and the sound of water splashing the tiles slipped further away. Slivers of her soul floated in his darkness, glittering around them like the night sky.

"Our bargain included a kiss, Princess," he warned.

Astrid's temper spiked and the haze of fury cut through the allure of his touch. The bargain was more than a kiss. He wanted her emotion. Her passion.

She would make it real—then cut his heart out of his chest.

She leaned into her captor and reached for the fantasies she'd buried, now no more than bitter notions of a love she would never have. Their lips met and Astrid closed her eyes. She imagined Dimitri was the union she'd dreamt of in her youth.

Her tongue swept against his and he met her with a half-hearted effort. Astrid squeezed his throat, wishing she could cut off his air. He wasn't getting out of this bargain. She kissed him harder. Devouring. Taking.

His fingers thrusted deeper as she stroked his cock. He kept pace with her frantic rhythm and Astrid moaned into his mouth, desperately clinging to her fantasy. This was her king, a male who wanted more than her body and respected her mind.

The pleasure building within her tightened and coiled. She fought it viciously, even as she arched her back to take him deeper. Her body shook as the first tremors of her orgasm squeezed his fingers.

It was her king who touched her and owned her body. He was her equal and she would rule beside him, hand in hand.

Astrid dug her night-tinted nails into the sides of his throat as she came. It crashed over her in waves, each more brutal than the last.

Dimitri groaned and his hand closed over hers. He pumped his cock, and it pulsed in her grip. Warmth struck her breasts and slid down to her belly. She scarcely noticed it as her golden eyed king sucked on her tongue.

Astrid jerked away and was met by the golden eyes of her imagined king.

No, Astrid choked. This male was none of those things.

His shadows dissipated, allowing fragments of orange, yellow, and white to part the fading darkness. The firelight illuminated the oversized shower and evidenced what they'd done. What she'd done.

Astrid stood, looking down at herself. Her stomach knotted and the bitter taste of bile rose to the back of her throat. She took a step back. Then another. He'd come on her, and Mothers save her, she'd loved it. Shame and outrage brightened her cheeks.

"Don't look so distraught, neva," Dimitri said from the bench. "I'll come inside you next time."

Temper burned her cheeks. This smug bastard didn't get to win. She wiped his cum off her belly and stalked toward him.

"Touch my face and I'll make you lick me clean," he threatened.

It might be worth it if she could get him to choke on some of it first...

As though he could hear her thoughts, he stroked his still hard cock once and specified, "*All* of me, neva."

Dozens of scenarios raced through Astrid's mind and each ended with him fucking her in a compromised position. He would be dead before the sun rose. The knowledge gave her solace, and she wiped her hand on his chest.

"The bargain is done," she said, and stepped out of the shower.

Chapter Twelve

Dimitri remained seated as Astrid wet a washcloth in front of the mirror. A grin tugged on his lips. The spoiled princess scrubbed herself like his cum might stain her if she didn't remove it immediately.

She finished cleaning herself and lifted her pauldron. Most females would have covered themselves with a towel or fled the room. His neva stood, inspecting the damage to her golden costume piece, completely bare. Well, not completely. She'd bargained for the jewels dangling from her dark sweeping curls.

"I need clothes." Her demand dragged him from his musings.

"You need a meal," Dimitri corrected before getting to his feet and rinsing off.

Astrid shot him a withering glance and snatched the peacock silk off the floor. She regarded it, then the golden pauldrons that once held it and unceremoniously dropped the blue-green material.

Winter was thick in Ledivion. The thin silk wouldn't keep her warm and the intricately woven gold that was more jewelry than armor wasn't imbued with heat by a fire weaver. Her garments served no purpose beyond showcasing her station—which had fallen considerably these past few days.

His vicious neva was the displaced princess of a conquered kingdom and more importantly, his.

Astrid stalked toward the linen shelving and yanked out a rolled towel.

Such a hostile creature, Dimitri mused as he turned off the faucet. He snapped his wings in a sharp motion, flinging thin arcs of water against the marble tile. Astrid's head whipped toward the sound and by the blood, a tempest of rage coiled behind her midnight eyes.

His magic sang for her, famished for the honeyed heat of her vibrant soul. The shadows unraveled and Astrid regarded them, taking a step back. Not out of fear, but calculation, Dimitri realized. He knew the E'lan Vital could see his death magic, just as he could see souls. His little neva was studying him.

He pulled the hunger back and his shadows retracted. Astrid said nothing and wrapped the black cotton around herself before exiting the bathroom.

Dimitri dried off and idly called after her, "Don't try to escape, Princess."

"Wouldn't dream of it," Astrid answered sardonically, on the heels of his warning.

He bristled, stepping into his bedroom. Astrid walked the perimeter of his space, stopping at each of the arching floor-to-ceiling windows. Was his little stray searching for a way out?

Dimitri moved to his closet, retrieving a fresh suit. "Stay here," he said as he dressed. "There are fates far worse than me waiting for you."

A metallic click sounded between them and midnight eyes met his. Astrid stood before the furthest window and rested her fingers against the handle. Dimitri pulled his boots on and shrugged into a maroon dress shirt. His garden, like most green spaces in the palace, were walled in, and his little neva didn't possess the wings to scale the thirty-foot walls. If she wanted to play in the snow barefoot, he would give her a few minutes before he dragged her back in.

He casually fastened the buttons of his shirt as he ambled toward her. "You belong to me by right of conquest. Do you have any idea how many males would line up to fuck you just because you're mine?"

Astrid pushed the window a few inches, as though she could outrun him in nothing more than a towel.

Does she think she could make it to the stables and flee on horseback? That she could ever escape me?

"In here…" Dimitri said, gesturing to his grand space, "you only have to deal with me. If you're captured?" He gave her a sympathetic look. "You can expect to be tied to a sawhorse and given to the legion."

Astrid gripped the window lock tighter, her knuckles turning bone white.

"If you took them three at a time," Dimitri said with a shrug. "It would still take more than a year for all the soldiers to have their turn."

He turned to leave.

"This is a palace, not a fortress," Astrid said to his back. "One of your soldiers could fly in while you're gone."

Her distinction had a grin pulling at his lips. He opened the door into the hall and glanced back at her. "You'll be safe here, I assure you."

Chapter Thirteen

Safe? Her jailor was delusional. She was not safe here. He'd murdered his own males. They would offer him no respect or loyalty. Worse, she was now a trophy they would attempt to take and break to strike at him.

Astrid closed the window and secured the lock. She assessed the space again, pausing on his desk. Firelight glinted off the decorative scrollwork on his scabbard. Twin short swords lay on the oak edge. Astrid rushed to the small table and pulled the closer blade free. She flicked her wrist, twirling the handle as she tested its balance. The weapon was exceptionally crafted, and the leather warmed between her fingers. Her hold felt secure and lethal. If one of his winged comrades came for her, she would tear their souls from their bodies and hack their wings off.

Astrid glanced at the other sword. Thin, dark wisps colored the leather-wrapped handle. It wasn't weathered and the erratic, overlapping pattern didn't accentuate the lines of the blade. Astrid examined it and dread hollowed her, turning her blood to ice.

Her hand trembled and Dimitri's short sword slipped through her fingers. The tip struck the oak planks with a metallic *ring* before its deafening clatter marred the hardwood floor.

Her virgin blood stained the leather. His rough treatment, memorialized, and now mocked her.

Hot rage and shame twisted inside her. She was an E'lan Vital. The strongest of her kind. She was above being at the mercy of males. Of anyone.

But here she was—helpless.

Her eyes burned. Astrid clenched her teeth, pushing the tears back. She wasn't helpless.

Without thinking, Astrid snatched her fallen weapon and swung. The short sword crashed against the desk, hacking at its twin's stained handle.

She was trapped.

Astrid swung again, harder this time.

All she could see was the evidence of how he'd used her. Hurt her.

Astrid swung blindly, sending leather chunks and wood chips across the floor.

She hacked until her arms went numb. Until the rage left her. Until the table was in ruins and the bent, warped weapon Dimitri had used on her was nothing but mangled steel.

A wail of hurt, rage, and shame tore from her chest, and she hurled the twisted metal with all her might. Steel met the windowpane with a loud clang and the ruined sword clattered to the floor. She struggled for a deep breath, forcing her mind to clear. Her fury plateaued and she gingerly touched the unbroken glass.

Ledivion was a war-mongering kingdom. They had as many fire weavers as Clorea had E'lan Vital. Their weavers would reinforce and enchant their glass and steel.

Astrid peered through the window at the snow-covered garden. There were no archways leading out, *because why would you walk when you have wings?* She supposed she should be thankful there were stairs in the palace at all. It would have been far more difficult to escape had he flown her to a tower.

Once her jailor was bleeding out on his sheets, she would slip away. She refused to be caged behind these imposing stone walls, confined to a pond and a few skeletal trees. If a guard or two got in her way, a trail of bodies would litter her path to freedom.

Astrid frowned at the ruined desk and the scabbards she'd hacked to pieces. Dimitri would rampage about the damage she'd done, but *fuck him*. She glanced at his mangled weapon. Rage curled in her chest like an animal crammed into a cage much too small. Astrid picked up the weapon by its twisted blade and stalked to the fireplace. Eradicating it from existence would soothe her fury.

There'd be no sword—or Dimitri—by sunrise.

She stood close to the fire as steel blackened and leather burned. Occasionally, the logs shifted, emitting a plume of tiny embers. The sword rolled to the edge of the flames and Astrid cursed. She reached for the fire poker then stilled…

Why would I use this crude iron when I could use the blade's twin?

Astrid retrieved Dimitri's remaining weapon and prodded the broken sword back into the center of the blaze.

She hugged her arms and let the glowing warmth comfort her.

Minutes passed before the door clicked.

"Finally catch a chill, neva?" Dimitri asked from behind her.

Astrid adjusted her grip on the handle, leaving the tip lowered as she tracked his movements without turning.

Metal clanked together behind her. "Did my desk upset you?"

His booted steps approached her, and Astrid spun, brandishing her weapon.

Dimitri exhaled a harsh laugh and slowed to a stop. "You raise my swords against me?" He assessed her. Then, his attention lowered to the flames and the remains of his sword.

"What the fuck did you do?"

Astrid swung and his wing lashed out. The hard, boned edge scraped down the top of the blade until it met the guard. A sharp twist yanked the sword from her hand, sending it flying.

The rough edge of his wing jammed into her chest next, slamming her back against the arched window. Shadows burst from him and engulfed the flames. They suffocated in an instant and even the smoke was claimed under Dimitri's death magic. He bent to retrieve the blackened remains of his weapon.

"You did this?" he asked, holding the mangled metal near her face as though she were a misbehaving animal. The cold glass bit into Astrid's back and she leaned away from the blade. "You've stolen your virgin blood from me, Princess," he said, leaning into her. "Touch my swords again and I'll refashion them with spiked pommels."

Astrid looked past him, focused on the dark wood beams intersecting the vaulted ceiling. His breath fanned across the shell of her ear as he rasped, "You'll still take them into your cunt, and I'll fuck your ass with them as punishment."

He shoved her away and stalked to his desk. Astrid remained silent while he picked over the splintered wood. Her jailor calmly opened the large window near his closet then lifted the heavy desk. Astrid swallowed dryly as he hurled it out the window with far too much ease. It crashed into the snow, tumbling through the garden, followed by its chair.

Astrid tensed, ready to fight when his malicious attention returned to her.

Dimitri paced in front of debris, running his hand through his dark hair. "Sit there and do not move." He pointed at the foot of his bed.

A blinding rage flushed Astrid's cheeks and her voice dripped with vitriol. "You cannot command me."

Dimitri rushed toward her and his hand closed around her throat. Astrid held her ground and leaned into his grip, lifting her chin. She would survive their ordeal, and his lifeless corpse would greet the dawn.

"I am your god," he hissed, further constricting her breath.

She was weightless the next moment. The crushing pain on her neck was amplified by the angle at which he'd lifted her. Dark curls fanned across her vision and Astrid twisted to right herself. She got her legs under her and braced for her knees to meet the hardwood floor.

The impact was painless and giving. Astrid bounced against his mattress, grasping the bedding as she dug her feet into his sheets to slow her momentum.

"I am your fate," he yelled, stabbing two fingers into his chest.

He ripped the furs and blankets off the bed and Astrid created more distance, slinking from the mattress to place the bed between them. She healed the bruising around her throat as he continued his tantrum and proceeded to throw the blankets out into the snow.

"You will curl to me for warmth," he said bitterly.

"You won't have anything to eat if I freeze to death," Astrid shouted.

"It's not that cold," Dimitri answered, moving to the armoire.

Astrid shivered and rose to close the window. An icy breeze drifted between the towel folded around her body, and the furs she'd been eyeing now laid wet in the snow. She debated retrieving them.

A click drew Astrid's attention. Dimitri withdrew a broom and dustpan from the wardrobe she'd believed to be a weapons cache. Folded cloths and cleaning supplies filled the shelves while larger tools were stored in the open cabinet beside them.

What kind of noble kept cleaning supplies in their quarters?

Astrid closed the window and stood silently as he meticulously swept the leather and wood debris. He took several passes over the already-clean area and placed the bin in the hall before returning the broom to its place.

Astrid expected the brunt of his attention, but he retrieved his swords instead. Her jailor glared at her then. Betrayal flickered through his molten gold stare so quickly Astrid questioned whether she imagined it. Warriors treasured their weapons and Astrid frowned at her mistake.

She should have destroyed them both.

Dimitri leaned his weapons against his nightstand and ran his hand through his onyx hair. Astrid observed him meticulously arranging his dark strands before straightening his suit jacket. His near compulsive grooming mirrored his cleaning a spotless floor moments ago, but the ritual seemed to calm him.

Dimitri inspected himself one final time before taking a seat on his bed. Astrid remained at the window as he picked up the plate of braised meat. The food was tempting but she was more interested in the black pouch he'd left beside the gray marble tray.

"Come," he said in a calm tone she didn't trust.

Astrid's mouth watered but she refused to get any closer.

"Now, or I'll tie you to my bed," Dimitri grated.

She needed her hands to command souls, and escape would be

impossible if she were restrained. Astrid took one step, then another, and sat stiffly beside him. His wing curled around her, and she arranged herself so the thick bones framing his additional appendage didn't touch her.

His proximity took the chill out of the air, a fact she would never admit. Dimitri lifted the plate between them and held up a morsel of meat, pinched between his thumb and forefinger.

Astrid leaned away and inspected the cuts on the plate. "What is that?" she asked.

"What I eat each time I return home." Astrid glared at him, and he clarified, "Swan. White swan, if you want to be specific."

Astrid leaned closer and inhaled. It smelled similar to duck with an undertone of rosemary. She lifted her eyes, and his molten gaze was watching her mouth.

She leaned forward and carefully bit down on the meat. He didn't let go like she expected. Astrid drew back and managed to tear a small strip free, and that dick was still holding on to the swan meat he offered.

He expected her to lick and suck her dinner from his hand. Temper overran logic and Astrid leaned forward. Her eyes remained locked with his as she parted her lips. The tip of her tongue caressed the tension between his index and thumb. His eyes hooded and Astrid smiled opening her mouth wider.

She bit down on the joint of his finger and clenched her jaw.

Astrid expected him to snatch his hand away and maybe get a taste of his blood, but he shoved her back instead. His weight pinned her; his knees trapped her arms. Astrid choked as he shoved two fingers past her teeth and into her throat.

She thrashed violently and tossed her head, but it was no use. He'd trapped her beneath him. His fingers pressed deeper, and Astrid gagged as he leaned in. Her eyes watered and he pulled back a fraction.

"Now, now," he said, languidly stroking his fingers over her tongue.

His knuckles forced her lips wider, and rage saturated her thoughts. Astrid instinctively angled her wrists. The hard muscles of his thigh met her fingertips. She commanded his soul, but it didn't answer.

Astrid glared up at him while he idly fucked her mouth.

"Bite me again and I'll shove my dick in your ass. Are we clear, my vicious neva?"

The amusement in his voice burned her. He deserved an eternity of pain, but his immunity to her magic necessitated a quick kill. Sharp and efficient.

Astrid swallowed her humiliation and relaxed her jaw.

"Good girl," he purred, letting her up.

He removed a handkerchief from his jacket, then calmly wiped his fingers. Astrid stiffened when his attention returned to her. He folded the linen square in half and curled his index under her chin. Astrid remained still as the handkerchief caressed her skin in soft, quiet strokes. This deranged lunatic thought she was his pet and expected her to willfully accept her new position.

His membranous wing curved around her, tugging her closer. Astrid resented his warmth and hated the feel of his boney wings. She swallowed the impulse to bash her elbow across his smug face.

Prey at ease die quickly, she reminded herself.

Dimitri lifted the plate between them and offered her another morsel of swan pinched between his thumb and forefinger. Amusement danced in his molten gold eyes, and her silent threat hung between them.

Go to sleep so I can kill you.

Chapter Fourteen

Astrid nibbled her dinner from Dimitri's fingertips, and he smirked, all too comfortable in his victory. If the idiot thought this was all it would take to yoke her, let him. She finished the plate and when he stood from the oversized bed, she quickly moved to the center.

"Don't look so frightened," he said, slipping out of his embroidered jacket. "I'm weary from travel and the way you made me come in the shower… we'll sleep tonight."

The male was an infuriating enigma. He did as he pleased—killed as he pleased—without a second thought, but in this space, everything had a purpose. Astrid imagined he would be careless, tossing his belongings haphazardly for the maids to tidy. Dimitri neatly folded each article of clothing he removed before meticulously placing them in the hamper.

What is wrong with him?

Astrid banished the thought the moment it arose. He had a plethora of issues and none of them were her concern. The cold began to bite, and Astrid lifted her chin, announcing, "I need a nightdress and blankets."

Dimitri raised a brow and climbed onto the bed. His muscular shoulders flexed as he prowled toward her on all fours. He leaned in, forcing Astrid to remain still. The bed shifted under his hands on either side of her hips. Was this how the war mongering Ledivites showed affection? Her jailor said he was done fucking her tonight. Surely he would give her clothes.

His wings drew forward and encircled her, confining her in his warmth. The backs of his first two fingers trailed down the front of her throat in a gentle caress. They continued their descent, stroking between her breasts and hooking into the hem of the towel. The fan of his dark lashes lowered, and he pulled her covering away.

"You'll need neither," he rasped.

Serpents, devour this arrogant male. Astrid shoved his wing and abandoned the towel he held hostage. The chilled floor met her feet, and she marched to his closet. If he wouldn't provide her with clothing, she would make do with his.

"Come. You can sleep under my wing. I'll keep you warm, neva," he said casually.

She wasn't curling up to him and she definitely wasn't doing it naked. Her hand grasped the closet door handle just as the warning of Dimitri's wings, rustling across the sheets, made her pause.

"Come to bed, Princess."

Astrid turned to find him lying on his back with an arm comfortably tucked behind his head, watching her. One wing lay folded beside him and the other was stretched over her side of the bed. She recoiled instantly. There was no *her side* of the bed.

Nothing here was hers.

She stood taller and tossed her dark curls over her shoulder. The ornamental rubies arranged in the picks and combs throughout her hair twinkled with the motion. She approached his outstretched wing.

"Keep your boney hammock on your side," she said, shoving the scaled edge of his grotesque appendage. It was like pushing a blanket, the membrane between the bones folded and creased.

A blanket lined with veins, she thought.

He withdrew his wing and Astrid slowly crept onto the bed. She pulled her pillow closer and lay at the very edge. He remained on his back and Astrid scrutinized his body. He was muscular and honed, unblemished and unscarred.

Her captor wasn't a hardened warrior. His callused hands might have been earned by performing drills with swords, but this male had never seen a day of true battle. She vowed to be his first and final wound.

Astrid closed her eyes, feigning sleep. Time stretched. The bitter cold sank into her bones as the night deepened. Dimitri's slow and steady breathing marked the passing moments. She'd curled her hands under her chin for warmth. The harsh winter chilled her feet and pinpricks needled her shins before she finally opened her eyes.

He'd moved since she'd last seen him. His head angled toward her and his wing draped across his body. Astrid eased closer and lifted her hand to the large ruby at the end of her hair stick. She turned it slowly, studying his relaxed features. The soft click felt as though it echoed through the silent, expansive room. She held still, not daring to even breathe.

Dimitri remained still, his breathing deep and even. Oblivious his death loomed mere feet away.

Astrid withdrew the stiletto dagger hidden in her curls and rose to her knees. She crept closer. Her gaze lowered from the strong angles of his face to the smooth muscle over his chest. She would slaughter him, steal his clothing and boots, then steal a horse and be racing to her cousins before dawn broke.

Astrid's arm rose and fell in a practiced move. Her fist met the chiseled muscles of chest. The thin blade slipped between his ribs, slicing his aorta.

Dimitri's golden eyes snapped open, and his dark gift exploded from his chest, consuming her. Astrid screamed as the sensation of serrated teeth tore across her body in every direction, but the sound strangled in her narrowing throat.

She couldn't breathe. Couldn't scream. The agony paralyzed her.

Dimitri's wing flung out, knocking her onto her back. He was on her the next instant. His weight crushing her into the mattress. Dimitri pinned her by the throat and glared down at the ruby-tipped dagger lodged deep his chest. The attack on her soul stopped the moment he pulled the blade free.

Astrid gasped, drawing greedy breaths as she struggled beneath him.

Dimitri cruelly squeezed her jaw and lowered the bloodied stiletto to her face.

"Open your fucking mouth," he hissed.

Astrid shook her head violently and managed to land a punch across his cheek. "Get off me," she screamed before biting down on his hand and aiming her next strike at his throat.

He flung her weapon with a malicious growl. Astrid threw an elbow, narrowly missing his jaw as he roughly flipped her over. The gray sheets pressed against the side of her face as Dimitri captured her wrists. He yanked them over her head, securing them beneath the talon protruding from the top of his wing. His hands spanned her waist as he moved lower. Heavy thighs straddled her legs, and the length of his cock dragged over her ass.

His hard cock.

Astrid doubled her efforts to escape and turned her head to glare at him. "If you shove your cock in my ass, I will slit your throat to your spine!"

The unyielding planes of his chest pressed against her back and the heat of his body surrounded her.

"I wouldn't *shove* my cock in your ass." His dark laughter tickled her ear. "I would place it there. Slowly. Teach you to like it, my vicious neva."

Every muscle in her body tensed as he shifted his hips, stroking his erection between her ass cheeks.

"I'm going to kill you," she snapped.

Dimitri's hand dug into her waist as he lifted off her and braced his weight on his palm on the small of her back.

"You've already failed, Princess. But I understand why you bargained for your hair now. I'll be taking all your trinkets," he teasingly whispered the last.

Astrid could feel his eyes on her rear. He took himself in hand and rocked forward, prodding her ass. She stiffened waiting for him to hurt her.

He leaned over her again, coaxing her apprehension with his

steady pressure but not thrusting into her.

"Bargain with me. There must be something you want," he crooned near her ear.

Astrid contemplated her situation. She was pinned beneath a brute who used his disgusting additional appendages to trap her. He would take what he wanted from her. At least this way she could have some control. Bits and measures to use against him.

Astrid wiggled, attempting to get the pressure off the tight ring of her ass. He pressed harder, making it sting, and Astrid stilled. She glared at him over her shoulder. "I want my own room."

"No," he answered with a chuckle. Astrid remained silent a moment as Dimitri trailed kisses over her shoulder.

"Do you see us as lovers in your demented mind?" she asked.

"Bargain with me, Princess, before I stop pretending your willingness matters." He prodded her harder to punctuate his point.

Astrid gritted her teeth, needing something small she could exploit later.

"I am to bathe myself," she said.

Dimitri lingered, his lips hovering over her skin so close she could feel his breaths.

"You may bathe yourself. And in exchange, you will give yourself to me—"

"Once," Astrid interjected.

Dimitri adjusted his hips, and his cock rested between her cheeks again. He braced himself on his forearms over her and purred, "Each time you bathe yourself, you will give yourself to me."

Astrid deliberated his words then added an additional stipulation. "And you will allow me correspondence with my cousins."

"Begging them to save you will only usher them to their graves," he said sweetly as he kissed her spine. "You will never be free of me."

Astrid clung to her rage. She would shape his obsession into a weapon she could use against him. "Do we have a bargain?"

"We have a bargain," he answered and lifted off her.

Astrid sat and rubbed her wrists. "Your boney talon cut me," she hissed, healing the lacerations.

"You would be uninjured if you didn't struggle," he said idly as he opened the top drawer of his nightstand.

I wouldn't be injured if you weren't such an asshole, Astrid thought as she studied his chest. She'd struck his heart—felt the blade slide between his ribs. The expanse of muscle over his broad chest was clean and whole. His shadowed death magic siphoned her essence to heal him. Which meant her next strike must be distanced.

She glanced away when Dimitri turned to her. He set a small, circular tin beside the pouch he'd carried in with her meal on the oak nightstand. He turned it over and three metal cylinders with flared bases fell into his hand.

"I'll start you off easy," he said with a grin.

Heat rushed to Astrid's face as Dimitri arranged the devices in a neat row. They were each of different thickness, the smallest still wider than his thumb. He picked up the metallic container and unscrewed the top, turning toward her.

No, no, no. She knew exactly what that was. Astrid pulled further away. "You are *not* sticking that in me."

Dimitri chuckled and circled the pad of his index and middle finger in the clear viscous fluid. "You'll enjoy it if you're prepared. I'll enjoy your screams if you're not..."

Astrid's gaze shot to the phallic metal placed innocently on his nightstand. The second was twice the girth of the first and the third. It was nearly as thick as his cock.

"Come here and turn around, neva," he instructed from the edge of the bed.

When Astrid didn't immediately obey, he grinned and said, "I had these made especially for you since you don't want anything I've used on my... 'whores,' I believe you called them."

Astrid didn't want the length of metal shoved inside her. She didn't want him or his touch. He should be dead. Her dagger struck true, but there wasn't even blood on the sheets. The vortex of shadows churning at the center of his chest saved him.

She silently weighed her options for the space of a heartbeat. The outcome remained the same whether she fought him or played into his stubborn fixation. He would claim her body. It was inevitable. With her bargain in place, she would at least be able to write her cousins.

Astrid swallowed her pride and crawled toward him.

Chapter Fifteen

Dimitri stifled a groan as Astrid slowly leaned onto her hands. She placed one in front of the other and crawled toward him. Her movements were elegant and controlled —completely at odds with the calculation and rage burning in her midnight gaze.

He imagined her lips around his cock and wondered if she would stare up at him with the same intensity.

His attention rose to the elaborate combs and golden sticks arranged in her hair. His princess gracefully turned at the edge of the bed and sat back on her heels.

How cute.

A part of him wanted her ass in the air and her shoulders on the bed. He wanted her desperate and begging for his cock, giving him anything he desired. A grin spread over his lips as he soothed the impulse.

This small female had stabbed him. The wound would have been fatal had he been a normal Fae. The famished hunger that consumed his soul wouldn't grant him death. Not if anything living was within its far-reaching radius... His heart constricted at the unwelcome recollections.

He buried them deep.

Learning the extent of his nature had been costly. An eternal price, one he'd paid today and every day of his undying life.

Dimitri dismissed his memories and focused on the female before him. His right of conquest. He placed the shallow jar of lubricant on the bed and gripped her throat, dragging her up until her back met his chest. Her skin was soft and cool against his, and her scent... Dimitri leaned into the waves of her curled black hair and inhaled. Wildflowers and honey surrounded him.

"Spread your legs for me," he crooned. She remained still and Dimitri squeezed the sides of her throat.

"I said I would give myself to you. Obedience wasn't part of our agreement," Astrid choked out.

He glided his fingertips up the back of her thigh and skimmed the curve of her ass. "Would you rather I make you kiss the bed and fuck your ass with the hilt of my sword?" Dimitri rasped, low at her ear.

She startled when he touched the entrance of her ass and bowed her back as though it would save her. There was no part of his little neva he wouldn't have. Dimitri traced her ass, spreading the lube before applying more pressure.

"I have two swords," he said. By the blood, her shortened breaths made his cock ache. Her pulse was a wild flutter against his lips, and he smiled at her ear. "And you have three places you can take them."

Astrid stiffened as the tip of his finger pressed inside.

"I could tie you down. Fuck your ass and cunt with my swords." Her heartbeat accelerated and he dropped his voice an octave. "Would you like that, Princess? My cold steel working you to orgasm. The ways I can make you come... I won't stop until you're begging for my cock in your throat."

"I do not beg," she growled, vicious but breathless.

"You will," Dimitri promised. He parted his lips, loosening the constant hold chaining his hunger. Wisps of his shadowed magic reached for her. Coveting. Possessive.

He ran his chin along her shoulder. His neva was so responsive. The scent of her arousal maddened and bound him to her. The arch of her back. The intimate pressure squeezing his fingers as he worked her. Every whimpered moan she prayed he didn't hear.

Dimitri drew on Astrid's essence. The honeyed spice of her soul electrified his senses. Her essence engulfed his awareness until all that remained was her.

The seas would drown the very stars before he tired of her.

Her breaths grew ragged, and Dimitri pressed his fingers deeper. "I'm going to teach you to crave me."

He pulled back and pressed in harder, working her into a steady rhythm. Claiming more of her with each thrust.

"You'll come to me. Little by little. Every kindness I offer you. Every time you come for me. You try to hide it." Dimitri groaned, nuzzling her thick dark hair. "I feel you coming. Every quiver. Every spasm you fight. I taste it, neva."

He pulled back and added a second finger. Astrid struggled, twisting in his grasp but unable to escape.

"Take it neva," he said with a chuckle, fucking her harder. Another slow draw on her soul had her shuddering. Her ass squeezed, pulsing around his fingers as she came. "You are so responsive. Remember who you're coming for."

He folded his wing in front of her and delicately slid the tapered edge over her clit.

"Look how wet you are." Dimitri brought the edge to her mouth. "Clean my wing."

Chapter Sixteen

A strid's mind swam with pleasure. She struggled to hold her thoughts. The serrated teeth of Dimitri's death magic gentled to a caress. It overlapped, stroking her until the euphoria left her dizzy.

The stinging pain of his second finger jolted her out of the blissful haze blanketing her mind. But even then, he'd twisted that pain into pleasure... then ecstasy. Orgasms racked her one after the other and Astrid's lashes fluttered. Her head lulled back against his muscular shoulder and his wing tip rocked against her pussy. The friction on her clit had her coming again. Astrid tensed, fighting the moan at her lips.

"Clean my wing."

His deep, accented voice pulled her back to the present. She blinked and the tip of his wing was so close to her mouth she only had to lean forward slightly to touch it. Temper and rage flared within her. She held on to it and turned her head away even as her breaths turned to pants.

"Clean it or I'll fuck you with it," Dimitri said, bending the last joint of his wing until the two tapered bones folded against each other. His lips brushed the sensitive point behind her ear as he whispered, "Choose."

"This isn't part of our bargain," Astrid argued. "I've given myself to you. Release me and provide what I am owed. I need stationery to write a letter to my cousins."

His laugh was low and soft, dancing over her shoulder as his stubbled chin scratched her skin. "My cock will be stretching you when I have you. This is foreplay, neva. Now clean my wing or I'll make a mess of it in your cunt."

Astrid closed her eyes. She didn't want his wings touching her—least of all *there*. She swallowed and leaned into his grip. She'd never tasted herself before. It was a few inches. Nothing, really. She was more concerned with the cleanliness of his wing than the way she tasted.

Her tongue flicked out, licking the roughened bone. It was hard, but not as terrible as she imagined. Her teeth grazed the ridged tip, and he shuddered a groan. She quietly wondered if his wings were sensitive. If he would scream when she sank her teeth into them.

Astrid suppressed the impulse. She'd ruptured his aorta. Her jailor should have lost consciousness and bled out in moments. She should be riding to her cousin's stronghold.

But she was still here. Trapped as a winged brute's plaything.

Astrid swallowed her indignation and licked the last bit of her arousal off his wing. She turned toward him over her shoulder and asked, "Are we done?"

"Hardly."

Dimitri released her throat and flattened his hand between her shoulder blades before shoving her down. His fingers slipped from her and Astrid breathed a sigh of relief. She needed more information before she could lash out at him again. Play into his attention and placate his deranged appetites.

At least he won't share me, Astrid thought bitterly. *Thank the Fates for small mercies.*

Astrid jerked as something cold touched her ass.

"Relax, neva," he murmured as his callused palm traveled down her spine.

She hissed as the chilled metal stretched her. "Is that your fucking sword?"

"Have you already forgotten the feel of my sword?"

Astrid closed her eyes as the inches of metal pressed into her. She'd expected it to hurt but the pain never came. It was odd. Heavy. She was uncomfortably aware of its presence.

"I like you wearing my metal," he said, wiggling the flared base. Astrid drew a sharp breath, and Dimitri squeezed her ass cheek. "You'll sleep in this, and I'll fit you with the next size in the morning."

He stepped away from her and Astrid sat up. She must have misheard him. He couldn't truly mean…

"I'm not sleeping with this."

Dimitri kept his back to her as he closed the tin and placed her phallic torture devices in their velvet pouch. Astrid scrutinized him as he placed his belongings into the top drawer of his nightstand.

"Take it out if you like," he said calmly. Before she could respond he walked to the bathroom and began washing his hands. "You'll take the next size tomorrow regardless," he called from the sink.

Astrid blinked as her captor got back into bed as though this were a normal night for him. He turned to her and outstretched his wing across her side of the bed. The center black bones were spread wide, offering her an expanse of the leathery membrane.

She'd rather sleep in the snow. "Get your wing away from me."

The corner of his mouth lifted into a lopsided grin, and he slipped his hand behind his head. His wing rustled the sheets as he retracted it to his side, leaving her portion of the bed bare. "Sleep. When you are chilled you can curl into me."

He was delusional if he thought she was going to snuggle up to him. Astrid moved to her side of the bed, laying on the very edge and turning her back to him. His wing shoved beneath her roughly, abrading her side. She shoved at the heavy bones, but his leathery wing curved around her and scooped her beside him.

"Get off me," Astrid snapped, attempting to right herself.

Dimitri's wing constricted even tighter around her and he began plucking the combs and clips from her hair. "You will wear your hair down from now on," he said as he removed her second stiletto hidden in her jeweled hair stick.

"I will not," Astrid said, turning sharply. She pushed herself up and reached for her collection of jewelry.

His wing twisted like a rug under her and shoved her away. Astrid wanted to stab him. The smug bastard opened the top drawer of his nightstand and let her gold embellishments fall into the drawer.

"You will also be waxed and pierced tomorrow morning," he said, settling onto his back once more.

This male was truly insane. "I'm not going to allow you to mutilate me."

He chuckled at that and closed his eyes. "Good night, neva."

Chapter Seventeen

Astrid scarcely slept. Partially because of the metal plug her captor shoved up her ass and partially because when the morning came, she would be pierced. Her ears, like most Fae, were looped in gold and adorned with dangling gemstones, but she had no interest in jeweling anything beneath her clothing. Her gaze lifted to the degenerate sleeping just a few feet from her.

She'd bargain with him again. Astrid thinned her lips. The Mothers only knew what he'd demand in exchange. The cold seeped into her bones throughout the long night, but Dimitri remained unbothered by the chill. The crescent of his dark lashes rested against his high cheekbones and a wing fanned across his waist like a sheet.

Astrid refused to give him another area to exploit. If he could withstand the cold, so could she.

Astrid flattened her hand to her sternum and relaxed the hold on her magic. The vortex of shadows came into sharp focus. She scrutinized its violent churning and wondered if the sharp, twisting mass was correlated to his hunger. She would monitor it the next time he fed on her. Learning her enemy was the only way she could devise a way to kill him.

She focused her power, and a golden haze glittered past her body. Dozens of starlit strands rose and looped back, stitching her soul in place. When Dimitri was gentle, his magic didn't break the strands binding her soul. It left her weakened, but ultimately unharmed.

A soft tapping on glass drew her attention.

The sun had risen, but the rays did little to warm the room. Sitting on the frosted window ledge was a fluffy, white and gray cat looking in on them. Its melodic cry was muted from outside. It rose on its hind legs, pressing its nose to the pane.

Dimitri took a deep breath, and his wings stretched. Astrid shoved at his boney appendage before it encroached into her space. He glanced over and blinked at her before wiping his hand over his face with a groan.

Irritation shot down Astrid's spine. Had he forgotten she was here?

The cat pranced in a tight circle as Dimitri approached the window. He opened it and the feline hopped in. It purred happily as it walked in a figure eight around his feet, rubbing along his shins. Dimitri glanced down and tapped his bare chest twice in quick succession. The cat bounded into the air and Dimitri caught the creature. He lifted the pet, allowing it to walk across his shoulders and it peered at her over his head.

"We'll leave for breakfast when I return," Dimitri announced before walking into his closet.

Astrid got to her feet and yanked the fitted sheet off his mattress in three tugs. She wrapped the damned thing around herself and stalked toward him. "I need clothes, shoes, and stationery. Paper and a pen to send letters to my cousins."

"Keres will bring you clothing after you're waxed and properly pierced," he replied as he pulled on a pair of black slacks.

Astrid stared at his cat, who'd slung itself over his broad shoulders like a shawl. It looked perfectly content in its place, blinking at her with its blue, luminous eyes. She would never be so comfortable with her demented jailor. Astrid turned her attention back to Dimitri.

"I want another bargain," she said, folding her arms.

Dimitri selected a shirt and grinned at her. "And what do you intend to trade?"

There was nothing he hadn't violated but he seemed to want her *active* participation. "I don't want your piercing. I'll—"

"No," he cut her off.

Anger flushed Astrid's cheeks. "I won't let you," she said, stubbornly.

He chuckled as he pulled on a fitted topcoat. The embroidering was subtle but there was nothing subtle about the way the black material hugged his muscular frame and emphasized his lean waist. He straightened the sleeves and said, "You will wear the metal I select for you, or I will have you pierced every morning, neva."

The feline chirped at her unwanted pet name and Dimitri scratched behind its ears. "You are my *sweet* neva," he whispered to the animal before lowering his face to it. He glanced at her between its gray ears and spoke like he was plotting her death. "She's my *vicious* neva."

"She won't wear your metal," Astrid snapped.

He moved toward her and Astrid stepped back when he brushed his wing in her direction.

"Get on your hands and knees," he said, lifting his chin toward the bed.

"No. I want a pen and paper. You owe me letters. Paper that I've written on."

A smug grin curled his lips. "I haven't—"

"Consider it foreplay," Astrid snapped before leaving him for the fireplace.

Dimitri didn't pursue her. He affectionately stroked his white cat, and its gray tail swooshed happily. "Shall we find breakfast, Graymalkin?"

This fucking male. "Replenish the fire before you leave."

A line furrowed between his brows. "Are you cold?" Dimitri asked, outstretching his wing. Astrid narrowed her eyes and remained still. "The only comforts you will find here, will be with me, Princess."

"Your death is the only comfort I'll find in you."

He hummed his agreement and turned toward the door. "I welcome your attempts."

The black stained door clicked shut behind Dimitri and Astrid stared at the smooth wood grain a beat. She paced the room, deliberating her next move. She needed information. There had to be a way to kill him. Everything dies, and that arrogant, winged asshole was no different.

The chilled wood floor bit into her steps until her soles went numb. Astrid stared down at her bare feet, then his bed. If he thought she was his belonging, she would extend his hospitality to the rest of his things.

Astrid let the silken sheet fall and stepped into his closet. His clothing was neatly arranged. Too neatly. Astrid leaned forward and scrunched her nose at the hangers. Each article was spaced evenly. If she had a ruler, she would bet they were exactly an inch apart. She shoved the closest jacket back and the metal screeched as topcoats piled together before his dress shirts bunched behind them.

He could hurt and demean her, but he wouldn't break her spirit. Astrid flipped through his dress shirts selecting a black one with sapphire blue embroidery. She yanked its matching jacket free, leaving the hanger to jut out of place with the other tightly-packed articles of clothing.

Armed with her new outfit, she hurried into the bathroom. Fates, she needed to get his tapered, torture device out of her ass. She laid her stolen garments on the counter and gingerly felt the flared base. Her fingers hooked beneath it and Astrid gasped as it moved inside her. The pressure made her painfully aware of how empty her pussy was, and she strangely wondered how it would feel if Dimitri filled her there as well.

Mortified, Astrid banished the intrusive thought and quickly removed the metal that invaded her. She cleaned herself and eyed the shower. Washing his touch away entirely was tempting, but she'd bargained to bathe herself. She wouldn't waste what little time she had away from him when she could force his separation upon his return.

Astrid tugged on his dress shirt. There were large slits in the back for his wings that allowed a breeze to dance across her ribs. Even his clothing tormented her. Astrid's gaze lifted and her reflection stared back at her. Dimitri's shirt swallowed her, the end of it stopping mid-thigh. She donned his jacket, and the sleeves ended inches past her night-streaked nails.

She exhaled and shrugged out of his jacket before venturing back into the bedroom. She went to Dimitri's mangled twin swords and hesitated for a moment.

Astrid took a breath. She couldn't damage them anymore than they were, and she needed her hands to defend herself.

Decided, she carefully lifted the less ruined of his two swords and sliced several inches off the end of the jacket sleeves. It cut effortlessly and Astrid paused to admire the blade before putting it back, exactly as it had been.

She returned to the bathroom mirror, and in it, inspected the elaborate topcoat. It was a beautifully crafted piece of tailoring. She rolled the cuffs of the dress shirt over the raw edges of the topcoat and clipped her lotus belt in place. It cinched the clothing tight at her waist, giving her the silhouette of a dress.

The door clicked and Astrid turned. A female entered. Her wings were lighter than Dimitri's. Where his wings seemed to be framed in black bones, hers were an ashen white. Against the gray membrane, the complementary blotches gave her wings the appearance of snow on granite. Astrid loosened the hold on her magic and the golden haze of the female's soul shone through her brown skin.

Astrid's gaze lowered to the small hardcase duffle in her hand and seethed. "Get out."

"Lord Dimitri wants—"

"I don't care what he wants," Astrid snapped. If this bitch came any closer, Astrid would tear her soul from her arms and legs and toss her in the snow.

The female exhaled noisily and met Astrid's eyes. "None of his playthings last more than a week. Lay down and stop making this harder than it has to be," she said, setting the satchel on the bed.

"You won't last the hour if you don't leave," Astrid hissed.

The female removed chunks of raw gold and a tray of needles, then arranged piles of precious gems. She narrowed her eyes. "Let me explain, since it doesn't look like you've grasped the severity of your current predicament. Lord Dimitri wants the hood of your clit pierced and to have you fitted with gold. I know what you are and if your gifts worked on him, he'd already be dead," the female said.

She removed several chunks of steel and piled them to the side. Her eyes lifted to Astrid, and she folded her arms. "He's a Death Spirit. You cannot kill him. So, you can fight me—and trust me, you would not be the first—or I can leave."

"Leave," Astrid snapped.

"And Lord Dimitri will tie you to a table, naked, and spread for the entire Royal Legion to see," the female continued as though she hadn't spoken. "You don't want him to do your piercing. I'm the better choice. Trust me."

Astrid weighed her words. "How many have there been before me?"

The female spread a cut of black cloth over the bare mattress. Her hands slowed at the edges, and she spoke in a flat tone. "More than I care to count."

A trail of bodies proceeded her, yet her demented captor bargained with her. Obsessed over the taste of her soul. Made her come to humiliate her.

Astrid shoved the thought away. If he'd kidnapped other princesses or queens, the news would have reached Clorea. She was willing to bet she was the first royal he'd taken and leaned into her station.

"King Ambrose allows this behavior?" Astrid questioned. "I'm the King's betrothed."

"It's complicated. Lord Dimitri was the Queen's Royal Assassin. King Ambrose... inherited him."

From Ledivion's previous reign. Astrid's mind raced. Dimitri obviously had no loyalty to his king. Sunlight reflected off the row of needles and Astrid resigned herself. This would be like the brand she carried behind her ear, and she would heal it, too, when she escaped him.

This was the better choice. Astrid glanced at the female. "My name is Astrid."

"Keres," she answered absently, lifting a small metal pot from her duffle. Astrid scrutinized the blue wax beads she spooned into the container. Flames lit in her palm, licking up the sides of the rounded bowl before lowering to flicker at the bottom.

Keres was a fire weaver.

"Why did you bring steel when you're here to adorn me with gold and jewels?" Astrid asked.

Keres spared the pile of dark metal a glance. "I need to repair Lord Dimitri's weapons."

"Are you his blacksmith?" Astrid clipped.

"Metallurgist," she answered in the same fashion.

Astrid's gaze shifted to the nightstand. "Did you make his phallic figurines, too?"

"Butt plugs?" Keres answered pleasantly. "Yes."

Astrid swallowed her rage and laid back, staring up at the exposed dark wood beams. "Is it fulfilling?" she asked. "Making weapons and sex toys?"

"Every sword needs a sheath, and some sheaths need to be trained," Keres replied.

Astrid held her tongue but made a mental note to learn the location of the fire weaver's chambers. If she wasn't too far out of the way the sun's rays would shine on her corpse the morning Astrid escaped.

While fantasizing about Keres's demise was satisfying, Astrid needed to focus on her escape. Lord Dimitri wanted her waxed and she wanted him dead. Her methods of approach had to change if she wanted to survive. She'd stroke his ego and get closer to him. The moment she unearthed his soft underbelly, she'd gut him. Astrid laced her fingers, resting them over her middle.

"Are there many Death Spirits at court?" she asked.

The gentle scrape of the wood against metal suddenly stopped. Keres didn't answer, but her reaction explained a great deal to Astrid.

"Many call him a curse among us," Keres murmured.

Astrid met her pale, yellow eyes and couldn't decern if it was pity or sorrow that hid behind her cold stare. She folded the skirt of Astrid's makeshift dress into her belt and began the waxing Dimitri ordered. Astrid winced and counted the seconds a cold compress was held to her freshly bared skin.

Dimitri killed members of his own court. They were too frightened to enter his chambers. He remained after the King and Queen were assassinated. Prince Ambrose became King Ambrose and was forced to keep him.

Why? The tension between Dimitri and King Ambrose was a

blatant disrespect her father would've never allowed of a subordinate.

Astrid tensed as another strip of wax pulled free. The compress relieved the pain and Astrid exhaled slowly.

Her dagger should have killed him, yet he'd slept unbothered on *clean sheets*. He hadn't even bled.

Keres moved the tray of precious gems closer. Small clusters of rubies, sapphires, and diamonds glittered against their black housing. "Do you want a gem in your piercing?" she asked.

Astrid turned her attention back to the ceiling, desperately concealing her panic. She wasn't afraid of pain, but needles in such a sensitive area... Astrid squeezed her fingertips together as cold forceps pinched her hood.

"I want it encrusted in diamonds," Astrid answered plainly.

She contemplated her captor in an attempt to distract herself. He did as he pleased because nothing could bring him to heel. He was immortal, whether cursed or blessed by death.

An unstoppable weapon.

The needle glinted in Astrid's peripheral and she exhaled.

A weapon she would wield... or break.

Chapter Eighteen

Astrid examined the mirror. Her reflection appeared unharmed, but an ache lingered between her legs. It was another mark he'd won against her. Small, fleeting victories she strategically offered to lure him closer.

She brushed the brand behind her ear and two bangles twinkled together as they slid down her wrist. Her gaze shifted to her newest adornments. Apparently, being "fitted with gold" meant wearing two bracelets on her wrists and one on each ankle. The simple hoops were nothing she would choose to wear on her own and Astrid was positive they indicated Dimitri owned her.

Keres had encrusted the piercing her captor ordered with diamonds. A choice Dimitri granted her. A minor victory in a battle lost.

It had been fascinating to watch. Astrid had never seen a fire weaver work before. A crimson aura flared over her fingertips, and she manipulated the gold as easily as Astrid maneuvered souls. The only piece of jewelry Astrid appreciated was a delicate chain that looped her waist three times. It was thin, but Keres assured her it was infused with fire magic and wouldn't break.

The door opened once more, and Astrid tracked Dimitri's movements through the mirror. He paused, raking his gaze down her body. She knew he would fixate on her wearing his things—think he owned her. Astrid smiled, waging her silent war. She would have him at her feet by the end.

Crawling or dead. It made no difference.

"Your gold is plain," Astrid gibed, sliding the cuffed sleeve higher so the twin ringlets rested against her hand.

The corners of his mouth lifted, and those liquid amber eyes gleamed in the fading morning light. There was a beat of silence. Two. He was more attractive when he wasn't speaking. Or hurting her.

And when I can ignore his wings, Astrid thought dryly.

"You look at home in my clothes," he finally said.

"Shouldn't I match you?" Astrid asked, sauntering toward him. She reached for the piled cotton Keres left and tossed the muted whites and browns on the floor. "These clothes make me look like your servant."

His brows raised a fraction, and he crooked his finger, beckoning her closer. Astrid took a step and immediately halted. Her new jewelry shifted against her clit. The initial pain had left her oblivious to the way the metal moved with her, but now that she'd healed herself...

She was too aware of the curved bar's relentless teasing.

Bemusement lit his golden eyes, and he purred, "Come here, neva."

Astrid swallowed the curses she wanted to hurl at him. She strolled toward him, fighting for composure while a flush rushed past her cheeks.

His gaze darkened as he tracked her movements. She came to a stop before him, and he leaned into her. "Lay down and show me your metal."

Astrid sat back on the bare bed, craning her neck to stare at him. "Why aren't you pierced?" she asked.

"You'll have to offer me a much sweeter bargain if you want me to wear *your* metal," Dimitri said, stepping into her.

He parted her legs with his knee and Astrid leaned back. Rough palms traveled up her thighs and she didn't fight him when he spread them apart. Her dress rose up, but not enough to expose what he wanted.

"Allowing you to destroy my bed and rummage through my closet awards me your obedience?" he asked, smoothing his repurposed dress shirt and jacket up her body.

Astrid half shrugged one shoulder. "It awards you your life, for the time being."

His features lost their predatorial edge. "I'll outlive your temper," he said, lowering to his knees.

His strong hands gripped her waist, and her breath caught as he yanked her to the edge of the bed. Her legs stretched past his broad shoulders. She couldn't breathe.

She'd fantasized about having a male's mouth on her. Wondered what it would feel like to have her clit teased and licked. Her foot met the hard bones framing his wings and Astrid's illusions shattered. She anchored her heels on the joints between his should blades and fought a smile. She'd settle for Dimitri's tongue in her needy cunt and block out his hideous wings.

He lowered his head and glanced up at her through his lashes. "Not fighting me?" he whispered, so close his breath fanned over her.

The sensation sent her heart racing. "Were you planning on hurting me?" she asked.

"Not if you behave," he promised before licking her clit in a slow, deliberate movement, all while holding her gaze. "Are you going to behave?"

Astrid's heart pounded at the dark promise in his words. She should be discerning his weaknesses and plotting his death, but her mind blanked each time his tongue circled her clit. A gasp rushed through her lips when he flicked her jewelry. The momentary tug and friction sent her reeling.

His lips closed over her clit, and he sucked lightly at first. Astrid fell back on the bed, oblivious to Dimitri's wing shifting beneath her sole. He fished the black pouch out of his bedside table drawer with his talon, followed by the tin of lube.

Astrid fought to collect her thoughts. She loosened the hold on her power and examined the vortex of shadows in place of his soul.

His magic washed over her. The serrated teeth, capable of ripping her soul from this plane, caressed her instead. It over-sensitized her skin, leaving her breathless. The brilliant haze of glimmering stars, spiraled toward him, circling his churning shadows. Twin spires lit, creating an axis in his shadows. They matched her soul's brilliance as her essence extinguished within the consuming darkness of his.

Dimitri's mouth felt hotter and his skin warmed until he felt feverish. Her eyes met his molten gold, the same color as the burning spires lit at the top and bottom of his shadows.

He licked, then drew on her soul, alternating her torture until Astrid teetered at the edge of her pleasure. His finger dipped into her cunt, followed by another. Astrid dragged her bottom lip through her teeth and rolled her hips. She was so close, devoured by the pleasure he offered.

He withdrew from her, and she scarcely heard the scrape of the metal lid. His fingers returned lower, and Astrid moaned as he circled her ass.

"I'll have you here tonight," Dimitri groaned between licks and kisses.

Astrid's breaths became ragged. She stared skyward as his touch invaded and overwhelmed her. The game she played was on a knife's edge and she was losing her footing. He worked a second finger into her ass and Astrid's nails raked over his mattress. She couldn't think. She could only feel. She wanted his fingers in her cunt and rocked her hips as he pressed into her deeper.

She lifted her hips, silently demanding he show her cunt the same treatment.

Dimitri chuckled and licked lower, outlining her entrance with the tip of his tongue. Astrid reached for him needing more. She fisted his dark strands and ground against his mouth. He didn't turn away or drag her hand from his hair. She'd been flushed and demanding and he rewarded her by tilting his head to one side. His tongue teased her cunt, pressing in slow.

Astrid gasped, spreading her legs wider. She moved with him as his thumb circled her clit. Her jewelry shifted with each motion, adding another layer of delicious friction. Dimitri thrust his tongue into her and Astrid came apart.

Dimitri growled as she orgasmed, roughening his strokes into her ass while he tongued her cunt.

Astrid's fingers slipped from his hair as she came down. Undone and short of breath, she stared up at the exposed dark beams angled across the vaulted ceiling. Her lashes fluttered closed when Dimitri withdrew. He returned a moment later and roughly flipped her onto her stomach.

Astrid's temper rattled through the pleasure fogging her mind. Before she could right herself, the leading edge of his wing pressed heavily across her back. His callused hand smoothed over the curve of her ass and apprehension threaded the echoing euphoria of her orgasm.

It grew exponentially when Dimitri stuffed a pillow beneath her hips and peaked when something wide, blunt, and cold touched her ass.

"No," Astid hissed, struggling beneath the weight of his wing.

His lips met the small of her back and a tremor whispered through her as he trailed kisses up her spine.

"You can take it like this, Princess, or across my knee." His wing shifted and the warmth of his chest met her back. "Choose," Dimitri murmured. The word grazed her ear, flashing her memory back to the night before, when he'd held her down after she'd stabbed him through the heart.

They'd struck a bargain because he wanted a willing meal.

The pressure on her ass intensified. It was thicker and far less giving than his fingers. Astrid contemplated her situation. He dragged her into depravity, but his insidious touch made her come harder than she had in her life. If she was forced to make concessions, he would as well.

"Here," Astrid said, then added her own stipulation, "but don't touch me with your wings."

A dark chuckle rolled from him and his teeth left a stinging kiss on the nape of her neck. "Done."

Astrid tensed, expecting the pain of a vicious intrusion. She blinked. It never came. His shadows curled around her as he drank her essence. Her skin hummed, amplifying every brush of his lips. It heightened the way his shirt felt against her breasts until each of her panting breaths teased her nipples.

She was coming when Dimitri worked the tip of the phallic-shaped steel into her ass. He pressed it deeper, and she didn't care about his gray wings crowding either side of her.

He smiled against her ear and spoke in a low rasp. "Relax, neva. We're almost there. You're taking it so well."

Flush colored Astrid's cheeks but she couldn't discern whether the heat stemmed from embarrassment or elation. Dimitri withdrew the plug an inch then pressed it farther. The metal stretched her, stealing her breath. It didn't hurt, but the sensation was so much more intense than the smaller one he'd fit her with last night.

Dimitri seated the plug inside her and kissed her shoulder. "I have one last piece of gold for you, neva," he said.

Astrid gasped when something thin pooled between her shoulder blades. He held the tip and trailed it down her spine. It warmed quickly and felt like the delicate chains looping her waist.

He clipped it to the back of her existing chains and got out of bed. His magic released her. "Come, we're late for breakfast. Stand."

Her jailor strolled to the basin like he hadn't made her come half a dozen times.

Astrid didn't trust her legs to hold her. And now that his magic wasn't consuming her senses, she could feel the dull pressure of his shiny new toy shoved in her ass. She stared daggers into his back as he washed his hands and muttered, "Serpents devour you."

She straightened the shirt and topcoat she'd stolen, repositioning the lotus belt lower on her hips. A light brush tickled the back of her thigh and Astrid twisted to see two dainty chains hanging a few inches above her knees.

"Your gold is plain and pointless," Astrid said as she straightened her outfit.

Dimitri toweled off his hands and she turned so he could see the twin chains peeking beneath her shirt dress as he returned to her.

Her captor lowered to his knees and Astrid took a step back. He caught the bend of her knee and drew her closer. The backs of his fingers glided up her inner thigh and Astrid shifted on her feet. "We're late for breakfast, my Lord."

"I know," he said, collecting the chains between her legs.

Astrid realized it was a single chain that split into two as the delicate links slid between her ass cheeks like a thong. She felt Dimitri fasten the gold to the plug, then lift the two chains. They ran along either side of her pussy and he fastened them to the front of the gold looped around her waist.

"You'll wear this while I fuck your virgin cunt," Dimitri groaned as he yanked her forward and set one of her legs over his shoulder.

Before Astrid could react, his mouth was on her pussy. He licked her, but it wasn't like before when he teased her clit. His tongue was wide and flat, swiping from her cunt to clit.

"Let go of me," Astrid hissed, instinctively curling forward and drilling her elbow into the base of his skull.

Chapter Nineteen

Pain cracked over the back of Dimitri's head and radiated down his spine. He jolted with a roar, taking Astrid off her feet. His fingers blindly found her throat before slamming her onto his bed.

The impact stunned her momentarily. She blinked, choking for breath. Astrid lifted her chin and wedged her fingers between his, creating a sliver of space for air. Her midnight gaze narrowed on him, full of accusations.

Suka. "I think you'd be better behaved if I starved you for a day or two," Dimitri bit out.

Astrid struggled to free herself, thrashing her head forward in a sharp motion. "If I die, you'll have nothing to eat."

"You're an E'lan Vital, Princess. Tell me your soul hasn't been stitched to your body since the moment your abilities manifested. I could starve you to death and you would rise the next day." Dimitri's death magic tore from him and engulfed her. He didn't bother tempering it or slowing the ravenous gouges it left on her soul. His vicious neva tensed, hissing out a breath.

She'd repaid his kindness with violence and deserved to hurt. He took what was necessary to heal his injury and withdrew his shadows.

An unfamiliar twinge scraped at his heart, but quickly faded when Astrid slapped his hand away from her throat. His princess drew ragged breaths and flattened her palm over her sternum. Golden threads arched over her before pulling tight and the twinge in his chest returned.

Dimitri ignored the nagging feeling. "Clean yourself," he commanded, straightening his topcoat. "We're joining the royal table for breakfast, and I can't have you making a mess on my thigh."

"I've lost my appetite," Astrid snapped on the heels of his order.

Malice swirled through Dimitri's thoughts. He fastened his sword belt and turned toward her. "You are accompanying me to breakfast. You will walk beside me, or I'll fit you with a collar and drag you by a leash."

Astrid remained still, glaring daggers at him. Dimitri took a step forward. She recoiled and snapped to her feet.

"I need my combs and jewelry."

He stepped closer again, and laced his fingers through her loose strands, making note of her micro-expressions. The tension beneath her starless eyes. The minute downturned curl at the corner of her mouth. Reactions that lasted for a fraction of a moment, but he'd seen them.

"I prefer your hair down," he said.

The strain and tension left her eyes, and she gazed up at him with feigned longing.

"Please," she whispered the word, leaning into him.

His princess had a penchant for theater. Dimitri stroked her cheek, soft and gentle...

"No."

Astrid's mask fell away, and distain once again radiated from the depts of her gaze. "I need real clothes. My legs are cold."

"Wrap them around me and I'll keep you warm," he murmured.

She shoved away from him and Dimitri let her go. Her steps were as awkward as Graymalkin's first brush with snow. The diamond-studded piercing would tease her clit, making his little neva wet until she grew accustomed to it.

Astrid tidied and adjusted her makeshift dress. She'd ruined one of his jackets, but the view of her bare sex as she carefully bent over to slip into her heels more than made up for it. His grip had left a dark tinge of bruises along her ass and hips, and he reconsidered why he'd even allowed her out of bed.

A smile curled the edges of his lips as he contemplated the hours she would spend tied to his bed beneath him. The little sounds she'd make as she learned to take his cock into her throat, cunt, and ass.

Dimitri adjusted his cock. He did enjoy when she fought him, but what they shared in the shower… her wanton passion was addictive. The way her soul sweetened with spiced notes of desire rather than the overwhelming heat of her rage.

Dimitri outstretched his hand when she straightened. "Come. You need a meal."

Astrid moved to his side but didn't take his hand. As though that would stop him. Dimitri caught her wrist and turned, but she dug in her heels.

"I'm not a pet you can command," she snapped.

She twisted her wrist and smoothed her fingertips up his forearm. Her magic slid over him, cool on his skin like a breeze in the springtime.

Dimitri pressed an amused kiss to her temple and stepped into the hall. She followed to his disappointment. The thought of her neck wrapped in his collar had him hardening for her again. He chuckled as he led her through the halls, tucked beneath his wing.

His spoiled princess would demand her collar be encrusted with diamonds. *And rubies,* he thought, recalling the trinkets she used in her hair. He would have Keres make one for her. Astrid had bargained with him last night and Dimitri found himself silently hoping that meant she'd accepted her fate at his side.

The corridor opened to the large dining hall, rowed with dozens of tables. The room was constructed in a mixture of stone and wood like the rest of the palace. Spacious windows to the right overlooked a green space turned white by winter and the scent of grilled meats, bread, and pastries invaded his senses.

Astrid slowed her steps, and he ushered her closer with his wing. He led her to the royal table, centered between the two rows. His king sat with a redhead he didn't recognize, and Dimitri sat to his left. The nobleman occupying the seat beside Dimitri abandoned his place along with his breakfast. Astrid reached for the chair beside his, and Dimitri yanked her down onto his lap.

"There's a chair, right there," she hissed. His feral neva shoved against him and the tips of her claws bit into his chest.

He circled his arm around her waist and leaned closer. "I like having you close," he purred, bending the taloned joint at the top of his wing to brush her long black hair behind her shoulder. Astrid shoved at the thick bones raising from his back and he exhaled a chuckle. "How long is it going to take you to realize I am *much* stronger than you?"

Astrid ignored him and examined her surroundings. Dimitri pulled her closer, curious as to what she was cataloging.

A way out? A weapon? A means to escape him? Dimitri mused as he caressed her toned thigh.

She would find nothing useful.

He leaned forward and filled his dish with a bit of everything. A pair of males strolled too near. The closer of the two turned his attention to Astrid. His gaze swept over his neva, from the golden hoops along the curve of her ear to the curve of her ass perched on his thigh. Wrath coiled in Dimitri's chest and his palm smoothed over the end of makeshift dress, keeping her covered.

The male stretched his wing, commenting to his companion. It disturbed the air around Astrid as they passed, fluffing the end of her skirt.

The leading edge of Dimitri's wing shot out, embedding the talon into the base of the male's skull. He withdrew and the male fell to his knees before slumping to the floor in a growing pool of blood. Hushed murmurs broke out as the royal table was abandoned completely.

Leaving Dimitri and his king.

Astrid kept still as a guard dragged the bleeding corpse away. No one stood within twenty feet of Dimitri but his king... and Ambrose made no attempt to hide his contempt. What Astrid couldn't understand was *why* King Ambrose allowed him to behave like this? Killing his own people. Sowing unease and discourse through his court.

Maybe they were lovers? Astrid thought wryly but abolished the thought. His disdain ran far deeper than infatuated machinations.

Astrid turned her attention to her meal. Sourdough, meats, what looked like more swan, and slices of cheese covered the plate. Did these idiots not eat fruit? Where was the jam? And why was this bread not toasted? She reached for the spongy loaf and Dimitri caught her wrist.

"You'll be hand fed until I've tamed you," he said, loud enough for those remaining to hear.

Astrid straightened her back. She'd expected to placate him in private, but if he wanted to make a spectacle of her, she would certainly give their audience something to watch.

She glanced Dimitri's way. "You don't have fruits or sweet wine."

"You will eat as we do," Dimitri said, selecting a cut of swan and bringing it to her lips. "Sweets don't hold off the winter."

Astrid took his hand and the room fell silent. His molten gold stare held her as she sensuously opened her mouth. She licked the space between his index and the succulent meat he pinched. Her lips closed over his fingertip as she tasted the juices before daintily catching a strip of meat between her teeth, pulling it free. She licked his hand again, a longer swipe of her tongue.

She sucked until every male in attendance imagined she was on her knees, attending to another part of their anatomy.

Astrid could play a docile pet. Their audience held no loyalty to Dimitri. The nobles and battalion would want and envy him, and in turn, Dimitri's jealousy would kill more guards. An endless cycle her jailor would perpetuate until the entirety of court avoided him, leaving her a clear path to freedom.

Dimitri leaned into her, and his voice dropped an octave. "Do you enjoy sucking on my fingers, neva?" he asked. Astrid smiled sweetly. Quiet and obedient as he tore off a small piece of bread and used it to sop up the herb-infused oil of the swan.

He jogged his leg without warning, bouncing her on his knee.

The motion jarred her back and drove the plug further into her ass. Astrid held still, waiting for the invasive pain to subside and he laughed, holding the bread to her lips.

"Or are you hoping one of them will save you, Princess?"

Astrid's temper scorched her schemes, and her plots blanked from her mind. She snatched the closest utensil and swung, burying the fork's prongs into Dimitri's muscular chest.

She scarcely heard the gasps and chatter that broke out. The rest of the King's court abandoned their meals and fled. The entirety of her focus centered on the golden irises that seemed to glow in the firelight.

He roughly captured her wrists and shoved them behind her. The talon at the end of his wing sliced her as it threaded the bangles she'd been fitted with. Realization struck, exposing the true function of her new jewelry. His wing pulled her arms behind her, taut, and held them there. He ripped the fork out of his chest and gripped her face, squeezing her jaw until the joint groaned.

"Open your fucking mouth," he growled, raising the bloodied utensil to her lips.

Astrid did as she was told and extended her tongue to flick the crimson coated tip. The coppery tang spread over her tongue as she swallowed and the fury in his eyes paled, replaced with another kind of heat.

She leaned into his hold and hummed at him. "Do you have a blood kink, *my lord?*"

Fingers pulled through Astrid's hair. An angle, Astrid noted, that could not be Dimitri's.

"You seem to be making yourself at home with things that belong to me," King Ambrose said, idly twirling her hair.

Dimitri yanked his king's hand away, taking several of her strands with it. In a smooth motion, he slammed Ambrose's hand down and staked it to the table with a steak knife. Astrid could only stare as Dimitri possessively crushed her to his side.

"Ona moia po pravu zavoevaniia," Dimitri growled.

Astrid didn't need to understand the implication to know she had no desire to be caught between these two volatile males.

"I am your king!" Ambrose bellowed, ripping the blade from his hand. The steel knife came away broken, the tip jutting out of the table.

Dimitri's dark laughter filled the room as he brushed the side of his face through Astrid's hair. He clutched her tight and she remained still, waiting for Ambrose to intervene. Dimitri would be executed for attacking their—

"No one is above our law. Not even you, *my king*."

Astrid blinked. *No. Dimitri aggressed his monarch. Injured him. Attacking your king was treason in any kingdom.*

She met Ambrose's eyes, silently pleading. His irises gleamed like sunlit honey. He lifted his palm. The ruined flesh gapped and bled, but his voice remained calm. "Mend my wound, soul weaver."

Dimitri stood, carrying Astrid away from his king.

"Nyet," he crooned, palming her breast. Astrid gasped as he squeezed her curves through the embroidered suit jacket she'd re-purposed. "My soul weaver is occupied. She'll be too busy taking my cock to afford you attention."

He turned to leave, and Astrid met Ambrose's sunlit gaze. Her eyes turned pleading as she mouthed, *Save me, my king.*

He remained seated, doing nothing as Dimitri carried her away.

Chapter Twenty

"You made your point. Put me down," Astrid snapped as she twisted her body and kicked her legs in retaliation.

Dimitri's grip tightened, crushing her against the unyielding planes of his body. The air squeezed out of her, but his hold loosened the moment she stopped struggling. Astrid glared up at her jailor, and the slightest hint of a grin curved the edge of his mouth.

"Asshole," she breathed.

They passed guards and well-dressed Ledivites Astrid cataloged as nobles. The Fae parted for Dimitri, keeping their heads down but turned and stared after her when he passed. Astrid supposed she should be grateful his arm tucked the skirt of her dress against her bottom.

Astrid stared up at him. Her vantage point gave her an attractive view of his jaw, the hard lines of his throat. The perfect indented hollow beneath his Adam's apple begged for her stiletto. She longed to slip her blade behind his windpipe and slice forward.

Wasteful daydreams, since his death magic would consume her to heal himself.

Astrid missed her chambers—her clothing and books. The weapons she'd designed to annihilate the Ledivites. Her latest creations included crossbow bolts with barbed hooks chained to the end. She'd love to spike Dimitri's wings to ground with them and fill him with a quiver of arrows, safely out of his shadow magic's reach.

"Are we dining elsewhere since you interrupted my meal?" Astrid asked as he climbed a flight of stairs.

His thumb stroked her side, and he glanced down at her. "Is my neva hungry?"

The words rankled her temper. She wasn't a belonging, but he was far too thick to comprehend nuance. Astrid rested her head on his shoulder. She tilted her chin down and lifted her gaze to stare up at him through her lashes before saying, "I'd like a private meal in the gardens or a library."

Harsh tension lined his eyes, but he blinked, and it was gone.

"And what do you hope to find in a library?" he asked.

"Knowledge," she answered. *And the means to kill you.*

Dimitri turned down a long hall and set her on her feet. Winter's chill snaked up her bare legs and Astrid suppressed a shiver. His wing curled around her, and Astrid slapped the boney appendage away.

It swung back harder, pressing her to his side. "You're cold," he grated.

"Then get me a coat," Astrid snapped, again shoving away from his wings. She'd meant to stalk ahead of him, but her piercing shifted, and Astrid drew a sharp breath.

Humor colored his voice as he chuckled. "The library is this way."

Astrid took a careful step and Dimitri's palm met the small of her back. He ushered her forward, sending a jolt of pleasure through her. The curved bar of her diamond-studded piercing swept over her clit with each tilt of her hips. It felt like Dimitri's hand was up her skirt, and the bastard knew it. Her pulse elevated with each step, but she held her head high.

Dimitri would do worse if she tried to stop him.

They strolled through a few winding corridors and approached a tall archway. Aged stone columns streaked in tiny, black hairline fractures, framed either side. The Ledivion crest was mounted at the center of each pillar. Astrid scrutinized the three intersected swords. Well-maintained and polished, they gleamed in the firelight against the ancient stone.

Leave it to the Ledivites to show such care to decorative steel but ignore the stone structure beneath it.

Her gaze moved to the space beyond the archway. It was cold and soulless. Dark walls and winter-frosted glass bordered rows of towering bookcases. Ledivites crowded the tables throughout the library, each engrossed in their studies and research.

A male stopped between two shelves and outstretched his wing. The clawed tip looped through a ring affixed at the top of a tome. Astrid watched as he pulled it free and added it to the pile he held. The male started toward the tables before catching sight of Dimitri. He froze and the book he'd acquired tumbled to the ground.

The others glared up from their work with annoyance, but their pinched expressions stiffened when their attention fell to her winged captor. The stillness was upended by the shuffling of feet and closing of books. The crowd retreated, milling through the smaller archways on the eastern and western walls in a hushed panic.

Astrid chanced a glance at Dimitri. He wore the same smug grin of self-proclaimed victory he did each time he maneuvered her into a compromising position.

The robed male who dropped his book bent to retrieve the tome, gray fabric pooling around him. He stood before hurrying toward them.

"What can I do for you, my lord?" he asked, bowing his head.

The rough edge of Dimitri's wing scraped the back of Astrid's dress. "My neva seeks knowledge," he said, shoving her forward.

Astrid took two quick steps before regaining her balance. A mixture of heat and temper tinted her cheeks, but she remained elegant and composed.

"What can I help you find?"

"Princess Noctis, priest," Dimitri interjected.

Tiny beads of sweat broke out over his forehead and the male clutched his books to his chest and bowed formally. "What can I help you find, Princess Noctis?"

Astrid expected the priest to meet her gaze, but his eyes remained fixed at the floor between them. Priests and priestesses who served the Three-Faced Mother held the same station as nobles in Clorea. Astrid smoothed her hands over her skirt and curtsied, as she would to any priest of her own faith.

The priest upturned his face and blinked.

"I would like books on your traditions," Astrid said gently before adding, "and anything you have on Death Spirits, like him."

"There is no one like me, Princess," Dimitri purred against her hair. His hand dragged across her waist as he prowled by. He lifted his chin at the priest and said, "Send a footman to bring us a breakfast platter and inform the cooks I want swan on it."

"Of course, my lord," the priest said with a nod and scurried off.

Dimitri took a seat at the closest table and spread his legs far enough for her to stand between before patting his thigh.

At least he wouldn't force her to walk every aisle in search of her books, Astrid mused. She took a seat on his lap and asked, "Do your priests manage your library?" It would be the last place she thought a Vinceret devotee would frequent.

Dimitri drew her closer and slipped his fingers through the wing slits of her dress. He traced idle circles on either side of her spine. "They oversee our history and archives."

"Is this your palace's only library?" Astrid asked.

"No, but it is the biggest."

Muted footsteps drew her attention and Astrid turned to find the priest holding three leather-bound books. He placed them on the table's blackened wood top and opened the thickest volume.

"These are religious texts," he began as he flipped through the book.

Leather and the comforting scent of aged paper filled the space between them. Astrid took a deep breath. Her mind had always been her greatest asset. She'd spent countless hours in her libraries, cultivating her weapon.

Until it sharpened into an advantage.

The priest opened the pages to the inked image of an imposing winged male. His hands were folded over the pommel of his sword and the hood of his cloak obscured his face.

"Death Spirits are a curse, Princess Noctis." The priest's voice was as still and solemn as a fathomless lake.

Dimitri pulled the corner of the book closer and read over her shoulder.

"Queen Arina boasted that the son she carried would become a greater warrior than Vinceret, the God of Conquest and Blood. Offended by such blasphemy, Vinceret cursed the infant to be born beneath death's shadow and blacken the veins of any close to him."

Astrid continued reading and the final passage sent a chill through her.

To appease the god and end the blood-cursed plague, King Lev tied his wife and son to a stake and put them to flame.

Chapter Twenty-One

Dimitri held Astrid, committing the feel of her smooth skin to memory. They spent the day in the library. During the first hour, he'd believed she used the books as a shield to wedge space between them. He reconsidered his assessment after she'd eaten her meals from his fingertips without argument.

His little neva was an academic. She savored the words, tracing her index and middle finger over each line of text. He hadn't expected her to relax against him in increments as she flipped the pages. The subsequent hours gave him a taste of what life would be like once she accepted her place at his side.

The day had given way to night when she finished the first book. Astrid set it aside and reached for the next leatherbound tome. Dimitri flattened his hand over the embossed cover and pushed it away, only to have her glare at him.

"You've spent the entire day here, neva," he murmured against her temple. "I'll have your affection now."

She turned into him, her lips drawing near. "I'd prefer to read."

Dimitri leaned in, taking a soft, chaste kiss. "I'd prefer your pretty wine-stained lips around my cock," he said, whispering the last.

Her lashes lowered and her laughter fanned over his mouth. "No."

"You forget I own you, Princess."

Dimitri stood, cradling her in his arms. Her dark hair draped across his chest, and he squeezed her closer. She didn't fight him as he guided her wrist across the back of his neck. Astrid's midnight eyes narrowed, then widened when he dropped the arm supporting her back. Her nails racked over his topcoat, and she clung to him while he supported her weight with one arm hooked underneath her legs.

Dimitri pressed a kiss to her forehead before saying, "I don't need your permission to take what I want from you."

"If you bring your cock anywhere near my face, I'll bite until my teeth connect."

Dimitri chuckled. "I could have a metal ring made for your mouth within the hour, neva. Should I pin your hands behind your back and fuck your throat until you learn to like it?"

Astrid didn't hurl her usual threats or insults as they made their way back to his room. She remained silent but Dimitri picked up notes of her arousal. He wondered if what he'd said got her wet or if dredging up her next plot to kill him made her cunt soft.

He would take either. His vicious neva's schemes would fail and he would invent new and creative ways to punish her.

They passed a filigreed mirror, and Dimitri plucked it right off the wall. He carried it with them and Astrid pulled herself higher to peek over his shoulder.

"Just the mirror?" she asked. "Don't you want the flower vases, or the table beneath it?"

Dimitri didn't reply. She'd find out what he intended soon enough.

He entered his room and kicked the door closed. "Seeing my clothes on your body makes my cock hard," Dimitri said, lowering Astrid gently onto their bed. He lifted her wrists overhead and looped the golden bangles with the talon topping of his wing.

Astrid yanked against her restraints but stilled when he turned her until her back met his chest. The sheets twisted beneath her knees and Dimitri inhaled, breathing in her scent of honey and wildflowers.

Dimitri set the mirror down in front of her and began unbuttoning the dress shirt she'd stolen from him. He took his time, enjoying the methodology of the task. The scent of her arousal heightened with each inch of skin he uncovered.

"Are you wet for me, neva?" he asked, pulling her shirt open to expose her breasts.

"The only thing I am for you, is murderous," Astrid countered.

"Look how hard they are. This isn't for me?" Dimitri rolled her nipples between his thumb and forefinger until her breaths were short. Then, he tugged until Astrid gave voice to her pleasure.

He softened his touch, circling her nipples to soothe the hurt. "Should I pierce these, too?"

"No," she answered immediately.

Dimitri palmed her soft curves. "Are they sensitive?"

His princess remained silent, and Dimitri curled his wing in front of her to angle the mirror. Their eyes met in the reflection and Astrid held his stare. She was flushed and beautiful, but it was the defiance etched in midnight that made his cock twitch.

"You can say you like it, neva," Dimitri purred. "Do you want to sit on my face while I play with your tits?" He applied more pressure, pinching until Astrid moaned. "I'll have clamps made. You can wear them every morning. I'll hold your hands behind your back and flog your ass while you ride my cock. I promise to stop after you make me come."

"You're disgusting," Astrid breathed.

"Filthy… is the word you're looking for, Princess," Dimitri said, reaching between her legs. Arousal coated his fingers, and Astrid thrashed. Strands of her dark hair caught in the stubble across his cheek and Dimitri restrained his prey.

"You'll never escape me," he rumbled as his callused hand slipped down her body. Dimitri reached between her thighs, toying with her piercing, before moving lower and spread his fingers in a V.

"I want you to see how wet you are, neva," he whispered, positioning the mirror between her knees, "and you're going to watch while I fuck you."

Chapter Twenty-Two

Astrid yanked against the simple gold bangles caught on Dimitri's talon. His harsh caresses tormented her, and worse, her body betrayed her, reacting to his touch. Softening as his warmth and the scent of winter nights in a darkened forest surrounded her.

His fingers found her clit and a spike of pleasure ricocheted through her. Dimitri toyed with her piercing, and she twisted in her bindings.

"I want you to see how wet you are, neva."

Astrid blinked up at the thin gold bands anchoring her to the top of his wing and cursed the mystically-reinforced metal.

Another reason to eviscerate Keres when she escaped.

Cold metal chilled her knee and Dimitri's sword flanked her memory. She jerked as her heart drummed—and stilled when she realized it was the mirror from the hall.

"And you're going to watch while I fuck you," Dimitri rasped.

He held her, open and exposed. A coward's act to intimidate her. Astrid knew she was wet. The heat pooling between her legs was undeniable, but this wasn't about proof. This was about power. A show of how much he wielded and how little he believed she held.

Astrid glanced at him over her shoulder. Firm lips and the strong cut of his jaw filled her vision. "Is that what you want? For me to watch, my lord?"

She turned back toward the mirror when he didn't reply. Did he expect her to contort herself and cry? To hide from him? Her body was a weapon, and like the rest of her arsenal, she wasn't ashamed of it.

"I prefer to be called by my name," Dimitri said, casually toying with her piercing.

The heady sensation consumed her. "Is that so, my lord?"

Wood groaned, and she found him opening the top drawer of his nightstand with the clawed edge of his wing. He hooked the round tin, setting it on the bed. The black velvet pouch followed. He'd said he'd fuck her with the metal plug in her ass, but she'd hoped he'd get caught in the moment and forget himself. She gazed skyward and concentrated on the illicit feel of his hand between her legs.

"Watch the mirror, neva."

It was too soft to be an order. Astrid recognized the skewed words he conveniently posed as a suggestion.

This is a test.

Astrid lowered her lashes and met the gleam of his molten gold eyes in the glass. He'd angled it so she'd see exactly what he did to her while having a view of his predatory gaze. What was meant to shock her instead felt like a layer of separation. Now this was a narrative she could lose herself in.

The reflection was a female with a noble who loved and cherished her. A scene from a book played out before her. Astrid moaned and rolled her hips in time with Dimitri's touch. She would pretend tonight, and focus on her imagined couple. A letter to her cousins was all that mattered.

Navigating her emotions was infinitely easier when she considered her enemy in terms of war. She would win on this battlefield and position the next front. But it didn't mean she couldn't enjoy the warfare.

Astrid's midnight eyes met Dimitri's. "Do you think she wants you?" she asked, rocking into his hand. A smile teased the corner of his mouth as the tension thrumming beneath her skin intensified.

"I think I own her," Dimitri purred at her ear. Before she could argue his point, he brought the third plug to her face.

Astrid's temper flared and she turned away. "I said I would give myself to you, not sink into your perversions."

Dimitri's palm pressed into the corner of her chin and forced her to face the mirror once more. The way he held her made the phallic metal tip press against her lips and Astrid thrashed.

She only accomplished the scrape of gold on bone and Dimitri's dark laughter.

"Shh," he soothed. "It's clean. Open your mouth."

Astrid clamped her teeth shut and glared at him through the corner of her eye.

"I won't make you swallow it." The politeness in his tone waltzed with her rage as he shrugged and added, "Tonight."

Astrid didn't budge. Her jailor was absolutely—

Dimitri's shrouded death magic engulfed her without warning. She moaned as the gentle serrated teeth entwined with her soul, seeking every crevice. Owning every part of her.

Astrid came hard, tremoring against the unyielding planes of Dimitri's chiseled body. She kept her jaw tight as her captor drew out each wave of bliss as they rained over her. He teased her clit in unhurried circles and her pleasure intensified into rapture. A second orgasm crashed over her and Astrid's lids fluttered closed.

"Open for me, Princess," Dimitri purred. "It's this or I have a ring made for that pretty mouth of yours. Decide."

If he commissioned a ring, it would undoubtedly come equipped with the metal plug he held. She would choke while he forced it down her throat.

"You only have to take a few inches." Dimitri kissed her temple and smiled against her browbone. "Show me how badly you want to suck my cock. Convince me, and I won't work it into your ass." He chuckled and raised a brow, catching her reflection's gaze. *"Tonight."*

Shame branded her, leaving fissures in her soul. Astrid swallowed her pride and shored up her cold logic as waves of ecstasy battered her resolve. *His desire was her weapon.* And if the plug was in her mouth, he couldn't shove it in her ass.

Astrid went rigid and parted her lips, ready for him to jam the phallic metal into her teeth. The assault never came. She hesitated in the space between her heartbeats, then opened wider. Its weight rested against her mouth, cold and heavy. Astrid leaned forward, licking the tip as it breached her lips.

"Take the head in your mouth," Dimitri crooned from behind her.

She obeyed, sliding the smooth steel past her lips as she sucked. Dimitri stopped teasing her clit and Astrid sighed at the reprieve. He unfastened his pants, and she stilled as the hard length of his cock glided along her pussy.

"Did I tell you to stop?" Dimitri asked.

The plug at her lips pressed deeper, forcing her to open wider, but stopped before she gagged. Astrid struggled to time her breaths as its girth slid in and out of her mouth.

"Spread your legs for me, neva."

Another order. She hated them, but complied nonetheless, fantasizing about the dawn finding his mutilated corpse.

Dimitri took himself in hand and the broad crown teased her clit, then moved lower. He wedged the blunt tip into her cunt and Astrid arched her back, unable to escape the invasion.

He thrust a knee between her thighs, hooking her leg over his. Astrid braced herself, squeezing her eyes shut. She was too vulnerable in this position—could do nothing to stop him from impaling her.

"I'll offer you a bargain," Dimitri purred.

Astrid's attention darted to the glass, but his amber gaze was fixed lower. The veined length of his cock stood proud, poised at her entrance.

"I'll stop fucking your mouth for the night, but only after you've buried my cock in your pretty cunt."

Astrid cursed as she looked away. *Serpents devour you.*

Dimitri palmed her breast, pinching the tight peak until she cried out around the steel trapping her voice.

Humor colored his words as he said, "Watch the mirror."

Astrid cast her eyes down. The sooner she fulfilled his bargain;

the sooner she could rest the ache developing in her jaw. She rolled her hips tentatively and watched the reflection beneath her. The head stretched Astrid's opening and electricity fired through her. The serrated teeth of his death magic caressed her as the golden hue of her soul shimmered against Dimitri's shadows.

He drank, savoring her with quiet pulls. Pinpricks of glittering light caught in the current of his appetite swirled around her. Dimitri's shadows curled, darkening the room until she was surrounded by a night sky lit with pieces of her flickering soul.

Dimitri tugged on her nipple, teasing the very tip, but Astrid kept her eyes fixed on the reflection.

This was the lady and her nobleman, Astrid reminded herself. She clung to her invented narrative, envisioning silk, candlelight, and fresh flowers.

The head of Dimitri's cock spread her open and pressed inside. *A night of lovemaking after years of pining at court.*

Her lashes fluttered with the next fall of her hips.

He would take his time, working his cock into her with gentle strokes.

Tension strung her tight as she rose and fell slowly on Dimitri's cock. A bitter corner of her mind wondered how many females Dimitri had taken to his bed to master his specific brand of cruelty.

He knew when to hurt her. When the bite of pain against her tight nipples would add to the crescendo of pleasure building inside her. More than that, the soft touch he administered after the hurt beckoned something dark crawling through her.

She could deny the desire he kindled in her, but her traitorous body sang and ached for him. She couldn't stop the orgasm threatening to break her. Couldn't stop from arching her back and taking his cock deeper. Her cunt rhythmically squeezed his thick length and Astrid cried out around the steel.

Dimitri's groan answered. "I'll never get enough of your greedy cunt coming on my cock."

He continued fucking her mouth and Astrid tossed her head. The phallic gag remained firmly in place and Dimitri chuckled.

"I said I would stop when you took all of me, Princess. You still have another inch." He leaned back and Astrid gasped at the change of angle. A callused hand squeezed her ass, and he added, "Maybe two."

Chapter Twenty-Three

Dimitri groaned low in his throat while Astrid wiggled and ground against his cock, desperate to take his entire length. He withdrew the butt plug from her mouth the moment she completed her task and chuckled. His little neva slumped forward, limp and boneless, still suspended at the wrist by the talon on his wing.

He gently settled her on the bed. Astrid's shoulders met his sheets, and she didn't fight him. She was quiet and flushed with a sheen of perspiration.

His little neva was recovering and regaining her balance. Dimitri knew better than to believe he could fuck the fight out of her.

The shadows of his death magic churned around them, catching the golden stars lighting her soul in their current. She tasted exquisite—a sweetness spiced with her temper.

He unlatched the thin golden chains securing the plug in her ass and set the chains aside. She was still dressed in his shirt and topcoat. While he admired her naked body, he thoroughly relished fucking her while she wore his clothing.

Dimitri pulled out and Astrid slumped onto her side. Her midnight stare raked over him and stopped on his erection. Her brow squeezed together, and he chuckled.

Did she think I came?

"We're not done," Dimitri said, unbuttoning his shirt. "Put your ass back in the air."

Her hand fisted over his sheet, and he wondered if she silently wished for the daggers he'd taken from her. He would take everything she had before he was done.

"Now," he said, shrugging out of his jacket.

Astrid lifted her hips but angled herself away from him.

"Eyes on me," Dimitri instructed.

Hatred iced her features as she met his gaze over her shoulder. If she begged, he might be kind and come on her instead of fucking her. But he wasn't kind and his vicious neva would never beg.

"Pull the plug in your ass halfway out and push it back in," he said.

Rage glittered against midnight. "No."

Dimitri undid his cuff and shook his wrist. "Fuck your ass, neva, or I will."

Notes of heat spiced the honeyed taste of her soul. Her rage was quick to ignite but tempered when she orgasmed in his arms. She would learn to crave him, to need him.

Astrid reached behind her and slipped her fingers under the flared base.

The sight of her made his cock ache. He could teach her obedience. And the way she responded... his little neva was so sensitive. The nobility at her court had no idea what lay beneath her silk.

She twisted her wrist, drawing the plug out. Then, she pressed it back in.

Dimitri took a seat and unlaced his shoes. "Again."

Her lips parted as she continued.

"Take more of it," Dimitri said as he stripped. "Good girl. Harder. Fuck yourself. Show me how much you want it."

Her cheek pressed into the gray sheets as she panted. Dimitri climbed into bed, positioning himself behind her, but she didn't stop.

"You're so responsive," Dimitri crooned. He teased her clit, coating his fingers in her arousal. "I'll never share you, but you'll know what it's like to be fucked with all your holes filled."

The flush across her cheeks deepened and Dimitri gripped the curve of her hip. The scent of her arousal spiked. The taste of her soul sweetened as he drank her essence. She was coming and trying to hide it from him.

Dimitri thrusted into her, burying himself deep. Her cunt pulsed around him, and he groaned. "You're mine, neva. Fate delivered you to me."

Her brow drew together, and she panted a breath, working the plug in and out of her ass. Dimitri couldn't decide whether he preferred her bound while he worked her lithe body with toys or on his bed with her legs spread, instructing her.

He had eternity for both.

Dimitri pulled out and flipped her onto her back. Astrid was out of breath. her starless eyes staring to the ceiling. He hooked her knee and dragged her into him, smiling as her night-streaked nails bit into the muscle of his chest.

He thrusted into her, and she moaned, arching her back. She met his thrusts, raking her nails over his shoulders. Dimitri leaned down, holding her in the cage of his arms. His wings folded low, surrounding her. She clung to him, panting against his ear, but her magic didn't snake over him.

"Slower," she breathed. "Dimitri, you're too big."

"I'll teach you to like it. You'll crave me, Princess," he said, though he gentled his harsh strokes. He pressed all the way into her before rolling his hips and she choked on his name.

"You'll take me here," Dimitri said as his lips brushed her throat. "And here." He thrusted into her, punctuating his words. "You'll beg me to drink you while I fuck your ass."

He drove into her, letting his pleasure build. It climbed each time Astrid screamed his name, intensified as her nails scored his back, and compounded each time her cunt squeezed his cock.

Dimitri pulled her closer, palming the back of her head. He fucked her harder as his pulse raced, so close to his release it agonized him. His back tensed and with a hard beat of his wings he came deep inside her.

His breaths were ragged as he lifted his head. Astrid's lashes fluttered against her cheek. Her dark hair was damp with sweat, and her skin was flushed. He'd either taken too much of her soul or fucked her too hard for too long. Probably both.

"Let's clean you off, neva," he said, kissing the corner of her mouth.

She murmured unintelligible words but didn't open her eyes. Dimitri lifted her out of the bed, and she curled into the cradle of his arms. Her breathing deepened, and slowly evened out before they even reached the ensuite.

Chapter Twenty-Four

Astrid woke beside a purring ball of white and gray fluff. Graymalkin sprawled beside her, and Astrid roused enough to realize why her legs were warm. Dimitri had outstretched his wing sometime after she dozed off.

"Get off me," Astrid snapped. Her ire startled Graymalkin and her preferred method of warmth darted for the window.

The scaled bones of his wing scraped over her hip as it traveled higher.

"Don't touch me with your animal parts," Astrid hissed, kicking him away. Her leg caught on the leathery membrane, and it engulfed her foot like a warm blanket. She felt his pulse against her ankle and snatched her foot away. Bile rose in her throat, and she scurried back, falling to the floorboards. She righted herself and backed away. A few feet separated them when the wall beside the bathroom door chilled her back.

Dimitri's wings folded to his side as he sat. His molten gold stare drifted over her curves before pinning her. "Keep insulting me, neva, and I'll fuck you with them."

Astrid couldn't discern if he was bluffing. He couldn't possibly—

As though he could hear the question forming in her mind, he bent the last joint of his wings until the two bones rested side by side. He gave her a knowing grin. "I'd teach you to like it."

A twinge of pleasure shocked her. Her unbidden memory reminisced on the rough feel of his hands holding her down. The thick pressure of his cock invading her. Forcing her open as he stroked deep and hard. His lips brushing the shell of her ear as his unwanted voice replayed through her mind.

I'll teach you to like it. You'll crave me, Princess.

Astrid shoved the traitorous memories away and stepped closer to the bed. "You've had me. I demand stationery. You will have my letters delivered to my cousins."

Dimitri lifted his chin toward the new desk that occupied the same spot against the wall. She hadn't noticed it the night before when Dimitri kicked the door open and placed her on his bed. She moved to his closet first and paused. Every article had been placed back in its original spot.

"Shove my clothes into piles and I will flog your ass red," he warned.

Astrid ignored him, but minded his threat. Her fingertips brushed the hanger, and she stopped. She didn't feel anything inside her. No weight. No invasion. Astrid shifted her hips and reached between her legs. There was a dull ache, and she was tender, but her piercing was the only thing he left on her. She smoothed her hand over the side of her neck, confirming the raised scar.

The piercing and his brand, Astrid thought.

She carefully removed a white shirt. Well, not exactly white, but a light blush embroidered with gray threads. The material slipped over her, and she hurriedly fastened the buttons before cinching her lotus belt over her waist. She made her way to his desk and tossed the wooden hanger onto the bed. It bounced, nearly hitting Dimitri.

She took a seat and smoothed her hand over the oak ledge. It was an *exact* replica of the desk she destroyed with his sword.

His soft footfalls sounded behind her. Dimitri curled a length of her hair around his finger as his winged shadow fell over her.

"Take your pick of my stationery," Dimitri said, leaning over her. She remained still as his arm brushed her shoulder. He reached past her and opened a cabinet door to reveal stacked trays containing different parchments. He pointed at the pristine white pages. An embossed symbol, a red sword flanked by wings, served as a header. "If you want to send a letter with my royal seal, they are on the bottom."

He opened the drawer beside her next. Pens were arranged in a carved tray, each carefully placed along two notched wooden brackets.

Astrid selected a black pen and avoided his royal insignia. She took two sheets from the tray above it and began her letter.

Her jailor lingered, reading as her script spilled over the page. He had to know she wouldn't spell out what she truly wanted to convey to her cousins. He stepped away and dressed as she signed her name.

"I need my things from home—"

"This is your home," Dimitri interjected as he shrugged into his coat.

"This is *your* home," Astrid snapped. "I don't have clothes, or my royal seal." She prayed daily and needed the peace of her temple. The quiet hiss of the Mothers' Serpents. The gentle rasp as they slithered through the sacred space.

"Take me to your temple of the Three-Faced Mother."

Dimitri chuckled. "We worship blood and conquest. If you need a god, you can pray to me."

Astrid bared her teeth. Even her father commissioned temples of all religions to be built and allowed her subjects to practice their faith. "There are more than a dozen gods. Does Ambrose deny them to his people?"

He cruelly seized her jaw and jerked her face up before leaning in menacingly close. "Do not speak his name in my presence."

Temper bought her punishment. And while their religious text claimed he could be killed by tying him to a stake and lighting him on fire, getting him into such a position would be a difficult task.

Astrid swallowed her rancor and softened her features to plead, "I need my temple and serpents."

Dimitri's grip eased and he glided his fingers down her throat. "And what are you willing to trade, my feral neva?"

Ire heated her face. "If I am yours, I would expect you to provide me with my basic needs.”

“I see to all your needs,” he purred, leaning into her. The pad of his thumb dragged over her mouth, forcing her lips apart. “Do I not, Princess?”

“A temple would give me a place to commune and reflect. Such a gift...” Astrid gazed up at him through her lashes and warmed the tip of his thumb with a kiss. “Would carry favor, my lord.”

A lavish gift, certain to infuriate the court's nobility, Astrid mused to herself.

His mouth widened into a grin. “Will you demand the stars next?”

Astrid leaned back in her chair and hummed at him in mock sympathy. “If you wanted a female who was easily impressed, you should have kept to your rabble.”

He scrutinized her then turned his attention to her letter and neatly folded it into thirds. “Which cousin should I send the courier to?”

“Sorin in the Vermillion Palace.”

“Stay here,” Dimitri said, tapping the letter beneath her chin and lifting her face. “We wouldn’t want that pretty cunt to suffer the horrors of the Royal Legion.”

Chapter Twenty-Five

Dimitri closed the bedroom door and strolled into the hall before coming to a stop. He turned, finding a shadow hindering the morning light beneath the door frame. He watched as Astrid paced at her point of escape, daring her to disobey him. Minutes passed and the glow beneath the doorframe brightened, unobstructed.

Good girl, he thought before continuing his path.

The King's apartments occupied the same wing. Dimitri had taken residence here after the battle at Incarnadine Fields. His footsteps echoed as he descended the stairs and turned down the first hall. Their rooms were relatively close, and Dimitri couldn't help but laugh. He hoped Ambrose heard Astrid's screams as she came.

By the blood, he hoped Ambrose heard every moan and whimper he tore from Astrid's soft lips. Dimitri had claimed her in their oldest custom, but the fact that she'd been promised to Ambrose was salt he would endlessly pour into his king's wounds.

A groan met Dimitri in the corridor and he grinned at the door. It was closed, save for a sliver. A request for privacy Dimitri had no intention of honoring. Disturbing his king was one of Dimitri's few joys in life, and he cherished every opportunity.

He kicked the heavy oak door open and strolled in. Ambrose was seated at his desk, but it was the little blonde on her knees who drew Dimitri's attention. His entrance startled her, and she'd struck the back of her head on the desk.

"It's a bit early for philandering," Dimitri said, strolling passed bookshelves and a map of the Eight Kingdoms mounted against the eastern wall.

His king glared at him and fisted the female's hair. Her dark gray wings sank to the floor as a muted whimper escaped her.

"Did I tell you to stop?" Ambrose sneered.

"I'm sorry, Your Majesty," the blonde said quickly. Her voice shook as she added, "The noise frightened me."

Ambrose dragged her face to his cock and held Dimitri's stare with a look of satisfaction.

This was nothing new to him, and Dimitri approached his king as wet choking sounds filled the space between them.

"Give me your wings," Ambrose said amidst a moan.

The female reflexively tucked her wings against her body and Ambrose shoved her head down until she gagged.

"Now," he whispered, holding her in place.

A broken sound came from her, muffled by Ambrose's cock. She opened her wings to flank either side of his desk chair. His king unfastened a pair of daggers and staked the female's wings beneath the arm rests. He stroked her blonde curls affectionately and leaned back.

"You can leave after you swallow my cum," he said, tracing his thumb over her cheek as he turned his attention to Dimitri. "And what can I do for you, assassin?"

Dimitri's gaze fell to the female's wings. She tried to keep them still, but they shifted with her movements. The membrane split against the blade with each bob of her head. Dimitri was no stranger to cruelty, even enjoyed it on most occasions, but this—like all his king's strategies—was purposeless.

He yanked one dagger out of the chair and tossed the bloody

steel onto the desk before biting out, "Leave us."

"You do not command anything," Ambrose snapped, holding the female's head in place by her reddening scalp.

Dimitri flicked his wing over the far end of the chair and the second dagger clattered onto the polished floor. "You'll suffer his rage or mine. You may not survive his, but you will certainly die screaming under mine," Dimitri said.

He allowed a lash of his magic to bite and harrow her soul. Ripping pieces free. The female wailed as her soul crested his tongue. The putrid flavor of decay coated his mouth, and Dimitri's stomach curled. After his taste of Astrid's honeyed soul, the rotten tang of fear made his stomach roil.

The female scurried away, and Dimitri smiled. "I think she disagrees with you," he said, leaning his hip on his king's desk.

"You forget your place."

Wrath hardened his features, and he tossed Astrid's letter onto the desk. "I forget nothing," Dimitri hissed in a low whisper.

Ambrose returned his stare and lowered his gaze to fasten his trousers. "Your plaything would look good on her knees. I want a taste of her. Can she swallow a cock, or does she cry and choke?" he asked.

"Touch her," Dimitri said, smiling cruelly, "and the promises I made won't protect you."

"We both know your promise binds you," Ambrose said dismissively before waving at his desk. "Your next assignment is in the folder."

Dimitri retrieved the folder, not bothering to open it. When the previous queen ordered a death, he'd complied happily. Her absence weighed on him, and in the years without her, the elation he found serving her had vanished beneath his new monarch.

"I need a letter sent to Sorin at the Vermillion Palace," Dimitri said, gesturing to the letter. "Redact most of it. I'm sure my feral neva is attempting to inform her family on how to best ambush us."

Ambrose picked up the letter and flipped it over before carelessly discarding it onto a pile of letters. "No one is coming to save her. I split Clorea with her neighboring cousins." He flicked the letter against the name again and laughed. "This very one she's writing to."

Dimitri was shocked into silence. His king sulked from the battlefield, but this went against every foundation Ledivion upheld. The kingdom was ripe for conquest. Blood.

Malice slipped through Dimitri's voice as he spoke. "You *surrendered* half a kingdom when it was primed to take?"

Ambrose leaned forward on his desk and steepled his fingers under his chin. Annoyance crossed his pale, yellow eyes. "This is why you could never sit on the throne. You're an abomination, too blood-thirsty and simple to understand *gaining* half a kingdom is better than laying siege for the *possibility* of one."

"You think the Legion would follow a king who cowers from battle?"

Ambrose flicked his hand in the dismissive way Dimitri despised. "A king doesn't need to *enter* the battlefield. A king *commands* it."

A muscle ticked in Dimitri's jaw. "You don't command me, and you seem to have forgotten. My hands placed that crown on your head, little brother."

Chapter Twenty-Six

Astrid stood at the door, listening to the soles of her captor's boots scrap the polished stone tiles. They slowed to a stop, and agitated rage scraped her nerves.

He wanted to punish her and thought she was fool enough to immediately disregard the rules he'd set.

She paced a few steps, reassessing his space. The window near the closet yawned open a few inches. Astrid rubbed her arm and moved to the glass. She clicked her tongue against her teeth, unsure if Graymalkin would understand her meaning.

"Graymalkin," Astrid called.

A trail of snow had been disturbed, leading from the window to the hedges boarding the wall. He would be sitting in inches of snow and had to be cold. Astrid waited for the fluffy cat. Minutes ticked by and the cold chilled her legs. She left the window open a crack and took a last look over the wintery landscape for her fluffy companion.

He's not out here, Astrid reminded herself. The cat probably had more than a dozen rooms he frequented.

Turning away, she went to Dimitri's nightstand and opened the drawer. Her brows drew together. Her pins and combs were organized in neat vertical rows, arranged by size, but it was the dark pouch that commanded her attention.

He'd held her in the cage of his arms, fucking her while the metal plug filled her ass. The weight of her shame crushed her. She hadn't endured the things he'd done to her. She came for him more times than she could count, arching her back and begging him to fuck her slower.

Astrid snatched the pouch, and the ring of metal deepened her rage. She marched to the window and hurled it into the snow garden. Dimitri would never touch her—

Graymalkin bounded out of the hedge dragging the black pouch by its drawstrings. He dropped it on the window ledge and tilted his head up as though he expected head scratches.

"No," Astrid hissed as she retrieved her torture devices and frantically brushed the snow away. She glanced at the door and rushed back to the nightstand. The metal contents clanked as she arranged the pouch in its original position.

She took a calming breath and shifted her attention to the embellishments he'd stolen from her. Astrid settled on the two smallest combs and carefully slid the drawer closed. She stood before the mirror and twisted her hair beside her temple.

Astrid examined her reflection. With everything he'd done to her, taken from her, leaving her hair down without ornamentation made her feel the most vulnerable.

The most naked.

Royal females were distinguished by their combs and pins. Brilliant decorations indicated their house and standing. Astrid slipped her first comb in place. Delicate golden flowers accented with phoenix feathers gleamed in the firelight; teardrop rubies dangled from delicate chains.

Astrid positioned the second comb and exhaled. If she'd known she would be taken prisoner, she would have worn her jade and diamond set. Rubies were worn in times of aggression, signifying the blood she was willing to spill. What she'd worn as a warning was now all that remained of her threats.

The door clicked and Astrid's pulse accelerated. To her surprise, it calmed when Dimitri stepped in. *The evil you know is better than the anticipation of a threat*, she self-soothed.

He spared her a glance and strolled to his desk with a folder and a plate piled with meats and bread. The scent of rosemary and beef braised with red wine ignited her hunger.

Astrid held still as he approached. He bypassed her and went to the adjacent sink instead. Water flowed and he leisurely washed his hands before leaving her to take a seat. The male occupied the only chair in his room and turned to face her. A quick inventory of his desk had her frowning at the lack of utensils.

She approached him, centering her attention on the folder instead of her breakfast.

Dimitri narrowed his eyes, then glanced at the folder and back to her. His next move surprised her. She was certain he would dismiss her curiosity as her father had. She'd lost count of how many times her father slid letters, maps, and documents away from her, assuring her it was nothing she should concern herself with.

Astrid stared at the folder as Dimitri lifted it from the desk and offered it to her. She took it, scrutinizing the powerful male. Was it a test? Would he punish her for daring to open it? She tensed, ready to retaliate if he attacked her the moment she opened the folder.

She flipped the thick parchment and exhaled a breath to steady herself, anticipating his assault...

He didn't move. Only stared at her.

Astrid blinked. Her heart slowly found a calmer rhythm. She said nothing as she studied the portrait of a winged male. He wore layers of wool and mink. A puffed hat decorated with a feather topped his dark hair. The page beside it contained information. Apparently *Morstril* enjoyed hunting and left a portion of his kills as a weekly offering within the temples dedicated to conquest. The page listed his routine, where he could be found each day. His habits.

"Who is he?" Astrid asked.

"A lord who profits on information," Dimitri answered, bemusement alight in his golden eyes.

A traitor then. "Are you setting an example or arranging a disappearance?" A smile broke over Dimitri's lips, causing Astrid to bristle. She snapped the folder closed. "What? Should a female not understand the distinction?"

"I would expect nothing less from the princess who carved my chest and split my aorta."

His words cooled her temper. Soothed it.

Dimitri leaned forward and lowered his voice. "Would you have done the same to my king?"

He baited her with words of treason. What game was he playing? Did he want her brought to the throne room and whipped?

"Would you protect him?" she asked. Testing his loyalties without incriminating her own.

Dimitri's laugh startled her. It was full and rich, reaching all the way to his molten gold stare. "No. I would send you to his bed… but I'm not a male who shares."

Astrid weighed his words.

"You obviously hold animus for each other. Why are you here?" she asked.

His features dimmed as his humor drained from him like streaming droplets in a steady spring rain. "We're cursed with each other through unfortunate circumstance."

Astrid hadn't expected him to answer, and his cryptic words made her wrinkle her nose.

He gazed up at her, considering her for a moment. Two.

"I promised my mother I would serve this court," he said.

Astrid moved closer, stepping between his legs until she brushed his knee. She had the errant urge to smooth his hair and comfort him. Astrid buried the impulse. She would not let idiotic sympathy cloud her calculations.

"Why this one? What court does she belong to?"

Dimitri's stare shifted to the snowy landscape through the window. "My father killed my mother. I was his intended target, and she was an unintentional consequence," he whispered. A smile woven in bitterness exposed his straight white teeth. "I killed him all the same."

Astrid let his words sink in. Before she could contemplate a response, he curved his wing. The heavy bones pressed into the back of her thigh, ushering her closer.

She glared at his offending appendage, and he drew his wing

away. His fingertips replaced his wing, caressing her and stopping beneath the hem of his shirt she used as a dress. His touch intimate, instead of demanding.

"I learned to control my curse after her death," he said, tracing light circles on the side of her thigh. He chuckled then and lifted his chin toward his bed. "Which is why you survived your little assassination attempt. Soul Drinkers, Death Spirits of legend, require proximity to consume their victims," he said. His eyes lowered to her lips. "Usually during an embrace."

His ravenous stare lingered, and his gentle touches heated her blood.

His voice lowered. "My abilities reach a mite farther."

He parted his lips, and the slow drag of serrated teeth covered every inch of her skin. Gentled. Exquisite.

And capable of causing horrific pain, if he so chose.

She was caught in the jaws of a monster. Instead of devouring her, he held her captive. Delighting in every breath—every utterance—he elicited past her lips.

Her senses heightened, drowning her in ecstasy. The trace of his fingers. The pull of her garment over her nipples as she swayed on her feet. The ache between her legs only he could ease.

The haze of excruciating pleasure receded, and Astrid's mind cleared. Her heart pounded, her skin was flushed, and this fucking male looked all too pleased with himself.

He pulled her down and she took her place on his thigh. He pinched a cut of beef and lifted it to her mouth. Astrid took his hand and leaned in, taking hold of the morsel with her teeth. She pressed her thumb to his forefinger, and to her surprise, he let go of the slice of beef. She took it into her mouth and chewed, astonished he didn't demean her by making her lick and suck her breakfast from his fingers.

Dimitri lifted another cut of meat and smiled at her.

"After you finish your meal, I'll have your lips on my cock."

Chapter Twenty-Seven

Dimitri smiled as Astrid took a bite of bread from his hand. She was seated on his thigh, relaxed. A far cry from her arrival. She was acclimating to her new life and obedience suited her. His little neva could be difficult at times, but he expected the female gracing his side to be as fierce as he.

Astrid's full lips warmed the tips of his fingers. Her teeth gently grazed the side of his thumb as she took a bite of beef. He upheld the silent truce between them. If she affectionately accepted what he hand-fed her, he wouldn't clutch each morsel and force her to lick his hand clean before offering her another piece.

Her acquiescence, while pleasant, was a strategy he recognized. She was cunning with a vicious temper. A feral cat would never know it wanted to live indoors until you captured it. He would domesticate her—curate the role she played until it was so pleasant she preferred it.

His gaze lifted to the two glittering combs she'd arranged in her hair. What he saw was not defiance. Astrid had a taste for fine things and jewelry. Defiance would have been slipping every pin and comb in her possession through her silky black strands. What's more, she'd chosen a pair of combs instead of her daggered hair sticks.

This was her asking permission.

He ran his hand through her long hair, admiring how the jewels in the shape of teardrops swayed. "You wear rubies in your hair, but you selected diamonds for your piercing."

"We wear rubies in times of war," Astrid answered plainly.

Dimitri chuckled, lifting another cut of swan to his princess's lips. "Were you at war?"

"You rode in peace and ambushed my court," she said before trailing her dark nails along his wrist. "Have the release negotiations begun for my mother?"

Astrid leaned closer, resting her shoulder against his chest as she savored her meal. Her scent of honey and wildflowers surrounded him, but it was her teasing mouth that had his cock growing hard.

A momentary touch of her lips.

The gentle graze of teeth.

The way her tongue swirled over his fingertips.

He wanted to fist her hair and shove her to her knees. She would learn to swallow his cock, working those pouting lips up and down his shaft. Beginning her education was tempting, but they were having a discussion.

"You question the Queen's release, but not your own?" Dimitri asked, idly tracing circles over her hip.

Astrid huffed a breath and glared through the corner of her eye. "I know my freedom lies directly over your bloodied corpse."

"You'll never be rid of me. Not even death can separate us, neva," Dimitri crooned. He admired her jeweled comb. Small rose-gold blossoms with rounded petals were daintily placed on an elaborate feather plume. "Are your gems the only message? Do the feathers or flowers hold meaning?"

She stilled, hesitating a moment. Dimitri grinned. They did. He remained silent, patiently awaiting what his princess would divulge.

"Phoenix feathers are an indication of royalty," Astrid recited.

The calm mask of her expression was meticulous, but she

smoothed her hair and repositioned the comb. Dimitri noted her self-conscious mannerisms. Her words were a ripple, but their true meaning ran far deeper.

"Nobility are distinguished by combs and pins with plum blossoms, orchids, bamboo, or chrysanthemums," Astrid continued.

Dimitri pulled her closer and pressed a kiss to her temple. "I could strip you bare, and you would still be a princess, neva. These are things they can't take from us."

"Then return them to me," she argued.

The raging abyss reflected in her stare made his cock ache. "I think I should stretch your pretty cunt and make you come until you turn docile again."

Astrid blanched as her lips parted.

"Oh yes, Princess, you even curled up to my chest when I picked you up."

She rose and Dimitri trapped her in the curve of his wing, close but not touching. He methodically cleaned his fingers with a linen cloth.

"Get on your knees."

Astrid blinked, swallowed, then said, "I need to see your apothecary. Or a healer."

Stalling wouldn't save her. Dimitri stood and spread his fingers through her hair, sensuously caressing her scalp, until he palmed the back of her head. Her dark eyes slid closed, and a muffled sigh slipped past her lips. His feral neva liked to be pet. Dimitri smiled before pulling the strands taut. She drew a sharp breath, and his gaze dipped to her mouth before returning to the rage filled depths of her midnight gaze.

"Why?" he asked, stepping into her.

Astrid pulled against his hold, but her struggles were futile. She exhaled heavily and glared at him before snapping, "I need a contraceptive brew."

Dimitri breathed a laugh. He would sire young in her, eventually. The corner of his mouth pulled into a smirk. "Why?" he asked again. Amusement flickered through him as she blinked.

She lunged forward, yanking against his grip on her hair. "A bastard with your wings will kill me."

Hardly. "Ledivite females have far easier births than your kind."

Astrid's brow pinched and her mouth went slack. "Does anything I say make it through your thick skull? You common-bred—"

Dimitri closed his hand over her throat, cutting off her argument. Malice tinged his vision. "You are mine, neva. Your births, when they happen, will be easy... And I can remedy the bastard part."

Astrid shrieked when he hoisted her over his shoulder and turned toward the door. She shoved against his spine and screamed, "Put me down!" as he stepped into the hall.

She bounced on his shoulder with each step, and he palmed her thigh, moving higher. He found her ass bare and lowered his touch to fall between her legs. His fingertips brushed her waxed pussy, and he chuckled darkly.

"Did you forget to finish dressing or is this for me?" he asked as he toyed with her diamond-studded piercing. Dimitri folded his wing over his princess's lack of modesty as she wiggled and squeezed her legs together.

When Astrid couldn't free herself, she hissed, "Don't touch me."

Dimitri bounded down the stairs, rattling her with each step. Her silken strands felt divine against his wings. She wouldn't stroke them, but her warm breath fanned the membrane folding from his back.

"Why wouldn't I touch you? Are you afraid of me finding out how wet you are?" Dimitri asked as he glided a finger through her slick folds. "I don't need to touch you, Princess." He nuzzled her hip as he turned down another corridor. "I can scent how wet you are."

"I'm going to kill you."

Her words sounded like a vow.

Dimitri entered Vinceret's temple. It was empty. His booted steps echoed through the large cathedral. Stained-glass windows arched into the vaulted ceilings, depicting scenes of battle and death. Fire and blades.

Empty pews rowed either side of him. Astrid's fist closed over the leading edge of Dimitri's wing, and he slowed his steps. He rested his chin on the curve of her ass while she twisted her body in an attempt to catch the wooden back of a pew.

He stepped closer, allowing her to clap her hand over the curving woodwork. Amusement crinkled the corners of his eyes as she pulled and yanked. Did she really think she could stop him simply because she grabbed a wooden bench?

"Lord Dimitri, what can I do for you?" The male's long crimson robes rustled as he strolled to the center of the dais, standing between the large obsidian altar and a grand, carved statue of a winged male in full battlement. His carved features watched over his people; his hands rested over the pommel of the sword before him.

"Bind us before Vinceret," Dimitri said, resuming his march to the altar. Astrid's black-tipped nails raked the wood. She was strong for a little thing, but no match for him.

The priest faltered as Dimitri met him on the dais. He set Astrid on her feet and gripped her wrist, keeping her beside him.

"Bind?" Astrid asked.

She viciously fought his hold, and he herded her closer with his wing. His feral neva exhaled heavily, then reached up as far as she could before dragging her pointed nails down the leathery membrane. Dimitri bared his teeth as the burning sting bit, leaving thin, bleeding lines in their wake. He snapped the joint of his wing into her side and Astrid sucked a breath, holding her ribs.

"I am not marrying you," she spat.

Dimitri smiled in answer.

Astrid's desperate plea was turned to the priest. "You can't marry us. I don't want to marry him."

Dimitri ushered her closer to the altar, trapping her waist against the gleaming black edge. He leaned closer, pressing his chest into her back. She struggled, until she felt the hard length of his cock against the curve of her ass.

His feral neva was taking her lessons quite well. Each step she surrendered brought her closer to him. He slipped his hand down her wrist, intwining his fingers over hers.

"We worship Vinceret, God of Conquest and Blood," he murmured against the shell of her ear. He placed their intertwined hands on the obsidian altar and outstretched his arm to the slot carved at its center.

Astrid couldn't quite reach, but he dragged her forward, forcing her to bend at the waist. An angle Dimitri could appreciate.

This altar is the perfect height to fuck her against. He would need to tell the priests to leave. If they looked upon his naked wife, he would have to kill them and Vinceret needed his priests to perform his rituals.

"You are mine through right of conquest," he said, crowding the altar on either side of her with his massive wings. Dimitri pitched his voice lower as his gaze lifted to the priest. "And I wish us married."

Chapter Twenty-Eight

Astrid suffered the indignity of being stretched over the obsidian altar. The stone beneath her embodied the winter surrounding them. Its chill bit through her shirt dress and tightened her nipples, but Astrid kept her vicious glare on the winged priest. He removed a gilded ceremonial dagger from his wide leather belt. The gray linen of his sleeves billowed as he approached.

Astrid researched Ledivion wedding ceremonies the instant her match left her mother's lips. This portion of Ledivite marriage had been a footnote, whereas pages upon pages were dedicated to the Royal Hunt, a spectacle where Dimitri's kingdom gathered to watch their future queen flee her king.

Until he overpowered and claimed her.

Astrid glowered. She was no hind.

Tearing the priest's soul from his body would remind her demented suitor *she* was capable of dispensing death as well. Using Dimitri's hand for leverage, she lunged across the altar without warning.

The tips of her night-streaked nails grazed the priest's robe and Dimitri's talon came down hard, slicing into her wrist. Black chips of obsidian flew as he pinned her—like an offering to his god.

Her captor yanked her injured arm behind her back, leaving a trail of bloody droplets on the gleaming surface.

"Don't let her touch you, priest," Dimitri said calmly.

The robed male stammered for a moment then smoothed his clothing, regaining his composure. "I must remember the Anima Carnifex stands before me," he said, lowering his gaze to her hand clutched beneath Dimitri's.

"I do not consent to this," Astrid shouted.

The heavy bones of his wings dug into her back as she fought to pull her hand from the accursed gold trapping her. "I may not have my hands now, priest—but I will. And I vow, you won't die. I'll keep you, and make you watch as I kill everything and everyone you have ever loved. I'll drive you mad with their suffering, and keep you as an ornament."

Dimitri's hard cock ground into the curve of her ass, bruising her hips on the obsidian ledge. He leaned over her, the heat of him against her back made the chill of the altar bite that much harder.

"You've never said such sweet things to me, neva. Are you trying to make me jealous?" he purred.

Astrid ignored him. She lifted her fingers through Dimitri's curled ones, while his palm remained atop hers, reaching for the robed male.

The priest swallowed thickly. His knuckles whitened as he clutched his dagger. "My lord."

"Make her my wife," Dimitri demanded, patting their intertwined hands on the gleaming obsidian.

Astrid fought harder as the priest gripped the ceremonial blade with both hands and lifted it overhead.

"May the blood binding you, forge an alliance. United in all things, never turning from the other—"

"—Serpents devour you. You are a dead man—"

"—Bind them by their blood spilled. Their pain shared. Bless this union, never undone."

The knife came down, piercing Dimitri's hand and hers, bottoming in the empty slot carved into the altar.

Pain burned through Astrid's hand and clawed past her elbow as their blood welled together. It spilled in thin rivulets across their knuckles, pooling beneath their entwined fingers.

Astrid clenched her teeth, seething as she committed the priest's face to memory. The robed male immediately retreated, nearly tripping over his long gray robes. His large, unblinking eyes were reminiscent of a deer before the arrow struck its mark.

"Finish it," Dimitri commanded.

The priest hesitated and Astrid wiggled her fingers at him, embracing the burning licks of pain it sent up her tendons and down her ligaments.

"If... if you could cover her hand, my lord," he stammered out.

Dimitri chuckled and leaned his weight into her. Her chest squeezed against the obsidian surface, pushing her breath past her lips. Her jailor covered her exposed digits and outstretched his wing, securing her uninjured hand by the cursed gold circling her wrist.

"Satisfied?" Dimitri asked the priest at her ear.

His deep voice caressed her, and the memory of his death magic coiling over her breasts and between her legs lingered too near. Mothers save her. Astrid twitched her fingers, focusing on the pain. She would pray and reflect on why she associated Dimitri's rough treatment with the ecstasy his touch promised after he subdued her.

The priest pulled the knife from their hands. Pain anew seared up Astrid's arm and she stiffened, baring her teeth. The priest touched the bloodied wound on Dimitri's hand and it mended, leaving a thick, pale scar in its wake.

"A moment, my lord," he said as he hurried around the altar and out of Astrid's sight.

Realization dawned on Astrid, and she struggled, stomping her bare heels on Dimitri's boots.

"You will not disfigure me," she screamed, turning her head to find her view completely obstructed by Dimitri's disgusting wing.

A soft hand, timidly settled on her ankle and Astrid kicked blindly.

"Stop kicking my priest," Dimitri said, pinning her knee to the altar with the bend of his.

The priest's magic oozed over her, and Astrid obliterated it with a lash of her own. "I'm going to skin you, and you'll exist as my blanket," she screamed. Then, she turned to snap at Dimitri, "I'm going to kill you and commission your spine into my next pauldron!"

"My lord, her magic is greater than mine," the pitiful soul weaver confessed on his knees.

A warm, expansive breath fluffed her hair. Dimitri's firm lips brushed her temple as he said, "Let him scar our bond, neva, or we can renew our vows every morning."

Astrid took a breath to clear her mind.

Then another.

"I can scar my own hand. I don't need this idiot butchering me," Astrid replied coldly before struggling again. "Get your sweaty hand off me."

To her surprise the clammy palm lifted, and the sound of sandaled feet shuffled behind her.

Dimitri ground against her ass and said, "You are not a priest."

"You worship conquest, right?" Astrid turned and snarled, "Get on your fucking knees, priest, before I kill your entire family."

Robes rustled behind her and, what she imagined was the priest's forehead touching the stone floor, met her ears.

Astrid turned her head as far as she could and stared into Dimitri's golden eyes. "I conquered your simpering priest, and I claim him by right of conquest. Now get off the floor and make me a priestess," she yelled the last loudly.

More rustling fabric.

"M-my lord?" the male mumbled.

Dimitri chuckled, and the vibrations danced along her spine.

"You're learning our ways," he said sweetly, like he was proud of her. "But your attempts are misguided. Right of conquest is a victor's prize when we are at war."

"Oh, I'm at war," Astrid seethed. "I'm at war with everyone he's ever loved!" Dimitri chuckled again and Astrid bristled. "I am scarring my own hand, or we will be here every morning, *my lord*."

"Bargain with me," Dimitri purred.

Impulse seized Astrid and she uttered an impossible task. "My kingdom. The Serpents' Crown on my head."

"Always the stars with you," Dimitri exhaled. His weight lifted off her and he turned her in his arms, encircling her in the barricade of his wings.

To protect that cowardly priest and his fading footsteps.

Blood covered both her hands, one from his talon and the other from his disturbing nuptials.

He held his mended hand between them. "Scar it, like this."

Astrid stared up at him, judging his compromise.

"It should be thinner than yours. Your hand is bigger than mine," she argued.

He brought her bloodied palm to his mouth and placed a stinging kiss to his mark of devotion. Crimson stained his lips and dripped down his chin. "Make it a scar. Visible to others," he instructed.

Astrid knit her magic through the wound.

Closing it.

Healing it.

Until a white scar, half the width of Dimitri's, ran along the back of her hand, between her index and middle finger.

"Satisfied?" she asked, momentarily glaring up at him as she healed the talon gouge on her wrist.

Dimitri grinned and drew her closer. "Yes."

Chapter Twenty-Nine

Dimitri's lashes lowered as he uncurled his wings. The metallic taste of Astrid's blood clung to his lips and sang on his tongue. Sharper than her soul. Sweeter. *Binding*.

She was his. By right of conquest. Bound to him before Vinceret himself.

He lifted her against him, forcing her legs around his waist. His neva jerked when her ass touched the cold, obsidian altar.

"What are you doing?" she hissed.

Dimitri prowled closer, invading her space until she leaned back on her palms. His gaze lowered to the place where his collared shirt folded to a point between her full breasts. Then, drifted lower, to the junction of her toned thighs. Her makeshift dress did nothing to cover her. Dimitri admired the radiant gleam of more than a dozen diamonds decorating her piercing.

"Fucking my wife," Dimitri purred, meeting her midnight eyes. "Now, lift your knees."

Astrid turned on her hip and Dimitri caught her ankle before she could get far. He dragged her back to him, spreading her legs wider. He pinned her waist and drove two fingers into her cunt.

His neva squirmed, grasping his wrist in attempt to stop him. "This is a temple."

"Vinceret won't mind," Dimitri said with a grin. He thrusted into her harder, working that little spot he'd discovered inside her that made her scream his name. Her thighs constricted over his waist with bruising force. She was so desperate to pull her legs together. To get away from him.

"Come for me, neva," Dimitri crooned, stretching her to take another finger. A flush spread over her cheeks and bloomed down her throat. "I feel you tightening over my fingers. Stop fighting it."

Astrid tossed her head, fanning her dark strands over the obsidian altar. Craven, beautiful, and his. She panted beneath him, instinctively rocking in time to his hand.

Her lids fluttered and she stared up at Vinceret as though he might save her. "There are priests here," she breathed.

Dimitri bent over her but sustained his harsh rhythm. "They won't return," he murmured against her throat. His lips met her skin, and he savored the lingering kiss of salt from her perspiration.

With her fingers tangled through his hair, she asked, "How do you know?"

A grin bloomed over Dimitri's lips, and he moved lower. "Because if anyone looked upon my wife's naked body," he said, exposing her exquisite breasts. "I would revoke the privilege of their existence."

"I'm not your wife."

Astrid's words breathed into a moan as his teeth clamped over the tight peak. She fisted his hair, tugging the strands taut and pulling him closer. Her scent of honey and wildflowers surrounded him, coalescing with the heated notes of her arousal.

Dimitri kissed the hurt and his princess shuddered. He licked and sucked, lifting his eyes to hers.

"You wear my clothes," he said, gliding the backs of his fingers up her thigh. He found her piercing and teased her clit. A strangled cry slipped from her, and she arched her back high off the altar.

"You eat from my hand," he reminded her as he unfastened his slacks. A low growl rumbled from him as the head of his cock met the wet heat of her cunt. He thrust inside with a long, hard stroke. On the second, Astrid trembled beneath him. Her greedy cunt squeezed, and Dimitri groaned, letting his head fall back. "And you come on my cock."

He spread her legs wider with his wings and dug his fingers into her waist. She took each thrust, writhing for him. Her nails raked over his chest and left crescents in his shoulders, drawing him closer. He fucked her, jarring her lithe body with each thrust, waiting for the next orgasm to crash through her.

"You, neva," he more groaned than said, nipping at the tapered point of her ear as she came beneath him, "are whatever I say you are."

Astid blinked when Dimitri pulled out. The obsidian still chilled her back, an ever-present reminder of the sacrilege they'd committed.

Dimitri flipped her onto her stomach and captured her wrists in one hand. Astrid yanked against his hold viciously but stilled when the length of his cock slid between her ass cheeks.

Mothers save me. He's still hard.

Astrid glanced back at him and pointed at the ominous, hooded statue. "Not here. Dimitri, your actions will offend your god."

He chuckled and leaned over her, grinding his cock into her backside. "I've long neglected the temples and sermons. I should have brought an offering weeks ago," he said, drawing her hands forward until she was bent over the altar with her arms outstretched. "Your orgasms will be my tribute, wife."

"Take me back to bed, my lord." *Anywhere but this huge temple, where anyone could stroll in.*

"Keep your hands on the altar," Dimitri rasped, flattening her palms to the hard surface, "and I won't make you beg me to fuck your ass slower."

His hands released hers and Astrid contemplated a dozen scenarios. Running would only delay the inevitable. She could scream, but her cries would only draw an audience—one Dimitri might not mind fucking her in front of.

Astrid slid her palms closer and straightened, pressing her back against the unyielding planes of Dimitri's chest.

"It's cold. Wrap me in your wings," she breathed.

His voice was a low rumble as he enveloped her and the altar both in the warmth of his gray wings. "I thought you hated my wings, neva."

She did, but if her only other option was having her naked body on display while he fucked her… Astrid learned in that moment she would take the wings.

He tucked the end of her dress into her golden lotus belt, then shifted his wing to keep her covered while he retrieved a thin, silver vessel. "Spread your legs."

Astrid obeyed and Dimitri trailed kisses down the back of her neck. He reached between her legs and toyed with her piercing before focusing his attention on her clit.

"You're so wet for me," Dimitri purred.

Astrid shut out his voice. The sooner he came, the sooner this would be over. Astrid closed her eyes and craned her neck back toward him. Her lips met his in a soft kiss. Then another. His scent coiled around her, earthy but crisp, like snow falling in a forest with the barest hint of pine.

She opened to him, sucking on his tongue as he licked into her mouth. Pleasure thrummed beneath her skin as he claimed her mouth. She rocked into his hand behind her, needing more friction.

Dimitri groaned, then acquiesced, thrusting two fingers into her cunt. Astrid's lids fluttered, and she arched her back, giving him greater access. She took him deeper, focusing on the sensation of touch— his kiss and the way his hands moved. He stopped playing with her clit and added a third finger. Astrid pushed against him, taking each stroke.

The tension within her pulled taut, as each thrust pushed her closer to the orgasm that threatened to break her. She scarcely registered when Dimitri poured oil over her ass and moaned when his fingertips returned to her clit.

His fingers left her and Astrid arched her back, silently begging him to fuck her. His touch returned, higher this time, circling her ass. Astrid stood on her toes, unable to escape him as he pressed inside. He fingered her ass slow while he mercilessly teased her clit.

Astrid broke their kiss and leaned forward onto his wings. Shame twisted her pleasure. She closed her eyes. She couldn't come for him. Not like this. Not with what he was doing to her.

"Give yourself to me," he rasped.

Astrid said nothing. His wings tightened around her, drawing her near.

"Come for me," Dimitri crooned, "because you're *mine*."

Astrid panted as he stroked a second finger inside her.

"Because I want every part of you," he murmured.

Astrid curled her night-streaked nails around the thick edge of the obsidian as the tension in her snapped. Pleasure crashed over her, so intense she trembled. Astrid drowned in the sensations cascading over her senses, one after the next.

She wasn't sure how long Dimitri held her there. When he finally withdrew from her, she sagged against the frame of his wings. They lowered, but remained folded beneath her as she laid bent over the altar. His death magic then washed over her. Gentle, yet claiming, echoing remnants of her orgasm until she was coming again.

Astrid gripped the heavy bones of his wings as the broad tip of his cock touched her ass. She held on as he stretched her; panted as he fucked her with the tip until she was moaning and rocking her hips to take him deeper.

"I'll never tire of the way your soul tastes," he growled, taking her in longer strokes.

His magic rippled over her and Astrid's pleasure spiked to ecstasy. He was drinking her soul, but with the haze blanketing her mind, she couldn't remember why she should fight it.

"Pinch your nipples for me."

Astrid obeyed his purring voice and was rewarded with a groan.

"Harder. Tug on them."

"Dimitri," Astrid breathed against his wing.

Astrid moaned as his fingertips bruised her hips. He took her in a harsh rhythm, and she arched her back, in need of more. *Wanting* more. She sighed his name, and his cock twitched. His grip tightened and he thrusted into her a final time, coming inside her.

Chapter Thirty

Dimitri brushed his lips over the side of Astrid's throat. He licked the straining tendon, and felt her pulse thrum against his mouth. He grinned as she caught her breath.

"Once I clean up, I want your lips on my cock, wife," he purred.

Astrid shoved her elbow into his ribs as though she weren't pinned beneath him. Then, she sighed. "I can't."

"Is this all you can take, Princess?" he asked, languidly rocking his hips. He leaned over her, catching her lips in fleeting kisses as she gasped and moaned beneath him.

He gripped her face, holding her firmly, but gentle enough not to hurt her. Her eyes fluttered open, midnight glazed with pleasure.

"I need an apothecary," Astrid said between deep breaths. "Contraceptive, Dimitri. I don't want the consequences you intend to wrought on my body."

Because no one would willingly carry cursed heirs.

Dimitri buried the chasms of hurt her words unearthed. He covered his ill-omened birthright with violence and temper but for the first time, he didn't want to inflict pain to cover his own. He withdrew from her and fastened his trousers. A numbness crept through him as she sat. His princess was flushed with a thin sheen of perspiration, and quickly buttoned her stolen garment.

There were no playful stares between them. No sweet smiles. None of the easy affection he'd witnessed of established couples he'd observed during his years at court.

Your cursed blood is an abomination. Dimitri's father's voice boomed through his mind, just as it had each time he'd slipped past his mother to approach the fallen king.

He *was* an abomination, and Astrid would run at the first opportunity. Love would never strike between them, but he might earn her loyalty.

Dimitri stepped into her and was surprised when her arms encircled his neck. He lifted her against him and guided her toned thighs around his waist. He smoothed his shirt over the curve of her ass, holding it in place as he made his way to the temple's balcony.

Her arms tightened around him, and her teeth chattered. "Dimitri, it's cold."

The winter chill kissed his wings as he squinted against the sun. He patted her thigh and assured her, "It's a short flight."

"What?" Astrid gasped as he leaped onto the railing.

He waited and she squeezed closer before turning her head to peek at the pines lining the cliff below. His princess immediately buried her face in the crook of his neck.

"Put me down. I want to go down," she insisted through her chattering teeth.

Dimitri leaned forward, embracing the transient moment of weightlessness he loved. Astrid shrieked and with a powerful beat of his wings they were airborne.

"I am going," Astrid yelled between his wingbeats before her feral nature overwhelmed her, "to feed you to the Mothers' serpents myself."

"You're holding me so sweetly," he teased, nuzzling her temple. "I need to take you flying more often."

"I'm getting frostbite."

He reached behind himself and cupped her chilled toes. A warm breath fanned over his throat, and she shoved her foot into his palm.

Dimitri couldn't help but chuckle. "You are not very tempered for someone who threatens murder as often as you do."

His neva remained silent as he scaled the next cliff. Dimitri crested the trees and shadows gave way to sunlight. The air was thicker here, warmed by the billowing pillars of steam that stretched over the thermal spring. He had the impulse to fold his wings and dive, opening them in time to level and skirt his wingtips in the spring as he soared. The female clutching him would need many more flights before she was seasoned enough for such a maneuver.

He gave her an easy descent and landed quietly before gently lowering her to the pebbled stones surrounding the spring.

"Undress," he instructed, shrugging out of his suit jacket before folding his wings through the slits.

His neva hugged herself and moved closer to the thermal spring. "I'm not taking my clothes off outside. Anyone could stumble upon us."

"I'll protect your modesty."

He withheld the fact he'd grown tired of coming here only to be shunned by the other members of court. They made a show of huddling together as to not get within ten feet of him, claiming his cursed blood contaminated the waters. Dimitri's patience had frayed too thin, and he'd slit the side of his throat, pouring his cursed blood into the spring.

They fled and never returned.

Astrid gave him a sidelong glance and began unbuttoning her shirt dress. "If someone flies over here, I expect you to bring them to me," she said. Then, Astrid tossed the shirt on the smooth rocks and waded into the pool.

Dimitri finished stripping and joined her before asking, "And what will you do with them once I've dropped them at your feet?"

She stepped deeper into the spring and took a seat, allowing the clear blue water to—somewhat—cover her breasts. "I'll take their eyes." She glanced at him over her shoulder.

Dimitri wandered to the water's edge and plucked a small yellow flower from one of the plants bordering the pond. He took a seat behind her and pulled her closer, until her back met his chest. The heat from the water seeped into his wings and Dimitri groaned, stretching them out. They spanned either side of them and he hooked his chin over her shoulder.

"For you," he said, holding the small flower in front of her.

Astrid took the yellow bud, smelled it, then flicked it away.

"I won't accept the wildflowers you bring your simpering females." She said this with no bite in her voice as she leaned into his chest.

He collared the front of her throat and tilted her face upward. "It's the contraceptive you've been shrieking for," he said, maintaining the bloom's proximity with the curve of his wing.

Astrid shook from his grasp and retrieved the flower from the water's surface. "Do you make it into a tea?" she asked, glancing back at him.

"You eat it, or the leaves. The leaves are bitter, though there is some sweetness to the petals," Dimitri explained.

He stroked her back while she scrutinized the yellow petals and pink center. After a few moments, she shoved his wing out of the way so she could approach the thorn-stalked plant and examine its heart-shaped leaves as it grew from the ground.

"Do you eat a flower daily?"

"No," Dimitri replied simply. "Ingesting the plant monthly will keep you free of the consequence you think I want *wrought* upon your body."

Astrid laughed, then took a delicate bite of the flower's petals and chewed thoughtfully.

"Should you find yourself housing an unwanted guest," Dimitri outstretched his wing and touched his talon to a small, hanging bud. "One seed from this plant will cleanse you of it."

"Will a handful cause hemorrhaging?" Astrid asked before popping the remainder of Dimitri's flower in her mouth.

"Who are you trying to kill?"

"Anyone who stands between me and the Serpents' Crown." Astrid leaned against Dimitri once more, and lifted her gaze skyward.

"Your kingdom is fallen, and still, you cling to it."

Astrid glared back at him then turned her attention to the reflective surface of the water. "It's my birthright—something you could never understand."

Bitterness tugged down the edges of his smile, but he ignored the barb she unknowingly hurled. His neva didn't truly want a kingdom. Her crown equated to privilege and freedom. Those were things he could provide.

"And if I were to offer you a wardrobe?" he asked.

Astrid glanced back at him again. Her midnight eyes glittered with calculation. "In exchange for what?"

He took her hand, bringing it to the surface. She splayed her fingers as he traced circles on her palm. "Would an array of gowns brighten your mood?" he asked.

"Not as much as your severed head," Astrid said, lacing her fingers with his, "but it'll do."

"I'll set an appointment with my clothier." Dimitri pressed a kiss to her temple.

Chapter Thirty-One

Astrid could play the part of tamed concubine. She soaked in the thermal spring, contemplating her next move. She'd penned her letter to Sorin and was due another letter after being bent over the altar. Astrid smoothed her fingers over the muscular arm caging her ribs.

"Has my mother's release been negotiated?"

Dimitri remained silent, but drummed his fingers on her side.

He's thinking up a lie, Astrid thought viciously. She longed for Sterling's dungeons and how easily it was to extract the truth from her victims. Her jailor was immune to her magic, but not *her.* Astrid turned in his arms and positioned her naked self to sit across his lap. She laid her head on his shoulder and waited for his lie.

"No," he said after a time.

Astrid blinked. She'd been dismissed and excluded from any

political strategies or battles in Clorea, but Ledivion was better and worse in equal measure.

"Can I see her?" Astrid asked.

His callused hand glided over the small of her back. "No."

Astrid suppressed the fury coiling inside her. There was no pause, no thoughtful reflection. He simply denied her request—dismissed her, as her father and cousins had.

She swallowed her rancor and curled into him. "Seeing her would help set my mind at ease. I would sleep better, knowing she's not being mistreated."

If her mother was claimed a war prize, Astrid would dice her captor into meaty chunks and keep him as a puzzle for her guests to arrange.

Dimitri's deep voice interrupted her thoughts. "I am sure her release is being negotiated. You will not be imparting any messages for her to take back to your cousins."

"I made a bargain with you to write letters to my cousins. I don't need my mother to carry words I can write. I want to see her," Astrid said before a thought occurred to her.

Guilt festered through her resolve.

Is a winged male hurting my mother right now?

Astrid's stomach knotted. "Was Clorea's Queen claimed as a right of conquest?"

"One must make a kill to claim the right of conquest. I was the only being to make kills in your palace, neva. Your mother is a prisoner, but otherwise, she is unharmed."

Dimitri's strong arms circled her waist. He held her in silence and Astrid was content to soak in the steaming pool. She postponed the frigid cold until pangs of hunger drove her from her heated sanctuary. Her captor was kind enough to let her dry herself with her makeshift dress and even helped her into the shirt and jacket he'd worn. The heavy linen kept the bite of winter off the skin it covered, but did nothing for her exposed legs.

Dimitri flew Astrid back to the palace and landed in the green space outside his bedroom. She rushed to the roaring fire as he casually strolled to his closet. She peered at him as he painstakingly considered a number of sleeves before selecting his shirt. Her gaze drifted to the muscles along his back, the way they flexed and shifted as he dressed.

Mothers save me. What am I doing?

She turned her head, glancing around, desperate to find anything else interesting as she rubbed her hands together. She exhaled and tilted her hand, examining the pale scar.

She could cut it off and heal it, along with his brand when she escaped. Thank the serpents he married her on a whim. The knowledge of their marital bond would die with him and his priest.

Movement caught her eye, and the very priest she planned to massacre stepped into the hall before turning his back to her and continuing on his way.

"Priest," Astrid called as she stalked into the hall.

The male glanced back at her. When he saw the intent in Astrid's eyes, he frantically gathered his gray robes and sprinted down the hall.

Astrid darted after him.

"Neva!" Dimitri roared behind her.

Astrid ignored him. She needed to catch this fucking priest before his winged ass found a window he could squeeze through.

Booted footsteps pounded behind Astrid and she ran harder. Dimitri could have her after she ripped the priest's soul from his body.

She gained on the robed male, her nails scraping his rough wings. The dark-haired priest unleashed a shrill scream, and her next swing made contact. When the smooth edge of his wing grazed her fingertips, her magic seized him, gathering his soul.

In the next instant, a muscular arm circled her waist, and Astrid was hoisted off her feet, away from her prey.

She bared her teeth, still reaching for him as he crashed to the ground. His soul no longer obeyed her, but she'd taken his legs before Dimitri interrupted her.

"My—my lord," the lean male stammered as he worked to redistribute his soul to his useless limbs.

"You cannot kill the priests."

His voice was bemused, and Astrid found herself hoping he wouldn't jam his cock in her ass for her outburst. He pressed a kiss to the back of her head and gently set her down. The priest rose on trembling legs and bowed at Dimitri.

To him. When *she* was his real threat.

Astrid's temper spiked and she no longer cared what his life would cost her. She shoved Dimitri's hand and lunged at the priest, breaking free of her captor's hold.

She caught strands of black hair and Dimitri tugged her waist at the same moment the priest flinched out of reach.

Astrid screamed her frustration, flailing in Dimitri's arms. He chuckled and the priest paled until she thought he might faint.

Her back met Dimitri's unyielding body, and she calmed. Her heartbeat slowed, joining his quiet rhythm. Fighting him was pointless, but it did ease some of her hostility.

"You cannot kill the priests," he repeated, smoothing his hand down her side as though she were the one in need of reassurance.

Astrid glared at the pallid, robed male and said, "Oh, he'll live—"

Her words were choked when Dimitri tossed her over his shoulder. His palm warmed her bottom and Astrid remembered she wasn't wearing panties.

"Avert your eyes, Dobromil. I'd hate to kill you for gazing upon my unclothed wife," he rasped, lower and on the precipice of violence.

Astrid heard cloth rustling, followed by a rushed, "My lord."

Dimitri turned and Astrid used his wings as leverage to lift herself. "I own you, priest. You may live as my servant. You will gather my laundry each morning—"

"He is not helping you dress," Dimitri interrupted.

Astrid struck his wing and continued her tirade. "You will make my bed, and you will find me fruits."

"Yes, Princess," the priest said with a bow. Then, he scurried away.

Dimitri nipped Astrid's thigh hard enough to sting and she jerked.

"You shouldn't dish it out if you can't take it," he said smoothly.

Astrid exhaled and lowered herself along the muscular expanse of his back. She examined his pressed slacks. The polish on his black shoes. He was always so neat and tidy. Astrid rolled her eyes, half tempted to slide her hand beneath his embroidered court jacket and untuck his shirt.

"Your priest is gone. You can put me down now," she sighed as she cataloged the hall.

No guards. No servants. No one had approached when she

made the deafening attempt on the priest's life.

Astrid smiled and lifted herself by his wing again. She twisted her waist to lean over his opposite shoulder. He turned toward her as they entered his bedroom and arched a brow.

"If you want to wear me like a scarf I can wrap my legs around your neck," she offered.

His features softened and he tossed her onto his bed. The fool male thought the Anima Carnifex could be led by a leash.

Perfect. Prey at ease dies quickly.

"Dress," he ordered halfheartedly. His golden eyes raked over her body before meeting hers again. "Or don't." His laugh surprisingly brought a smile to her lips, and he turned toward the hall. "I will return with a meal."

Astrid rolled onto her side with a huff. "Bring me fruits, and sweet wine," she grumbled after him.

She stood and wandered to the door, watching him, playing the part of a smitten female. Her lashes lowered and her pale scar glared at her accusingly.

The tamed wife, she thought as she counted the halls Dimitri crossed in the torchlight glinting off his dark hair as he passed.

Chapter Thirty-Two

Dimitri strolled to the Royal Legion's mess hall. The mundane chatter silenced the moment he set foot inside the large dining hall. It had been nearly a decade since he graced them with his presence in this place. His chest tightened into a bitter knot. He'd fought beside them once. Was one of them.

Once.

He'd been an awkward whelp the first time he'd stepped foot inside these walls—a youth of only fifteen. Inexperienced and foolish. Always attempting to win the affection of his father, the King, when the male was never capable of the sentiment.

It seemed like a lifetime ago, but the lingering purpose he'd once felt within these walls grounded him. No matter how many years transpired, or how much he denied it, the unwanted ghost of a life that could have been never left him.

The brutal drills and training came easily, and he'd found the place he belonged.

Dimitri's thoughts turned bitter. His comradery vanished when he turned eighteen. A fully grown male assigned to his first legion, tasked with his first assignment.

Dimitri ran two fingers along a buffet table staffed by a handful of footmen. They made regular trips to the kitchen, ensuring the dishes remained piled high with meats, bread, and potatoes. He smirked at the wide bowls of rich brown gravy, a common condiment on the royal table, but a rarity here. A treat the battle-hardened earned for the legion through particularly vicious victories.

He strolled past the delicacy and wondered if his father would have served the legion gravy if his plan had succeeded.

Dimitri was dispatched with a small team for his first assignment. It was unusual for a male as young as he'd been to be assigned such an honor, but he'd mistakenly thought his dedication to the craft of war was noticed and rewarded. A foolish young male, so blinded by his pursuit of belonging, he didn't recognize the ambush his father orchestrated.

The enemy knew they were coming. Seventy males waited for their arrival, dwarfing their force of ten. Fear had never chilled Dimitri's blood. He worshiped Vinceret and there was no better death than on the battlefield, wrought in steel and blood.

He cut down the enemy forces with cold precision and the inevitable happened.

Pain had exploded through his chest, and Dimitri glanced down, scarcely recognizing the spearhead jutting through his armor. His magic culminated in a torrent of famished shadows, lashing at the closest soul. Then the next.

Dimitri broke the spear and ripped it from his rapidly healing body. His curse was finally a blessing. He could save his friends *and* win this strategic foothold for his father.

He'd yelled for them to fall back, to stay out of range, and began his assault with no regard for the shriveled, black-veined bodies he left in his wake.

When it was done, his team survived, but at a cost. The males he'd fought with kept their distance. Instead of regarding him as an asset, he became a menacing threat. The same males he'd saved spread whispers of the Death Spirit through the Royal Legion. His place of belonging and the friends he'd made died before him, as lifeless as the contorted corpses he'd left on the battlefield.

None of it mattered, Dimitri reminded himself. He was above them, by birth, skill, and intellect.

Dimitri found his quarry at the end of the table. Several bottles of wine with cups stacked tall beside them. He uncorked and sniffed several bottles before finding the honeyed wine he searched for. The footman stood exceedingly still, and Dimitri grinned. The male pulled his wings tighter to his back and sweat began to bead on his forehead.

"Do you think if you hold still, I won't notice you?" he asked, recorking his neva's wine.

The footman swallowed. "N-no, Lord Dimitri. I can have a new bottle brought to you, my lord."

"No. I have what I came for," he answered, glancing over the silent mess hall. Dimitri held the bottle of wine out and wiggled it at no one in particular. "You don't mind if I take this do you?"

The silence continued and Dimitri casually strolled down the three steps separating the buffet from the rows of tables. Hundreds were packed into the long tables, and not one Fae moved.

They were hardly breathing.

Dimitri lifted his hand, admiring his scar for long moments before turning his palm in to display his wedding mark. "My wife is in my chambers, and I've been assigned to a target. If any of you so much as look in her direction while I am gone, I will kill all of you and your families. Do you understand me?"

The silence continued, but their eyes followed him.

"Should I kill all of you as a message? I asked, 'do you understand me?'" Dimitri yelled the last.

"Yes, Lord Dimitri," they answered in unison.

"Good," Dimitri said, lifting the bottle of wine at the legionaries. "Enjoy your meal."

Chapter Thirty-Three

Astrid would be grateful and obedient. The corners of Dimitri's eyes crinkled at the thought. Whether she gave him an affectionate smile or a vicious sneer made no difference to him. He thoroughly enjoyed punishing his feral neva. If she dismissed his thoughtfulness, he would tie her to a rafter and flog manners into her. And if she appreciated his efforts, he would make her come until she passed out.

He carried her stolen bottle of wine and bite sized pastries filled with chicken, cheese, and beef. The chefs said nothing when he filled his plate with selections reserved for the royal table. They would rearrange the dishes to disguise his pilferage. His younger brother would never know he'd taken food off his table for his little neva, but he knew—and it brought a smile to his lips.

He'd searched the kitchen, but knew the fruits his neva desired were in short supply. A handful of individually wrapped chocolates—the ones his brother kept for the unfortunate females who found themselves in his bed—would have to do. Chocolates weren't fruit, but Dimitri speculated it was the sweetness she missed.

He entered their room and glanced at Astrid, then set her dinner on his desk. She met his eyes as he passed. His princess looked at home, seated on the edge of their bed. Graymalkin lounged over her legs, occupying her entire lap. She continued stroking his cat's chest as he washed his hands.

Dimitri noticed Astrid watching the way he lathered his hands under the warm water. Her midnight gaze trailed up his forearms and a faint flush brightened her cheeks when she reached his chest. Her brow knit together, and she turned her attention back to Graymalkin. Her scrutiny bemused him. He was a striking specimen of a Ledivite male. And shouldn't a wife freely admire her husband?

Dimitri strolled back to his desk and took a seat. Astrid stood, to Graymalkin's disagreement, and sauntered toward him. His shirt was too large for her frame but the way it hugged her curves… His female in his clothes. *What more could he want?*

"If you're going to insist I sit on your lap while you hand-feed me, could we get a bigger chair?" she asked. Her nails ran along his embroidered lapel as she lowered herself onto his thigh. A smile curled her full lips, and she toyed with the collar of his shirt. "A couch or settee." She leaned closer and whispered, "A throne."

Rage and jealousy coiled through his muscles. Her ambition turned her gaze toward his brother.

"A would-be queen," he rasped, daring her to admit her betrayal.

She curled up against him, laying her head on his shoulder. "It's my birthright. Clorea is unoccupied. We could rule as Queen and King Consort."

Relief flooded him and a low laugh slipped past his lips. He wrapped her in his arms and tucked his neva against him. Her quiet scent of honey and wildflowers gave his mind peace. She wouldn't abandon him now.

"My cousins would aid me. We would be unstoppable together. The Death Spirit and his soul weaver. Who could stand against us?"

His soul weaver.

Her words left a hollow ache in his chest. Dimitri smoothed his hand over her thigh before retrieving the plate. He held the dish in front of her but instead of taking one of the pastries, she pushed off his chest and stilled.

He lifted the plate a fraction. "You've pleased me, neva. Eat."

Astrid's midnight eyes flicked from him to the golden puffs and returned to him. Her back tensed as she studied him. She slowly reached for a flaky square, shifting her weight away from him. Dimitri thinned his lips. His feral neva still distrusted him deeply. He'd been rough with her. Demanding.

Nothing good or kind survived within him. Gentle emotions equated to pain, and he'd crushed them years ago.

But his vicious neva housed even less. He would feed her violent impulses and worship her as his queen. He had an eternity with her and with time—and tributes—he would win her loyalty.

She was his, and he would never let her go.

He trailed his fingers along the dip of her spine as she took delicate bites of the stuffed pastry.

She finished her first piece and raised her chin at the glass. "Can you pour me some wine?" she asked before selecting her next flaky square.

Dimitri did as she asked and handed her the thin, fluted glass. Astrid took the glass and swirled its contents before bringing it under her nose. She inhaled and a hint of a smile touched her lips. She sipped the dark liquid and glanced at him. "I thought you'd said you didn't have honeyed wine here. This is almost as good as home."

"This is home," Dimitri corrected as she set the glass on his desk. He pressed two fingers onto the base and slid it from the precarious edge Astrid left it on. "Sweet wine is a lowborn libation here. The nobles drink red. It pairs best with the meats served at their tables."

"Do the lowborn not eat meat?" Astrid asked.

Her curiosity appealed to him. Most noble females only cared to understand how far their male's influence reached and what it could afford them.

"Mostly rabbit and fowl," Dimitri answered.

"Swan is a fowl." Astrid glanced down at his signet ring. She lifted her lashes, and a mischievous smile crossed her lips. "Did a lowborn female cook it for you before you came to court?"

"Are you jealous?" he asked.

She licked the flaky remnants of her last square from her finger and laughed softly. "I'm trying to understand you."

"My mother was lowborn. Her family raised swans. They're bigger than ducks, yield more meat. She was a soul weaver and caught the eye of my father."

"Your mother was a soul weaver?" Astrid blinked at him. "Why don't you follow the Three-Faced Mother?"

"Because, neva, fate is not kind. Why would I bend to her? Vinceret is who we worship here. It always made more sense."

"Do you have other family? Keres told me you came to court as a distant relative to the King."

The lie his father perpetuated.

"No one worth mentioning," Dimitri answered.

As Astrid savored her meal, the muscles knotting her back relaxed. She turned toward him and held a stuffed pastry bite to his lips.

"Do you eat?" she asked.

Dimitri leaned forward and opened his mouth, kissing her fingertips as she hand-fed him. The same way she'd done to him. Her cheeks flushed, adding a hint of lavender to her complexion and Dimitri chuckled.

"Miss my tongue, neva?" he asked darkly.

The color on her face deepened. "I'd like to return to the library."

Dimitri humored her change of subject and placed the empty dish on his desk. He held his little academic, committing the feel of her satiny skin beneath his hands to memory.

Life with Astrid would be agreeable once she accepted her place beside him. He imagined books piled into towers beside their bed. She would lay on her stomach and read with the sheets bunched low on her waist.

"Do you have a subject you'd like me to bring back to our room, neva?" Dimitri asked, smoothing her hair to one shoulder.

She glanced at him and arched a brow. "In exchange for..."

"Consider it... an act of kindness," Dimitri murmured. He lifted her hand and pressed his lips to her wrist. Astrid went so still he wondered if she held her breath.

"I want the war archive. Every Ledivite battle over the past fifteen years," she said after a beat of silence.

Dimitri took a deep breath, contemplating her request as her scent of wildflowers and honey enveloped his senses. "The knowledge you desire is far from commonplace."

"So are the things you desire, my lord," Astrid retorted. "If your present kindness extends to my mother, I would like her released."

"Do you want her naturalized as a Ledivite?"

Astrid wrinkled her nose. "No. I want her released to my family."

Dimitri held up a finger, countering, "One battle from our war archive."

"Twelve years ago, there was a battle at Incarnadine Fields."

Dimitri blinked. He knew the details of that particular battle intimately.

"Your people lost," Astrid continued, "and I want to read about the massacre."

Cunning little neva. "How long have you been researching Ledivion?"

"Since the moment I realized my hand would be sold to the highest bidder."

Dimitri nodded and pulled the folded parchment on his desk closer, tapping its center. "I will be leaving shortly. I need to set an example, and will return in two nights' time. The servants will bring you furs within the hour so you may sleep comfortably in my absence."

"You're leaving me alone?"

He glanced up at her and found her scrutinizing him. "There is no place in all the kingdoms where I would not find you."

"Your absence will be known. What do you expect me to do when the enemies you've made come for me?"

Dimitri stroked her cheek and smiled. "Kill them."

Chapter Thirty-Four

Dimitri was being sent away on an assassination mission. Astrid hid her smile. She couldn't ask for a better opportunity to escape.

A knock sounded at his door. "My lord?" a female's voice called from the other side.

"Come," Dimitri answered.

The door clicked open, and he made no move to stand or release her. Three females entered holding furred bundles. They placed the blankets at the end of his imposing, four post bed and bowed before hurriedly retreating.

Astrid untangled herself from her demented host and moved closer to inspect the bundles. They were thick and soft. She took the ends of the gray one and flung it open before popping it over the bed. A light floral scent met her senses. Dimitri must have requested they be freshly laundered.

He appeared behind her and smoothed his hand over her waist. The heat of his touch warmed her skin. He drew her into him, and her back met his firm body.

"Keres will bring you a gift while I'm gone," he rasped against her hair.

Astrid nodded in agreement, then asked, "You're returning after two evenings?"

"I hope to be sleeping beside you on the second," he murmured.

Astrid turned in his arms and studied his expression. Tension hid behind his eyes and the corners of his mouth were downturned. This was a male torn. He would complete his task as quickly as possible and rush back to her. A single night wouldn't give her enough time to escape. She needed him *at ease*, which meant she needed to prove she would be here...

Obediently waiting for him.

"I'll write my letter in the morning. You've exhausted me," Astrid said, flattening her hand over his lapel.

"Lay back. I'll do all the work," he said, leaning into her.

His insistence grated her, but arguing would only set Dimitri on edge. She wrapped her arms around his neck and kissed him sweetly. "You had me on the altar before your god," she whispered at his lips. "Let me rest, my lord."

A rakish grin flashed across his lips. "Am I too rough with you?" he asked, as he unbuttoned the topcoat she wore. Then, he started on the shirt beneath it.

"I'm not acclimated to your... size," she said, gracefully stroking his ego.

"I'll have another set of plugs made for you. You'll wear them during the day until you can take me."

Astrid paled as Dimitri pushed her clothing over her shoulders and they fell in a heap. She blinked, searching for a response. "You're too kind, but that won't be necessary."

Dimitri stroked her hair and lifted his chin toward the bed. A command.

She reconciled her fate, tucking herself under the furs and curling up on her side of the bed while Dimitri stripped. He placed her golden lotus belt on his desk and their clothes in the hamper before joining her.

Astrid rolled onto her side, facing away from him as she pulled the furs up to her chin. The sheets rustled and a muscular arm circled her waist and dragged her backward. The length of his cock prodded her ass as her spine met the chiseled planes of his chest.

"Dimitri," she hissed, unable to break free from his hold.

He wedged an arm under her and palmed her breast, squeezing her curves as she fought. Dimitri rolled her nipple between his thumb and forefinger. Pleasure ricochetted through her, and Astrid kicked her legs.

The head of his cock glided through her pussy, and he groaned at the warm pressure. "You're so wet for me already, neva," he purred, tugging on the tight peak until it plucked through his fingers. He immediately pinched her again. "Do you like being overpowered? Having your legs spread?"

The blunt tip of his cock pressed against her cunt and Astrid swallowed a moan as he stretched her. He was rough, purposefully hurting her, and his treatment made heat pool between her thighs.

What's wrong with me?

Astrid stilled. Keeping the illusion of his tamed wife was essential to her escape. This was an asset. He knew how to make her wet, but it meant nothing. He was nothing.

Dimitri gentled his touch, circling her stinging nipple with the pad of his finger. She fought the sensation and prayed he couldn't feel how close she already was to coming.

"I'll never share you, neva," he said before kissing the tapered point of her ear. "No one will ever know the things I do to you, or how hard I make you come."

It was freeing, knowing everything he'd done to her would remain with him. Her secrets encapsulated in one male. They would die alongside him when she found a way to *liberate* his soul from his body.

"I'm exhausted and tender. I don't want to be fucked. I want to rest," she said.

He shifted his hips and Astrid braced for his brutal rhythm. He moved slow, thrusting deeper with each of his calculated strokes. When she'd taken his considerable length, he tangled his legs with hers and held her against him.

Astrid's brow drew together when he laid his head on the back of her pillow. His wing draped over her legs, and he remained still.

"What are you doing?" she asked, perplexed.

"Sleeping," he answered from behind her.

Astrid's temper spiked. She shoved away from him and gasped when inches of his hard cock slid out of her and slowly pressed back in.

"Dimitri, I can't sleep like this."

He held her tighter, and murmured, "You will."

Astrid stewed, counting his breaths warming her hair.

"If you're sexually frustrated, you can ride me until you come. But I'll be sleeping with my cock inside my wife."

Chapter Thirty-Five

Astrid blinked against the morning rays brightening the room. The dull ache that steadily grew behind her eyes had developed into a stabbing headache over the course of the night. She'd thought Dimitri had done his worst when she first arrived, forcing her to sleep with a plug in her ass—and she was wrong.

Dimitri's cock inside her was so much worse. It was more than the intrusion he thrust between her thighs. It was the way his chest rose and fell behind her. How the angle of his cock moved when he squeezed her closer. The heat building each time he shifted position, drawing his length away, only to press those inches back into her.

Astrid had been trapped beside him all night. Caged in his arms and impaled.

It was morning, and she'd had enough of this. Astrid struggled to untangle herself, but her demented jailor only hugged her tighter.

"It's morning and I haven't slept," she said, prying at the muscular arm barred over her waist. His callused fingers dug into her waist and Astrid's temper flared. She kicked, hoping for his knee but was satisfied when her heel connected with his shin. He grunted and she continued thrashing against him.

"I'm fucking tired, Dimitri."

He caged her throat with one hand while the other hand caught her wrists. "Did you spend the whole night thinking of me?" he asked at her ear.

His voice had taken a deeper pitch, one Astrid may have appreciated if she didn't want to ram his swords through his ribs.

Astrid relaxed in his hold and softened her voice. "I'm tired, my lord. I just need a few hours."

"Do you think I can be managed so easily?"

"How can I manage you when I'm exhausted and you don't allow me to rest?"

Dimitri's death magic enveloped her and Astrid exhaled loudly, squeezing her eyes shut. The entire room was too bright. The rays of morning light were like needles in her eyes, stabbing at her brain to the rhythm of her pulse.

"I fuck you because you're mine," he murmured, "but I also care for my belongings."

The scathing retort on Astrid's tongue never left her lips, as waves of his magic swept up the back of her neck and crashed over her scalp. This wasn't the gentle serrated teeth that pricked her soul, intensifying every sensation in her body.

This was like being stroked with the side of a blade. There was no pain, but the potential was there, if it were turned. It dulled the throbbing behind her eyes, taking a little more with each pass. The fatigue clouding her mind thinned, but didn't entirely lift.

Astrid's brow drew together. "You're a healer," she stated. But not like her. Lack of sleep wasn't an injury and certainly wasn't something she could correct.

"I'm a Death Spirit," he corrected.

Astrid relaxed and her magic engulfed her in a rush. She glanced down at her body, examining the aura of her tiny soul stars gleaming through her skin. Dimitri's shadowed magic slithered over her. Black hazy coils traversing her curves in the same way serpents would. The sight was oddly comforting, and Astrid contained her power once more.

"What did you do?" She felt sharper. Clear headed.

His lips traced the angle of her ear, and he rasped, "I returned some of what I took." Astrid narrowed her eyes, and he added, "I'll drink from you and replenish myself tonight."

His magic pulsed and changed. Like needles scraping over her skin, thickening as they moved, transforming to serrated teeth. Ecstasy swallowed her and she bit back a moan.

Dimitri rocked his hips, and murmured, "Beg for my cum, wife."

"Serpents—"

No. Insulting him would only push him to do worse. Astrid focused on her breathing. The pleasure that fogged her mind made the grip on her throat feel like an embrace and her brow drew together. Something was wrong with her, but she couldn't think. Dimitri withdrew the length of his cock before sliding back in, fucking her slow and deep.

Astrid's lashes fluttered as she breathed, "A husband should worship his wife."

"*Worship?*" Humor colored the word, and his breath skimmed over her ear. "If you wanted my tongue in your cunt, you'd only have to spread your legs, neva."

She imagined him between her thighs. Her fingers tangled in his dark hair.

Dimitri pulled out of her and Astrid gasped as he lifted her onto her hands and knees. His hand smoothed over the curve of her back and he sat back against the headboard.

"Ride me," he commanded with an arrogant grin. "Show me how you want to be worshiped."

His magic curled over her, giving her no quarter. It was as addictive as it was maddening. The shadows beckoned her to lay on her back and spread her legs. To let his touch consume her entirely.

Astrid fought the overwhelming sensations and clung to the physical sensation of his touch. The satin beneath her knees. The hard muscle of his thigh under her palm. How her night-streaked nails glided across his skin as she crawled on top of him.

She pressed her hands to his chest and lowered herself onto his cock. Astrid's head fell back as the crown stretched her. Her breath caught as she took his head, working him into her body. Ecstasy rained over her as she rose and fell, taking him deeper each time.

Fingertips brushed her cheek, moving to her parted lips. Astrid opened her eyes and met Dimitri's amber stare. His dark gray wings framed him against the stitched leather headboard. His thumb brushed over her mouth as she took more of him.

"You're so gentle."

Astrid kissed his fingertips and drew his hand down the front of her throat. "You only think it's gentle because you can't see the difference between fucking and breaking."

His grin widened at that, and he lifted the leading edge of his wing. Astrid stilled, tensing as the curved talon brushed her hair behind her shoulder.

"Why do you hate my wings?" he asked, settling his bony appendage beside him.

Astrid ignored him and rolled her hips.

"Tell me and I won't fuck you with them… *tonight.*"

Her gaze lifted to the taloned points. "You've said you take care of the things that belong to you, but you'd torture your wife with those jagged bones?"

He chuckled, taking her wrist and Astrid leaned against his chest. She ducked her head beneath his chin not trusting her expression. The sheets rustled and her hand lifted higher, meeting roughened scales.

"This is the leading edge of my wing. The bones here are larger, denser, and difficult to break. The edge is meant for battle. We use it to deflect blows and impale our opponents."

Astrid cataloged the information and nodded. It must have pleased him because he caressed the small of her back.

He moved her hand lower, brushing the tips of her fingers over the membrane, and Astrid's breathing betrayed her.

"I know you have quite the imagination. Think of it as leather," he said, before adding, "a fine suede."

"Suede doesn't have a heartbeat," she breathed as her stomach knotted.

"Is it my pulse that bothers you?" he asked, bemused.

His pulse did bother her, but not for the reason he was thinking.

Dimitri kissed her temple and leaned up, circling her in his arms.

"The inner bones are thinner. Smooth," he said, curling his wing toward her.

Dimitri intertwined his fingers with hers and folded the last joint of his wing onto itself. He made a loose fist and thrust the folded joint through her grip, fucking her hand.

"I can fill your cunt with one and fuck your ass with the other," he whispered at her ear.

Astrid jerked her hand away. "They're animal parts." *Never meant to be fused to a Fae.*

"They are *part* of the male you belong to," he said, catching her throat.

This again. Astrid lifted her chin, giving herself a sliver of air. She needed to steer her demented jailor's attention. Keep from losing what ground she'd gained this morning.

She leaned into his grip, then resumed rising and falling on his cock. She took his hard length as she stared into the depths his molten gold eyes. Her fingers dug into either side of his jaw and the callused grip on her throat fell away. She leaned down and kissed him, taking him deeper as she sucked on his tongue. His cock twitched inside her and Astrid's lips curled into a smile.

Attention starved male.

"Compromise with your wife," she whispered against his mouth. "I'll be a little rougher. You fuck me a little slower." He chuckled, his breath fanning over her. She snapped his bottom lip between her teeth, biting hard enough to draw blood. "And if you touch me with your wings, I'll cut them off the next time you fall asleep."

A thin line of blood fell from his lip and trickled over his stubble. Dimitri was on top of her the next moment. He thrust into her, each brutal stroke jarring her body. Her earrings clinked and swayed as he fucked her hard and Astrid spread her legs—*welcoming* him.

His dark wings unfurled above them. Outspread and menacing.

He was hatred and power.

Death embodied.

And she wielded him.

Astrid didn't fight the orgasm as it crashed through her. She raked her nails across Dimitri's shoulders, down his back. "Deeper," she cried. "Dimitri, come for me."

He groaned and thrusted into her once. Twice. Astrid's nails tore the sheets as he yanked her hips toward him. Dimitri had risen to his knees, holding her ass more than a foot off the bed while her shoulders remained on the mattress. The veins along his forearms bulged as he fucked her.

Astrid couldn't move; couldn't get away or shield herself. She could only take his relentless thrusts and come for him. Writhe for him. Astrid let the ecstasy of his touch engulf her. It consumed her, permeating her very soul.

Marking her.

With a hard beat of his wings, Dimitri thrust into her a final time. His cock pulsed as he came deep inside her.

Astrid wasn't sure how long he held her or when he'd sat against the headboard and pulled her close. She rested against the unyielding planes of his chest, counting his heartbeats.

"La nikogda v zhizni tak sil-no ne konchal," Dimitri said in a language she didn't understand.

"What did you say?"

"Your cunt is exquisite, neva."

Astrid grabbed his jaw and hissed, "That is not how you speak to a princess."

Dimitri seized her throat and dragged her closer. Astrid bared her teeth then parted her lips for him, letting his tongue slide across hers as he ravaged her mouth. He smiled after a few moments, breaking their kiss and asked.

"Jewels, then?"

Chapter Thirty-Six

Astrid strolled into Dimitri's ensuite, expecting an hour to herself. The reprieve she'd been looking forward to was short lived when he followed her in. Her bargain to bathe herself was negated with a shrug of his broad shoulders.

"I didn't say I wouldn't help you. Or watch," Dimitri said, taking a seat on the edge of the black porcelain tub.

He wouldn't let her out of the water until she'd washed and scrubbed every inch of skin. His compulsion for cleanliness scraped at her nerves, but it was far from his strangest characteristic.

The male seemed impervious to the bitter cold. Astrid couldn't discern if he was simply acclimated to the winter that embedded itself into every stone and tile of this palace or if he was warmed by the souls he consumed.

Dimitri left his perch to shower as she toweled off. Astrid

watched as he tilted his head back and hot water sluiced over his chiseled body. His muscles bunched and flexed as he moved, sending a shiver down Astrid's spine.

She turned away, retreating to his closet but her mind betrayed her, replaying the way his chest heaved when she rode him. The build of pleasure as she lowered herself onto his cock. The intensity of it.

Astrid dug her nails into her palm and focused on finding clothing. She chose a linen shirt and the thickest topcoat he owned. It was black wool trimmed in leather with blood red embroidery of smoke or clouds over the back and down one lapel. She slipped his garments on and stepped into her heels.

Dimitri strolled up behind her as she fastened her gold lotus belt. "Don't butcher my coat. We're fitting you for a wardrobe this morning."

She glanced toward him over her shoulder. "Will this wardrobe include shoes? Jewelry?"

His hand smoothed over the curve of her ass and he pressed his lips to her damp hair. "Always asking for the stars," he murmured and turned to dress.

They strolled through the palace and Astrid cataloged their route to the eastern wing. The chatter of a large crowd echoed through the stairway they climbed. When they reached the top, Astrid blinked. She'd never seen so many winged Fae in one place. Dozens upon dozens of Ledivites shuffled through the wide corridor. She knew King Ambrose kept a large court, but there were several hundred people here. The overlapping voices quieted as their arrival was observed. Shortly, the only sound heard were the shuffling feet of a parting crowd as Dimitri stalked forward.

Whoever these people were, they knew enough to fear him.

They passed large archways leading into grand rooms with polished floors—ballrooms that had been repurposed for merchants' wares. She'd seen this on a smaller scale in Clorea but the array of goods here were astounding. Fae crowded into the elegant rooms. As Dimitri and Astrid shuffled, shoulder to shoulder through the indoor market, the reflection of candlelight off polished steel and elaborate jeweled tiaras caught her eye.

Tables covered in black velvet rowed another room, Astrid observed as they entered. Ornate armor and weapons were neatly rowed. Intricate carvings of animals decorated breastplates, and a snake coiled across a pauldron caught her attention. She slowed and within seconds, Dimitri caught her wrist, pulling her forward.

"My wife will not shop amongst commoners," he said.

Peasants could never afford the luxuries lining those rooms.

"Is another court visiting?" Astrid asked. Trading between courts during visits were a common occurrence and would explain the mass of Fae gathered.

Dimitri led her up another flight of stairs. "They are gathering for the upcoming Ascension and to congratulate King Ambrose on expanding our borders."

"Is that a Ledivite holiday?" If Dimitri was truly her sword, she should learn his culture, if for no other reason than to make managing the demented male easier.

Her winged male answered, but his words were emotionless. "It's an annual celebration marking the end of the last reign and the start of the new."

A constant reminder of his lover lost, Astrid mused, surprised by the bitterness lingering in her thoughts.

"How is the Ascension celebrated?" Astrid asked as they reached the top of the steps.

The floor was the same as the one below, but instead of the bustling crowd, this corridor was empty. The cadence of Dimitri's boots echoed through the hall and the hum of the crowd below them rose again.

"Viktor," Dimitri called as they walked farther into the hall.

A male stepped into the archway and answered, "My lord," before disappearing into the ballroom.

They followed Viktor, and he bowed in a flourish along with two females who appeared to be his assistants. "Always a pleasure to see you, Lord Dimitri. And of course, your beautiful new wife, Princess Noctis."

The clothier was tall and lean. His black wings and hair starkly contrasted his fair skin. Astrid studied his eyes, one amber and the other a clouded, milky gray. There were no scars around his eye, which either meant the healer wasn't skilled enough to save his sight or these were the eyes he was born with.

Viktor sashayed to an exquisite suit on a male dress form. It was the darkest black she'd ever seen. The color seemed to draw the light out of the room, a feature which highlighted the gold thread embroidery along the lapels and cuffs. Beneath it was a vest stitched in the same golden thread. The clothier leaned back, scrutinizing his work. He tugged the lapels down and dusted the shoulders.

"I think a white shirt would suit this and your skin tone," he said, turning toward them once again. Viktor drummed his fingers over his sternum as he narrowed his eyes at Dimitri. "Thin gold chains to tie to the embroidery?"

Dimitri nodded and asked, "Where is my wife's dress?"

"I need *inspiration* before I can make a gown," he replied, taking Astrid's hand.

She braced for Dimitri's hot-tempered retaliation and assessed the females. She would have time to shove them behind a fabric table and make her stand, while Dimitri killed the clothier.

To her astonishment, Dimitri allowed her to be led away.

"How long has this brute been making you wear his clothes?" Viktor asked as he guided her onto a hexagon platform before a three-paned mirror. He tilted his head, studying her reflection, then chuckled and flicked the edge of her makeshift skirt. "I suppose you're grateful he's so much taller than you. This would be indecent otherwise."

Astrid blinked. They were easy with each other. Some of the tension slipped from her and she said, in a lower tone, "He would keep me locked in his room if he had his—"

"Tied to my bed, if you continue conspiring against me," Dimitri interjected from a table across the room.

His back was turned toward them as he browsed yards of lace hanging in neat rows. Astrid took in the open space. Different materials were displayed alongside dress forms clothed in beautiful garments.

"Is all of this for him?" Astrid asked. Surely the crowd below them would shop here once Dimitri finished.

Viktor nodded and stepped behind her. He flicked his fingers in arching sweeps and yards of fabric flew off their respective tables. Astrid remained still as satins, silks, and linens, in diverse colors momentarily fell over her shoulders before taking to the air once more, replaced by another.

Air weavers excelled at textile arts. Their ability to embroider, sew, and create tapestries were far faster than those forced to operate looms by hand.

"My work solely belongs to Lord Dimitri. In exchange, I reside here, as a member of the royal court with my wife and children. I also have access to any material I desire."

"Your work is exquisite, but is living at court enough?" Astrid asked. He might make a fortune off Dimitri, but he would make that and more if he were permitted to sell to other nobles.

"There are other benefits of having Lord Dimitri as a patron, with which I am sure you are familiar. I live in a kingdom of war, but have no interest trading my needle for a sword," Viktor said as he brought another swath of silk across her throat, this one the same deep black as Dimitri's suit.

"No one would dare touch my family," he continued. "My children have the same education as any high ranking noble." A broad smile spread over his lips and the corner of his eyes crinkled as he straightened silver lace trim against the black. "I'm permitted to dress my family in my creations and with only one customer, I have an abundance of the rarest commodity of all: *time*. And I spend it with my wife and children instead of slaving over fabrics."

Astrid dissected his words, comparing them to Keres's. The male they knew, while still terrifying, was kind in his own way. She watched Dimitri's reflection as he browsed the tables collecting fabrics. He was protective and generous.

And jealous. And overbearing, Astrid reminded herself.

Viktor and Keres obeyed him because he offered them a comfortable life. Astrid didn't need a life gifted to her. She wanted her presence acknowledged, her mind respected. She needed to be an equal to a male who valued her.

Dimitri started toward her. As his image vanished behind hers in the glass, his wings spread, extending past her shoulders. A marriage of their forms. Staring back at her was a mirage of a daughter grown, with Astrid's features and Dimitri's wings.

Astrid dismissed the thought as Dimitri stepped onto the raised platform, breaking the illusion. His chest pressed against her back as his lips warmed her temple.

"Add some lingerie to the wardrobe Viktor creates," he whispered, placing the material he'd collected in her hands.

Astrid straightened her back and met his gaze in the mirror. "What style would you like?"

"Surprise me," he murmured. His fingertips grazed her scalp as he ran his hand through her hair, sending tingles cascading over her skin.

Astrid closed her eyes and let Dimitri's touch consume her. When the last of her strands slipped from his hold, she opened her eyes. He left her to cross the ballroom. He took a seat to wait patiently.

The two females worked in tandem with Viktor, but it was the flowers pinned in the shorter female's dark hair that caught her attention. Snow plants, sprigs of vegetation dotted with tiny red flowers.

Was she one of Sterling's spies? Was he here?

Astrid fidgeted with the lace, feigning interest in the pattern until Viktor turned his back. "Do you make these or are they purchased?" Astrid asked, taking the opportunity to arrange her fingers in the subtle sign language Sterling taught all his spies.

Are you a friend? she asked beneath the conversation.

"We make all of these by hand. The density and quality of the threads are carefully selected," she answered while her gestures read, *Be ready to escape.*

Sterling had planned her extraction, but she wouldn't leave her mother here. Dimitri would send her mother to Clorea in pieces for Astrid's betrayal.

Free my mother first, she gestured against the lace as she held it to her throat. "Can you add jewels to this, Viktor?" she asked.

The clothier scrutinized the lace on her throat, then replaced it with another. "We can sew in jewels. Give you a neckline that glitters like the night sky."

Astrid smiled, turning toward the dark-haired assistant.

She simply smiled and turned her back, arranging bolts of silk on a table before excusing herself and leaving the ballroom.

Chapter Thirty-Seven

Dimitri spent the next few hours admiring his feral neva. Viktor crafted her a stunning gray dress with flowing sleeves. It was an amalgam of their kingdoms' fashions. She proudly wore her gold pauldron and lotus belt over the sleek dress. Warmth settled in his chest as he gazed at her. She was a vision—one befitting a queen.

The pair discussed garments and materials, sampling the plethora of swatches Viktor traveled with. He took her measurements and curated notes as she toured his creations. If she planned on wearing Clorea's royal attire, he would need Keres to imbue her metalwork with heat to keep his little wife from catching a chill.

Astrid returned to him as Viktor carefully notated final details his pocketbook a step behind her. He tapped the point of his pen in the book and snapped it shut. "I think that's everything. I'll have your wardrobe delivered in three days' time," he said to Astrid before turning toward Dimitri and adding, "and a footman will deliver your suit this evening."

Dimitri nodded and stood. Astrid took to his side without his prompting and the warmth that had settled in his chest radiated through his soul. She'd accepted her place with him.

"Thank you, it was wonderful meeting you, Viktor. I hope to meet your family one day," she said with a genuine sweetness Dimitri had never heard.

Viktor bowed and placed his hand over his chest. "It would be our honor."

Dimitri inclined his head at his clothier and led Astrid into the hall.

"His clothes are beautiful. How did you two meet?"

Gifts were apparently the way to his princess's heart. She fell in step beside him, so close her fingers brushed his as they walked. He caught her hand, and she hesitated for the briefest moment before interlacing her fingers with his.

"Ambrose selected one of Viktor's suits for his coming of age ceremony. I had the garment burned and appointed Viktor as my personal clothier," Dimitri recounted.

"How do you hold so much say here?" Astrid paused, seemingly mulling over her thoughts. He remained silent. In a muted whisper, she pushed further, "This isn't your court and you're not the King."

The bitter exclusion of his birthright iced over his composure like a winter frost on glass. This wasn't his court, and he would never be king. His father reminded him often enough before he found his death beneath Dimitri's bloodied fists.

Dimitri gazed down at the lithe female beside him. He didn't need his birthright. Cursed blood ran through his veins. "The question you should be asking isn't why my word holds sway, but who among them could stop me?"

"If no one could stop you, why aren't you king, my lord?" she asked sweetly.

They reached the end of the hall and stepped onto the balcony. The unforgiving chill cooled his wrath and Astrid stepped into his side. "Come. I'll return us to our room," he said, lifting her into his arms.

She clung to his neck as a winter-kissed flush spread across her cheeks. He started toward the railing.

"I'd prefer to walk," she stammered. "Dimitri, put me down."

She squeezed to him tighter, burying her face in his throat as he stepped onto the railing. He should have flown here. Now, he had no intention of walking through the crowd of nobles who vied for his brother's favor and attention.

He pressed his lips to her forehead and murmured, "It's a short flight, neva."

Dimitri lifted off the railing with a powerful beat of his wings and smoothly glided along the eastern wall of the palace. He suspected she wasn't used to the weightless feel of falling and spared her the sensation. She didn't loosen her strangling grip, but she lifted her head a fraction, watching the pines peek over the outer wall as they passed.

He pumped his wings, gaining height, and his little wife jerked in his arms. He chuckled and squeezed her closer. "I won't drop you."

Astrid remained stiff as they crested the palace's outer walls and softly landed in his private green space. He gently set her on her feet and Graymalkin burst from the snow-covered bushes with a weathered leaf in his mouth. He bounded to Astrid, and she cradled him as she hurried to the window.

"Have you brought me a gift, my fearless hunter?" she laughed, taking the crunchy leaf from his mouth. Graymalkin purred loudly, content with the pets and snuggles Astrid provided.

Dimitri followed her into their room. She bent forward to place his oversized white cat on the foot of their bed and he couldn't help but admire her ass. The cut of the silk dress accentuated her curves beautifully. He would ask Viktor to make her a shorter, sleeveless version of this dress in red with lace over her breasts.

Dimitri's thoughts were interrupted when Astrid prowled toward him. Her fingertips slid down his chest in a smooth caress and he grew hard in an instant. Mischief glittered in her midnight eyes as she asked, "Do you think you could convince an earth weaver and a fire weaver to create a fruit garden for your wife?"

He smiled and stroked her cheek. "Always the stars with you."

She hooked her finger between the buttons of his shirt. "My blood belongs to Clorea. We could take it... Rule side by side."

Her words shocked and subdued him in equal measure. She'd

offered him a crown. A title and seat in exchange for securing her kingdom. This was transactional. It didn't mean she wanted him. Dimitri smothered his soft feelings, even as a small, desperate part of him clung to the sentiment.

It was more than he's ever been offered... More than he deserved.

Dimitri smoothed his thumb over her lips, willing them to speak the truth instead of honeyed lies.

"If I had your loyalty, wife, I would lay the very stars at your feet."

She smiled against the pad of his thumb and took his hand in hers. Anticipation scraped beneath his skin as she traced the scar binding them. Her breath caressed the top of his hand, and the touch of her lips followed. A reverent kiss.

A promise.

Her midnight eyes lifted to meet his.

"Place the Serpents' Crown on my head and I will be yours as long as you breathe, husband."

Chapter Thirty-Eight

Be ready.

Astrid seethed, trapped beneath silk, furs, and the weight of Dimitri's outstretched wing. Anticipation had been a constant scrape against her nerves the first week. The news of Clorea's Queen escaping Ledivion should have reached her quickly, but nothing came. The days had dragged into weeks and now, nearly two months had passed.

Without a word.

Without a sighting.

Without a signal.

The letters to her cousins went unanswered and Dimitri had yet to leave her side. He refused the assassination he'd been assigned, disobeying his king. The only positive outcome Astrid had in these weeks was the war archive.

Dimitri brought her the volume which included Incarnadine

Fields, as promised, but the only documentation within the heavy tome was the location and the date. Both pieces of information of which she'd already known. When she glared at Dimitri, he'd shrugged and said, "The war archive chronicles an entire year. You'll have to research a different battle, neva."

Dimitri's wing lifted off her legs and straightened like a cat stretching its limbs after a nap. His callused fingers caressed the side of her throat and Astrid closed her eyes.

When he was gentle, his touch consumed her.

"I need to finish a kill before the Ascension," he groaned into her hair. "I'll return before you can miss me too terribly."

Astrid sighed as Dimitri kissed the point of her ear and trailed his lips over the slope of her shoulder. He'd learned her body over these weeks. The black velvet pouch had grown into a suede box. He introduced new pieces to his arsenal every few days—Nipple clamps, steel replicas of his cock, vibrating plugs of various shapes and sizes.

Last night, Dimitri worked a vibrating plug into her ass and tied her to the bed before turning it on. She moaned his name when he teased her nipples. Pinching and tugging on them until she cried out. Until they were stinging and tender. She'd writhed for hours as her pain wove into pleasure.

He pushed her to orgasm again and again, but it never satisfied him. He was relentless until she was breathless and unable to move.

Dimitri's callused fingers closed over her mouth and pulled her head to the side. "Are you thinking of my cock, neva?" he asked at her lips. He leaned into her, the quiet routine of their morning kiss. His hand moved lower, caressing the front of her throat. "I can smell your wet. You can sit on my face once I've returned."

Astrid turned into the tight circle of his arms and ran her night-streaked nails over the stubble on his chin. "Leave tonight, and spend the day with me," she pleaded. If the spies were waiting for Dimitri to leave, she needed to buy as much time as possible for her mother's escape.

"I should have left last night, but I can make up for it," he said stroking her hair. "I'll be back before dawn."

A promise steeped in yearning.

Astrid hid her curse behind a smile. "May I go to the library while you're gone?"

He chuckled and pulled away, getting out of bed. "Keres will take you. She's bringing you a gift this morning."

Dimitri disappeared into his closet and when he emerged, her brows came together. She'd expected him to don armor, but the common-born, understated clothing in which he dressed gave her pause. The trousers and collared shirt would allow him to blend into a crowd, to slip in and out unseen.

Astrid doubted he could do *anything* unseen. The male could dress in moth-eaten rags, and they wouldn't diminish his molten gold eyes or striking features.

Her gaze fell to his sword's pommel as he fastened his belt. The sight of his sword handle alone had been enough to send her into a roiling fury when she'd first arrived. Astrid stared at the gleaming pommel and leather-wrapped handle. She'd lost her virginity to a crude thrust of metal.

Where was her rage?

Dimitri's actions simultaneously enraged and soothed her. He'd used her body, but also brought her pleasure. He'd forced marriage onto her but never dismissed her.

I would expect nothing less from the princess who carved my chest and split my aorta. He recognized her intelligence—her viciousness—even if he was too foolish to believe she wouldn't turn on him.

Astrid wrapped herself in gray fur and sauntered toward him. She hooked her fingers into his belt and stood up on her toes, still not quite tall enough to press her lips to his.

"Will you leave me one of your swords so I can defend myself?" she asked, playing the part of his tamed wife.

He chuckled and unfastened the scabbard at his hip. Leather trimmed in metal pressed into her palm and Astrid wrapped her fingers around his weapon.

"Tonight then," she said.

His palms warmed her arms, and Astrid closed her eyes as he lowered his head.

"Tonight," he agreed at her lips. He lingered a moment. His thumb slid across her jaw as his fingers tangled in her hair. Instead of a kiss, he cupped the back of her neck and gently drew her forward until his forehead touched hers. Their breaths mingled for the space of a heartbeat.

Two.

Then he stepped away from her without a word and opened the tall window. Snow crunched beneath his boots as he stepped out into the garden. His dark wings seemed even larger against the stark blanket of white snow.

He was gone the next moment, launching into the sunlit sky.

Chapter Thirty-Nine

The winter breeze infiltrated the bedroom and curled a small drift of snow at Astrid's feet. She lingered as the unforgiving season's chill crawled up her legs. Astrid closed the glass when a muted knock drew her attention.

"One moment," Astrid called before pulling on a heavy fur-lined robe and making her way to the door.

The timid knock came again, followed by a trembling voice. "Your breakfast, Your Highness."

Astrid opened the door, and the maid paled. Her tarnished yellow gaze darted around the room before meeting her own.

"He's not here," Astrid assured her.

The female's wings sagged with relief and slid her fingers across her neck before muttering, "Thank Vinceret."

She muttered what sounded like a prayer as she wheeled Astrid's breakfast beside Dimitri's desk. Garlic, thyme, and the scent of grilled beef wafted from the covered dishes. Astrid's mouth watered. She silently wondered if this had been ordered by Dimitri in his absence or supplied by the priest she forced into servitude.

Astrid lifted the decanter of sweet wine and poured herself a glass.

"Am I too early?"

A voice she recognized. Astrid turned toward Keres as she entered with a footman close behind her. The last time she'd seen the winged female she'd been pierced at Dimitri's command. An experience she wouldn't be repeating.

"Why is he here?" Astrid asked, lifting her chin at the footman and the four leather bags he carried in each hand. Dimitri had told her Keres would bring her a gift, but the word held different connotations to Astrid.

Keres flicked her hand toward Dimitri's bed and the male silently obeyed, laying the satchels in a neat row.

"Raw materials," she said, strolling over to Astrid's dining cart.

The maid shrank away with a curtsey. "We'll bring your next meal at midday, Your Highness."

Astrid nodded and the female retreated with the footman a step behind her.

Keres lifted the metal domes covering the platters one by one, revealing eggs, toast, and grilled meat. The white patches blotching her wings gleamed as she moved through the beams of sunlight that did nothing to warm her room.

"I should have asked the footman to rekindle the fire," Astrid said absently.

The fireplace blazed to life, startling Astrid. Keres giggled. "How warm do you want the room?"

Astrid blinked at the female's generosity and answered, "As warm as it is in Clorea."

The flames burned brighter, and Astrid contemplated her sudden kindness. Was her new demeanor a result of Dimitri's threats or an interest in friendship? She'd outlived Keres's original prediction of one week with Dimitri by nearly two months. It would be nice to have a friendly face at court, but she was hesitant to trust Dimitri's metallurgist.

The room warmed quickly, and Keres turned her attention to the satchels. Chunks of platinum and gold, along with an array of precious gems, glittered against the dark sheets.

"The Ascension will be held next week. Dimitri said you wanted corsets and jewelry."

Astrid glanced over the sapphires, diamonds, and rubies. "Do you have jade?" She asked, picking up the weighty platinum ingot. "Is the Ascension celebrated with a feast?"

"There are feasts. Hunts..." Keres gently took the metal from Astrid and met her gaze. "Be mindful with Lord Dimitri. His mood sours and it's best to avoid his company."

As if she could. "I won't be able to avoid him."

Keres opened a small leather pouch tied to her belt and removed a thin vile. She took Astrid's hand and squeezed. The glass was cold in her palm, and she closed her fingers over it.

"He drinks heavily every year. Add a few drops to his glass and he'll sleep through the night. You've lasted this long. It'd be a shame if we lost you now," Keres said with a smile that didn't reach her amber eyes.

"Why does he stay at court if he holds such animosity for Ambrose?"

A breath of a laugh devoid of emotion slipped past Keres's full lips. "You weren't here during the old reign," she said, then lowered her voice to a whisper. "Many believe he was in love with Queen Vesta. He obeyed her without question, and the way he looked at her in court..." Keres blew out a breath and shook her head. "There were rumors of an affair, which is why King Constantine hated him. It's probably why King Ambrose hates him now."

A pang of betrayal stabbed Astrid's chest and her mouth went dry. She held her expression as she shoved the biting emotions down, but they persisted, clawing at her.

"They must be rumors. He would have been executed," Astrid insisted.

Keres quirked her lip. "You've met him. *Personally*. He's a Death Spirit."

Who among them could stop me? Dimitri's voice replayed in Astrid's mind and she grappled with her misplaced jealousy over a long dead queen.

The robe became oppressive as the room's temperature rose. Astrid changed into a flowing, black silk robe embroidered with rubies. She returned to find Keres toying with liquid platinum floating between her hands.

"Are there many fire weavers at court?" Astrid asked.

"There are several. We're offered positions at court and our stipends are better than most."

Because a nation who worshiped conquest would need worthy steel at their beck and call, Astrid thought. "Are you betrothed to a fellow fire weaver?"

"No," Keres answered flatly. "Take off the belt."

Astrid analyzed Keres's features. The minute downturn of her lips. The tension in her eyes. Keres's amber gaze lingered on the scar marring the top of her hand and Astrid's heart sank. She was far too familiar with the dwindling light in the metallurgist's eyes. Astrid wore the same look many times. The quiet hope for her cousins' acceptance and respect. And the slow realization it would never come.

"I'm sorry. I didn't care for the match my father set for me either," Astrid volunteered. After a beat, she asked, "Has another captured your attention?"

Fire weavers were born from earth weavers; their abilities manifested once every thousand souls. And while not guaranteed, the chances of passing magic through the generations rose dramatically when both parents carried the same gift. It wasn't uncommon for the rarer weavers' betrothals to be strategically arranged.

Keres didn't meet Astrid's eyes as she opened her hands on either side of Astrid's waist. The metal hugged her hips and tapered higher as silence stretched between them. When Keres finally spoke, her voice was as dull and lackluster as her eyes. "My flames secured my place in court, but even they can't overcome what I lack."

Keres's dejection plucked a raw nerve within Astrid. Males had inherently insisted she was lacking, but unlike Keres, she never allowed their assumptions to poison her sense of self. Male prejudice would never define her.

"And what is it you think you lack?" Astrid asked, quieting the venom in her voice. Anger sparked in Keres's eyes and pride bloomed through Astrid's chest.

The female's wings shifted, raising behind her. "My discoloration," she answered, biting off the word.

Astrid studied the source of Keres's insecurity. Her wings were daintier than Dimitri's with the same pointed talons on the first joints. Fine serpentine scales covered the boned frame. The white, speckled scales caught the sunlight from the shadows and seemed to glow from within.

"I see nothing wrong with your wings, but if anyone breathes otherwise, bring them to me," Astrid said sweetly.

Keres's brows pinched, her lips parting as she met Astrid's stare.

"I'll bar their soul from their wings, and you can burn them away as quick or as slow as you like."

A soft laugh escaped Keres's lips as she returned her focus to the fluid platinum. The metal caging her middle reformed into thin branches. "I see the rumors of your viciousness are true," she said, continuing her work. Leaves sprouted while plum blossoms budded and bloomed over her waist.

Astrid tilted her hip, admiring the intricate branches before sharing a smile with the winged female. "A well-placed example tends to silence wagging tongues."

Keres's smile finally reached her eyes and Astrid held still as she began placing diamonds into her design.

"I'll start by melting their weapons," Keres said.

Causing pain would be better revenge, but Astrid did not say so. Destroying a war-mongering Ledivite's weapons *would* be a devastating loss. Astrid frowned as her thoughts wandered to her sword. "Does Dimitri ridicule you for your wings?"

Keres shook her head and stood taller. "His only concerns are quality and craftmanship."

The same way he hadn't dismissed her for being female. Astrid buried the soft feelings welling in her. *She was meant to wield her sword, not desire it.*

"He did barge into my room in the middle of the night after his latest war prize mangled his sword," Keres continued.

"He deserved it," Astrid retorted.

Keres leaned back, rubbing her thumb over her palm and studying her handiwork. She muttered, "I'm sure he did."

"Do you think I could bother you and an earth weaver to make a garden in this green space to grow some fruits?" Astrid asked. Typically, she would only need an earth weaver but in the winter, a fire weaver would be necessary to keep the frost at bay.

"The earth weavers are occupied, but I can see what I can do in the next few days."

"Surely they could spare an hour for their newest princess," Astrid argued. It took minutes for seeds to grow into fruit bearing trees under an earth weaver's coaxing.

Amusement lit the amber depths of the metallurgist's eyes. "He didn't tell you."

"Tell me what?" If Dimitri thought he could ban fruits from the palace and force his diet of sour bread and meat on her forever, she was going to set him on fire the next time he slept.

"He ordered the earth weavers to build a temple to the Three-Faced Mother as grand and tall as Vinceret's."

Every thought of vengeance blanked from Astrid's mind. He was erecting a temple to please her. The male was ill-tempered and violently unpredictable… but did her bidding. The Three-Faced Mother couldn't have fashioned her a better sword.

A leashed and obedient Death Spirit.

Chapter Forty

Astrid spent hours with Dimitri's metallurgist, creating pauldrons, corsets, and glittering ornaments for her hair. Keres took her leave when the midday meal arrived. Astrid rowed her new belongings in front of Dimitri's collection of polished leather boots.

She straightened and looked around the closet she now shared with him. Clothing, hung with a maddening precision, surrounded her. The servants clearly knew of his idiosyncrasies, and the consequences of error, terrified every time they entered his room. The court had to be aware, too, but none were bold enough to mention his compulsions.

What is so out of control in your life that you need absolute control over your things and space? Astrid wondered as she brushed her fingertips along the sleeves of his shirts. Silks, cashmere wool, and fine linen—materials of luxury met her touch. Dimitri's belongings were curated, emanating wealth.

A sophisticated noble. High-born.

But he'd said his mother was low-born. A soul weaver whose family raised swans. Had he been with her when she caught the eye of his noble stepfather or did his mother bring her comfort recipes to court?

Her real curiosity was the previous queen. Astrid donned her coat and strapped Dimitri's blade to her thinner, more delicate sword belt. She could wield the weapon, but the gleaming metal wasn't for protection. It was a not-so-subtle reminder of the hate and rage that would descend upon this court if they so much as touched her hair.

The click of her heels echoed through the empty halls. She reached the library without incident. The expansive room was bright and airy, and full of scholars. The priest who'd forcefully married her to Dimitri cautiously approached, while the other seated Ledivites made note of the weapon on her hip and hastily retreated.

"Princess Noctis," Dobromil said with a bow. He clutched a stack of books to his chest as though they might shield him from her. "I have not been able to locate more text on Death Spirits, Your Highness."

Astrid held up two fingers. "I want the life of the previous Queen. Her betrothal to the King. Ambrose's birth. All of it."

"Yes, Your Highness," the priest said with a small bow, before rushing to the shelves.

Astrid removed her coat and took a seat at the table closest to the fireplace. The roaring flames popped and crackled as her attention slipped to the tall windows. She glanced over the sea of pine trees. Their pointed tops and outstretched branches were topped with fluffy clumps of snow.

She missed Clorea. The warmth and beauty of her palace gardens. The scent of dozens of flowers drifting through the open windows. The melodic birdsongs at dawn and dusk.

Ledivion was quiet and cold—a blank canvas her people painted in blood.

"Your books, Princess," Dobromil said, interrupting her thoughts.

He placed two books in front of her. They weren't the heavy leather-bound tomes she'd read previously. The volumes were covered in pale ivory. Astrid brushed the textured surface.

Linen.

Astrid opened the cover to a portrait of a beautiful female. Her dark hair was swept up and pinned, highlighting her delicately pointed ears. Every detail was painstakingly recreated, from her jeweled nails to the throne she occupied. The Queen's luminous blue eyes were so life-like, swirling with unspoken secrets Astrid was eager to uncover.

She read, content in the glow of the hearth. The silence and warmth reminded her of home where reading had been her constant companion. Her father dismissed her desire to campaign with her cousins and expand Clorea's borders, but even he couldn't silence her mind.

Queen Vesta was a priestess and served the Three-Faced Mother. Astrid curled the corner of the page up, tapping her nail on the point as she read. Vesta had traveled to Ledivion with a dozen other priests and priestesses, erecting temples for soul weavers within the Royal Legion.

Astrid read pages upon pages chronicling her pilgrimage and King Constantine's notice of her. Vesta abandoned her service to the Three-Faced Mother and took the crown Constantine offered.

A pang of betrayal struck Astrid. Queen Vesta turned her back on the Mothers to please a male. Traded her purpose for wealth and power. This female didn't deserve to be remembered as a soul weaver.

Astrid continued reading, growing increasingly irritated with each new detail. Vesta acclimated to life in Ledivion and grew pregnant their first year of marriage. Astrid blinked. The child was still born and in a fit of rage Constantine killed everyone in the birthing chamber.

The soul weavers.

The archivist.

Everyone.

He ordered the earth weavers to level the temples dedicated to the Three-Faced Mother. After his tantrum, the only temples that remained were conscripted to the God of Conquest and Blood. The Queen didn't fight for the priests and priestesses she'd traveled to Ledivion with. She was hardly seen at all. Queen Vesta mourned for years, and little was recorded of her during that time. She bore Constantine's sole heir nearly seven years later.

The spine creaked as Astrid closed the book with a soft *thump* and pushed it away. She couldn't fathom how Vesta willingly cast her faith aside and allowed the desecration of so many temples. This female was spineless, but somehow managed to rein in Dimitri's loyalty and devotion.

Astrid stood and the sword at her waist wobbled. Her hand covered the rounded pommel, and the metal chilled her palm. Did Queen Vesta welcome his depravity? Bow to him and his compulsive requisite to be superior?

It didn't matter, Astrid told herself. She couldn't stomach subservience. The serpents would guide her home before she allowed Dimitri to fuck her at his convenience. She wielded her Death Spirit well enough now, and her explorative research of the prior monarchs gave her little insight.

"Your Majesty," Dobromil said, loudly enough for her to hear, but it was the tinge of fear in his voice that drew her attention.

Did he fear for his king or was it that a male was in the same room with her and Dimitri could choose to lay the offense on his shoulders?

When Ambrose approached, Astrid slid her hand down the hilt of Dimitri's sword, pushing it behind her as she curtsied. "My king, it is a pleasure to see you this evening."

Dobromil walked into her line of sight behind Ambrose and shook his head once.

"It would be a *pleasure* to have you in my bed," Ambrose crooned, brushing his index and middle finger along her jaw and ending on her chin.

The urge to rip his soul from his extremities and step on the arrogant male's throat was overwhelming, but Astrid smiled and leaned into his touch.

"Dimitri will return in a few hours," she said, burying her instinct to bite until she tasted blood. Instead, she kissed his fingertips. "His next assignment could be farther. It could take him three days to complete, if it pleases you, my king."

Time enough for her mother to escape this frozen prison.

"And how would *you* please me, soul weaver?"

Ambrose crowded her, gliding his hand over the small of her

back. The bitter taste of bile flashed in Astrid's mouth and she stifled her revulsion. His touch was soft and smooth. There were no battle-hardened callouses. No roughness from laborious work. Not a day of hardship. Nothing earned.

So unlike Dimitri.

The errant thought surprised Astrid, and she banished it as it formed.

"You'll have to teach me how to please you," she answered, stepping out of his arms, "the next time you send Dimitri away."

Chapter Forty-One

Astrid left the library, abandoning her coat. She turned into the hall and thanked the serpents Ambrose remained with the priest. Her drumming pulse quieted when she entered Dimitri's room. She stripped and drew a hot bath, stilling when the usual chill didn't seep into her bones.

Her attention shifted to the fireplace and the flames burning within it as she leaned in the doorway. Keres's magic kept the space comfortable. Astrid's only regret was not bringing books with her. She would ask Dimitri to take her back to the library in the morning.

Astrid stepped into the bath and moaned. Comforting heat enveloped her as she lowered herself using the black porcelain rim. She bathed, scrubbing each place Ambrose's hands lingered until her skin pinkened.

She leaned back, resting the back of her head on the lip of the tub. What should have been a relaxing moment of peace was eerily quiet instead. She'd unknowingly grown accustomed to Dimitri's constant, unwanted attention.

Memory echoed his booted footsteps behind her and Astrid cracked her lids. The steam curled, and her imagination configured the shape of Dimitri's figure seated on the side of the tub. The arrogant bastard wasn't here but she could still feel his amber stare traversing her skin.

Did she want him here? The thought led her to a far more worrisome inclination. Did she… *miss* him? Astrid ran her hand over her face.

Serpents guide me. What is wrong with me?

Astrid stepped out of the bath and roughly toweled off. She slid into bed, tucking herself under the furs and pulling them up to her chin. She was warm and comfortable, but it wasn't the same. The heat radiating off Dimitri sank in deeper, branding himself on her.

She blinked, willing herself to relax. It wasn't long before her gaze swept the room and stopped on his pillow. The empty place in his bed. She should be glad for his absence—a day of reprieve.

Astrid closed her eyes, listening to the wind howling in the courtyard. This should be the best sleep she'd had in weeks.

Why did she yearn for his presence?

Astrid laid still but her restless mind refused to quiet. She threw back the covers and paced the room. If she were home, she would have gone to her temple. If King Constantine hadn't destroyed every remnant of the Three-Faced Mother, she would be there now.

Frustration swelled within her and Astrid stilled. She closed her eyes and visualized the cloaked statues. The rasp of scales over stone.

Mothers hear me, Astrid voiced in her mind.

The words rang hallow.

She wasn't home, wasn't in her temple. The Mothers' serpents couldn't guide her because they weren't here. Because Queen Vesta abandoned her faith and condemned every soul weaver who remained in Ledivion to her fate.

Astrid gritted her teeth, glaring around the room. She returned to her pacing, in search of an outlet for her turmoil. Moonlight glinted off the scabbard she'd left on Dimitri's desk. Astrid stalked to it, ripping the blade free and letting its sheath clatter to the ground behind her.

The darkened corner of the room called to her. Foxglove would have coiled in the shadows there, blissfully unaware his bone-colored scales disrupted his camouflage. Astrid approached the wall and pressed her hand to the wood.

Ambrose's father desecrated her temples. She would remake the first one here.

The point of Dimitri's sword bit into the wood. Astrid dragged it over the paneling, carving sweeping lines into the wall. Curling slivers dropped at her feet as she etched three robed figures.

She took a step back, examining the hooded silhouettes. They stood taller than her, crowding the corner of the room. Tension slowly left her body, and she returned Dimitri's sword to its scabbard. She laid the blade across his desk, examining the oak face. It would make a poor altar with the drawers and files disrupting the flat surface. She turned, searching the room for the best-suited piece of furniture.

Minimal alterations would be required for the smaller set of drawers situated on Dimitri's side of the bed. Astrid dragged his nightstand before the carvings and wedged it into place. It was lower than she'd like, but it would serve its purpose.

Astrid moved to the dining cart and piled the best cuts of meat onto a plate. She set it on the altar and lowered to her knees.

Mothers hear me, she began in her mind.

What was she asking? What did she need?

Astrid listened to the wind, silently wishing the sound originated from the Mothers' serpents. She longed for the familiarity of her temple. The crackle of fire. The rasp of scales. The quiet security.

Is Foxglove even alive? It didn't occur to her to ask Dimitri what happened to the rest of the court. They couldn't have killed everyone. People would be needed to run Clorea. The internal workings were passed from one king to the next.

Astrid's lashes lowered and she stared into the shadowed corner. Foxglove wasn't hers, but she missed him. The ill-tempered cobra hissed and snapped at everyone but her. Her hands spread over the cold wooden surface of her makeshift altar.

"Mothers guide me. Show me my path," she whispered.

Why have you led me here?

She sat back on her heels and exhaled. Without the serpents to guide her, she was simply talking to herself in front of a drawing. She turned and glanced at the empty bed covered in furs.

When Dimitri returned, she would bargain for Foxglove...

Astrid tucked herself back into bed with a final thought. If Dimitri killed the Mothers' Serpents, she was going to cut his dick off.

Chapter Forty-Two

Dimitri soared over snow-covered pines. The glow of the southern palace illuminated an orange haze into the night, that grew brighter as he approached. His wings burned and the pain spread through his back as he pressed on. The desiccated corpse of his target had been left as an offering to Vinceret in the early evening. Normally, he would have spent the night at a tavern, but the rancid taste of the male's fear-rotted soul lingered on his tongue. He'd cleanse his palette with Astrid's fiery soul and sleep with his wife's soft curves beneath his wing.

Guards and archers perched in the towers while soldiers patrolled the exterior wall. Most windows were dimmed, the occupants fast asleep at this late hour. Dimitri glided lower, allowing the guardsmen to identify him as he passed. His head pounded with each beat of his wings and exhaustion sapped his strength.

He crested the exterior wall, acutely aware of his brother's men. The snow crunched beneath his boots as he landed in his private green space. Dimitri rolled his tense shoulders as he approached the tall, arched windows and stilled. Dots of condensation beaded the glass.

Dimitri leaned back and took silent inventory of the other windows. His neva had apparently made changes during his absence. The corners of his mouth lifted in a grin.

She's accepting these quarters as her new home.

He glanced down at the sill. A strange, red plant had been placed against the frame. Dimitri picked up the stalk covered in small red blooms. Graymalkin must have found it during one of his adventures and left it when Astrid didn't come to the window.

He opened the glass panel and the summer's warmth poured out of his room.

By the blood, my little wife likes the heat.

He closed the window and approached his bed. Astrid lay on her side dressed in one of his shirts with a sheet pulled up to her waist. She curled up to Graymalkin—no more than a fluffy mass sprawled on his back.

He turned to drop his cat's foraged trophy on his nightstand only to find his furniture missing. Wrath needled beneath his skin as he assessed the rest of his room. He located his nightstand, and his gaze lifted to the robed silhouettes carved into his wall.

Dimitri glared in his wife's direction. After he set his room to rights, he was going to flog her until she begged for his forgiveness. He stalked to his nightstand and paused. A dish was placed at its center with chunks of cooked beef piled on it. He turned toward her and choked back his searing fury.

She made this room her own and left offerings to her goddess.

His rage quieted as he approached her sleeping form. He discarded the flower on his desk and assessed his entitled wife. The sheets were tangled around her legs and hugged the curve of her ass. His shirt was too large for her and all but two buttons were unfastened. The collar gaped open over her bare shoulder and her dark hair pooled behind her.

She was stunning—and his.

His gaze raked over the carved Three-Faced Mother and lowered to her offering. *What had she asked her goddess for?* He would sacrifice anything Vinceret required to keep his vicious beauty by his side.

The moonlight reflected off the scar marking the top of his hand. He splayed his fingers, admiring it, then headed to his ensuite. He stripped and bathed quickly, cleansing himself of the sweat and grime from his travels. The room was uncomfortably warm, and Dimitri wondered how his little wife could sleep so soundly, completely oblivious to his return. The crackle of flames drew his attention. He would order Keres to tame the fire to a manageable temperature. She was likely the only one who'd dare make changes in his room.

Dimitri slipped into bed over the warmed sheet and laid on his side behind Astrid. Her honey and wildflower scent surrounded him, and the tension of their separation dissipated. He'd found a kind of peace with his feral neva. Craved her presence. She would sleep in his arms tonight and like it. He smoothed his hand over her waist and dragged her close, disturbing Graymalkin who left her with a lyrical chirp.

Astrid took a deep breath and wiggled against him. Her ass ground against his hardening cock and she ran her nails along his forearm in the same way he imagined she would pet his cat's belly before stilling once more.

He spread his wing over her legs and brushed his lips over the delicate skin at the nape of her neck. The beat of her heart and her quiet breathing soothed his pounding temples.

A whispered sigh slipped past Astrid's full lips as she leaned into him. He held her close, content for her to dream quietly in his embrace. Exhaustion blanketed his mind, and his eyes closed.

The gentle scrape of her nails pulled him back. Her fingertips traced twisting lines down his forearm in a featherlight caress, and on her next breath she jerked away from him.

Dimitri tightened his hold, and her power flared over him the next instant. He smiled, nuzzling her soft hair. The feel of her magic heated his blood. Soft ribbons, gliding over his body like warm silk.

"It's me, mýlaja," Dimitri crooned.

"What did you call me?" Astrid snapped.

Dimitri caught both her wrists in one hand and angled his wing to hook the talon through her golden bracelets. His muscles ached as he straightened his wing and lifted her to her knees. He languidly rose behind her, pressing his chest into her back. Her arms stretched over her head and, after a few stubborn tugs, she calmed. Dimitri palmed her thigh and lifted his hand up her bare waist.

"Always, you insult me," Dimitri purred at her ear.

He lifted his wingtip and slid the talon between the buttons of his shirt. It took no pressure to cut them free. He traced the edge of his wing along the underside of her breast and parted his lips, drawing against her soul. Her taste coated his tongue, spiced and sweet.

He lingered over her, savoring every moment. She arched her back and Dimitri's breath caught when the curve of her ass dragged along his cock. He sliced the remaining button and teased her nipple with the edge of his wing.

Astrid tensed and yanked against her restraints.

"I can scent how wet you're getting for me," Dimitri whispered. He reached higher, palming her breast before pinching the hard peak. Astrid's breathing turned ragged, and he lifted the wing hooking her bracelets, forcing her to lean into him.

"I'll teach you to like them," he promised, caressing her cheek with the edge of his wing.

Astrid twisted away from his touch. "I'm not a dog you can train."

"You could never be something so mundane," he said before bringing his lips to her throat. Dimitri released her wrists and lowered his wings around them. Not touching her, but visible. He swept her glossy hair over one shoulder and hooked his fingers under the collar of his shirt. She didn't fight as he slid the cashmere linen down her arms.

"You're not a pet to be trained," he murmured, before flipping her onto her back and prowling over her lithe body. "You're my wife," he whispered at her lips.

She met his stare and softened beneath him. Dimitri leaned closer, stilling when her fingertips met his sternum. Her touch was gentle, tracing the hard, chiseled muscle of his chest before following his collarbone to his shoulder.

Dimitri rocked against her. The head of his cock slid over her silken flesh. She was wet for him. Needy. He angled his hips and thrusted, driving into her warmth. Pleasure racked him and her legs closed around his waist. He stroked into her harder, burying himself in her cunt.

He let his shadows unravel and caress her. His magic swept over her, mingling with the tiny golden stars of her soul. He savored her taste and fucked her harder, completely entranced. She took every thrust, arching her back for more as she moaned his name. Her nails raked over his chest and shoulders. Her cunt squeezed his cock each time she came.

"My wife," Dimitri groaned at her lips as he took her with desperate strokes. "The only female as bloodthirsty and vicious as I am."

Her fingers tangled in his hair, and she pulled him closer. Dimitri couldn't think and didn't care to. She surrounded him. Engulfed him. Her lips met his in a heated rush and he drank her affection. She could take another stab at his heart, if it meant she was his, fleeting as this was.

Her tongue glided against his, stroking into his mouth. She nibbled on his lip and sucked on his tongue. Dimitri followed her, even as his mind screamed it was a trap. He clung to each moment, waiting for the sting of her bite.

He wrapped her in his arms and thrust deeper, forcing her to take every inch of his cock into her greedy cunt.

She broke their kiss long enough to cry, "Harder," but kept him close.

Her nails dug into his shoulder as she trembled beneath him. Dimitri nearly came as her breaths fanned over his ear. As she moaned and panted for him, he thrusted into her, desperate and harsh.

Dimitri came hard, completely entranced by the female in his arms. She caught the side of his chin with her index and turned him to face her. Her lips were swollen, and her cheeks were flushed with strands of her dark hair clinging to her forehead. There was no tension in her midnight eyes. No calculated focus or fiery viciousness. She wore a smile, and the emotion glittered in her stare.

She sensuously dragged her thumb across his mouth and said, "You don't have to fuck me like you'll never see me again. I'll be here in the morning."

He knew better than to believe her, but Vinceret save him, it felt like she meant it.

Chapter Forty-Three

Astrid woke with the dawn wrapped in Dimitri's warm embrace. He slept on his side with his wings outstretched behind him. The morning light cast shadows over his sharp cheekbones and his dark hair had dried at odd angles while he slept. She brushed aside the strands that had fallen into his eyes. Her touch was soft and gentle as it followed the arch of his brow.

Her sword was strikingly handsome. The corners of her mouth lifted as she breathed in his scent of winter night with a hint of pine. He'd been sweet last night in his own way, cleaning her and changing the linens. He'd tucked her into bed, and she'd grumbled, protesting the sound of running water a few moments later.

Graymalkin chirped from the windowsill and Dimitri groaned, squeezing her closer. The fluffy gray and white cat cried again, and Dimitri's lips grazed her shoulder before muttering, "I'm coming you little tyrant."

Astrid smiled as he dragged himself from bed and trudged to the sill. She believed she could manage a life with him. A love match was never part of her future anyway. Royal marriages were strategic and served their kingdoms. At least the cock she was tied to was useful and…

Her thoughts drifted as she admired the unyielding planes of his chiseled body. How they flexed and coiled with his movements. He turned his back to her, opening the window for Graymalkin. The sunlight shone through his gray wings as he stretched, backlighting the membrane from mauve to pink amidst the dark veins.

She'd prefer to bar his soul from his wings and remove the unsightly appendages from his perfect back. Astrid dismissed the notion. Most Ledivites would choose death over losing their wings and Dimitri was no different.

He closed the window and returned to bed. His callused palm rasped along her side before he pulled her to him. The room was comfortably warm, but the heat he radiated soaked into her bones.

She turned toward him and smoothed her fingertips up his forearm. "Keres told me you commissioned a temple for the Three-Faced Mother."

"Keres talks too much," Dimitri muttered as he closed his eyes.

"Why didn't you tell me?"

Dimitri slipped his wing beneath the silk sheet instead of responding. The serpentine scales dragged across her thighs as he moved them higher. Astrid caught the leading edge of his wing and strained to keep her voice neutral, if not understanding. "I do not want your wings on me."

"I'll teach you to like them," he said, overpowering her and dragging his wing up her middle.

Astrid shoved at the joint of his wing, tenting it over her. "No. You will compromise with me." The imposing weight of his wing lifted, and she tentatively released it, relieved when it remained above her.

He lazily blinked at her and grinned, flashing his straight white teeth. "What would you like to bargain?"

"I'm your wife, you need to make room for me," she insisted. His wing neared and Astrid shoved it back to its original position. "*Compromise*, Dimitri. I want to cut your wings off, and you want to rub them on me—things neither of us want. So, we'll meet in the middle. You keep your wings, but you don't touch me with them."

His eyes hardened and a malicious gleam lit behind his eyes, staining his molten gold stare. "No."

This stubborn male was impossible. Astrid brought his hand to the side of her face and kissed his palm. "You can touch me, just not with your wings," she said, smoothing her fingertips down his forearm.

A muscle twitched in his jaw and Astrid tensed. She cursed herself for not having the foresight to slip one of her hair stick daggers under her pillow.

To her astonishment, he lifted his wing. The black silk sheet billowed and fell, piling low on her waist. He pulled his hand away from her face and fisted the material, yanking it up until it came past her shoulder. His wing fell over her next. The heavy bones squeezed her as his talon tucked between her and the mattress.

Astrid struggled against her silk confinement and kicked at Dimitri. "Get your disgusting wing off me."

"My wing is not touching you," he countered, slipping his hand beneath the sheet and over her hip.

Astrid took deep breaths, calming her seething fury. Managing him would take time. He was too obtuse to understand curling his wing over her with a thin silk barrier was still touching her. The constriction of the membranous cage eased when she stopped struggling and Astrid shifted to her side to face him.

"Your wing is too big and it's heavy. You're hurting me," Astrid said.

An arrogant grin curled the corners of his mouth, but he relented. His wing unfurled and he drew it away, leaving the far edge of it spread over her thighs.

"Sleep, neva. It's early." With that, Dimitri closed his eyes.

Serpents devour him.

She wasn't a throw pillow. If he expected her to lie still while he slept on her for a few hours, she was going to slit his throat. Astrid recalled her failed assassination attempt. Stabbing him wouldn't get her out of his bed, and if she tried to leave, he would swaddle her in the curve of his grotesque appendages.

Physically fighting him was pointless.

She inched closer and Dimitri made room for her, lifting his chin over her head. This close, his clean scent surrounded her—snowfall deep in a forest. She pressed a kiss to the hollow at the base of his throat and did her best to embody the defenseless, whiskered moniker he'd given her.

"I'm hungry," she whispered, tracing small circles on his chest.

He was silent for a moment and Astrid soured. She'd been a moment from nipping the tendon running along his neck when his abrupt exhalation shifted her hair.

"I'll bring you breakfast," he said before smoothing her strands back into place and rising from the bed.

Astrid rose with him, slipping into the smoke colored, strapless dress Viktor designed for her. Dimitri donned his court finery and arranged his hair. He stepped into her, running a finger along the plum blossom branches comprising her newest corset.

"I see you appreciate my gift," he said, scrutinizing the tiny flowers.

She took his hand and when he met her eyes, she motioned toward his closet. More than a dozen intricately-designed corsets and pauldrons lined the walls. She leaned into him and whispered, "I need my own closet."

He chuckled and stepped away from her. "I'll have an earth weaver adjust my walls and add a new closet."

"I'd like to see the temple," she said, desperate for the solace only found kneeling before the Mothers.

Dimitri pinched her chin and leaned into her, stopping before his lips met hers. His lashes lowered as he gazed at her mouth. "Anything else you'd like to demand, neva?"

Astrid stood on her toes and met him in a soft kiss. "I'm asking, not demanding, my lord," she said, tracing her night-streaked nails over the sleeve of his topcoat.

He squeezed her closer then turned, leaving the room.

Astrid cataloged her victory. Dimitri was eager to please her. Starved for affection. She'd secured her Death Spirit, and now all that remained was steering him toward the Serpents' Crown.

Astrid watched the sway of his wings as he strolled down the hall. Would he be willing to decimate Ambrose's court as he'd done to hers? They could take Clorea and Ledivion both, merging them into a single kingdom and ruling side by side.

A besotted King and his soul weaver Queen.

She would need the Mothers' guidance. Astrid started toward her makeshift altar but froze at Dimitri's desk.

A snow plant rested on its side at the corner of the desk. She picked it up, inspecting the tiny red flowers over its thick stalk. The bottom had been cut cleanly. There were no teeth marks or other evidence to signify it as Graymalkin's latest discovery. Astrid set it back down and took a shaking breath.

Sterling and her cousins were coming for her.

Chapter Forty-Four

Astrid couldn't pinpoint when sharing her meals with Dimitri became pleasant. He'd returned with her breakfast, and aside from dismissing Dobromil who arrived with a small bowl of wild berries, Dimitri had been surprisingly well-behaved.

Astrid finished eating and set her plate on his desk before picking up the snow plant. She turned the stalk, admiring the blooms. "Is this a present from your travels?"

He took the parasitic flower and gently traced the petals along her jaw. "A gift from Graymalkin. He says you're an awful hunter and wouldn't survive if he didn't generously share his kills with you," Dimitri said, laying the plant beside her dish. "Come. I'll show you to your temple."

Astrid stood and followed Dimitri through the labyrinth of halls. They stepped onto a veranda and the cold bit into her, sinking deeper until it chilled her bones. Dimitri stepped closer and curled his wing around her. The membrane of his wing molded over her back and shoulder. Astrid stiffened, her reaction immediate and sharp. It was like walking into a cobweb. She hurriedly brushed it off, in hopes to remove the irate spider before it bit her.

Only there was no way out of the cobwebs Astrid found herself tangled in, and she had to reason with, rather than flee, a much larger spider.

She traced the bones of his wing and swallowed the bile rising in her throat before turning toward him. "Your jacket would keep me warmer."

Dimitri wordlessly pulled his wing away and Astrid welcomed the winter chill. He glanced down at her with an expression she'd seen many times—the slight narrowing of his molten gold eyes. The tension in his jaw. Anger danced with annoyance as he decided on how he would punish her. Astrid held his stare for the space of three steps, daring him to drag her back to his room.

But what good would that do? Bending him to her will was meaningless if she pulled so hard he snapped.

Astrid stared forward through the snow of the frozen garden space and stepped closer to him. The edge of his wing brushed her sleeve as they walked. She kept silent, willing it to be enough.

Dimitri shrugged out of his jacket and Astrid's pulse quickened. He placed the cashmere wool over her shoulders and Astrid smoothed her hand over the embroidered lapel. "Thank you."

They stepped into the frosted, open space and the building towering above them stole her words.

The large archway opened to the temple's interior and through it, Astrid caught a glimpse of a robed female carved out of marble. Her facial features were obscured beneath a hood and in her outstretched hands was a coiled serpent. Astrid's heart squeezed and the pinprick of tears threatened her resolve.

Her boots crunched through the thin layer of snow that had fallen the night before. A wave of heat struck her the moment she crossed into the temple. Astrid blinked back her tears. There had been a void in her chest since she arrived. Dimitri had taken so much from her. Stripped so much of her—but this...

This felt like home.

Astrid approached the altar, staring up at the three robed statues before gazing down the east and west walls. It *was* like home, down to the placement of the pews and the fountain at the start of the aisle.

Everything... but the Mothers' serpents, she realized.

Dimitri's booted steps echoed behind her as he strolled through the silent temple. Without the familiar rasp of scales, it felt empty.

"How did you recreate this? Did you send the earth weavers to my palace?" Astrid asked.

Dimitri nodded. "It was a few days' travel, and they began construction immediately upon their return. I asked Keres to warm it, since you're more comfortable in a furnace."

Astrid laughed and turned to spread her hands over the pristine altar. Every piece had been replicated from the silver-veined marble to the shadowed corner Foxglove napped in.

Dimitri moved to her back. He outstretched his wings, and his shadow cast over hers onto the altar. A sensuous shiver ran down her spine as he ran the back of his fingers down her arm. He leaned into her. His chest pressing into her back. Astrid's lips parted as his callused hand smoothed over hers—the warmth of his hand a stark contrast to the cool marble beneath it.

Their binding scars overlapped.

His breath fanned over the shell of her ear, sending tremors of anticipation through her as he whispered, "Is this to your liking, neva?"

Astrid swallowed and tilted her chin upward. The Mothers stood silent and in their upturned hands, they cradled birth, life, and death.

The egg, the serpent, and the shed.

She'd asked the Mothers to guide her, to free her, in Clorea. Had Dimitri been sent to her? Was he meant to open her path?

Astrid leaned into his firm body and tilted her head back. "It needs serpents and offerings," she said, rotating her hand and lifting her fingers until they were intertwined with his. "There's a cobra at my palace temple who means a great deal to me. I would feel more at home if you brought him here."

Dimitri's arm encircled her waist, and his deep voice thrummed against her hair. "If I handed you the stars, you would still ask for more."

She lifted their entwined hands and pressed her lips to his brutal scar. He was powerful and handsome, though his affection was misguided at times. A striking addition to her arsenal. A Death Spirit she could deploy on her enemies.

A weapon she would temper and bend by degrees.

"Shouldn't my husband want to lay the world at my feet?" Astrid asked sweetly.

Dimitri chuckled darkly and answered, "If he possessed his wife's loyalty."

Astrid turned in his arms. His muscles flexed beneath her touch as she smoothed her hand higher to cup the side of his face.

"Have I not been loyal?"

He palmed her ass and roughly lifted her. Astrid gasped as the cool marble chilled her bottom. His hand closed over her throat and forced her back against the altar.

"No. Dimitri, this is sacrilege to the Mothers!" she yelled as he threw her skirt over her corset. Astrid thrashed beneath him, but her efforts were useless. He overpowered her, wedging his waist between her thighs.

"Serpents devour you. I don't worship conquest," she snapped.

He stilled and Astrid panted her relief. She lay still for the space of a moment and gentled her voice as she sat up. "You can have me," she whispered as his stubble scratched against her soft touch, "in your bed, at your thermal spring... anywhere but here."

Dimitri effortlessly lifted her off the altar, cradling her ass and trapping her against him. He leaned in and Astrid met him with soft kisses, stroking his cheek.

He pulled back but remained so close his lips brushed hers as he spoke. "I'll have you on your knees tonight. You're going to wrap those pretty lips around my cock. You'll spread your legs and moan for me as I stretch your cunt. And after I've made you come a dozen times, and you're trembling and flushed beneath me, I'm going to fuck your ass."

Images flicked through her mind as his promises fanned across her lips. Her traitorous mind replayed the feel of his callused hands gripping her waist. The way she arched her back and took each of his strokes. A flush crept over her cheeks as she cursed the heat pooling between her legs. As much as she'd tempered and bent him, he had done the same to her.

"You'll beg for me, wife," he murmured before smiling at her lips. "And I will relish every moment."

Chapter Forty-Five

Dimitri took a seat on a pew shadowed from the morning sun. The rays bathed the temple in golden light, but he cared little for it. His attention remained fixed on Astrid. He'd allowed her space to pray and scarcely recognized the silent female kneeling before the white marble altar. The vicious temper he'd encountered time and again vanished within this temple.

Unless he was trying to fuck her in front of her goddesses.

He strangled his dark amusement and smiled. He preferred this... more accepting side of her.

Time passed and Dimitri began to wonder if she bowed not in prayer, but to ascertain how long he would allow her to commune with her goddesses. He sat in silence as the passing minutes eroded his patience. This temple could be her sanctuary—a place to escape to and find solace from anyone but him.

He strolled to his devout wife and lowered to his knees, folding his wings behind him. "Teach me to pray to your three-faced goddess," he whispered.

Astrid ignored him and Dimitri's impatience gave way to wrath. The silence stretched between them and dragging Astrid to his feet by a fistful of her hair sounded more appealing by the second. He'd been a moment from acting on the impulse when her head turned a fraction.

Seething fury glimmered in the depths of her midnight eyes. She would kill him and leave his body as an offering to her robed statues if she were able. Her viciousness was a shield, intended to deflect male attention, but he found it intoxicating. Her rage sweetened the flavor of her soul, and he could think of nothing more pleasing than watching her rancor slip into surrender as she came.

"If this is where you wish to spend your time," Dimitri began, gesturing to the Three-Faced Mother, "I will spend it with you. Teach me."

Her features remained harsh as she scrutinized him. "You've admitted you don't worship Fate."

Her words were true. Fate was cruel and Dimitri believed blindly walking the mangled path set before him was a fool's errand. "I worship Vinceret. But should I not pay my respects to the goddesses my wife kneels to?"

Astrid eyed him suspiciously. Clorea was ruled beneath the shadow of the Three-Faced Mother. His little wife protected her faith viciously. Curiosity pestered him. Did she desperately cling to her temples because she was devout or was her time for worship restricted? When he returned for her pet snake, he would ask if she would like a collection of heads as a belated wedding gift.

Astrid gazed at the statues. "We pray to the Mothers, and she sends serpents to guide us to our fate."

His little wife was far too willful to be led by anything. The concept of her beliefs were marred by her actions. "If you believe in a predestined fate, why do you fight me? Your Mothers allowed me to capture you. Keep you. Is this not your fate?"

A small laugh slipped past her lips as she smiled. "Trusting in fate does not mean I am to roll onto my back and allow life to happen to me. You are an instrument of the Three-Faced Mother just as I am. I couldn't serve the Mothers beneath my father's suffocating grasp," Astrid said, turning toward him. "The Mothers sent you to liberate me."

"How are you sure your assumption is correct? The Three-Faced Mother could have as easily placed you in my path to be my faithful and smitten wife."

"Because you don't serve her," Astrid said simply. "The path she set before me isn't meant to be easy. It's meant to be traversed."

On the battlefield, he'd witnessed the dying and wounded scream for their gods. Begging for their intervention. Desperate cries to save them, to spare them. His feral neva didn't lament to her goddess. She believed her hardships served a greater purpose. A quiet serenity came over her as she closed her eyes in prayer, assured and unwavering.

Dimitri wanted her faith and passion. Her loyalty.

"What do you pray for?" he asked.

"Knowledge," Astrid breathed. "There is no doubt you're a sword. I pray to recognize if you were meant for my hand or if another wields you and you're destined for my throat."

"I am in your hands, neva, but a weapon can only perform as well as it is treated," Dimitri said, lowering his voice to a caress. "If you cared for your blade, sharpened and honed it... I would never fail you."

Astrid offered him a bemused smile. "Why would I care for a blade that cuts me more often than my enemies?"

"Why do you blame the weapon when your injuries are obviously the result of your poor swordsmanship," Dimitri countered.

Humor lit her eyes, and Astrid rose to her feet. She smoothed her hands over the altar, tracing the veins of glittering silver. She turned her head, not quite glancing back at him, and asked, "Would you've been kind to me if I spoke to you sweetly in the carriage?"

Dimitri shrugged his broad shoulders. "I would alter nothing about you, neva. There is no changing who we are."

Astrid's features softened in a way he'd only seen when she slept. She may have been a princess, but her court choked and silenced her. He'd thought to force her affection when all he needed to do was supply her with a space to breathe. He would still punish her when she turned her viciousness toward him, but he accepted her as she was.

Dimitri rose to his feet and brushed off his knees. "I will have snakes delivered. Is there a particular meat you prefer for your offerings?"

A genuine smile crossed her lips, and she sauntered toward him. "I carved offerings from our prisoners back home."

Dimitri stroked her cheek and smiled. "Then your serpents will be well fed."

Chapter Forty-Six

Astrid closed her eyes. The warmth of Dimitri's touch soothed a part of her that was never accepted in Clorea.

He stepped back. "I need to turn in my reports."

She intertwined her fingers with his and they strolled out of her temple. "I want to send another letter to my cousins."

He stopped suddenly and yanked her toward him. Callused fingers caged her throat, urging her chin higher. His teeth flashed as he spoke. Territorial and vicious. "They can't save you from me, neva."

"I don't need saving," Astrid purred, leaning into his grip. "I only wish to remind them *I* am the rightful heir, and tell them *we* are wed."

His fingers loosened and he pressed a kiss on her forehead before releasing her. "I'm... sorry."

The words were clumsy, but it was the first apology she'd received from him—and perhaps the first he'd ever given. He may believe he owned her, but during the passing weeks, he'd begun to value her.

They returned to his room and Astrid began writing her letter. Dimitri lingered for a few moments before leaving her side. She knew he read her letters before they were sent, but there would be no code to infer. This letter was a tactful declaration. She'd married and adopted Ledivite customs. Her throne would no longer fall to the first born male. *She* was heir to the Serpents' Crown.

A large shadow landed in the private gardens and Astrid smiled. Her besotted husband had returned unexpectedly quick. She stood, making her way to the window and froze.

The edge of a rust-colored wing was framed in the glass. Astrid stepped back and a male she didn't recognize pushed the window open. His eyes darted over the room.

"We don't have much time, Princess. Sorin sent me," he whispered with his hand outstretched.

His empty hand.

Sterling would have told this male his name, not her cousin's. Further, where was the snow plant to signal he was part of the plan? He should have carried it, or at least had a blossom pinned to him.

Dimitri's warning rang through her mind.

If you're captured, you can expect to be tied to a sawhorse and given to the legion.

Her magic snapped to her in an instant. The golden haze of tiny stars glimmered over the flesh and bone housing his soul. She hadn't made a kill in months, but would happily remind him why males wailed her title when she approached.

"I don't need rescuing. Save my mother," Astrid hissed.

"The orders were for you." The male stepped into the room and caught her wrist, tugging her forward. "We don't have time; he'll return soon," he gritted through his teeth.

"I'm ordering you to save my mother," Astrid commanded.

He dragged her forward, stepping onto the windowsill. Astrid's temper spiked. If he couldn't take orders from her, she'd send him back to the Vermillion Palace in bloody pieces.

Astrid clapped her other hand over his, squeezing it to her wrist. Her magic flared and she ripped his soul from his legs. The male crumbled to the ground and thrashed his wings in a wild panic.

"What've you done?" he cried, dragging himself onto the snow.

"Dimitri!" Astrid screamed, catching the male's ankle in both hands.

He flapped his wings harder, sending loose pages flying off the desk.

"Dimitri!" she yelled again, dragging her newest playmate back into the room. She raised her arms, making a dramatic show of dropping his useless leg. "I'm going to cut off your wings and use them to make a new pair of boots," she said sweetly.

She toyed with him, stepping on the back of his knee and barring his soul from one arm but leaving him the other. He wiggled back and forth like a fish tossed onto land. He posted himself up with his good arm.

"Princess—" His eyes widened as he looked past her.

Astrid smiled, delighted to see the blood drain from his face. It'd been so long since she killed. His death would be a glorious thing of beauty. She took his limp hand, intent on introducing him to her husband.

The leading edge of his rust-colored wing snapped forward and she twisted out of its path. His talon tore her sleeve and sliced her shoulder. Before she could right herself, the rust-winged Fae managed to take flight and fled through the window.

Her scalp burned the next instant as Dimitri held her by a fistful of her hair. She gripped his hand, fighting his unrelenting pressure.

"Do you think you can leave me?" he bellowed before dropping her.

Astrid's dark hair tossed across her vision with a powerful beat of Dimitri's wings. He was in the sky the next instant.

"Fucking idiot, jealous male," Astrid hissed, rubbing her stinging scalp. She watched their dark silhouettes against the crisp blue sky and her lips parted.

What was he doing?

Astrid squinted as Dimitri flew higher.

She leaned in the window frame as disappointment slumped her shoulders. Her prey was escaping, and Dimitri was as useless at hunting as Graymalkin.

Her sword's silhouette tightened. Dimitri's wings pulled tight to his body suddenly and he sang through the air like an arrow. Astrid watched, astonished, as he closed in.

Closer.

Closer.

The impact was brutal, and her prey tumbled through the sky in an uncontrolled spin. Astrid lifted her gaze to Dimitri. She recognized the steady beat of his wings but there was something large and flat covering his legs. Astrid stared, puzzled, as Dimitri tossed it.

It fell to the ground like a sheet of paper, falling after his opponent.

Astrid straightened as realization struck her. Dimitri had torn off the male's wing.

He dove again and his silhouette steadily grew larger. Heat flushed her cheeks and Astrid backed away from the window, searching for a weapon. She drew one of his swords and stood so the bed was between her and his grand entrance.

He landed a moment later. Blood splatter and pieces of what she recognized as bone covered him. His eyes were wild as he stalked toward her.

"I wasn't leaving you," Astrid quickly explained.

Her words stalled when his wing lashed toward his desk. He hooked his talon through the ring on his twin scabbard and caught the weapon in a smooth motion. The slide of metal against its sheath rang as he drew his weapon.

Fuck.

Astrid instinctively stitched her soul and raised her sword. "Dimitri, this was an attack."

Another step.

"I was calling for you," she exclaimed, frantically.

Dimitri lunged. He struck hard, knocking the blade from her throbbing hand. Astrid choked as his grip cut off her air. He dragged her forward, lifting her feet off the stone floor. He held her so close, his lips brushed hers as he spoke.

"Your blood is mine. Your orgasms are mine. *You* are mine."

Chapter Forty-Seven

Dimitri crushed his lying wife to his chest and launched into the sky with a powerful beat of his wings. He'd been foolish—letting himself believe she'd accepted her place beside him. He didn't deserve her, a princess with a mind as sharp as her beauty. A female who didn't cower from his magic and his curse. Pain infested his heart. She'd never truly be his.

But he would keep her.

Dimitri held her tighter, focusing his pain and rage into the ruthless crescendo of their flight.

She would never escape him.

He rose above the clouds and Astrid clung to him. Her shrill screams were lost to the howl of wind as they ascended. His neva locked her arms around his neck and shoulders. She hooked her ankles behind him, wrapping her toned legs around his waist.

"Dimitri." Her voice was breathless as her hand ran over the back of his head and down his neck. "We were attacked," she pleaded, squeezing him closer. "I wasn't leaving you, my lord."

Lies. Every word from her honeyed lips was a lie.

And Dimitri didn't care.

He needed her—wanted her—and he hated her for it.

Silk tore as he ripped the skirt off her dress. He tossed it and the black material twisted and fluttered downward through the open sky. Her panties followed and Dimitri palmed her ass, lifting her higher to unfasten his slacks.

The air was thin at this altitude, leaving him lightheaded and short of breath. Sunlight beamed down on them, and he glanced at the clouds rolling below. Dimitri engulfed her in his death magic and Astrid shuddered in his arms. His shadows curled around her, stealing the glimmering stars of her soul.

He took from her, counteracting the altitude.

"I'll never let you go," Dimitri growled, thrusting into her. She was wet and slick. The heat of her cunt squeezed his cock tighter as she took more of him.

By the blood, she was perfect.

"Dimitri, I— Dimitri, I can't breathe," she panted at his throat.

He wanted to punish her. He should be hurting her, but her pleas unearthed soft, buried emotions and twisted him.

His fingers dug into her hips, holding her while he fucked her harder. This was all that mattered. She belonged to him, body and soul.

And he would rain death over all eight kingdoms before he ever let her go.

"Slower," Astrid murmured.

"Take it," Dimitri growled. "Take all of me."

Her nails raked across his shoulders and Dimitri groaned at the burn. He held her against him, chasing the ecstasy he found in her. Everything about her intoxicated him —the spiced nectar of her soul, every sound he coaxed from her—it all drove him closer to release.

Astrid laid her head on his shoulder and her moans quieted to whispered sighs. He'd kept her too high for too long.

Dimitri palmed the back of her head as he came. Pleasure

coursed through him, and he leaned back, wrapping her in his dark wings. Bliss and weightlessness overtook him before his shoulders tipped back and they plummeted.

241

Chapter Forty-Eight

Astrid clung to Dimitri, dizzy and short of breath. Her breaths turned ragged, but she couldn't get enough air in her lungs. Her night-streaked nails bit into his back as her head fell to his shoulder.

Dimitri's death magic consumed her, hungry and seeking. It intensified her ecstasy until she craved each ruthless thrust. Until she needed him, rough and claiming.

Astrid blinked as dark splotches patched her vision and her mind began to quiet. The steady beat of his wings tossed her hair but all she could feel was the harsh rhythm of his cock and the waves of her orgasms crashing through her.

Pain cut through the haze that blanketed her mind. Dimitri cruelly gripped her hip and thrust into her a final time. He groaned, tilting his chin back and palming the back of her head as he came deep inside her.

Dimitri curled his membranous wing around her, then the other, molding them to her body. He leaned back and Astrid's heart raced as her view pitched forward. The cold bite of nerves shrieked through her body as weightlessness enveloped her.

They plummeted the next moment, accelerating as they fell through the clouds.

"Dimitri!" Astrid screamed.

She wedged her hand between their bodies, pressing her palm to her sternum. Golden threads burst from her and arched back into her body before pulling tight. Astrid stitched her soul again and again. She'd never seen a body fall from this height.

Would there be anything left of her body to regenerate?

From this high, the pine forest were mere patches of green and the southern palace looked like a figurine. They were falling, but the ground didn't grow closer. She knew once it did, she would have moments before impact.

Astrid yanked on Dimitri's shirt and struck his chest. His fingers, tangled in her hair, lazily caressing her scalp, was her only indication he was conscious.

Serpents devour you.

She wasn't going to die like this. Astrid grabbed his face, cupping her palm over his nose and mouth.

Dimitri shook his head and pulled her hand away. His wings constricted around her until she fought for breath. He rocked his hips, languidly sliding his cock in and out of her.

Astrid's temper spiked. She was trapped within his boney, membranous prison and could do nothing to stop their freefall or his invasion.

"Pull up," Astrid yelled, shoving her shoulder against the leading edge of his wing.

Her mind raced as the ground rushed to meet them. She couldn't escape this. The sword she had prayed for was maddened and he was going to kill them both.

Astrid tensed and tucked her chin, bracing for impending death. If she survived this, she was cutting off his *fucking* wings.

The suffocating compression eased as Dimitri altered the angle of their fall. Astrid counted her breaths, acutely aware her back would hit the ground first. His arm cradled her spine, and he held the side of her head against his chest with the other.

Dimitri spread his wings abruptly. The change in momentum was sharp and jarring. Astrid's legs flung back, her heels dusting snow as they pulled out of their dive. She would have been a red stain in the snow if Dimitri hadn't held her in place.

"Put me down!" Astrid screamed.

She shoved at him, struggling against his hold. A ten-foot drop wouldn't kill her. Astrid pushed off his chest and swung, catching his jaw with the point of her elbow.

Dimitri's hold faltered and she gasped, falling into open air. She would land hard, but she could heal a broken ankle.

A callused hand caught her wrist and Astrid's shoulder took the brunt of her weight as she jerked to a stop. She twisted, upturned her chin. "Let go of me before I decorate the snow with your organs!"

Dimitri flicked her wrist away and she landed on her ass in the snowbank. Astrid cursed, getting to her feet. She dusted the clumped snow off her skin, realizing she was naked from the waist down.

At least they were in a clearing in the middle of the forest. The cold bit into her feet and leeched up her legs. She stomped toward Dimitri and nearly fell when her bare foot came down in the snow, upheaving her center of balance on her remaining high heel.

"What did you think you were doing?" Astrid snapped, trudging toward him.

Dimitri fastened his slacks and sneered at her. "Reminding you who you belong to."

"*Belong* to?" Fury tangled her words and Astrid's magic engulfed him. His soul remained constant beneath her will, and she wanted to scream. "You parade me like a whore. Anyone could have seen us."

"You're mine, neva."

Her fury shattered beneath his declaration. "I belong to no one!"

"You're mistaken," Dimitri said, catching her by the throat, "*wife.*"

The title was her prison. Yet another cage a male sought to trap her in. Astrid clawed at his collar, dragging him closer. She dug her nails into either side of his windpipe and spat, "The only thing I belong to is my fate."

"I *am* your fate," Dimitri bellowed before shoving her back.

Astrid fell in the snow and scrambled to her feet. She needed a weapon and scanned the clearing for a branch. A rock. Anything. But fresh snow surrounded them, concealing anything useful.

Dimitri turned from her and his breath fogged as he exhaled.

"Give me your shirt," Astrid snapped. Her demented sword glared back at her over his shoulder, as though her demand was outlandish. "You ruined my dress. Give me your shirt, your coat, and your belt," Astrid ordered, shaking the melting slush off her foot.

Dimitri shrugged out of his topcoat and tossed it to her. Astrid caught the heavy garment and waited for his shirt. He stripped out of it and Astrid snatched it from his hands, shoving the coat to his chest before letting it fall.

He caught it before it hit the ground and Astrid donned his shirt. She cursed and welcomed the warmth locked in his clothing.

"Your belt," she said with a flash of her teeth.

Dimitri didn't fight her and removed his belt. Astrid took the remaining articles and fished his belt through the arms of his coat. She swung it over her hips and turned to straighten it over her ass. Dimitri's brows lowered as she belted the makeshift train around her waist.

"Take me home." The word shocked Astrid the moment it slipped past her lips.

A smug expression crossed Dimitri's features as he closed the distance between them. She dug her nails into her palm, wanting to cut the certainty off his face.

"Carry me nicely," she snapped when he bent to pick her up.

Dimitri paused for a moment, and she wondered if he was going to hoist her over his shoulder. To her amazement, he scooped the back of her train and held it to the bend of her knees, lifting her off her feet.

Astrid's temper cooled. She was covered and the heat of him seeped into her. Dimitri spread his wings and launched skyward with a powerful beat of his wings.

"Don't fly higher than necessary," she added. A muscle ticked in Dimitri's jaw, and she quickly added, "Please."

They glided toward the southern palace in silence—an uncomfortable truce struck a foot above the pines.

Chapter Forty-Nine

Days passed and Astrid's patience wore thin. She waited for a sign. For one of Sterling's spies to contact her. He wouldn't have tried to extract her while Dimitri remained in the palace. Sterling would have waited for Dimitri to leave, trusted her to extend his next assignment and buy the necessary time.

Sorin must have sent the winged male, or worse, her dear husband's enemies sought to punish him with her humiliation.

Astrid glanced at Dimitri as he shrugged into a black topcoat with understated crimson embroidering and fastened his sword belt. He'd been awake when Graymalkin's lyrical chirps woke her this morning. She'd been confined to this room since they returned, and the tension between them steadily grew.

He'd kept his terms of their bargain, taking the letters she penned to Sorin each morning. Astrid signed her latest message and held it up with two fingers as he strolled past her. He took the folded parchment, not bothering to open it.

"Dress in your finest gown. The Ascension will start in an hour," he said over his shoulder before leaving the room.

A Ledivite custom she had no experience with. If Dimitri let her out of their room, she could have asked Viktor what colors were typically worn. King Ambrose would lay a sword on his parents' grave to honor their reign. Dimitri dressed as though it were a funeral, but the accounts she'd read made it sound like a celebration.

Astrid walked into their shared closet. The earth weavers expanded it when they repaired the wall she'd carved the Mothers into. An array of tulle, chiffon, and silk gowns hung in neat rows greeted her.

She selected a sleeveless black gown of chiffon and lace. Following Dimitri's lead would be a safe choice. Astrid slipped into it and caged her waist beneath one of Keres's breathtaking creations. This one was gold with delicate, platinum lotus blossoms arranged over the thin boning.

The metallurgist enchanted each of her pieces to radiate heat, much in the same way Astrid could stitch a soul. The magic slowly drained out of the metal and Keres embedded her fire into them when she rejuvenated the hearth, keeping the room comfortable.

Astrid tucked her hair behind her pointed ear and opened the top drawer of Dimitri's nightstand. Her jeweled combs, pins, and sticks were meticulously arranged beside his suede box.

Her gaze lingered on the container.

Dimitri stored the toys he used on her within it, but hadn't opened it since their fight. He'd clung to her these past nights, forcing her to sleep with his cock buried inside her. Drank her soul and fucked her each morning, but the intensity between them was lacking—leaving a void Astrid refused to acknowledge.

She collected her jade pins and combs, before sliding the drawer closed. Dimitri would be in a bitter mood according to Keres, and the drug she'd given her was concealed in the gold-wrapped jade hair stick.

Dimitri returned as Astrid slid the last comb into place. Her irritation lifted when she caught sight of the red lilies in his hand.

"Neva," he said, turning toward the door.

Astrid took her place at his side and controlled her expression when he didn't offer her the flowers. They strolled through increasingly-busy corridors and the crowd parted for Dimitri as they had during her first visit to Viktor. The ambient chatter hushed, beginning again, louder, as they passed.

Sunlight poured over the steps she climbed, and Astrid's breath caught at the expansive courtyard. Her gaze shifted to the arena seating surrounding the meticulously manicured space. Pillars supported three stories surrounding the orchard. Winter had robbed the trees of their greenery, but there was an elegance in the way the skeletal branches framed a walkway to the matching pair of tombstones.

They were simple, curved stones embellished with Ledivion's crest, intersecting swords. Her gaze averted to the railings wrapped in red ribbons.

Astrid's attention was pulled away as Dimitri guided her to stand in front of him.

"Hold on to me," he muttered as he bent, hooking his arm under the bend of her knees.

Astrid wrapped her arms around his neck and Dimitri lifted her against him. They shot upward with a hard beat of his wings and rose above the canopy. She squeezed him closer as they floated to the boxed seats on the second floor.

They landed softly in the box closest to the graves and Dimitri set her gently on her feet. She approached the railing. The ribbons she thought adorned the railings were… flowers. The same blood red lilies Dimitri held. Their sweet scent drifted through the space.

More than six seats were arranged on this balcony and Astrid couldn't help but wonder if this box belonged to Dimitri or if he'd simply commandeered it.

He took to the air again and Astrid cataloged the crowd. Gowns of every hue speckled the seating below. She turned toward her neighbors and found them huddled at the far end of their box. A trio whispered to each other in a cluster, while other winged guests openly pointed as Dimitri landed at the foot of the graves.

Murmurs and frightened glances erupted through the arena as Dimitri lowered himself to his knees. He bowed his head and pressed his hand to the snow-covered ground in front of the grave on the right. His mouth moved as he spoke to the frozen earth.

"He has no right to be there," Astrid's neighboring female hissed from her corner.

"King Ambrose should exile him," the male behind her answered.

Astrid caught the male's stare, and his charcoal wings shrank to his back. He was quick to usher the two females accompanying him from the seating area and Astrid shifted her attention back to her sword.

Dimitri laid the flowers in the snow, adjusting their position several times before he finally stood.

Betrayal festered in Astrid's chest. How did this female maintain Dimitri's loyalty years after her death?

It doesn't matter, Astrid told herself.

Dimitri took to the air once more to rejoin her.

This volatile male was her sword, and his past was cold and buried.

Horns sounded as Dimitri landed. She stepped closer to the lily-covered railing and squinted against the sun.

King Ambrose entered the courtyard atop a massive black horse. Its mane and tail gleamed against the snow as it tossed its head and pawed the ground. Other winged members of the royal court were lined behind him as they marched beneath the curve of tree branches.

A scabbard with a jewel-encrusted hilt was strapped to the back of Ambrose's saddle. Astrid studied it, curious if it was the sword Ambrose would lay before the graves.

The scrape of glass sounded behind her and Astrid was lifted off her feet the next moment. She clung to Dimitri as they flew above the courtyard and towering spires. The palace was much larger than she'd originally thought. She searched the architecture, desperate for a wing to stand out, or for evidence as to where her mother was held.

Nothing seemed out of place and Astrid leaned into Dimitri, shielding herself from winter's bite.

They landed in the white garden outside Dimitri's room. Astrid rushed into the comfortable heat, leaving the window open behind her.

He entered behind her and rasped, "Take the gown off, wife."

Astrid bristled. Her title lacked affection. It was a noose around her neck and Dimitri tightened it every time they fought.

He dropped the bottle of wine he'd stolen from their seating on his desk and began to strip. Astrid unzipped the side closure of her dress and let it pool at her feet. She moved to the desk in nothing more than her black lace thong and heels before opening the bottle of wine.

Her sword's compulsion would force him to retrieve her dress and fold it before placing it in the hamper.

Dimitri did as expected while she poured his glass. She removed the pins and combs from her long dark hair, extracting the jade stick last. When Dimitri turned his back on her, she opened the hidden vial. Keres said a few drops would put him out until morning, but Astrid didn't have time to measure the dose.

She upturned the gold-wrapped jade, emptying the contents into his red wine. This wouldn't kill him, and should he sleep for a few days, it would be a welcomed reprieve. She could get her mother's location from Dobromil and free her before Dimitri woke.

He returned to her, murmuring against her hair. "Get on the bed and spread your legs." The seductive purr in his voice was laced with violence.

Astrid had no intention of laying still and letting him take his pain for a dead lover out on her. She pressed the glass into his hand and caressed his fingers when she pulled away.

"Yes, my lord," she whispered, sauntering to their bed. She arched her back as she crawled onto the mattress.

He approached as she sat back, swirling the dark contents of his drink in its glass. Astrid held his molten gold stare, willing him to drink his fucking wine.

Dimitri lifted the rim to his lips and drank deeply, emptying its contents. He set it on his nightstand and Astrid suppressed her victorious smile.

Chapter Fifty

Astrid's back met the hard planes of Dimitri's unyielding body as he got into bed behind her. His callused grip caged her throat, and she leaned into it, lifting her chin. She blinked skyward, silently cursing herself for not asking Keres how long the drug would take to knock him out.

The length of Dimitri's cock prodded her, and it wasn't the feel of him that spiked her temper. It was his hands skimming over her waist while he thought of his dead queen. She wasn't a surrogate for his grief, and she'd fight him so hard there'd be no room in his mind for his mistress while he fucked her.

Dimitri nuzzled her hair and inhaled deeply before curling his wings around her.

"Get your wings off me," Astrid snapped, shoving at her boney prison before she threw her elbow into his chest.

The wings constricted tighter and his arms circled her middle. He inhaled again and grazed his teeth over her throat.

"I'm… tired." Dimitri's words were slurred but he didn't release her.

His death magic reached for her, but it wasn't the sharp sensation of serrated teeth that occurred when she stabbed his heart. It was gentle, drawing little more than a taste as he held her.

"What are you doing," Astrid breathed as the feel of his body against hers created a pleasured haze over her mind.

"I like the way you smell," he murmured.

Astrid ignored the way his breath fanned under her jaw and along her throat. Ignored the fact she wanted to lean forward and rock her hips while he fucked her.

She held still, clinging to her logic and reason. "What do I smell like?"

"Dreams," he groaned, "and forgotten times."

Dimitri pulled her onto her side to lie beside him. Being used as a throw pillow was little better than being fucked while he thought of another female. And his words… Her sword was a poet, and her traitorous mind bloomed with the red lilies he carried.

He'd never brought her flowers.

Astrid struggled to turn in the tangle of his arms and wings. When she faced him, his ever-present mask of arrogance was absent. Anguish dulled his features, and his luminous eyes were muted beneath his turmoil.

"Do you bring her flowers every year?"

"Yes," he answered immediately.

The corner of his lips lifted, and his expression softened like he was remembering a fond memory. The moment was short lived, and he pulled her against his chest, resting his chin on the top of her head.

Astrid contemplated her situation. The drug Keres gave her hadn't knocked him out. She suspected his death magic took enough from her to keep him conscious. Much like he had done when he fucked her above the clouds. He was more talkative under the drug's influence, and she wouldn't waste the boon the Mothers' serpents laid at her feet.

"Tell me about Queen Vesta," Astrid said against the hollow at the base of his throat.

"She was kind. Beautiful," he replied.

Astrid stroked his side, mirroring his actions, as she plotted her interrogation.

"Did you love her?"

"Very much."

His confession hurt far more than it should have. Astrid breathed in his winter scent and buried the sting of his betrayal. Dimitri was here with her and any feelings he once felt were irrelevant. She needed information. How did Queen Vesta earn his loyalty and how could she replicate it?

"She favored you in court. How did you win her loyalty?" she asked, certain Dimitri would chronical every depraved encounter—

"A son is born with his mother's loyalty," he answered flatly.

Astrid blinked, fighting the touch of his shadows and the bliss of his hands on her body. "You're Ambrose's brother?"

"Yes."

Astrid recalled what she knew of Vesta. Dimitri was Ambrose's older brother. "You were documented as still born," Astrid whispered more to herself than him.

"I was."

Which was why King Constantine killed everyone in the birthing chamber. Vesta wouldn't surrender her infant, and Constantine wouldn't give his queen to the flames. The Queen isolated herself for seven years.

It wasn't in mourning.

She was raising Dimitri.

Astrid pushed away from him to gaze into his molten gold eyes. "Why aren't you King of Ledivion?" she asked, cupping the side of his face. "You're the rightful heir."

His lashes lowered and he looked away. "I'm an abomination. My blood is cursed."

Astrid's chest squeezed. Constantine fed him that lie, and self-loathing sprouted from every scar his father carved into his soul.

She drew his hand from her waist and brought it to her lips. Dimitri drew his wings higher, as though they could shelter them from the rest of the world.

"You're not an abomination. You were just born in the wrong

kingdom," Astrid whispered reassuringly.

She folded his fingers down until only his index remained and snapped her teeth over the point. He winced, but didn't pull away. She ran her tongue over his finger in a slow, deliberate swipe and swallowed.

"If you were born in Clorea, you would have been revered as a god."

Dimitri smeared his injury over her bottom lip and pulled her into a searing kiss. Astrid opened for him and his tongue swept over hers. The metallic tang of his blood filled her mouth, and she moaned, deepening their kiss.

She wrapped her leg over his waist and rocked her hips. The head of his cock slid over her pussy and Astrid made an exasperated sound, needing him.

Dimitri broke their kiss and leaned away as he palmed her ass. Astrid's night-streaked nails dug into his chest as his cock stretched and filled her. He pulled her in, claiming her mouth as he moved inside her. She took his thrusts, each deeper than the last until she'd taken his entire length.

He toyed with her piercing and devoured the sounds he elicited from her. Dimitri was never gentle, but he took her slow as his shadows caressed her soul. Making her feel every inch of him—every tilt and rock of his hips.

Astrid tossed her head back and he trailed kisses down her throat. Dimitri nipped her collarbone and moved lower to lick and suck on her nipples. She cried his name and arched her back, clinging to him.

He worshiped her, raining bliss through her body as he drove her to orgasm after orgasm. Astrid tangled her hands through his dark hair and pulled him closer, needing the rough feel of his hands while he fucked her.

Dimitri caught her wrists and lifted them above her head. The curve of his talon threaded the gold bracelets circling her wrists and sharply pulled her away.

He held her waist, not missing a beat as he gazed down at her. He slid his palm down her sweat slick body, between her breasts.

"I want to see you, neva," he rasped, thrusting into her harder. "I want to watch you come and know you're mine." His eyes lifted to meet hers. "Are you mine?"

"Yes," Astrid cried.

Each stroke tightened the tension coiling within her. It strained so tight, Astrid could hardly breathe. He pinched her nipple, tugging, and the pain mixed with pleasure had her coming so hard pinpricks of light glittered on the edge of her vision.

Dimitri rolled Astrid onto her back and fucked her harder. He drove into her. Once, twice, and stilling on the third as he tensed above her. His cock pulsed as he came, pouring himself into her. Astrid panted and his hand spanned over the back of her head.

"Say you're mine," Dimitri purred, languidly thrusting into her.

"I'm yours," Astrid whispered.

She'd been delivered to her sword just as he'd been delivered to her. The Mothers' serpents led her to him.

He wrapped her in his arms and kissed her throat before murmuring, "Nikogda ne ostavliai menia."

She didn't understand his words, but the longing in them was unmistakable. Astrid ran her fingers through his dark hair and whispered, "I promise."

Chapter Fifty-One

Dimitri woke to the beating of his heart throbbing behind his temples. He blinked against the morning light and frowned at the female sleeping against his chest. Astrid never curled up to him. He held her through the night, keeping her close.

The events of the previous day whispered through his mind. The Ascension. The lilies he'd left on his mother's grave. He'd left with Astrid before Ambrose could honor their father. They'd returned here…

But what happened after that was like trying to recall a dream. It slipped from him, as brittle as ashes in a breeze. The tumbling flickers of memory without context mocked him. One after the other they fell into place, painting the night he'd spent with Astrid.

Malice colored his vision.

She'd interrogated him. Dug through his private thoughts and moments. His hand closed around her throat, and he shoved her onto her back.

"You fucking drugged me?"

Astrid flailed, clawing at his grip, then those infuriating midnight eyes met his. Rancor glinted in her stare as she slipped two fingers beneath his grip and pivoted on her shoulder. She kicked at him, her heel aimed to break his jaw.

His reflexes were diminished by the lingering effects of her drug, but the leading edge of his wing deflected her blow and he was able to avoid its trajectory.

By the blood, he hated her. Dimitri leaned into his grip as she fought. He'd told her about his mother. Begged her not to leave him.

Astrid choked and twisted, managing to wedge her foot under his arm. She straightened her leg, lifting his weight off her airways.

"After everything you've done to me," she spat, "*drugging* is where you draw the line?"

Dimitri freed his famished shadows. His cursed magic ripped at her soul, feeding and rejuvenating him as she screamed.

Astrid crumbled and he bent low to whisper, "Suffer, wife."

Her palm slid over the side of his face. She would beg for mercy. For his forgiveness.

Pain radiated over his scalp as she fisted his hair and yanked him to her chest. His crazed wife shrieked, driving her elbow into his cheekbone and eye. Dimitri pulled away after the third blow and his feral neva scrambled to her feet.

He withdrew his ravenous hunger, and his princess stalked to his desk completely naked.

She dragged his twin weapons off his desk, sending loose papers cascading to the floor in a flurry.

"I drugged you, and you took my virginity—" She launched his weapon at him. "—with your fucking sword."

She unsheathed the second and hurled it at him. The blade would have embedded in his chest if he hadn't caught it.

"We. Are. *Even*," she seethed, stomping toward him.

Her vicious beauty made his cock hard, but he wasn't finished with this. He caught her by the throat once more and stepped into her. "Who gave you the drug?"

Astrid bared her teeth and yanked him closer by his collar while standing on her toes. "Gave me? I was *sent* here to kill your brother, before your little ambush derailed my plans."

Suka. Dimitri shoved her away and bellowed, "Answer my question."

"Do you remember anything we talked about last night?" Her vicious gaze searched his eyes. Her expression dropped as she exhaled, and her shoulders slumped. "All the plans we made?"

The ghost of her lies echoed through his mind.

Help me take the Serpents' Crown. We'll rule Clorea side by side, my king.

Dimitri stripped her venom from his thoughts. Whether it was real or imagined, it made no difference.

Her promises were lies.

"Was it Viktor or Keres?" he insisted.

She shook her head, and the curl of her lip added small wrinkles to the corner of her nose. "You should reevaluate your standing if you think your own people would betray you," she said before turning her back on him.

Wrath sank into his heart and his knuckles whitened around the handle of his sword. He discarded the weapon at the foot of their bed and followed her into their closet.

"Should I kill them both to be sure?" Dimitri snapped, entering the large space.

Astrid jammed her arms into her black silk robe. "You could have been so much more, but you relish your part as the broken sword who can't help but to cut its master," she snapped as she cinched her belt over her waist.

Dimitri closed the distance between them. "I have no master."

"Nikogda ne ostavliai menia," she said, craning her neck to challenge his gaze. "You told me that last night."

"I was drugged—"

"You were honest," Astrid yelled. "Maybe for the first time in your life."

The fragmented memories of the night he'd spent with her, stitched into a picture. She'd taken his cursed blood. Said she was his. Promised to never leave him.

"Put your hatred aside," she said, caressing his cheek like she had last night. "I am everything you want. Everything your birth entitled you to."

Her lips brushed his and longing twisted in Dimitri's chest. His eyes trailed down her body as her fingertips ran through his hair. She touched her forehead to his and whispered, "We can leave Ledivion to your brother."

His mother wouldn't want him to strip Ambrose of his crown, but how could he trust the bloodthirsty female in his arms?

"This kingdom has done nothing but betray you," she said at his lips. "Reclaim Clorea with me. Rule beside me."

Dimitri pinched her chin and lifted her face. He tasted her lips. Longed for her loyalty. "If you betray me, wife, I'll make you beg for a death I'll never grant."

Astrid snapped her teeth over his bottom lip and licked away the blood. "Betray *me*, and I'll burn everything you love to ash."

Chapter Fifty-Two

Astrid lowered her head in prayer alongside her fellow parishioners. Constantine forced the soul weavers of his kingdom to live in the absence of the Three-Faced Mother, yet demanded their service.

Ambrose's father was as foolish as he was shortsighted. He bemoaned the serpents and cursed the gift they bestowed upon him.

A Death Spirit son.

Astrid wouldn't discard Dimitri. In the wake of cruelty repeated so often and by so many, her sword clung to the tiniest fragment of affection.

Mothers hear me, Astrid began. *Thank you for the weapon you've delivered to my hand.* A blade honed so sharp he struck down her enemies as easily as he cut her. Doubt festered, souring her soul. Could she trust him? Would he hold her above his brother or would he force her to bow?

She replayed the conversation they had last night. How much of their evening did Dimitri remember? He'd objected to his brother's assassination while she rested her head on his chest.

"I could seduce him and kill him for you," Astrid had offered, tracing the lines cut through his chiseled muscles.

His chest rose and fell before he'd said, "He won't have you."

Astrid laughed. Dimitri knew nothing of males. "He would. I see the way he looks at me."

"I'm not a male who shares my belongings, but my blood is cursed," he'd said as his fingers wove through her hair. "The whole court saw you swallow my blood after you stabbed me in the dining hall. You're as tainted as I am, neva."

His self-loathing was evident in his voice, rooted in decades of pain.

Ledivites put too much weight into their ridiculous superstitions. A few public kills would rectify their backward opinions.

One, if she made it bloody.

"I could kill him with a touch," she'd offered sweetly. "No seduction necessary."

He'd hugged her closer. "I promised my mother I would take care of him. Set your sights on Clorea, and I'll retrieve your crown."

Astrid put their evening out of her mind and glanced up at the three hooded statues. At the egg, the serpent, and the shed they cradled in their outstretched hands.

Would his mother's wishes always come before her? Would his brother?

The rasp of scales on stone surrounded her. Comforted her. Dimitri had been true to his word, adding snakes to the temple of the Three-Faced Mother. She missed Foxglove's presence, but Dimitri would deliver her albino cobra when he returned from his next assignment.

A female, dressed in a white blouse and a long gray shirt—the uniform of a maid or kitchen help—strolled up beside Astrid. She emptied a silver bowl of raw meat onto the altar and placed the empty dish to the side.

"Princess Noctis," she greeted, bowing her head in respect before lowering to her knees.

Astrid watched her hands. She folded them, holding her index and middle finger together beneath her other palm.

She had a message. *Finally*. If the female didn't have a team ready to help her mother escape, Astrid would send a message of her own. Perhaps in the form of the spy's soulless body left as an offering to the Three-Faced Mother.

Astrid straightened her skirt while gesturing, *Are they ready?*
We'll free your mother the next time Dimitri leaves.

Chapter Fifty-Three

Astrid strolled the halls with Dimitri. He'd been surprisingly well-behaved, sitting in a pew while she prayed. He didn't interrupt her, or insist she'd spent enough time with her goddess as her father had.

He stood as she rose, and Astrid made note of the Ledivites seated adjacent to him. Did they believe they were safe in a holy place or had her proximity softened their view of him?

Astrid recalled her neighbors during the Ascension and relegated her opinion to her first notion. Her volatile male worshiped conquest and blood, but his respect for her seemingly extended to her temples.

She took his hand as they made their way back to their room. Dimitri opened their door, and the scent of grilled beef wafted to her. She glanced over the cart beside their bed. It was topped with covered dishes and Astrid couldn't help but wonder if Dimitri ordered this, or if the meal had been delivered so he'd leave the dining hall in peace?

Dimitri uncovered a dish and took a seat at his tidied desk.

His gaze raked over her body. "Sit with me, wife."

In the single chair occupying their entire suite? Astrid kept her expression pleasant and straddled his thighs. It was a tight fit, but the cushioned leather hugged the bend of her legs.

Dimitri meticulously unfolded the rolled napkin and removed the fork. He skewed a small cut of beef and softly blew on it before offering the bite to her.

The male craved control over everything in his domain and Astrid leaned into his compulsion. She flattened her hands over his waist, rocking forward. Her lips parted for the morsel he offered as she held his molten gold stare.

The corners of his mouth lifted and his eyes warmed. "You play the part of my devoted wife too well," he said, trailing the tip of the fork over the root vegetables. "Do you expect me to believe you love me now?"

Astrid took his utensil and laid it down. She contemplated her response. What he'd want to hear and what she should say, but ultimately settled into the constant she'd known to be true.

"Love is a privilege never meant for royalty. The best we can hope for is to be paired with someone useful," Astrid recited as she straightened his lapel.

Her night-streaked nails slipped between the buttons of his shirt and she stroked the unyielding planes of his chest beneath it.

"I find your… talents useful," she whispered, gazing up at him through her lashes.

Dimitri curled a strand of her hair around his finger. He watched it pull across his hand and fall before his gaze snapped back to hers. "Is that all?"

Humor brightened his molten gold stare to amber.

Astrid leaned into him, wrapping her arms around his neck. The warmth of his body lured her closer and their lips met. He didn't force her mouth open or catch her by the throat.

Her sword smiled against her lips and let her pace their kiss. The meeting of their lips. A moment of his tongue sweeping across hers. She pulled him closer, and his callused hands palmed her ass.

She pulled away and laid her head on his shoulder, blinking up at his bony appendages. "You could let me cut your wings off. Then I'd find you useful *and* attractive."

His dark laugh flowed over her. "You don't need to maim me to admit you're attracted to me."

His deep voice caressed her, and she could hear him grinning against her hair.

Relaxed. Quiet.

"You don't even have to admit it. I can scent you, neva," he purred.

Maybe not too quiet. He was still him, but his words were steeped in temptation and dark promises.

Astrid grazed her teeth along the side of his throat and kissed her bite. Her mind drifted to her mother's freedom. The King was a liability—a wild card between them she didn't trust.

"Does Ambrose know about you?" she asked.

Dimitri turned toward her, and Astrid reluctantly lifted her head off his shoulder.

"Of course he does."

Then where did he fit into this equation? Constantine despised Dimitri. He attempted kill his own son, and Dimitri's magic took his mother's life in place of his own.

My father killed my mother. I was his intended target, and she was an incidental consequence. I learned to control my curse after her death. Which is why you survived your little assassination attempt.

Her sword had killed his father, in turn crowning his younger brother King of Ledivion. Could she trust him to remain at her side if Ambrose stepped between them?

How could she test him without leaving herself open for betrayal?

"Your brother is going to send you beyond Clorea for your next kill." Astrid hesitated before adding, "I'm asking you to leave when he assigns your target."

Suspicion darkened his features, and his hands grasped her thighs. "And why should I be in such a rush to leave my wife's side?"

Because I need to free my mother. Because I want to test your loyalty. There was risk in every truth.

"Because I'm yours," Astrid answered.

"If you're mine, you should want me at your side."

"I'm asking you to trust me. Or would you rather strike a bargain?"

"I need no bargains when I have everything I want," Dimitri said, sweeping his hands beneath her skirt. His index hooked the lace trim of her thong, pulling it down.

Serpents devour you. "I'm asking for a simple favor. If you betray me, husband, I will destroy everything you love."

He caught her by the throat, firm enough to keep her close but not so hard he cut off her air.

"Love, if you betray me, I'll spend centuries making you regret it." Dimitri sealed his promise with a kiss and lingered as his breath fanned over her lips. "Now, tell me why you're in such a hurry to send me away."

Chapter Fifty-Four

Trust. Dimitri knew better than to linger on such soft and fragile emotions, but love… It was elusive and dangerous. Catastrophic and blinding.

By the blood, he wanted it.

Craved it.

His lips met Astrid's again. A whispered promise strung with rotted lies. He knew his little wife didn't love him. Knew she kept him close like the daggers decorating her flowing black hair.

But his neva wanted him. She might never admit it, but he had an eternity to shape her desire into love.

"Trust flows both ways, Princess," Dimitri murmured before pulling away from her. "Why am I leaving?"

Astrid studied him and he wondered if she scrutinized her prisoners the same way—while she decided which parts to cut off first.

"I have plots in motion," she said finally.

Malice enveloped his heart. "There is nowhere, in all of the king-doms, where I won't come for you."

He expected her to fight him. To leave. He imagined crushing that slender throat beneath the cage of his hand.

Instead, she squeezed her thighs over him, inching closer. "I am destined for the Serpents' Crown and you, dear husband, will rule beside me."

A truth and a lie—but a truth he wanted more than anything.

A vicious female who could never be taken from him.

"Will we have winged heirs?" he asked, painting his imagined future with her.

"That will be a bargain. One you'll have to strike centuries from now."

Because she didn't really want him.

Astrid touched two fingers under his chin and lifted his face. She smiled at him, her midnight gaze glittering with amusement.

"Don't look so disappointed," she teased. "Our reign will last an eternity. Or were you planning on dying, my lord?"

"Death and I are old friends." But she hadn't answered his question. Her words danced around the subject. She dangled things she valued in front of him, which gave him a glimpse of what she wanted.

She coveted her crown, her kingdom, and her Death Spirit weap-on.

Dimitri wished he could see into his neva's mind. He would give her all those things and lay the stars at her feet, if she truly wanted him.

"If I'm to trust you won't leave me, then you're plotting to free your mother," he said simply.

Astrid's eyes widened momentarily, and she hid her reaction, leaning closer. Her forehead touched his and he drank in her affec-tion.

It was a lie. A charade to push him away from her mother. And he didn't care.

"You could have asked me," he murmured into her hair.

Her shoulders tensed and she pulled away. His wife met his stare, and there he found rancor glittering within the depths of her mid-night eyes.

"I did," she bit out.

By the blood, her rage made his cock hard. "Ask me nicely," he purred.

Her eyes held their maniacal luster, but her voice sweetened and turned pleasant. "Dimitri, please kill the guards and escort my mother to Clorea."

"And ruin months of planning for you?"

Astrid snatched a tapered, golden stick from her hair. She unsheathed it and had the point biting into his throat before he could stop her.

"I'm going to skewer your organs and hang them over our bed," she hissed.

"You say such sweet things, neva," Dimitri said. He leaned into her, ignoring the stiletto slicing into his throat. The tension on his neck subsided and Dimitri smiled, tasting her lips. "I'll leave the day after I receive my target."

Astrid started to protest, and he quelled her with a second kiss. "I've never left the day he's given me a target and I'm not starting now."

Dimitri lifted her against him as he stood and gently set her on her feet. "Strip. Unless you want me to rip that dress off you."

The edges of her eyes tensed, and his little wife hid her aversion to orders. When she unlatched her corset, Dimitri began undressing. He folded his clothes along with her dress before placing them in the hamper.

Astrid watched him from their bed. Her gaze left his face to linger on his chest, before roaming lower. He chuckled and opened the nightstand drawer, retrieving their suede box.

"Are you coming to bed?" she asked as he strolled passed her.

He placed the box on his desk, flipping the lid open as he took a seat. Astrid studied him but made no move to leave their bed.

"Join me, wife," he purred, lifting a delicate gold chain.

Astrid sauntered toward him. Her midnight gaze never left the gold dangling from his fingertips. "Another bracelet, my lord?"

He took her hand and guided her to straddle him. Astrid climbed onto his lap and sat back on his knees. The corner of his mouth lifted into a smirk as he pulled her flush against him. She startled but recovered quickly. She should know he wouldn't allow her to be so far from him.

Dimitri leaned closer, trailing his lips along the point of her ear. He took her hands and crossed them behind her back before murmuring, "This gold isn't for you to wear."

He threaded the chain through her bracelets and clasped the link.

Astrid twisted in her bindings and eyes found his. "Dimitri."

"Yes," he answered, softly stroking the backs of his fingers between the swell of her breasts.

"Untie me," she breathed, leaning into his touch.

Dimitri palmed her soft curves, pinching her nipple until her breath shook. "You're mine, neva, and I want you tied," he said, tugging on her tight peak before kissing the hurt.

He opened the tin of lube and dragged his index and middle finger through it. Astrid shifted against him, following his hand then meeting his gaze when he reached behind her. She leaned in, meeting his lips in a soft kiss. Dimitri groaned as she opened for him. Her tongue swept over his and he smiled against her lips.

Affection consumed him but nothing would save her from what he'd planned. His wife broke their kiss as he reached lower, liberally coating her ass as he circled it without penetrating her.

"You're going to ride my cock while I use our toys to fuck you here. I'll stop when you've made me come," he said, nipping her bottom lip. "Or you beg for my cock in your ass."

Astrid stood on her knees and twisted away, causing the head of his cock to slide against the soft heat of her pussy. Dimitri groaned low in his throat.

"I'd rather have you tied," she whispered, lowering herself onto his cock. The heat of her cunt squeezed the head and she rocked her hips, taking him deeper.

"You have nothing that could hold me," Dimitri rasped.

"I have my words," she said, rising off his length before lowering again. "If I asked you to hold your wrists behind your back, would you?"

Dimitri spread the remaining lubricant over the metal replica of his cock and caged her in his arms. "If you were my wife in more than just name, I would obey every syllable."

Astrid rose to her knees, molding her breasts against him in her shortsighted means of escape.

"Take it, neva," Dimitri said at her throat. "I'll work it in slow before I fuck you with it."

His little wife shifted against him, caught between the chair and his arms. He applied more pressure and Astrid moaned as the tip sank into her. "I can scent how wet you're getting for me. You don't need to pretend you don't like this," he said as he worked another inch into her. "You're allowed your pleasure, wife."

He kissed her throat as she panted, grazing his teeth over her pulse. He fucked her ass with the tip, and it wasn't long before Astrid tentatively rocked her hips. She took his cock and the toy a little deeper.

"Good girl. Take it for me."

Astrid rose and fell on his cock taking the toy deeper as her breaths turned shallow. She leaned back and Dimitri lowered his head, sucking on her tight nipple.

Her body tremored and she went still with a strangled cry on her lips. Her cunt rhythmically squeezed him, and Dimitri lifted his head.

"You're riding me too slow, neva," he said, savoring the salt of her perspiration. "Do you need to be reminded of how I fuck you?"

He withdrew the length of metal and thrust it back in.

"Dimitri, it's too much," Astrid cried, arching her back.

He stroked into her ass harder and whispered, "Take it."

"Dimitri!"

"Come for me. I want to feel your cunt squeeze my cock." His shadows engulfed her, and the honeyed taste of her soul crested his tongue. And something else. Notes of warmth, but not the heat of her temper.

Astrid came with a scream and his focus shifted to her. He continued his harsh rhythm, grating, "Give me one more."

"Dimitri, please, it's too much," she cried.

"One more and I'll fuck you slow the rest of the day."

"You'll fuck *my cunt* slow for the rest of the day," Astrid clarified. "Is it a bargain?"

"A bargain," he promised.

Astrid moved with his shadows, frantically meeting his strokes. Her lips met his in a desperate kiss. The taste of her, the heat of her body, her scent of wildflowers and honey—all of it intoxicated him.

Burgeoning pressure rose through his shaft and Dimitri didn't fight it. He let his head fall back and groaned, "Fuck."

He came a moment before she did, emptying himself deep inside her. Astrid bit into his shoulder to muffle her screams. Dimitri smiled at the burn and held her close, smoothing his hand over the small of her back.

He wasn't sure how much time passed but his neva sat up with a moan. He reluctantly loosened his grip and gazed up at her. The blood coloring her full lips, hardened him in an instant.

Her hand closed over the front of his throat. "No. We have a bargain." He raised his brows, and she continued, "You're going to carry me to the shower so we can clean up. Then, you're going to lay me on our bed and fuck me slow." She leaned into him, kissing him greedily before dragging his lower lip through her teeth. "Slow. The way *I* like it."

Dimitri stood, carrying her with him. "Anything, wife."

Chapter Fifty-Five

Candlelight illuminated the room Astrid shared with Dimitri. She sat in the middle of their bed, bundled in silk and furs. Her Death Spirit kept his word, departing the morning after he'd been assigned his latest target.

Astrid ventured to the library in those early hours and requested Ledivion's most recent war archive. Dobromil reluctantly complied with her demand, and she'd returned with her prize.

She curled up in bed as she had in Clorea, dragging Dimitri's pillow across her lap to cushion the heavy tome. Hours passed as she immersed herself in the pages. Consuming knowledge calmed her nerves and Astrid leaned into her self-soothing habit.

The windows darkened as night's shadow fell over the palace. Her mother was to be freed before dawn. Sterling was capable and had proven himself time and again, but she couldn't help but worry.

The passing hours set her teeth on edge. She wasn't involved with this plan—didn't know how many soldiers made up their team. It was common to only know your part in the event of capture, but Astrid didn't even know where her mother was being held.

The pop and crackle of the fire did nothing to soothe her. She continued to read, absently scratching Graymalkin's chin. The fluffy beast sprawled next to her, purring as he flexed one paw then the other on either side of her wrist.

Astrid turned to the final entry and her hand trembled.

The Acquisition of Clorea.

A single paragraph chronicled how King Ambrose and Sorin Noctis conspired to assassinate her father's court and divide her kingdom between themselves.

She'd written dozens of letters to her cousin, and they'd all gone unanswered. He'd abandoned her mother—his queen—to this frozen wasteland for *half* a kingdom.

Astrid seethed, closing the leather-bound book. When Dimitri returned, they would depart for Clorea. Once she reclaimed her birthright, she would ask Keres to craft elegant bird cages large enough for a head.

Sorin and all her male cousins would decorate the pillars of her throne room. They would bear witness to her reign for all eternity.

An explosion ripped through the night.

This is wrong. Astrid vaulted from the bed and unsheathed Dimitri's sword. She dashed down the hall, ignoring the chill biting through her nightgown and the stones numbing the balls of her feet.

Serpents devour her, she should have demanded Dimitri tell her where her mother was being held.

Astrid's frantic pace slowed as the hall widened into a large room. Ledivites in various stages of undress shrieked and panicked, pouring from the stairways. Astrid chose the busier stairway, shoving her way upstream through limbs and wings.

On the next floor, cracks fissured the ceiling and a multitiered chandelier hung precariously. Her mother wasn't a soul weaver.

If they damaged the integrity of the wall…

Astrid spied chainmail-draped wings moving against the crowd. She followed, guided by the rattle of armor. They ran through another hall, and it opened into a small library. Bookcases were crushed beneath huge chunks of rubble and the story above was visible through the creaking beams.

Earth weavers stood at the walls. Their palms open as they reenforced the structure.

Astrid didn't have time to fight the crowd. Her mother could be injured. Dying. Her magic snapped to her and a sea of soul stars blinded her. There were so many of them. All blocking her path.

She laid her hands on the winged male directly in front of her. His body dropped and screams erupted.

Three more fell before the crowd parted for Astrid and she ran. She stitched her soul and focused her magic on regenerating her heart, lungs, and eyes.

The hall narrowed before her, but it was the unobstructed snow-covered pines that gave her hope. Fire erupted over the wall, shaking the foundation as more stones crumbled and fell.

Astrid charged for the room. Two guards met her and engaged. Astrid deflected the first's blow and pressed her hand over his chest. The male fell into a lifeless heap. When she turned to the other, the male dropped his weapon and fled.

Wreckage covered the room. Fallen stone. Splintered furniture.

A shadowed figure on horseback shouted orders as flames destroyed more of the exterior wall. The distinctive blend of leather and metal making up his armor was unmistakable.

Sterling himself had come for her mother.

A dozen black-winged Ledivites moved as one, badged with the serpents of Clorea. They stormed the room, and Astrid heard her mother scream.

One of the males hoisted Astrid's mother over his shoulder. She screamed, "Asti," reaching for her as she had across the table in Clorea all those months ago when Dimitri attacked.

Astrid lurched forward, catching her hand. Golden strands looped from her, arching back and pulling tight.

Astrid dropped her mother's hand and shoved at the male's back. "Take her! Go!"

He flew to Sterling and her steadfast ally secured her mother in front of him. His movements hesitated as his gaze lifted past her.

"Go!" Astrid screamed.

Sterling and his team raced their horses beyond the tree line.

Their hoofbeats and her mother's frantic cries faded into the night.

A slow clap sounded behind her and Astrid turned to see King Ambrose stepping over a guard's body to enter the room. A pair of spearmen flanked him, but it was crossbow in Ambrose's grip that concerned her most.

"You think anything happens in my palace without my knowledge?" he asked, taking aim.

She heard the thrum of the bowstring before pain exploded through her chest. Astrid's breaths drew short, and she focused her magic on the wound before ripping the bolt out of her heart.

It continued to beat. Mended.

The head of a spear cut through her ribs and tore from her back in the next instant. The momentum knocked her to the ground and Astrid's vision blurred and blackened. She tried to breathe, but coughed liquid. Tasted blood.

Astrid viciously clung to consciousness. She blinked and turned her head. Ambrose was barefoot, dressed only in a pair of pants slung low on his hips.

She reached for him, but her movements were uncoordinated and sluggish.

Ambrose shoved her a few feet, using the spear impaling her as though she were a mop. He turned his head and asked, "Is she stitching her soul?"

Dobromil stepped out of the shadows, looking stricken. "Yes, Your Majesty."

Astrid's fists closed over the handle. She would pull herself up, through this spear, and rip his soul out of his fucking face.

"Good," Ambrose said, ripping the spear from her chest with a twisting motion.

Astrid's vision flickered to darkness. The last thing she heard was the wet sound of bones and flesh against metal.

Chapter Fifty-Six

Astrid drew a deep breath as she squinted against the daylight. Her chest ached and the rancid taste of dried blood lingered in her mouth. She turned her head and spit, willing her eyes to focus.

Her magic was slow to unravel, sweeping over her in clumsy passes. She knit together the hairline fractures across her ribs. Straightened the misaligned vertebrae. Whoever healed her was a butcher, not a soul weaver.

Astrid's vision cleared and the distorted shapes sharpened into Dobromil standing beside the oversized window.

"Oh, you're dead, priest," she rasped, sitting up.

Her words were like shards of glass in her throat and Astrid realized her hands were bound behind her back. Coarse rope abraded her skin and limited her movement. She shifted her shoulders, twisting her wrist until her nails found the knot.

"Did you enjoy dressing me?" Astrid asked, glancing down at her pristine night gown when Dobromil met her stare.

"Keep your voice down," he hissed. His wings squeezed to his back as he crept across the room and leaned into the doorway. He turned back toward her, clutching the silver medallion hanging from his neck. "King Ambrose wasn't here when we mended you."

It was much colder in this room than Dimitri's. Her nipples were plainly visible through the black silk. They must have retrieved her garment from Dimitri's closet. She sincerely hoped they shifted his clothes, and he killed them all for it.

"Untie me," Astrid snapped as she worked a finger through the knot. "And I'll kill you instead of keeping you."

He dropped the sigil of his god and the talisman bounced against his chest as he hurried to the bed. "Lay back down, Princess Noctis, before he comes in here," he begged, gingerly touching her and pushing her back.

Astrid let him guide her, slipping her leg between his. "I'm going to rip out your entrails and make you into a living chandelier."

Color drained from his face, and he whispered, "Lay down, please. Close your eyes."

Astrid tangled her legs with his and rammed her shoulder into his gut. They tumbled to the ground and Astrid twisted her back, splaying her hands over his torso.

"Dimitri is on his way! He's coming! He's coming," Dobromil cried in a hiss as he hyperventilated.

He didn't scream. Didn't call for Ambrose.

Astrid rose to her feet, suspicious of the priest.

"Why would I believe—"

"Because if we helped take something from Dimitri, he would kill us all," the priest said, dusting off his robes as he got to his feet. He straightened and snapped his wings shut before glaring at her with a hate that rivaled her own. "And if you weren't such a self-absorbed cunt, you would know I don't want to see my brothers die."

Astrid didn't doubt his words. Dimitri would kill them, but would he kill his brother? He'd spared him—Even given him a throne.

But if she killed Ambrose, Dimitri would have little choice in the matter.

Astrid dropped to her knees and gripped her wrist. "I need you to dislocate my shoulder."

"If-if you'd just lay down, I can tell him you're still mending and aren't conscious yet."

Ambrose preferred his females awake.

What a gentleman.

Astrid dropped her shoulder and blew out a breath. "See where I'm holding my wrist? Stomp on it, priest."

"What?"

Mothers save me. "I need my hands to rip out his soul and I can't reach anything while bound. So, untie me or dislocate my shoulder."

Dobromil timidly approached her. His boot was hesitant as it touched her hand.

"Aim for the wrist. This one," she coached, shaking the arm she meant to sacrifice. "Think of it as a plank of wood and—"

Pain snapped through her shoulder, but not *enough* pain. The priest stomped down but only a few inches and immediately pulled his foot away.

"Stomp to the *ground,* you fucking coward," Astrid hissed over her shoulder.

A heavy door clicked shut from beyond the room and Astrid's head snapped to the entryway.

"He's coming. I'm begging you, Princess, go lay down."

Astrid glared at the priest who served Vinceret but upheld none of his tenants. "Stomp. To the ground. I'll handle him."

Astrid bowed her head, steeling herself.

Mothers, let this coward strike true.

White hot agony lit her shoulder, and her magic flared, dulling the pain. She panted and leaned forward, casting her hair over her injured shoulder before pivoting to Dobromil.

"Let me go!" Astrid cried loudly. Her curated tears wet her lashes as her voice cracked. "Lord Dimitri will be angry if he finds me missing."

The dull thud of heavy boots approached her. Astrid turned, blinking tears for Ambrose's benefit.

He crouched beside her and smoothed her moisture-streaked cheek. "Oh, sweetling. Didn't you ask to spend three days in my bed?" His hand slipped to her hair, and Astrid was dragged to her feet with him as he stood.

"Leave us, priest," Ambrose bit out, tossing her onto the bed.

Astrid screamed, cowering as she tucked her legs and curled onto her side.

Dobromil stared at her, bewildered and muttered, "My king," with a parting bow.

Ambrose's knee sank into the mattress as he leaned over to catch her ankle. He dragged her to the edge and forced her legs apart. The softness of his hands made her skin crawl and Astrid cried, "Please, my king." She struggled beneath his hold, positioning her injured arm.

He smiled, parting her thighs further. "What other piercings has Dimitri given you?"

Ambrose fisted the front of her nightgown and ripped it down the middle exposing her breasts. His lips thinned as he squeezed them before sighing, "How disappointing."

Astrid cried and squirmed as he pinched her nipples. She needed him closer, and she played her part as prey. Ambrose twisted her tight peaks until they burned, and she whimpered, "My king, you're hurting me."

"Isn't this how he gets you wet?" he asked, slapping her. Her cheek stung. "I hear you screaming under him."

She turned away, staring through the icy windowpanes as tears fell over the bridge of her nose.

"You'll have to tell me which one of us has the bigger cock," Ambrose said, unfastening his pants.

Astrid dropped her facade and wrapped her legs around him, pinning his arms between them. She yanked him forward, taking his crushing weight. His soul stars gleamed past his flesh as she flattened her hand over his thigh.

His soul flickered to her will, retreating from his legs, then his arms.

She sank into the mattress under his increasingly dead weight and Ambrose screamed, "Guards!"

Glass shattered and a winged shadow stretched over her.

Ambrose twisted toward it, gasping, "Help me, brother."

His weight was ripped off Astrid and she righted herself, pulling her hands from the loosened knots.

Dimitri's eyes were wild. He held Ambrose by a fistful of hair and his sword across his throat.

"You can't kill me," Ambrose yelled as his fear slid into rage. "I'm your king!"

"I would kill a god to possess her!" her sword answered, dragging his blade across his brother's throat.

"No! Stop!" Astrid yelled, clasping her hands over the wound. She stitched his soul and healed what would have been a fatal injury. Hatred shaped Dimitri's features and she smiled at the male who she now knew truly placed her above all others.

"I want his eyes, husband. Let him watch you fuck me for the rest of eternity."

"Guards!" Ambrose wailed. "Guards!"

Astrid's magic engulfed him. She separated his soul from his voice as she traced his quivering mouth.

"Do you really think your guards will storm in here to face a Death Spirit and his soul weaver?" she purred.

The large male began to tremble. His eyes pleaded for mercy as he stared up at his brother. Astrid patted his cheek twice and smiled when the sunlit honey of his eyes dulled.

"I can answer your question for you," she said, lowering her lashes to the shriveled skin of his cock.

"Dimitri is much bigger."

Chapter Fifty-Seven

Dimitri dragged his brother's shaking body a short distance to his room. He had no pity for Ambrose. He could have reigned over Ledivion for centuries, but he'd inherited too much of their father's cruelty and arrogance. Constantine had taken his mother from him and died for it—but Ambrose's sin was far worse.

He'd broken Ledivion's oldest law and trespassed on Dimitri's right of conquest. His prize for battles hard fought in Vinceret's name. Conquests were untouchable. Astrid should have been safe.

His brother should never have touched her.

"How long did he have you?" Dimitri asked as they entered their room. If Ambrose had raped his wife, his death would last lifetimes.

Astrid arched her brow and glared at him from the corner of her eye. "He didn't have me. I was killing him before you interrupted me," she answered, opening the top drawer of his nightstand.

His brother's scent lingered on her, but there was no arousal. No heavy odor of cum.

His little wife gathered all her jeweled hair sticks and gleefully unsheathed her weapons before rowing them on their bed. He'd need to speak to Keres and find out exactly how many hidden knives she'd crafted for his wife.

Astrid took her jade-handled stiletto and jerked Ambrose's face up. "Since you're so jealous of your brother, I'm going to take your eyes," she said, slicing into the delicate skin around the socket. "You can watch him fuck me with a cock much bigger than yours. Over and over."

Pride bloomed in Dimitri's chest as he watched his vicious neva work. She removed an eye, unbothered by the tears streaming from the other.

Astrid placed her bloody trophy beside her collection of daggers and Dimitri recoiled at the trail of gore it left on the white fur throw. He would have the bedding changed as soon as his wife was satisfied.

She extracted his other eye and dropped the pair into a wineglass. The nerves trailing behind them flapped like little fish and Dimitri cocked his head. He'd never encountered a soul weaver of her disposition, and her violent quirks made his cock hard.

"Hold his wing out," Astrid said as she stepped into the bathroom. She filled the wine glass with water and returned to him.

Dimitri let his brother fall face down and lifted one of his gray wings.

Astrid held the glass out toward the wing and the twitching nerves and veins acted as a tail, propelling the eyes frantically against the glass. Dimitri chuckled, amused with his wife's new toy.

"I'm going to cut off your wings, Ambrose. The skeletal display will be fixed to my throne here in Ledivion, and your membrane will upholster it."

The eyes swam faster, splashing the surface. Astrid giggled, flattening her hand over the top before they could leap out and fall to the ground. She lifted the glass to her face and breathed, "You're so dramatic."

Astrid placed her makeshift aquarium on his desk and balanced a book on it before turning to Dimitri. "Will you rule Ledivion as Dimitri Morana, my king?"

His father's name strung after his anchored a sharp, and visceral reaction. Rage and pain warred inside him. He would have done anything for his dead father's acceptance.

Once.

"No. My father's line never accepted me."

Constantine conspired to kill him for nearly a decade. If only he'd believed Dimitri when he told him he had no aspirations for the throne. Dimitri never wanted to rule.

But his neva did and demanded every star lighting the night sky.

He grinned at her. "I'll rule alongside you as your Death Spirit."

She smiled at that. A true smile, without calculation or scrutiny. "You should kill your brother's court and start fresh," she said, drawing his sword from his hip.

Astrid slid the blade beneath the base of his brother's wing, and it fascinated him. He'd hacked off his share of wings, had even torn them off on occasion, but his wife slipped the blade's edge between the bones. Carefully severing tendons and ligaments—like she was butchering a swan.

"It takes more than one person to rule an entire kingdom, wife," he said.

She nodded and gathered the folds of Ambrose's severed wing before flopping it onto their bed.

"Do you think if you make a mess of our bed, I won't fuck you in it?" Dimitri asked, flashing his teeth.

"I think I want a workroom, but we make do with what we have," she answered, gesturing for him to lift the other wing.

Dimitri raised the membranous limb as Astrid harvested her trophy. She moved to his head next, not taking the same care she had with his wings. Ambrose's corpse slouched forward and fell to the ground. Astrid swung at his neck and the tip of Dimitri's blade clanged against the wooden floor.

"Enough," Dimitri said, retrieving his weapon from her. He glanced over the room and frowned. "Where's my other sword?"

Astrid shrugged. "I don't know. He killed me," she said, kicking the maimed, bleeding heap. "You need to take his head to the court as proof of your Crimson Ascension, my love."

Dimitri's chest ached. Her words made this real. "You love me now?"

"You've proven no one stands between us," she offered. "Trust deepens over time."

Dimitri clasped her face, holding her jaw while squeezing her cheeks. His gaze fell to her full, pouting lips. "Does it, wife?"

She smiled, leaning into his hold. "Betray me and I'll add *your* wings to my throne."

Dimitri laughed, believing her. His lips met hers and she opened for him. Immediate. Trusting.

And he tasted blood.

A sampling of the violence she endured—and enacted. His queen was as merciless as she was vengeful.

"Love me, and I'll never betray you," he murmured at her lips.

Astrid pushed against his chest, and he took a step back. "Take his head to Ambrose's council and send Keres to me if you see her."

The playful stares and sweet smiles he'd once coveted were there between them, in their own way. Their affection wasn't soft, but he'd developed a bond with Astrid. The same deep connection he'd observed during his years at court among established pairings.

His feral neva loved him, she just didn't know it yet.

"Keres and the earth weavers will be here after I speak with the royal council," Dimitri said, collecting his brother's head. "Our room will be converted into Ambrose's grave."

Astrid's brow knit. "You build arenas where your royals actually died?"

Dimitri nodded.

"Will they care if he's still alive? Parts of him, anyway?" she asked.

"No," he answered, then reconsidered his response. "If they do, I'll kill them."

The way her midnight eyes glittered made him want to stay in bed with her for the rest of the day.

"I want to break a sword and throw it on his grave, too," she rushed out.

His wife knew Ledivite rituals. This pleased him beyond measure. "I'll amend any ceremony you wish, love."

Scrutiny returned to her stare. "We'll rule together, in all things?"

"I need only one thing," he purred. "You, in our new bed, waiting for me." A flush colored her cheeks and his chest squeezed again.

"Get dressed, neva. The earth weavers will arrive before I return. Keres will show you to our new rooms."

Dimitri strolled into the hall with the proof of his Ascension swinging by his hair as he whistled a tune. The length of his hall was empty, but it usually was.

A noble coming down the stairs froze as Dimitri entered the first communal space. The male paled and immediately fled. Others reacted the same and Dimitri began to grow suspicious after he'd failed to spot a single royal guard.

He pushed the door open to the royal council and raised his brows. More than a dozen royal guards were clustered with the courtiers. Their chatter ceased as he stepped over the threshold.

The nobility shrank from him, but the armored Ledivites held their ground.

At least they have the sense not to draw their weapons. Dimitri would hate to have to kill them all and his little wife needed guards.

Dimitri tossed the head into the room. It fell with a *thud* and rolled toward them, marring the stones with splotches of blood.

"My wife, Princess Noctis, killed King Ambrose in my room. Make the arrangements."

Chapter Fifty-Eight

The day brought with it a plethora of earth weavers and servants. They greeted Astrid with murmurs of "Your Majesty," or "my queen," as they bowed. She regarded them as they moved her things and began deconstruction of the room.

They weren't stricken or teary eyed. Did they hold any loyalty to Ambrose?

Would they show any to her?

A pair of earth weavers stepped into Dimitri's closet and began collecting his garments.

"Don't do that," Astrid said, rushing toward them. They immediately stopped and she gawked at the negative space among her sword's things. "Put everything back as it was. You'll have to move the *whole* closet. Dimitri is very particular."

She helped the females evenly space the hanging shirts before leaving them to their work. They closed the door and pressed their hands to the wall. Small vibrations ran beneath Astrid's feet and the entire closet began to sink into the ground.

"They'll raise the closet in your new room."

Astrid turned toward Keres's voice and beamed. "Can you make me a dozen birdcages? I want them to give the ambiance of a lantern. They'll be hung on the pillars in my throne room, when I return to Clorea."

"One kingdom isn't enough for you?"

"Clorea is my birthright."

"Just make sure you take Dimitri with you. He isn't as hateful in your company, and I don't want to see his temper without you." She laughed with Astrid then motioned toward the door. "He's selected a larger set of rooms with an adjoining green space."

Astrid retrieved the glass containing Ambrose's eyes and followed Keres through corridor after corridor. They crossed the arena where the tree branches intertwined above the graves of Dimitri's parents. More than a dozen earth weavers sank the seating area into the ground and unraveled the woven tree branches.

"What are they doing?" Astrid asked.

Keres glanced over before they moved down another hall. "The space is being converted back into an orchard."

They'd died in an orchard?

"There are several types of fruit trees there. Plums were Queen Vesta's favorite. Dimitri didn't allow any others to be planted after the arena was built."

"Plums or fruits in general?" Astrid asked.

Keres grinned at her. "Guess."

The court's view of Dimitri troubled Astrid, but his secrets weren't hers to tell. The nobles would be wise to align themselves with their new king. If they would not, she'd renovate the southern palace and keep them as furniture.

A pair of footmen stood before grand double doors—doors they opened as Keres and Astrid approached.

A wide hall stretched before them, lit by a series of beautiful chandeliers. End tables held fresh cut flowers and Astrid strolled past a hanging mirror that looked suspiciously familiar.

"Library and workroom," Keres said, pointing to the rooms on the left and right.

Astrid leaned in the doorway of the library. A single table with two chairs were placed at the center of the room and empty bookshelves rowed the walls, dividing the space.

Dimitri was short tempered and demanding, but the male listened.

"The priests will bring you books to fill the shelves. Let the servants know what tools you want in your workroom."

Astrid nodded, following Keres into her new, larger room. A pair of earth weavers were raising Dimitri's closet out of the stone floor and maids pulled linens over a four-post bed made of light wood.

She made her way to the winged females at Dimitri's closet. "Can you recreate Dimitri's room here. His desk. The bed," Astrid said pointing to their placement in the room. "He has a wardrobe of cleaning supplies in it that will have to be brought in, and if you could add a second closet, I'd be grateful."

The earth weavers nodded and pulled the room together in minutes with a small addition to the bed at her request.

Dimitri entered a short time later and Astrid strolled to him. "Your Majesty," she said sweetly at his side.

"I'll start work on your lantern cages," Keres said, exiting the room. The others bowed and immediately took their leave as well.

Tension riddled Dimitri's muscles as he glanced over their new space.

Astrid leaned closer, taking his hand. The color scheme was the same, but there were small differences that distressed her Death Spirit.

He calmed by degrees as she explained. "Your cleaning supplies are there. Your desk. They moved your closet exactly as it was. You might have to straighten a few things, but everything is in its place," she assured him.

"And this?" he asked, strolling to their bed.

A shelf had been built into the headboard, flush with the mattress. A metal framed, sealed aquarium was inlayed and trapped within the glass were a set of honey-colored eyes.

"Your brother's new home," Astrid answered. "Has the royal council recognized us as King and Queen of Ledivion?"

Dimitri took a seat on their bed and drew her into his arms. "You'll wear Ledivion's crown."

Astrid crawled onto his lap, straddling his thighs. She ran her fingertips over the point of his ear and caressed the hoops and dangling gold he wore. "The King and Queen don't have matching crowns?" she asked.

"The Ascension belongs to the one who inherits the throne, which you did when you killed the current ruler," Dimitri purred, palming her ass though the silk of her paneled skirt.

Astrid's temper iced her veins. One crown, like Clorea.

"But we'll rule together?" she asked, daring him to say otherwise.

Dimitri pulled back to meet her gaze as he squeezed her ass, pulling her closer. The length of his hard cock was unmistakable.

"I told them you killed Ambrose. The Crimson Ascension they're arranging is for you."

He didn't claim her kill. Didn't expect her to submit and be biddable. Her tension left her, replaced by her wanton need only he could sate.

"We shared the kill. We'll share the throne as well," Astrid whispered at his lips. She leaned in, touching her lips to his. Tasting him.

His callused hands rasped up her sides and Astrid moaned. His touch banished the ghost of Ambrose's hands. They branded her as his.

Astrid wrapped her arms around his neck and leaned away, breaking their kiss. "Tell me about the coronation. What other customs are we to perform?"

"The Crimson Ascension is the coronation," Dimitri said, nipping her bottom lip and holding her against the unyielding planes of his body. "Once the sword is broken and thrown on his grave, we are King and Queen of Ledivion. There is a custom… where the new Queen runs and her King captures her."

"You want to hunt me?" *Like a common hind.*

"It's not a hunt," Dimitri explained. "It's a claim. A promise. A public display showing the kingdom you are mine and nothing can take you from me."

"Why am I running?" Astrid asked, rocking her hips over the length of his cock. "What if *I* want to chase *you?*"

Dimitri groaned. "You'd never catch me without wings."

"I could cut yours off. Then, we'll be on an even playing field."

His hand wrapped beneath her jaw and his fingers pressed into her cheeks. "After you've laid your broken sword on my brother's grave, you'll run from me. Then, I'll catch you, neva, and take you to our spring. Our toys will be waiting and you're going to take them into your cunt, your ass, and this pretty, pretty mouth."

Heat pooled between her thighs at the heated promise of his words.

"Ledivion will bow to her Queen, and you, my love, will bow to me."

Chapter Fifty-Nine

The touch of Astrid's lips left Dimitri weak. Her tongue swept over his as she rocked her hips over his aching cock. She pulled back, trailing kisses along his jaw, down the side of his neck, to the hollow at the base of his throat.

Her teeth grazed his collarbone, and Dimitri smoothed his palms up her thighs as she unbuckled his belt.

"Will you show me how to bow to you?" Astrid asked. She pulled away before he could answer and kneeled between his legs.

He'd fantasized about the feel of her tongue. Her lips sliding up and down the length of his shaft. The way her throat would constrict around his cock as he fucked her mouth.

"You should be comfortable," Dimitri said, outstretching his wing. He dragged his pillow closer and handed it to her. "Can't have you hurting your knees."

"You're so thoughtful, my king." Astrid adjusted her cushion. She unfastened his slacks and gazed up at him. "You never forced your cock down my throat."

Dimitri hiked a brow. "Did you want me to start?"

Astrid pulled his length free. She angled him closer and leaned in while holding his stare. Violence glinted in her midnight eyes, and he smiled, welcoming it.

"I want to know why," she said, breaking the spell between them.

Dimitri chuckled darkly. He'd had her suck on his fingers while he fucked her. Fucked her mouth with the replica of his cock while she rode him.

"How many times have you bitten me and drawn blood?" he asked.

Astrid shrugged and flattened her tongue over him before licking the head in a slow, teasing sweep.

Dimitri groaned and she did it again. His imagination paled to the feel of her. He reached forward and tangled his hand through her dark hair.

"If you're rough with me, I'll do more than draw blood," she said before kissing the tip.

Dimitri raised his hands in surrender and leaned back on his arms.

"Move your wing."

"They're not touching you."

Humor lit her features. "I want your brother to watch."

His vicious, little wife. Dimitri shifted his wing, giving Ambrose an unobstructed view. He didn't bother to confirm his brother's dull yellow eyes were on them, too fixated on Astrid kneeling before him.

She took him past her lips and Dimitri groaned at the warmth of her mouth. Her tongue swept over the crown as she sucked. He wanted to fist her hair and shove the length of his cock past her wine-colored lips.

Dimitri flexed his hand into a fist then splayed his fingers open. He was the only male she would ever know, and he was all too willing to explore this with her. His fingers brushed over hers around the base of his cock.

"Stroke the shaft while you suck on the tip," he murmured. She followed his lead, trailing her fingers up and down his length.

He let her find a rhythm then closed his hand over hers. "Tighter," Dimitri groaned. "Yes, like that."

His cock pulsed and Astrid pulled away sharply. "Do not come in my mouth."

Dimitri glanced down at her, catching his breath. Her dark eyes were full of accusation. He drew two fingers across his throat and said, "On my swords." When his wife only blinked at him, he amended his oath. "I promise."

Astrid watched him as he unbuttoned his shirt with one hand while leaning back on the other. The chiseled muscle of his chest rose and fell with his breaths. She did this to him and the power in it was addictive.

She took him past her lips again and stroked his cock as he'd shown her. His reactions thrilled her. Every groan reverberating through his chest. Every flex and coil of his muscles.

He was hers to tease and savor. The power she held over him left her wet and aching.

Astrid opened her mouth wider, taking more of him. His head fell back, and he groaned her name. She sucked harder, stroking his shaft to the tempo he would fuck her in.

Dimitri shot forward, cupping her face in his hands as he pulled her away. "You're going to make me come," he said, gently stroking her cheek.

She stroked him again, running her thumb over the broad crown. "How terrible."

Her Death Spirit's grip moved to her jaw. His fingertips pressed into her cheeks as he lifted her face. "Get on the fucking bed," he said before kissing her.

Astrid laughed, crawling onto their sheets. Dimitri shrugged out of his topcoat and shirt before stepping out of his shoes. She turned her attention to Ambrose. His eyes swam to the front, and she tapped her nails against the glass.

The mattress dipped as Dimitri moved behind her. His shadows embraced her the same moment his hand smoothed up her thigh. He reached between the panels of her skirt and Astrid's breath caught as every touch heightened. The serrated teeth of his magic swept over her in a gentle caress, seeking every part of her, claiming every inch.

"Get on your hands and knees," he murmured.

Astrid obeyed and arched her back, needing him inside her.

Dimitri unlatched her pauldron, and it fell along with sashes that covered her breasts. Her corset dropped next, followed by yards of silk. His chest pressed into her back and his lips brushed the point of her ear.

"You want to be fucked in front of Ambrose?"

The scent of winter dusted with pine fell over her, blanketing her with notes of warmth. It permeated her soul, consuming her until all she knew was him.

"Yes," she breathed.

Rough hands clamped down on her hips and the head of his cock nudged her entrance.

"Dimitri," Astrid sighed, her body aching for him.

He thrust into her, stretching her to accommodate his size and she flattened her hand against Ambrose's aquarium to steady herself.

"Take it," he said, driving several more inches into her.

Pain laced through her pleasure, overwhelming her as she took his length. She tensed as Dimitri fucked her, as her orgasm crested and crashed through her. Pleasure drowned her, so intense she couldn't breathe—couldn't scream—as she came again and again.

Dimitri's shadows retreated and Astrid lay, collapsed amidst her pillows. He held her hips upright, but her shoulders were on the sheets.

"There you are," her Death Spirit purred.

He rocked his hips and Astrid gasped.

Serpents, save me. He's still hard.

"Come for me, Dimitri," she said, knowing he wouldn't. Her husband wasn't satisfied until he made her come so many times she couldn't move.

Dimitri's shadows crept over her body, and he stroked into her slow, tormenting her with a haze of ecstasy.

"After you've given me one more," he replied.

Astrid lifted herself onto her shaking arms. She rocked back, taking him at an easy pace.

Dimitri leaned over her and caged her throat. His lips traced the shell of her ear as he murmured, "Come for me, neva. Let my brother see what a female looks like when she orgasms."

He fucked her, deep and slow. Each stroke pushing her closer in a steady climb. Astrid pressed her hand against the glass as her long black hair swayed over their dark sheets.

Astrid called his name as she came, and he fucked her harder. His harsh rhythm intensified her orgasm—prolonged it. He slammed into her as his hands dug into her hips. His cock pulsed inside her and he barred his arm across her chest. Dimitri sat back, groaning as he came, emptying himself inside of her.

His shadows withdrew and exhaustion fell over her. He'd taken too much of her soul.

"Dimitri." The words slipped out as a murmured whisper.

She scarcely felt his lips brushing her temple before her lids slipped closed and sleep claimed her.

Chapter Sixty

The days bled together as Astrid met with Ledivion's royal council, the Earth Weavers' Guild, and more than a dozen chefs who vied for their culinary delights to grace her table.

She stood on the raised hexagon dais and Viktor circled her, scrutinizing his design. She'd asked to be wrapped in the night sky and his creation didn't disappoint. The strapless black dress hugged her curves and flared at the waist leading into a train. He pinned diamond-studded lace along the tight boning over her hips and draped it over the full skirt.

Astrid hoped the gown reminded Dimitri of their nights together, where they were surrounded by his shadows and glimmers of her soul stars.

The happiness touching her lips was momentary.

Her upcoming coronation should have thrilled her, but the ease at which Ledivites shifted their loyalty from one monarch to the next left her unsettled. Astrid had killed her predecessor, marking her ceremony a Crimson Ascension. Keres had taken Ambrose's sword and weakened the blade. Ledivite ritual demanded she break the brittle steel and toss it on Ambrose's grave.

Memorializing Ambrose's reign as a disgrace.

The court blindly aligned themselves to Astrid and she couldn't help but wonder if they fantasized about breaking Dimitri's twin blades over *her* grave. She admired the glittering gems and banished the thought.

Dimitri was kissed by death.

They would rule until the stars burned from the sky and the seas turned to ash.

Astrid devoted herself to the Three-Faced Mother, but Ledivion bowed to a different god. Her fears were revered customs and beliefs here.

"Did the Ledivites embrace Ambrose so readily when he took the throne?" Astrid asked. Ambrose hadn't killed for his throne, but he did inherit it suddenly.

"Vinceret is worshiped here. He's the God of Conquest and Blood," Viktor said as he pinned the edges of the lace to the train. "Ambrose's father was devout. King Constantine rode into every battle. Fought and bled alongside the Legion."

Astrid glanced over her shoulder. "And Ambrose didn't?"

Viktor shook his head as he stood. "He never enlisted with the Royal Legion, never marched onto a battlefield."

Confirmation of what Astrid already knew. Ambrose wasn't battle-hardened. His soft hands were a reflection of his comfortable life of luxury. Nothing he obtained was hard fought. He'd been gifted everything, yet squandered it and took it for granted.

"How did he become King if he lacked the very tenants Ledivites hold to their heart?" Astrid asked.

Viktor's brow drew together as he draped black silk over her arm. He pinched the fabric and his gaze lifted to hers. "It was quite the scandal. I'm surprised word never reached Clorea."

"If it did, my father wouldn't have told me."

Viktor laughed, returning to his task. "There were many who thought they were more deserving of the crown. Lord Ivan was the loudest. He was King Constantine's right hand. They worked in tandem through many campaigns."

Astrid cataloged everything Viktor didn't say. Ambrose never trained. Whether he thought he was above it or was too lazy didn't matter. He didn't have the respect of the court, nor of his people.

"Lord Ivan challenged Ambrose for the throne during one of the council meetings and Lord Dimitri killed him before he could stand."

The corners of Astrid's lips lifted into a smile. She would have handled it differently, but a desiccated, black-veined corpse would stop tongues from wagging. Dimitri's soul reaping magic was an astonishing asset, but she preferred to *keep* her playthings. Until she was bored.

"The nobles believe Queen Vesta wanted Ambrose on the throne. Lord Dimitri upheld her wish."

Her sword's loyalty never faltered and the knowledge soothed her.

"Did you know her?"

"Not truly," Viktor answered. "I saw King Constantine and Queen Vesta at feasts and celebrations, but I didn't move in their circles. She did come in from time to time during Dimitri's final fittings. I've heard the rumors, I think all of us have, but I saw nothing illicit between them."

The clothier thinned his lips as his wings tightened to his back and glanced at the doorway.

"Dimitri is overseeing the transfer of the war archive chronicling the past century to my private library. He'll be a few hours," Astrid volunteered.

Viktor's wings lowered an inch, and the tension left his shoulders. "He's really taken to you." He adjusted her neckline and continued without meeting her eyes. "There was a constant sadness that shadowed Queen Vesta's soul. I think she and Lord Dimitri quieted each other's pain. The Queen longed for the son she lost, and while he'd never admit it, Lord Dimitri misses his friends and family murdered in the raid that brought him here."

Viktor would never know how close he was to the truth. She smiled when he lifted his gaze.

"Lost souls will always find one another."

Chapter Sixty-One

Dimitri sat in bed with a drawing pad against the bend of his knee. He sketched in silence, his pencil gently rasping over paper, complemented by the crackle of the fire.

A strange sensation settled in his chest throughout the evening. An emotion akin to comfort he couldn't pinpoint. He glanced over his shoulder. Astrid lounged beside him, engrossed in her book.

His wife was the source of his ease.

She wouldn't leave him. Couldn't be taken from him. She'd fought for him, insisting upon a diadem to match Ledivion's Crown of Daggers.

Her kingdom would have two crowns.

Two thrones.

His neva wanted him to rule beside her, and he agreed. Not because he had any desire to reign over the Ledivites who saw him as a curse, but to stay close. If he was near, he could keep her safe.

Dimitri watched Astrid curl the page into itself before turning it. His little scholar sat cross-legged with her book laid open over Ambrose's aquarium. A short black silk robe draped over her curves and fanned over their sheets. He would slip it off her shoulders and use the sash to tie her wrists behind her back when she finished reading for the evening.

When he'd imagined their future, he'd known books would be piled beside their bed. He hadn't been prepared for the near dozen leather-bound towers set so close together he needed to raise his wings to keep from knocking them over.

She'd requested the war archive encompassing the past century, then sent Dobromil after any documented Death Spirits, which she devoured.

"There have to be more accounts," Astrid grumbled.

Dimitri arched his brow, and she exchanged the thin booklet for a heftier tome.

"There are only three accounts of Death Spirits. The start of The Blood-Cursed Plague, another royal, and you," she said counting her fingers. "How can there be no records of Death Spirits being born among the common folk?"

"Why would Vinceret curse commoners?" They didn't war and certainly didn't boast about their unborn children being greater warriors than the God of Conquest and Blood.

Aggravation gleamed against midnight, and she turned to face him fully. "Why do you still think it's a curse?"

Bitterness coated his tongue as he answered, "Because these famished shadows could be nothing else."

Astrid dragged the book off his brother's encasement and the eyes swam to the front of the glass as though they were listening.

"I think they are born and Ledivites kill them in secret," Astrid said, opening the book and pointing to a passage.

His ever-scheming neva saw conspiracies on every page, because she herself was constantly plotting. "Where are you going with this?"

"Fire weavers come from earth weavers. They're produced every thousand souls."

Dimitri nodded. This was common knowledge.

"I believe a Death Spirit is a rarer magic, like fire weavers and air weavers," Astrid announced as her expression lit with excitement. "But your union is a Ledivite and a soul weaver."

"And you're concluding this off two documents?"

"I've met your soul weavers. They're weak," Astrid said pointedly. "Death Spirits can't help they're born hungry. Your mother was strong enough to hold your shadows. She taught you to control it."

"She did," he confessed, mildly concerned about what else she would infer from his admission.

"I'm going to overturn the decree of the Blood-Cursed—"

"No," Dimitri bit out. "I have given you your temples. You will not commit heresy against mine."

Astrid tossed the book aside and crawled into his lap. She took his face in her hands and spoke softly, leaning so close her breath fanned over his cheek. "Death Spirits aren't a curse from Vinceret." Her forehead touched his and she caressed his jaw. "They're a blessing from the Three-Faced Mother."

We aren't. The painful truth replayed through his mind, and he couldn't find his voice. His chest tightened, and he couldn't breathe.

Astrid held him closer, smoothing his hair. "You were born in the wrong kingdom, Dimitri," she whispered to him. "The Three-Faced Mother fashioned you and her serpents guided you to me. You're mine now. My perfect sword."

She contradicted the foundations of his beliefs. His mother may have worshiped fate, but she lived beneath the shadow of the God of Conquest and Blood. Whether it was fate or his mother's own thoughts that offended Vinceret didn't matter.

Dimitri's voice hallowed and he grated, "My blood is cursed."

Astrid's lips met his and he leaned into her comfort, only to have the snap of her teeth across his lip. He caught her by the throat and squeezed as malice slipped through his heart.

The corners of his wife's mouth lifted into a smile. She opened her mouth wide and flicked the tip of her tongue over the injury she'd inflicted.

"Your blood is not cursed," she said, kissing him again and sucking on his bottom lip. "You are closer to the gods than any of us."

By the blood, she infuriated him and had him hard the next instant.

"I've sent letters to the temples in Clorea asking for their strongest soul weavers to join me here.”

"It doesn't matter how many soul weavers you bring to Ledivion. She belongs to Vinceret.”

"I don't want Ledivites to worship a new god,” Astrid argued. "I want every birth taken to the major towns to be registered.”

Dimitri pulled back. His wife was a tactician, and this was her first step, not her end game.

"And why would you want to oversee thousands of births?” he asked.

"Because your people spent centuries cultivating fire weavers, when they should have been searching for Death Spirits.”

Dimitri's lips parted. "You—”

"How many battles did you win single-handed?” Astrid pulled his hand away from her neck and held his gaze as she kissed his fingertips. "How many times did you turn the tides of war?” She smiled not waiting for his answer. "Now: what if there were a dozen of you?”

His little wife wanted more swords at her disposal.

"By your own logic, you and I would have the highest probability of producing another Death Spirit,” Dimitri purred.

Astrid reached between them and palmed his hard length through his slacks. "Stop thinking with your cock.”

"Lie back and I'll use it instead of thinking with it.”

Astrid held his jaw and slid the tip of her tongue over his mouth, collecting the blood from his lip. His cock ached and he needed to be inside her. Dimitri opened his eyes and found her staring past him.

"Do you see how big your wings are?” Her gaze lowered to meet his. "Labor would kill me.”

"You have a penchant for theater,” he said, stroking her cheek.

"If you suggest I lay back and allow myself to be butchered so you can cut your offspring out of me, I'll slice your dick off.”

Her threat sounded like a vow, but it was progress. She carried his heir in her statement.

"You'll need something bigger than those little daggers, neva,” he teased.

Astrid rolled her eyes and pressed a palm to his shoulder, attempting to rise from his lap. He dragged her against him and held her close as she squirmed.

"Dimitri, stop." Astrid laughed. "I want to read a few more chapters and I need to visit Keres before the Ascension tomorrow."

"She won't save you from me," he said, grazing his teeth over her pulse.

"I don't need saving," Astrid insisted, then softened her voice. "I want to add something to our box."

Dimitri grinned. "For when I have you at our spring?"

Astrid hummed her agreement and slipped from their bed. "This will be something you wear for me."

Chapter Sixty-Two

Astrid's horse came to a stop beneath the grand archway. Sunlight gleamed across the barren courtyard. The earth weavers had offered to grow trees across the expanse of snow and braid it into a walkway, but she'd declined.

Ambrose's grave would share nothing with Queen Vesta's resting place.

She'd ordered the deconstruction of arena seating, rebuilding it in shades of crimson to reflect Clorean architecture. The pillars were carved with flowers transitioning through the seasons, beginning with winter and ending in spring.

Astrid embraced the strange Ledivite customs. This was once the royal wing. The room she'd shared with Dimitri had occupied the space upon which the disgraced King's tomb now stood.

The blood red lilies that had lined the railings little more than two weeks ago had been replaced with glittering rubies. Astrid wasn't sure if they had taken the red gems she'd arrived with as her calling card, or if the Ledivites understood that in Clorea, rubies signified the blood she was willing to spill for her kingdom.

Astrid steered her horse closer to Dimitri's. "Did you tell them to decorate with rubies?"

Her sword gazed over the glittering stands and grinned. "I would have told them to encrust the railing in diamonds to match your piercing."

Astrid's lids narrowed to slits, and he chuckled.

Her attention was drawn to gray robed priests emerging from the opposite end of the courtyard. Four of them stepped into the snow and a hush fell over the crowd. They stopped beside the grave and Astrid urged her horse forward with Dimitri at her side.

Her train fanned over the white mare's rump and trailed behind. Black lace over silk stitched with diamonds stood out against the snow. Behind them, the royal council followed on horseback.

Astrid recognized Dobromil as they drew closer. He stood before the grave with his gray-winged brethren behind him. Two of the priests held white marble trays lined in black velvet. Ledivion's crown of daggers rested on one and a diadem with two blades positioned to mimic horns lay on the other. The last priest balanced Ambrose's sword on his upturned palms. One beneath the guard and the other near the lower half of the blade.

Dimitri dismounted first and swept her train to one side of her before offering his hand.

"Husband," Astrid said, taking his hand. Her boots sank into the snow and their horses were led away by the royal council.

"Your Majesties," Dobromil said with a bow.

Astrid curtsied and answered, "Priest."

Whispering murmurs broke over the crowd as Astrid straightened. Ledivites held Vinceret to their hearts but the priests and priestesses closest to him didn't receive the same honor. A disrespect she would rectify after she was crowned.

Dimitri flared his wings, and the ambient chatter ceased.

Dobromil nervously glanced at the crowd and outstretched his hands on either side of him. "May Vinceret guide your reign."

Astrid and Dimitri lowered to their knees as he brought his hands together.

The snow chilled her legs as it melted beneath her. Astrid kept her head bowed and Dobromil's gray robes turned away from her.

"Crown your Queen first," Dimitri bit out.

The priest froze. This wasn't what they'd rehearsed but Dobromil recovered quickly. He pivoted to Astrid's crown and lifted the intricately woven gold over his head.

"Vinceret bless you and may the blood of your enemies overflow your cup," he said.

The weight of Ledivion's crown settled among her jeweled combs. The Mothers' Serpents led her to this moment. Ledivion was now hers and her birthright, Clorea, would soon follow.

Astrid upturned her face as Dobromil pointed his index and middle finger together. He made the sweeping motion of a V in front of her throat and said, "Rise, Astrid Noctis, Queen of Ledivion."

She stood and the crowd roared, "May the blood of your enemies overflow your cup."

Dobromil lifted Dimitri's crown of daggers, and their audience quieted once more.

"Vinceret bless you and may the blood of your enemies overflow your cup," the priest said as he crowned her sword. "Rise, Dimitri—"

"Queen Astrid's Death Spirit," Dimitri finished.

Astrid ignored the whispers among the nobles and royal council behind her. She stepped into Dimitri and traced his pointed ear. The small hoops and hanging gold clicked across her night-streaked nails as he turned to gaze at her.

Desire and dark promises stirred in his molten gold eyes.

"Rise, Dimitri," Dobromil started again. "Queen Astrid's Death Spirit."

Her sword stood and the crowd didn't repeat the blessing she'd received. Astrid wasn't sure if it was because he'd forgone his title, or her subjects refused to acknowledge her sword.

Dimitri removed his crown and pressed the braided metal into her hands.

"No," Astrid argued.

Ledivion had betrayed Dimitri for the last time. These fools cursed the blessing he was. Astrid pointed to the snow between them. "We will rule side by side and if there are any objections... their bodies will line our court."

Dimitri chuckled and lowered to one knee before bowing his head.

Astrid crowned the male fate gifted her.

"May the blood of *our enemies* overflow your cup, my king."

Dimitri held her stare, vicious and predatory.

Her perfect sword.

Dimitri's lips warmed the scar across her palm, and he stood, turning to Dobromil. "Bring my wife Ambrose's sword, priest."

Dobromil retrieved the sword and stood between Dimitri and herself. Sunlight glinted off the blade as he bowed and held out the weapon.

The handle was cold in Astrid's grip, and it was heavier than she expected. She approached Ambrose's grave. The headstone was the same stone as his parents'—light gray rock curving to a rounded top. Unlike his father, the Morana crest of three intersecting swords didn't embellish his marker. No name was carved into the surface. Nothing identifiable.

Ambrose was entombed beneath a blank grave.

Astrid stabbed the point of his sword into the frozen ground. She held the pommel and drew her leg up, kicking through the face of the blade. The steel shattered, littering jagged shards over the snow while a few inches of the tip jutted upright. She tossed the handle, letting the remnants of Ambrose's blade clatter against his grave.

The Ledivites erupted into cheers and Dimitri's winged shadow engulfed her own. Astrid turned toward him. "Did you want to break a sword on his grave, too?"

Dimitri's wings curved around her as he pulled her in. He crooked a finger under her chin and their lips met. His kiss wasn't gentle, but he was reverent. The heat of him burned into her memory.

"The only thing I want is you."

Chapter Sixty-Three

The idle chatter of a thousand voices filled the courtyard. Astrid stood beside Dimitri beneath the grand archway leading into the palace grounds. The surrounding forest had been cleared into a snowy field, divided by the well-traveled road leading back to Clorea.

Astrid crossed this threshold months ago, but it felt like a lifetime had passed. So much had changed. The male she thought to kill was now her husband and the kingdom she planned to raze was now hers.

Dimitri leaned closer and his deep voice pulled her from her musings. "You're begging to be caught wearing this gown, wife."

Astrid smoothed her hands over the gold and platinum corset constricting her waist. Viktor had worked with Keres to create this work of art. She glanced over her shoulder at the yards of black silk and jeweled lace fanned over the snow behind her.

Ledivite nobility filled the palace courtyard behind a row of armored guards on horseback. They leaned one way, then the other, packed shoulder to shoulder in extravagant dress. Astrid couldn't fathom why they were so eager to witness their queen flee their king. Did they think Dimitri would catch her and fuck her in front of them?

Astrid turned away from the crowd. This ceremony was archaic, but the ritual meant something to her sword. She interlaced her fingers with his and stared into his golden eyes. "It's customary to give your queen a head start."

He lifted their hands, and his firm lips warmed the scar binding them. "I'll give you to the count of ten, love."

"When does my time start?"

"When you let go of my hand," he answered.

Astrid dropped his hand and dashed to the closest guard on horseback. She tore his soul from his legs, and he fell to the ground with a startled cry. Astrid was in the saddle the next instant, charging toward the tree line.

She glanced back as her horse raced to a gallop. Her train flowed behind her, creating the illusion of a glittering strip of night against Ledivion's snowy canvas.

Dimitri swept his hand through his dark hair, removing his crown. He handed the daggered circlet to Dobromil and spread his gray wings.

Fuck.

Astrid leaned forward, begging the mare to run faster.

Hooves pounded the ground. She was closing the distance to the pines.

Another few seconds.

She could outrun him.

Astrid reached the shade of the forest when a hard body crashed against hers. The collision knocked her off her horse and ripped the reins from her hands. Dimitri crushed her against the unyielding planes of his body. His wings snapped open, and their momentum shifted violently.

His wingtips dusted the snow and propelled them upward, cresting the pines.

"You'll never escape me, neva," Dimitri murmured.

Astrid laughed. They glided a few feet above the snow-covered treetops and her dark hair steamed across his shoulder. "You knocked off my crown."

"The priests will fetch it," Dimitri replied.

The air warmed and thickened as the flew between the billowing pillars of steam rising from the thermal spring. Dimitri began an easy descent and landed gently before setting Astrid on her feet.

Their suede box rested at the center of the tree stump near the spring. Excitement thrummed beneath her skin as she approached it.

"Did you bring my additions?" Astrid asked, taking a seat on the stump.

Dimitri grinned, strolling toward her. "I haven't opened it."

"Take off your clothes," she said as she lifted the lid. The thin wooden box Keres gave her was nestled amongst their assortment of toys.

Her sword shrugged out of his topcoat and folded it before setting it beside her. He began unbuttoning his shirt and lifted his chin at their box. "What did you bring? Is that a cock ring or a sleeve you want me to fuck you with?"

"Something more permanent," Astrid answered as she opened her kit.

A needle lay against the velvet beside a series of thin platinum bars.

She lifted the sharp instrument, examining the end. "If your shadows bite me, I'm adding another bar."

Dimitri stripped out of his shirt and folded it before glancing over the uniformed metal. "Are you sure they'll fit?"

"Keres made them," Astrid began, then arched her brow. "Off the mold she has of your cock."

"Did you expect me to fill you with another male's cock?" he asked as he continued to strip. "You will only ever know me, wife."

Dimitri stood before her, his imposing form a display of sculpted muscle and sharp shadows. Astrid appraised her sword, gliding her nails along the underside of his length.

"I'll place it here," she says, squeezing either side of his shaft an inch past the head. "And if you can't control your shadows, we'll add more." Astrid tapped the inches down his shaft. "All the way down."

"You are enjoying your new position far too much, neva," Dimitri rasped.

Astrid dug her nails into his waist and pulled him closer. She parted her lips over the head of his cock and stared up at him through her lashes.

Dimitri tilted his head back and his fingers curved beneath her jaw. He rocked forward, sliding into her mouth.

Astrid let him stroke over her tongue once more before pulling away. "You will wear every mark you placed on me, my king."

"Marks to bind us?" he asked.

Astrid smiled in answer and lifted the needle.

Dimitri tensed as she began.

"Don't move," Astrid whispered teasingly. "We're almost done."

She'd never done a piercing before, but it wasn't unlike stabbing a prisoner or cutting a piece of them free for Foxglove.

Dimitri remained still aside from a few hisses of breath. His shadows pulsed around him but didn't surge to her.

He healed quickly and Astrid admired her work. Astrid leaned back on her hands and pouted at him. "I was hoping to add a few more."

Dimitri caged her throat and tugged her forward. "We can bargain for that later. Now, open your mouth."

Astrid glanced at the sky.

"It's customary for all the guests to stay at the palace until we return, neva. No one will come looking for us," he assured her before adding, "and I'll kill anyone who looks upon my wife's naked body… *after* you've taken their eyes."

His words quieted Astrid's apprehension.

Dimitri caressed her throat and dragged his thumb over her mouth. "I need your lips around my cock, wife."

Astrid parted her lips, and his hand trailed into her hair. His fingers tangled through the strands at the base of her skull and she glared at him from beneath her lashes. If he thought a piercing suddenly allowed him to fuck her mouth as hard as he pleased, she was going to cut his balls off.

"I'll go slow, neva. Teach you to swallow my cock," he purred.

Astrid dropped her hand and parted her lips as he stepped into her. She held the shaft as he slid the head of his cock over her tongue. Dimitri groaned as he gently ran his fingers over her scalp. The sensation sent tingles cascading over her skin.

His affection left her easy. She let him fuck her mouth with the first few inches of his cock. Dimitri groaned as he watched her. His breaths were ragged and the way his chiseled body moved ignited her imagination.

She loved watching him fuck her. The power of his body taking her, again and again. But this was different.

She surrendered to him, but there was control in it. He came undone because she allowed it.

"Can you take me deeper?" he asked, caressing her jaw and tracing the corner of her mouth.

The heat in his molten gold stare seared her and she nodded. He stroked the hollow of her cheek and pressed forward, stopping when the head reached the back of her mouth.

"I'm not going to move," he assured her. "Take a breath and press the head into our throat, neva. It'll cut off your air, then pull back."

Astrid gazed up at him and remained still, testing his word.

"I won't force it." Dimitri ran two fingers across his throat. "On my swords."

His oath and promise. A gesture to his god.

Astrid leaned forward. The head of his cock wedged into her throat cutting off her airways. It wasn't unbearable. Watching his muscles strain was well worth the mild discomfort.

She pulled back to the tip and worked his length past her lips again. She stroked his shaft the way he'd taught her, taking a breath before she pressed the head into her throat. His reactions were exhilarating, and she moaned.

Dimitri tensed and lifted his chin before groaning, "Fuck."

"You like that?" Astrid studied him as she continued stroking his length. His pulse point thrummed along the side of his throat. The hard muscles of his broad chest rose and fell with his ragged breaths. All of it hinged on what she did.

Astrid took him past her lips and she moaned again. She beamed when his breath caught. This was a battlefield he could never win.

Dimitri took her hand and instead of showing her another way he liked his cock stroked, he helped her to her feet.

"I wasn't done playing with you," she whispered as he bent to kiss her.

"I can scent how wet you are. I've been neglecting you," he murmured at her lips. "You can swallow my cum another time."

That didn't sound as appealing as teasing him, but Astrid didn't argue the point as Dimitri unlaced her gown.

Black silk and diamond-stitched lace fell to her feet. Her sword stood silent for a moment then grinned.

"You weren't wearing anything under your dress," he said as she stepped out of the yards of silk.

"I knew you wanted to chase me." She glanced at him over her shoulder and sauntered around the tree stump. "We both know what you were going to do when you caught me," she said with a shrug. "I simply saved you some trouble."

Dimitri followed her and lowered to his knees. His fingertips trailed down the back of her thigh to her knee-high boots. "Maybe I enjoy undressing you," he countered.

Her sword removed her boot and dragged her leg over his shoulder.

"Dimitri," Astrid cried.

He tongued her clit and flicked her piercing. Astrid ran her fingers through his dark hair as he licked and sucked. His wings came forward, cradling her back as he lifted her off her feet.

Astrid lay against his wings as he yanked off her other boot and slung her leg over his shoulder. He thrusted into her with two fingers as he devoured her, and Astrid couldn't think.

"Put me down before you drop me," Astrid hissed between moans.

He lifted his head, holding her thigh to his shoulder. "I can fly for hours, neva," he said, stretching her to accommodate a third finger. "And I am considerably heavier than you."

Astrid squirmed against him as his shadows snaked up her body. She couldn't close her legs, couldn't escape him.

His mouth worked her, and she was helpless to do anything but come for him. She fisted his hair, yanking him close as she rocked her hips.

She moaned with relief when he withdrew his fingers, but her reprieve was short lived. The low hum of a vibrating plug filled the space between them.

The blunt tip pressed into her cunt and Astrid screamed as she came. He filled her with it while he sucked on her clit.

"Slower. Dimitri, please," she cried.

He ignored her, thrusting those hard inches into her. Making her take his length in the harsh rhythm he set.

She came again and he moaned against her silken flesh. His gaze lifted, pinning her beneath the crescent of his dark lashes.

"I think you're wet enough now," he said before kissing her clit.

Dimitri removed the replica of his cock and brought it to her ass. He applied more pressure, and Astrid sighed a breath as the tip pressed inside.

"You like when I fuck you slow?" he asked. Astrid moaned her agreement as she rocked her hips. "Slow and deep? That's it. Take it."

She let the onslaught of sensations drown her. She writhed against his wings, coming apart against his mouth.

Dimitri continued fucking her ass as he pressed a second replica into her cunt.

"Please fuck me," she begged.

"I am," he answered, stroking them into her in unison.

She came hard and clamped her thighs on either side of his throat. Dimitri pried one of her thighs back, continuing her torment.

"I can't come any more. Please, fuck me with your cock."

"You can have my cock when my wings get tired," he answered.

Astrid's lashes fluttered closed as another orgasm crashed over her. He fucked her with one, then the other, alternating before fucking her with both again.

She was boneless when he finally laid her over a soft patch of grass where snow didn't accumulate due to its proximity to the spring. Dimitri withdrew their toys and held her in the cage of his arms. He thrust into her as their lips met. She swallowed his groans, wrapping her legs around his waist. He fucked her harder and she took each stroke.

The golden stars of her soul glittered, suspended in his shadows that surrounded them. Dimitri tensed and thrusted into her a final time. He broke their kiss as he came, panting against her throat.

Astrid's heart hammered in her chest. She stroked his hair as they calmed by degrees.

Dimitri outstretched his wings after a time. He stood, cradling her in his arms as he stepped into the thermal spring. Astrid moaned as the heat of the water seeped into her bones. He cleaned her and held her in his lap. Astrid curled against him watching as the last of the sunset's orange hues fade from the sky.

Chapter Sixty-Four

Dimitri strolled through his mother's favorite orchard. The temperature maintained for the trees was uncomfortably hot, but he never complained. He happily accompanied her and picked fruits from the branches she was too short to reach.

The memories were bittersweet. His father murdered her here. He'd waited for Dimitri to leave her side. Constantine's arrow struck his heart, but his father had miscalculated. Dimitri's shadows burst from him, hungrily reaching for anything to fuel his regeneration.

They reached his mother.

The leading edge of Dimitri's wing shot forward. Constantine's headstone cracked beneath the impact and crumbled after the second.

Dimitri turned to his mother's grave and dropped to his knees. "Mne zhal-," Dimitri whispered, pressing his hand to the grass.

He couldn't contain his curse. Hadn't learned to control it yet.

When he'd realized what he'd done, he killed Constantine with his bare hands. By the time Ambrose had pulled him away, their father was unrecognizable. They'd burned the bodies, and Ambrose told the royal council the King and Queen had been assassinated.

They were buried side by side and Dimitri hated his father's proximity. He shoved his wing over the grass, scattering chunks of Constantine's headstone across the orchard.

"I have a wife. I think you would have gotten along with her," Dimitri said, reminiscing over all the times his mother had instructed, *Let the serpents guide you.*

Dimitri devoted himself to the God of Conquest and Blood. He'd prayed and left tributes, believing if he proved his loyalty to Vinceret, his curse would one day be lifted.

The curse Astrid insisted was a blessing from the Three-Faced Mother.

"She's overturned the decree of the Blood-Curse Plague. The royal council is afraid of her." Dimitri chuckled. "I didn't have to kill any of them. She wants to teach the Death Spirits to control their magic like you taught me."

"I'll teach them to hold the more dangerous aspects of their magic," Dimitri said as he stood. He smoothed his hand over her headstone. She'd been buried in Ledivion custom, but he knew her heart had always remained in Clorea with the Three-Faced Mother.

Dimitri took to the sky with a powerful beat of his wings. The air cooled drastically as he flew beyond the magic stitched into the orchard by the earth and fire weavers. He landed in the snowy court-yard adjacent to the temple he'd built for Astrid.

He passed parishioners as he entered the temple. Snakes covered the floor behind the towering statues of three robed females, while others basked in the sun streaming through the windows on the pews.

Astrid's white cobra glutted itself on red meat strewn over the altar as an offering. Dimitri wondered if his wife placed him there and moved to an unoccupied space to the side of the altar. He lowered to one knee.

Mothers, hear me. Thank you for blessing me with your most cunning daughter.

Chapter Sixty-Five

Astrid followed Dimitri up the stairway that once led to the arena. Warmth blanketed her as they stepped onto the thick grass that had nothing to do with the winter sun. The temperature was regulated by fire weavers while earth weavers maintained the fruiting trees. Surrounding them, beyond the reach of their magic, were shadowed, snow-covered pines.

The orchard had changed greatly since she'd last seen it. The trees no longer formed a walkway. They were grouped in small clusters and spread throughout the green space.

Even the graves were different. Queen Vesta's headstone had been replaced by a fountain. A statue of the Three-Faced Mother was positioned at the center of the water feature. The hooded females stood in a circle with their backs to one another, each holding the stages of life.

The egg, the serpent, and the shed.

An engraving, lettered in gold, graced the statue's base:

Vesta Morana

Beloved Mother

Queen of Ledivion

She glanced at her sword. Did he know being buried at the Mothers' feet was the highest honor a soul weaver could receive in death?

"It's a beautiful tribute," she said.

Dimitri smoothed his hand over the fountain ledge. "This was her favorite orchard. She had one at every palace."

"Because Ledivion is freezing and this place felt like home," Astrid replied.

He lifted his chin and gazed at the Mothers. "I suppose you're right."

"I usually am."

Astrid didn't mention the missing grave. She was curious if Dimitri moved his father or if he was here, unmarked and forgotten. He would tell her eventually during one of their nightly talks.

"I'm readying the legion to march on Clorea," Astrid said. "We'll ride ahead by half a day and kill Sorin. The nobility will fall in line—"

"Or I'll kill them," Dimitri finished.

"More than one person is needed to run a kingdom. The nobility will serve me, or I'll cage their heads, and hang them beside my cousins."

The *thrum* of a bowstring resonated through the warm air and Astrid tensed.

A heavy arrow struck Dimitri's thigh the next moment, slicing muscle and embedding in bone. He fell to his knee with a roar and Astrid dropped to his side.

Instinct overwhelmed her as her magic swept over him. She couldn't stitch his soul and Astrid's eyes narrowed at the wound. This was far too wide to be an arrow. She began stabilizing the injury and yanked the projectile free.

The arrowhead was wide and crescent shaped. These weapons were meant to cut rigging lines on ships.

More bowstrings thrummed in the distance.

Astrid caught Dimitri's arm and dragged him backwards. "Get

up. We have to move," she hissed, angling him closer to the fountain. Her magic pulsed over him, focusing on his heart and lungs while she slowed the bleeding.

Two more arrows struck his injured leg, severing it, and more struck his wings.

No. These were modified arrows—of *her* creation. Hooks attached to the back of crossbow bolts staked Dimitri's wings to the ground, immobilizing him.

Astrid scanned the snow-covered pines as she worked to stop the bleeding. There wasn't time to regenerate his leg. They needed cover and she couldn't move him on her own.

Another arrow struck, opening Dimitri's ribs, and his shadows engulfed her. Serrated teeth harrowed her soul and Astrid screamed, blinded by agony.

It suddenly stopped, and Dimitri clapped his hand over the back of her head, pulling her close.

Pink foamed at the corners of his lips as he choked on his words. "Stay out of my shadows."

"I'm strong; I'll survive this. Take what you need," Astrid cried, clinging to him.

Dimitri violently yanked his wing through the arrows pinning him. The membrane tore and the leading edge of his wing struck her.

Pain exploded over Astrid's side as the air was knocked from her lungs. She was thrown from Dimitri's side, weightless for the span of a heartbeat. Two.

She collided with the ground and tumbled into freezing snow.

Chapter Sixty-Six

"Your letters were very helpful, cousin," Sorin said as he dragged Astrid to her feet. Her equilibrium teetered and she struggled to regain her balance.

Dimitri's still body lay near the fountain. His shadows poured from him, wilting the grass, blackening the trees. Taking everything within their radius.

They stopped, churning a few feet from her.

"Dimitri!" Astrid screamed.

More arrows struck. They carved his torso, sliced limbs.

His shadows pulsed and began to retract.

"No!" Astrid screamed, but couldn't shake Sorin's grip.

She reached for a hair stick and ripped it from her curls. The thin blade glinted as she unsheathed it. Astrid rammed the blade into Sorin's gut. Her cousin grunted and curled forward, releasing her.

Astrid turned, grabbing the collar of his jacket with both hands. She fell back, rolling onto her shoulders as she got her feet under him. Their eyes met for an instant, and there she saw betrayal in his dark gaze.

Astrid smiled and threw him over her.

Sorin tumbled onto the grass and into Dimitri's shadows. Her cousin screamed as the shadows overtook him. He twisted, trying to escape. A hand, lined with black veins, burst from the thick, opaque shadows, before being engulfed again. His face surfaced next, screaming for her. Sunken, milky white eyes over gaunt cheekbones, pleaded.

"Astrid!"

She recognized the voice and turned toward Sterling. He stood at the far edge, two of her cousins between them and gestured, *Who are we killing?*

Throw them in, she gestured back and bolted to Desmond, her youngest cousin. His eyes widened and he quickly dropped his attention to his crossbow. Panic overwhelmed him as he fumbled with the bowstring.

Astrid tackled him and threw his weapon to Dimitri's shadows as males screamed behind her.

"Asti, what are you doing?" Desmond cried.

"What I should have done a long time ago," she answered, dragging him to his feet.

Another arrow sang through the air. Flames cascaded behind it and Astrid watched in horror as it struck Dimitri's body.

Astrid threw Desmond into the shadows and charged forward.

Strong arms caught her, lifting her off her feet.

"Let me go, Sterling! I need to heal him," Astrid screamed as she sobbed.

She thrashed, but Sterling held her. "You can't go in there. He'll kill you."

"Let me go to him," she begged. "He won't hurt me."

The thick shadows retracted, exposing four contorted, desiccated corpses. Dimitri's death magic churned into a sweeping vortex, returning to him. Sealing within him.

The four souls weren't enough.

"Dimitri!" Astrid screamed.

The shadows burst from him in answer. The same vortex she'd

seen twisting in his chest, but now on a larger scale.

It faded, and her sword stood before her. Healed and whole.

Relief flooded Astrid, but she realized he wasn't looking at her as he closed the distance between them. Sterling fell to his knees behind her.

The arms that held her were now lined with blackened veins.

"No!" Astrid sprinted toward Dimitri. Colliding with him as she took his face between her hands. "No, Dimitri, stop."

"He's with them," Dimitri grated.

"He's with *me*. You kidnapped me and I wrote him letters about you," Astrid confessed.

His attention turned to her and hatred gleamed behind his molten gold eyes.

"You betrayed me—"

"I *saved* you!" Astrid screamed. "If you love me, let him go."

Chapter Sixty-Seven

If you love me.

Malice and hate bled through Dimitri's vision. He'd allowed Astrid to cultivate these soft, bleeding emotions in him. The loyalty of his wife's heart was conditional, and he knew better than to believe her.

Knew every syllable slithering past her lips were lies. Sweet words he wanted to be true, but that was the crux of her poison.

Her venom had sunk into him like the fangs of the serpents she worshipped.

Lethal.

Corrosive.

And he'd welcomed it.

Drank it.

"Dimitri, don't do this to us," Astrid cried.

Her tears looked so real, but Dimitri couldn't discern if they spilled because he'd laid dying or if she wept for her co-conspirator.

"He helped me save you," Astrid hissed as she grabbed his jaw and shoved his head to the side.

Dimitri begrudgingly glanced over the battlefield he'd survived. Four black-veined corpses lay strewn over the gray, withered grass. Gaunt, ashen faces stared back at him; their expressions contorted in agony.

"Sterling helped me throw my cousins into your shadows." She stepped into him, standing on her toes as she caught his face between her hands. "I am loyal to you."

Her midnight eyes searched his and her expression fell with the last of her tears when he remained silent.

"Trust me," she whispered as her arms slipped beneath his topcoat. Her fingertips trailed over his side and Dimitri's wrath faltered.

He crushed the quiet feelings she stirred in him. This wasn't her affection. She manipulated the strings tied to his heart. How many times had she touched him like this before she curled to him to sleep?

"Don't break what's formed between us," Astrid said against his chest. "Please, Dimitri. Let him go."

Wrath and anguish clashed inside him. His need to hold her close was strangled by his desire to snap her neck. He caged her in his arms and rested his cheek on the top of her head.

He withdrew his shadows and Astrid squeezed him tighter. She pulled away and Dimitri cursed himself a fool. Then, Astrid yanked him into her by the collar of his shirt. Her lips met his in a desperate kiss.

She stole his breath, and he could say nothing.

"Trust deepens," she whispered before pressing her forehead to his. "I am yours, just as you are mine."

"La nikogda tebia ne otpushchu," Dimitri vowed. *I will never let you go.*

Astrid slipped out of his arms and went to her fallen ally. Golden threads arched through Sterling's body and pulled tight again and again.

His neva couldn't mend what he'd taken.

Dimitri moved closer and guided his magic over Sterling.

Astrid craned her neck to glare at him. "We saved you," Astrid bit out, shoving at his shadows. Her hand swept through his intangible magic. "Get your fucking shadows off him!"

"You can't restore what I've taken," Dimitri said simply. He couldn't separate the souls he'd consumed but he could return some of the essence his shadows devoured. Enough to restore the hue of life to his skin and fade the black veins.

Sterling burst to life with a jolt, wild eyed and gasping for breath as he shoved away from Dimitri.

"Sterling! Sterling. It's okay. You're okay," Astrid said patting his shin and she crept closer. "Take a deep breath."

Dimitri hated how familiar they were. Astrid's magic flowed over him, and the golden stars of his soul obeyed her every whim.

The dark-haired wingless male stared up at him. His palm ground over his sternum as his mouth worked, but no words came.

Astrid's midnight gaze shot to Dimitri. She blamed him for the male's panic.

"Stop contemplating his death. You crave loyalty. There is no one more loyal than him."

A cutting retort had been on Dimitri's tongue, but his little wife suddenly shifted her attention to the battlefield, then back to him.

Schemes glittered in her eyes as she asked, "Can you put Sorin's soul back in his body?"

Dimitri surveyed the mangled corpses.

"The one closer to you, with the rings," Astrid added.

His brow knitted. "No."

"Please?" Astrid beamed at him. "I'll bargain for him."

"I can't revive the dead, neva."

Astrid huffed as she helped Sterling to his feet. "I wanted to keep him."

The wingless male straightened as he frowned, rubbing his chest. He leaned toward Astrid and asked in a hushed voice, "How do you get the feel of the teeth out of you?"

"She doesn't," Dimitri answered, stepping closer.

Astrid stepped between them and her palms pressed against his chest. She kept her hand on him as she spoke to her ally. "Being attacked by a Death Spirit is—"

"Enlightening," Sterling finished, then hastily bowed. "My king."

The male's show of loyalty was performative, and Dimitri was under no illusion of whom Sterling was truly devoted to. This male was another weapon in his wife's arsenal.

"How many soldiers did you bring?" Dimitri asked.

"Five. River escaped. He's likely fleeing to Serpents' Dawn."

Returning to the halls where he'd massacred Clorea's royal family. Dimitri dragged Astrid against him and stared into her fathomless eyes. "Did my wife tell you where to find us?" he asked, searching her features for micro expressions.

Proof of her betrayal or innocence.

"I have spies here, Your Majesty."

Dimitri's eyes lifted to meet Sterling's. He recognized the detachment. Stern green eyes, fortified by years of hardship stared back at him. This male was prepared to be tortured. Dimitri didn't care if he'd developed these skills during warfare or as a criminal. His soul tasted of rot, just like all the others.

"And?" Dimitri prodded.

Sterling glanced at Astrid and his little wife nodded. He swallowed before he spoke. "And you come here often. It's isolated. I came to free Ast—"

"My wife," Dimitri corrected.

Sterling tensed and his attention turned to Astrid. "Are you willingly married?"

"Why wouldn't she be?"

"Because she hates your wings," Sterling snapped.

A predatory smile crept over Dimitri's lips as he stepped around his wife. "I taught her to appreciate them."

Astrid interlaced her fingers with his and tugged him back. "Stop posturing at each other. I've chosen Dimitri as my husband and king. Where is my mother? Is she safe?"

Sterling's gaze raked over Dimitri, and he slowly nodded. "She lives in an estate near the Vermillion Palace."

"Which one of my cousins has the Serpents' Crown?"

Sterling thinned his lips. "They rule together."

Venom dripped from her voice as she asked, "Which ones?"

"All eight."

Astrid leaned into Dimitri and pinched the bridge of her nose. "Collect their heads," she asked, stroking the center of his chest. "I wanted to keep them, but their skulls will do."

"Anything else, neva?" Dimitri asked.

His cunning wife smiled. "Tell the Royal Legion we march for Clorea tonight."

Chapter Sixty-Eight

Astrid accompanied the Royal Legion to Clorea's capital, Serpents' Dawn. The plush carriage she occupied was much larger than the one that brought her to Ledivion, but her company hadn't changed.

Dimitri sat beside her, watching the shops and buildings surrounding the palace parade past the window. Her people stared uneasily. Sorin had divided the kingdom, surrendering half of their lands to Ledivion. She wondered if word had reached them, and whether they knew of her cousin's demise.

They rode through the palace gates and followed the curved road to the entry. Dimitri exited first and spread his wings. "If any of you raise your weapons at my wife, I will personally deliver your husk to Vinceret."

Sterling's voice joined him. "Stand down."

Astrid exited the coach, surveying the guards lining the palace. She smiled as she took Dimitri's hand. "Don't kill all our soldiers."

He inclined his head, and his crown of daggers gleamed against the shadows.

Astrid climbed the steps. She was returning to Serpents' Dawn not as a rescued princess but as a ruling queen.

Viktor had woven beautiful sheets of silk for her and dyed them the deepest blood red. Astrid had Dimitri's shadows painted onto the ends of the skirt panels. Her pauldron featured elegant plum blossom branches with rubies fitted as the petals. They glittered in the sunlight as she stepped off the coach.

It wasn't the dress that captured the guards' attention. They stared at the diamond and ruby diadem resting atop her head and the daggered blades mimicking horns.

Astrid took Dimitri's hand and glanced at her friend. "Sterling, would you please bring my ornaments?"

He nodded and Astrid headed into the palace. The light clinks of metal sounded behind her, followed by a barrage of armored steps and breathless gasps. Astrid glanced over her shoulder to find Sterling with a length of chain slung over his shoulder. Four empty birdcages, sized for canaries, hung from the chain draped over his chest and legs. Her remaining cousins' heads would fill the other cages, just as Sorin's and the others' occupied the four strung across Sterling's back.

Astrid made her way to the War Room. The guards who'd once barred her entry shrank at her approach. Dimitri's shadowed magic swept over them as he ordered, "Open the doors."

They pushed the doors open before Astrid reached the doorway and fled their posts.

Warrick's eyes widened as they entered the room and he turned to River. "You said you killed the Death Spirit."

Her cousins scattered like insects. Dimitri's shadows engulfed them, and their screams followed.

Astrid leaned into her king and brushed her lips over the hollow of his throat. "Remember, I want to keep them."

The remaining nobles huddled in the far corner. They jumped as Sterling arranged the birdcages on the table dominating the room.

Astrid stepped over River's writhing body and spread her hands over the table's face. The Serpents' Crown lay in the center of the map depicting her kingdom.

An angry red scrawl divided her birthright, marking the half surrendered to Ledivion.

Weak plays for power made by weaker males.

Astrid removed her jeweled diadem and placed it at the center of the Ledivite-owned lands. She lifted the Serpents' Crown, holding it before her. It was heavier than she expected. The gilded snakes held a quartz crystal between their fangs as their eyes glinted.

Fate had led her here and she would steer Clorea onto the path the Three-Faced Mother set before her.

The circlet slid over her dark hair and rested against her ornate combs. She finally wore the Serpents' Crown as she was always meant to.

Astrid turned in a smooth motion. "I've missed my loving family." She bent and pressed her hand over River's forehead, stitching his soul to the skull she would keep.

"The family who took my strategies and conveniently forgot my name when they returned victorious," she said binding Warrick next. "My cousins who betrayed me at every turn. Who whored my kingdom out to rule half of it as dogs."

Astrid bound the last of them and returned for their delicate wire cages. "You will live as long as I reign, bearing witness to my throne."

She opened the hinge and turned to the cowering council members.

"For you, I will offer a choice: Serve me or join them as witness."

Chapter Sixty-Nine

Astrid had never realized how constricting the walls of her room were. It wasn't the size of the suite or her furnishings. It was the constant dismissals and hinderance of knowledge that strangled her by degrees. The silent slights accumulated over the years, becoming a burden she unknowingly carried. It weighed on her soul, threatening to suffocate her. The Three-Faced Mother opened her path and sent a Death Spirit to liberate her.

Dimitri had freed her, bound himself to her, and irreparably changed her.

He promised an eternity of devotion if she loved him, and Astrid was dangerously close to losing her heart.

Would it be so terrible? Her sword loved her. It bordered on obsession.

Astrid contemplated her options as she stepped around her four-post bed, surveying the destruction her cousins had wreaked. Her papers and documents had been scattered across the floor. The book-cases were emptied, their contents discarded in heaping piles. Even the stacks of books she'd organized by her urgency to read them had been rummaged through and carelessly strewn near the foot of her bed.

Sorin had used the information she'd sent him and rifled through her things in search of her inventions—her weapons she'd created. He couldn't be bothered to put anything back because he never expected her to return.

A comb jeweled with emeralds and its matching hair stick were tossed with her other jewelry across her bed. Astrid took the golden stick and unsheathed its hidden dagger.

"I fantasized about killing you and returning here," Astrid said as she examined the point.

"And what do you fantasize about now?" Dimitri teased as he removed his daggered crown and piled her books on their sides in the empty shelves.

She squinted, reading the titles. He was alphabetizing them. Astrid held her tongue as she gathered the loose pages scattered across the floor. If her room in disarray put her on edge, she could only imagine what it did to her Death Spirit.

She straightened the pages and placed them on her desk. The scar across the back of her hand caught the glow of the chandelier glittering overhead.

"We were bound before Vinceret," she said, tracing the proof of their union.

Dimitri set the books down and turned toward her. "We are married, wife."

There was an edge to his voice. A warning and a promise. He would defend his claim, and she would never escape him.

Astrid smiled.

"But not in Clorean tradition, husband," she answered.

The tension left his eyes, and he moved closer. "Beneath the Three-Faced Mother?" Dimitri asked, smoothing his thumb across her lips. "Do I get to chase you again?"

"It's a quieter ceremony," Astrid explained, taking his hand between hers. "We pour our wine into a single glass. It symbolizes our fates becoming one."

Dimitri leaned closer. "I will happily complete as many rituals as you desire," he purred.

His callused hands swept down her back and over the curve of her ass. Astrid gasped as he gripped her thighs and lifted her against him. He carried her to their bed, guiding her legs around his waist.

Dimitri laid her down and prowled up her body. She tightened her thighs around him and breathed, "You still owe me a mark, my king."

"I'll leave many marks on you, love," he rasped, trailing kisses down the side of her throat.

Astrid removed her crown and curled a finger under Dimitri's chin. Her sword lifted his head, and she caressed his cheek. "You owe me a brand. One you'll wear on your neck."

The corners of his eyes crinkled. "I'd forgotten you wear my crest," he said, sweeping her hair from her throat.

Astrid turned to the side, giving him an unobstructed view. Dimitri's firm lips warmed the mark beneath her ear as she asked, "If you don't recall me wearing it, does that mean I can heal it?"

"No," he grated. "I should fuck your ass for even asking."

Astrid moaned at the images his words conjured. Memories touched her. His strong hands tight on her waist. Her body pressed against his silk sheets as he spread her legs. The touch of metal before he filled her cunt with a replica of his hard length. His shadows sweeping over her while he worked the head of his cock into her ass.

Heat bloomed between Astrid's thighs, and she moaned as her lips met his. She pulled away and breathed, "Or you could let me ride you while you take my brand."

Dimitri rocked forward, grinding the length of his cock against her center. "You could just ask me to fuck you slow." His teeth grazed the underside of her jaw, then her throat. "You don't need to be on top."

The friction he gave her was perfection and she gripped her crown until her knuckles turned white. "I can't get a clean brand if you're moving."

Her sword hummed in agreement and held her against him. Astrid wrapped her arms around him as he lifted her. Dimitri sat on the bed with his back against the headboard. Candlelight danced over his features.

Her devastatingly handsome male.

Astrid held her crown over the candles, letting the flame lick the serpent's head. "Hold this here."

Dimitri obliged and she began unbuckling his belt. His molten gold stare never left her as she unfastened his pants. Astrid fisted his cock, and a groan rumbled from his chest.

"Keep the flame on the serpent's face," she said, pulling his length free.

The intensity of his gaze sharpened as his fingers dug into her hip. "I know where it is, neva."

Astrid rose to her knees and gripped the headboard. "Do you?" she asked at his lips.

Dimitri's hand slipped lower, hooking the front of her thong. He ripped the thin lace, and the tip of his cock glided against her.

"Ride me or lay back and spread your legs."

Astrid took her time, rocking her hips as she took the tip of his cock. Her grip on the headboard tightened as she leaned into him. She rose and fell in short motions, savoring the feel of him. How he stretched her as she took him deeper.

"Take it, neva," he groaned as his head fell back. His hand was a vice on her waist, leading her movements. He yanked her down, forcing more of his thick shaft into her with each fall of her hips.

"Now," Dimitri said after the length of his cock was buried inside her. He held out her crown. "Lay your mark so I can fuck you properly."

Astrid took the Serpents' Crown and pressed the point of her finger against his chin, turning his head to the side. "Don't move," she said sweetly.

Heated gold and flesh hissed as she rolled the snake head across the side of his throat. Dimitri tensed beneath her but otherwise didn't move. She counted five of her heartbeats and meticulously removed her brand.

Astrid's magic flowed over him. She attempted to heal the wound to a scar, but his soul refused to obey.

"I can't heal you," Astrid said returning his attention to her. "Make it scar, or we'll do this every morning, my king."

Chapter Seventy

Dimitri focused his magic, repairing the brand instead of restoring his smooth skin. Astrid rocked her hips over his cock as she watched her mark become permanent.

Possessive little thing.

He took the Serpents' Crown and laid it on the nightstand before sweeping his wing over the bed in a sharp motion. The metallic sound of her pins and combs scattering across the floor filled the room and Astrid's nails dug into his throat.

"You are ruining my jewels," she hissed

Her grip wasn't strong enough to cut off his air and Dimitri leaned into her, tasting her lips. "I didn't want a hidden dagger stabbing my wife while I fuck her."

He held on to her as he got his legs under him. Her dark hair fanned over the sheets as her back met the bed. He moved with her, withdrawing to the tip then thrusting the hard length of his cock back inside. She took his thrusts, sighing as he fucked her slow and deep.

Astrid's palm pressed to his chest. Her nails bit into him, flexing each time he drove into her.

Her panting breaths. The way she tossed her head and tightened her thighs over his waist. The breathless sounds she made when he was buried inside her and twisted his hip. The blush trailing down her throat to bloom between her breasts. He adjusted his tempo to her subtle reactions.

"Give me your shadows," Astrid breathed.

Warmth spread through Dimitri's chest and his heart squeezed. She wanted his death magic. She viewed his ravenous shadows as a blessing.

Dimitri kissed her, loosening his hold on the ever-present hunger burning within him. His magic reached for her, caressed her. The sweet taste of her soul coated his tongue.

His shadows churned around them, spilling over their bed as he deepened their kiss. Dimitri savored the feel of her mouth, the taste of her soul.

Wispy notes of warmth accentuated her taste. It was lighter than honey. The sweetness was airy, like spun sugar. He'd tasted the heat of her temper and the rich notes of her schemes but *this...*

It was new and—Dimitri groaned when she sucked on his tongue. He tangled his hand in her hair, isolating this new taste.

Is this trust?

No, she trusted him. He laid two kingdoms at her feet. He would bring her the very stars if she loved him.

His mind blanked.

Could it be love? The culmination of the bond between them?

Please, let it be.

Astrid moaned and Dimitri swallowed her cries as she came around his cock. His shadows surrounded them, darkness lit with glimmers of Astrid's soul.

Dimitri relished her nails raking over his back. Cherished each time she came, screaming his name. He kept her slow rhythm and let his pleasure build. He imagined the life they would shape together. How he would sleep with her in his arms, and wake to her each morning.

He was hers and nothing would separate them.

The muscles in Dimitri's back tensed as his ecstasy mounted. He drove into her once. Twice.

He came hard, emptying himself into his wife.

His queen.

His fate.

Dimitri held her in the cage of his arms and Astrid absently stroked his hair as her breathing settled.

"I'm not sleeping like this," she said after a time, tracing the point of his ear. He pressed his lips to her throat and pulled away. Astrid took him by the wrist and tugged him forward. "I'm blaming the compulsive desire to shower on you."

He chuckled and paused when they entered her ensuite. "This will need to be adjusted," Dimitri said. Her shower was far too small for his wings.

"I'll arrange a new set of rooms tomorrow. You'll need to make do with this tonight, my king." Astrid kissed him and turned, entering her miniscule shower.

His wife cleaned herself and left him to struggle in the tight confines of her bathing apparatus.

Once dry, Dimitri stepped back into the room his wife had occupied as a princess. He'd expected to find her asleep, but Astrid stood on the balcony wrapped in a black robe with splashes of red florals.

He approached from behind her and pressed a kiss to her temple as he wrapped her in his arms. She leaned into him, maintaining her gaze on the lights of the town surrounding her palace.

Astrid traced circles over his wrist. "The Mothers laid you in my path."

"As you've told me many times," he murmured, content to simply hold her.

"You're the only male who could love all of me," she said.

She was vicious and bloodthirsty. Loyal and fearless. "We are the same, neva. And I would have no one else."

"The only male I…could ever love."

Dimitri held her closer and whispered, "My heart has been yours since the moment you stabbed it."

Astrid laughed and interlaced her fingers with his. She guided him to bed and curled up against his chest. Her bed was too small.

His wings hung off the mattress at odd angles that would ache come morning, but a calm settled over him as she fell asleep. It reminded him of the ease he felt in Astrid's presence, but it ran deeper.

It was peace. And he'd found it in her.

Dimitri gently stroked her hair as she slept. He didn't need titles or riches. Kingdoms and crowns were meaningless to him.

An eternity with her was all he needed.

Epilogue

Astrid stood side-by-side with Dimitri before a towering pair of double beam doors. Being locked out of the Three-Faced Mother's temple left her uneasy. She couldn't recall seeing them closed before and silently counted the serpents carved into the oak to calm her nerves.

The overlapping chatter of the crowd seeped into the palace hall. Ledivites and Clorean nobles crowded the pews and argued over their perceived importance.

"I don't see why they are making you wait," Dimitri said, out-stretching his wing.

Astrid tugged him back before his talon reached the doors. "Our guests are taking their seats. They're anxious to meet the King of Ledivion and the Queen of Clorea."

"They will meet the Queen of Ledivion and Clorea, escorted by her Death Spirit," Dimitri corrected.

"You're the only royal I've met who hates his crown," Astrid whispered.

He leaned into her and curled his index under her chin. Their lips met—the same reverent greeting he woke her with each morning.

"The only thing I desire is you," he whispered.

Astrid straightened, running her hands down her corset. "In truth, you desired a larger bed and shower," she reminded him.

He chuckled and the sound felt like a caress. "Fate blessed you with a Ledivite male."

She leaned into him and didn't immediately shove his bony appendage away when his wing curled around her. During the past week, earth weavers had built them a new suite, installed her birdcages throughout her throne room, and added the aquarium for Ambrose's eyes into the bed she shared with Dimitri.

The ambient conversations hushed to silence when the heavy doors parted. White marble silhouettes filled her view. The statue of the Three-Faced Mother holding a serpent in her cupped hands was visible first, followed by identical statues on either side of her. The doors opened wider, revealing the robed female on the left holding an egg and the snake's shed held by the figure on the right.

Astrid walked with her hand curved in the crook of Dimitri's arm. Crimson silk laced through her pauldron and paneled over her breasts. Her platinum corset accented with phoenix feathers caged her waist and the train behind her bled the red silk into black. From the back of her corset, dozens of delicate chains studded with hundreds of diamonds spilled across her skirt. Viktor had hand stitched each hinge into place along her train, orchestrating her vision of stars against the night sky.

She glanced at her sword as they passed both winged and non-winged guests. The sashed, flowing robes worn by male Clorean royals didn't suit him, but he'd worn crimson silk for her. Their joint kingdoms would witness Dimitri dressed as the King of Clorea, if only for today. Her husband was happy to fade into the shadows, but she would make certain their joint rule was recognized and acknowledged.

They reached the dais and took three short steps to stand before the Three-Faced Mother. A priestess stood behind the altar, where the Serpents' Crown rested at the center. Her black hair gleamed against her vermillion robes. The hooded cloak she wore mimicked the goddess behind her, obscuring her face.

She raised her arms out to either side and called, "Fate has drawn these souls together."

"For the serpent guides them," the crowd answered in unison.

The priestess lowered her hands and interlaced them in front of her. Two other priestesses dressed in the same manner joined her. They slid two wine glasses in front of Astrid and Dimitri, then filled them with red wine. A single golden chalice was placed between them.

Astrid and Dimitri turned to face each other. The heat in his molten gold eyes consumed her and he lifted his glass first.

"I accept my path and bind my fate to yours, daragája," Dimitri said, pouring every drop of his glass into the chalice.

Astrid held her glass, pressing it to her heart before lifting it in Dimitri's honor. The male who'd laid the stars at her feet. The male she loved and could now recognize was always her fate.

"I accept my path and bind my fate to yours," she said, emptying her glass into the chalice.

She lifted the heavy goblet and brought it to Dimitri's lips. He swallowed, brushing his fingers over hers as he took the cup symbolizing their shared life. He lowered the rim to her lips and the honeyed wine coated her tongue.

The priestesses spoke in unison as Dimitri returned the chalice to the altar.

"May your union be blessed by the Three-Faced Mother."

"And may the serpents guide you," the crowd answered.

Dimitri lifted the Serpents' Crown from the altar. The weight of it settled on her crown, and she gazed up at the sword fate had gifted her through her lashes.

"Her Majesty Astrid Noctis, Queen of Clorea and Ledivion, and His Majesty Dimitri, Queen Astrid's Death Spirit. Long may they reign."

"As their fates allow." Their audience's reply was more a cheer than prayer.

"Until the stars burn from the sky," Dimitri murmured before tasting her lips.

Astrid smiled, returned his kiss, then promised, "And the seas turn to ash."

Looking for more works by Kalista?

Step into *Invoking the Blood,* an enemies to lovers in a dark fantasy setting with Hades x Persephone vibes and vampires.

KALISTA NEITH

INVOKING THE BLOOD

AMMEWNITION STUDIOS

ARTITHIA • ANARIA • NECROMIA • HELL • CHAOS

One

The only thing worse than being surrounded by dark-bloods
was being surrounded by noisy drunk idiots playing dress up.
Every establishment would be like this tonight. Faye had no idea
how this ridiculous Hunter's Moon tradition started, but she wanted
to slap the moron who brought it about. Glancing over the crowded
bar with a sigh, she picked at her dinner. The smell of cooked meats
wafted through the air, interrupted by the scent of cheap cologne.
Faye impatiently waited for the appropriate amount of time to pass
so she could conclude her birthday celebration without her sister's
objections.

Sparrow kicked her under the table, leaving Faye's shin stinging.
"At least pretend to be having fun, bitch. You're spacing out over
there."

"Do you see what we're surrounded by?" Lost and Found, a

popular pub in the merchant district, was full of people wearing glamoured fangs, elaborate costumes, and theater blood dripping from the corners of their mouths. Drunken masses decided it would be great fun to masquerade as vampires and prance beneath the glow of tonight's red moon.

Sparrow's eyes widened bringing her fingertips to her lips. "By the Darkness, people are having fun." She threw back her shot of whiskey, slamming it on the table. "You're having fun tonight even if I have to beat it into you."

She beamed, looking past Faye. Dark-blooded men were all the same with one exception, Vashien, her sister's beloved, coincidentally the only man to last more than a few months with her sister as well.

He was the only man who made Sparrow light up every time she saw him. Faye always thought he was kind and settled some of Sparrow's wild energy. Though she suspected Vashien's acceptance stemmed more from his relationship with her sister Sparrow than a liking for her.

Vashien moved through the crowd, shoving some of the more inebriated patrons with his green membranous reptilian wings. Artithians were a large, winged race, but even by their standards, he was big. Faye smiled at the colorful, glittering cake he held, looking tiny in his hands. A sparkler jabbed into it.

"Happy birthday," Vashien said, his smile warm and genuine. Giving Faye a squeeze with one arm, he set the cake down in front of her. Moving to Sparrow's side, he thumped her with his wing. "Are you behaving and keeping the birthday girl entertained?"

She snorted, shoving at him. "Faye doesn't want to be entertained."

He nodded, sliding his fingers under Sparrow's plate. "Are you done with this?"

Holding her fork like it was a weapon, she said, "Take my food, and I'll stab you."

Faye giggled as Vashien held his hand up in peace and leaned down for a kiss. Glancing at their drinks, he nodded to Faye. "I'll get you two topped off."

Sparrow leaned back in her chair, craning her neck to watch Vashien leave.

"What are you even staring at? You can't even see his ass when his wings are folded like that."

Sparrow fluttered her hand at Faye. Sister code for *shut up, I'm busy*. "Get your own man to ogle." Turning back, she lifted her second shot glass while pointing at Faye's drink. "I think Vash only keeps that shit on hand for you."

Faye raised her glass of pomegranate juice, swirling the dark red liquid and smirked at her sister. "What about that shit? I can smell it from here."

"Touché," was her only reply before throwing back another shot. Sparrow's gaze fell to the decorated chocolate cake. She leaned forward. "Are you going to eat that?" Without waiting for a response, Sparrow stabbed her fork into Faye's cake, taking a bite. "Wow, that shit is good."

Faye pulled the extinguished sparkler free and set it on the side of the plate before nudging the rest toward her sister. She didn't understand how Sparrow ate so much and stayed so tiny.

Faye's gaze rose to the open dark wood beams along the high ceiling. The tavern was warm and welcoming. Clothed tables were arranged through the front of Lost and Found for those who wanted a hearty meal. The back and loft hosted three bars, two on the lower level and one above. She smiled when she spied a large sign on the railing above. *No flying*. That was new.

Faye could only imagine the drunken Artithian who thought it would be brilliant to fly to the lower level instead of taking the stairs. She would have paid a gold mark to see Vashien's face if anyone tried.

"It's your birthday so you get to pick. And these are the only options. Either we sneak into the Hunter's Moon Ball at the High Queen's castle, *orrrrr* we sneak into the Hunter's Moon Ball at the High Queen's castle? Great options, right?"

Faye's brow furrowed. Sparrow had been this way since they were children, wanting to shove every experience into her life. Insisting, *the consequences will be worth the memory*. But this was a bad idea even by Sparrow's standards. Vampires lusted during the Hunter's Moon. The High Queen of Necromia was a Pure Blood, one of the only two left. A born vampire. She held her annual celebration for all her kind at her estate while the pretend vamps partied in places like Lost and Found.

Faye frowned. "You've lost your shit."

Her long, wavy blonde hair fluffed as she bounced in her chair, whining, "Come on, I want to see the vampire orgy."

Of course, she did. "We're not going. There are two kinds of attendees at the ball, vampires and blood whores. And we're not vampires so are you offering up your blood and flesh for coin this evening?"

Sparrow rolled her eyes and plopped her chin in her hand, pouting as she looked away. "They don't know we're not vampires."

Even with the best disguise, their heartbeats would give them away to start. Lack of fangs. Revulsion to drinking blood.

"Excuse me, ladies," a man said, interrupting their argument, flashing his glamoured fangs.

Sparrow straightened, returning a smile as Faye glared at her for encouraging him.

"May I inquire what court you beauties belong to?" The man clasped his wrists in front of him.

Faye didn't need to look at him further. The dark-blooded shard on his index finger told her everything she needed to know. All magic was a gift from the Darkness, borrowed through life and returned in death. Soul shards served as an external indication of the depth of power housed within the individual, divided into two castes: the dark-bloods and the day-bloods. The tendrils within the swirling mist determined which caste they belonged to. White tendrils were day-bloods, black tendrils, dark. The darker the mist surrounding the shard, the stronger the individual. These small marquise-cut crystals dictated a person's worth and social standing, as though magic was all that mattered in life.

She glanced up at the stranger, the words of polite refusal frozen on her tongue. Faye studied his face. "Who are you dressed as?" The man wore cheap costume accessories like everyone else celebrating tonight, but veined misted shadows swayed beneath his eyes, brushing the tops of his cheekbones. The light caught Faye's ring as she sipped her juice.

"A Pure Blood." The man answered cheerily, looking down at her hand. The corner of Faye's mouth turned down, instantly souring her mood. He'd been polite because he thought she was one of them. She shoved it underneath the table. Faye's ring was a fake, displaying a soul shard Sparrow charged with her power to mirror her dark-blooded shard.

"You have the wrong hair if you're masquerading as the Shadow Prince," Sparrow interjected.

This man's dark mass of curls was all wrong. Rumor said his hair was long and white. From her seat, she could pick out a handful of the crowd dressed as him, but she'd never seen anyone pair bad eyeliner with the glamoured fangs. She answered dark-bloods in the same manner as their requests. He had been polite, so she returned the favor.

Plastering a false smile, Faye inclined her head. "I'm sorry. I must decline your advances." The words of protocol within the dark-blooded courts to tactfully decline romantic interest.

The man placed his hand to his chest. "Of course. I belong to the Court of Silver Leaves if you have a change of heart." He bowed and turned away from them, disappearing into the crowd.

As an Anarian, she was either propositioned or ignored. The ones who deigned to speak to her acted as though she should be grateful to catch a dark-blood's eye. Eyeing her ring again, Faye glanced from her hand to Sparrow's, comparing the two, unable to discern the difference. This simple fraudulent piece of jewelry allowed her to walk freely in Necromia. The energy Sparrow put into it would fade over time, seeping from a shard never meant to hold its power. It would be empty by morning.

Many Anarians dreamed of being chosen by a dark-blood, their life ambition to live within their lavish dark courts. As a pet. They would have material things and want for little, but it came at a cost Faye wasn't willing to pay. Being a pet meant someone owned you. A possession to be stroked and touched when they pleased.

Sparrow slouched in her chair. "You should give them a chance."

Faye narrowed her eyes at her sister. She'd given them chances in the beginning, hoping to be seen for who she was, instead of the soul shard she lacked. Experience taught her how young and naive she'd been. But looking back, it had been glaringly evident from the beginning. Sparrow had waited a month for Faye to turn twenty so they could invoke their blood together. They traveled to Necromia. Sparrow insisted on invoking her blood at the largest of the blood temples, deeming it good luck, but when she failed, she knew what fate lay ahead. That day the entire walk back no one had met Faye's gaze. She'd come there full of hope and left an Anarian, a shardless, powerless mortal.

"No," was her only reply as she looked down at her drink.

Sparrow tapped the table, pulling Faye from her pained memories. "Vampire orgy?" Sparrow's green eyes lit with excitement.

Faye fell back in her chair, looking upward. "You ask every year."

"And every year, I hope you grow some balls so we can go." Sparrow tilted her head, staring at her expectantly. As though she were asking for something normal, like going to the bakery. "I can't *not* know things. Please."

"Dark-bloods already surround me. Why would I agree to be surrounded by more dark-bloods? *Blood sucking* dark-bloods."

Sparrow slouched. "They're not all bad." Her sister, forever the optimist. They weren't bad to her. She was one of them.

"They are, and I can prove it," Faye said casually, inspecting her nails. They'd baited each other with those words since they were girls. Sparrow leaned forward, her green eyes gleaming. "What are we betting?"

"We'll go to the Hunter's Moon ball. I'll give you five minutes to find me a day-blood among them. When you lose, we never go again. You stop trying to set me up on dates and let me die a virgin in peace."

Her sister narrowed her eyes, scrutinizing her. "If I win, you have to go on five dates and be *nice*. And we go to the Hunter's Moon ball every year. I need an hour to find a day-blood. Blood whores count, right? Anyone in attendance."

Faye nodded. "Ten minutes, unless one of them tries to bite me. Then you lose, and we leave."

Sparrow smiled, waving her hand. "They won't even see you. Thirty minutes."

"Fifteen."

"Deal." Sparrow beamed.

Vashien returned with their drinks. Sparrow took her glass of whiskey and swallowed the contents in one gulp.

She set the glass down and got to her feet. "Faye agreed to fun!"

She swatted Vashien's ass as she happily made her way to the door. Faye glanced at her pomegranate juice, feeling guilty for letting it go to waste. "I'm sorry."

Vashien smiled reassuringly at her. "I'll put it in the batch going to the cottage. What kind of fun did she talk you into?" Vashien stacked their dishes waiting for her answer.

"Sparrow said it was a surprise." Faye lied, knowing Vashien would stop them if he knew what they were about to do.

Vashien nodded, picking the dishes up. "Well, be safe. Don't let Sparrow make too many bad decisions."

Faye smiled and waved as she weaved through the crowded tavern, making her way to the door.

Sparrow already had their coats. Faye took hers, pulling it on. "In a hurry, hooker?"

Sparrow bumped the swinging oak door open with her hip, her winter coat half on. "I'm trying to get there before you change your mind." Pulling her coat on completely, she hopped in place, holding the door open. "Let's go. Let's go."

Faye stepped out into the night, the brisk chill biting her cheeks. She glanced up at the red moon hanging full in the night sky.

"This way." Sparrow took her wrist and led her through the city streets, lined with shops and tall buildings.

They crossed several blocks before Faye finally asked, "Do you know where you're going?"

"Darkness, walking sucks. Remind me to take phasing lessons next year."

Faye laughed. Sparrow would complain a few times every year but never learned the teleporting skill most dark-bloods used to travel anywhere they'd been previously.

"We're almost there." Sparrow pointed to a stone spire that rose above the shop buildings.

They stopped a block away, at the outskirts of the city.

Faye stared at the open courtyard. "I think we're underdressed." Dozens of people were entering the courtyard, dressed in ornate gowns. Their hair arranged and pinned, some in beautiful curls and others wore strings of glittering jewels woven into their elaborate braids. The men accompanying them wore tailored suits. "This doesn't look like the vampire orgy you've been dreaming of." Faye stuffed her hands in her pockets to fight off the cold of the winter night. She looked on at the people entering suspiciously. How were they not cold? None of them had coats. Not even a shawl.

"They're probably blood whores." Sparrow shrugged. "Orgies won't happen outside where anyone could see them."

Sparrow squeezed her wrist, and warmth spread over her body. "Sight shield. We're invisible."

Faye skeptically glanced down at herself, then Sparrow. "I can still see you."

"That's because it's the same spell." Sparrow punched her in the arm.

Rubbing her arm, Faye looked at her sideways. "Are you sure?" Sparrow shrugged. "New spell. Let's see."

Faye stood in shock for a moment as Sparrow bolted for the courtyard. Faye dashed after her, catching up as she waved a hand in front of a man in a gray suit. Faye mouthed, *What are you doing?*

"Relax, he's a baby dark-blood. You can talk. We're invisible, and they can't hear us." To the man, she yelled, "Can you?" Sparrow smiled at Faye triumphantly.

"Fifteen minutes," Faye whispered.

Sparrow waved her on, slipping further into the courtyard.

Faye followed cautiously and could scarcely believe what she saw.

The air carried a heavy floral scent. Twinkling lights laced intricate archways. Beautifully manicured plants and flowers surrounded grand fountains—pathways carved through the grounds with wrought iron benches scattered throughout. A string quartet played, setting the mood.

Beyond the hedged walls of the gardens rose a massive stone structure with several turrets arching high at different heights.

"I'm not burning my fifteen minutes here." Sparrow linked arms with Faye pulling her forward.

Faye followed, nearly tripping over Sparrow when they passed a woman seated on a male's lap on one of the benches. His mouth pressed to her throat as she clung to him. Her nails dug into the dark material of his suit jacket.

Faye could only watch, knowing she was invading the couple's intimate exchange but couldn't bring herself to look away. She abstained from sex, unwilling to surrender what little control she still had over her life. But this give and take between them appealed to her. Faye could see the woman led their exchange. Her vampire surrendered, receiving what she offered. An intoxicating dynamic Faye was nearly tempted to try.

The woman's moans of pleasure followed Faye as Sparrow led her further in. They snuck into the inner courtyard within the estate's towering stone walls. Sparrow followed the sounds of guttural groans and screams of pleasure. Faye knew vampires lusted tonight, but she expected them to have restraint. Or even modesty.

Vampires were no shy creatures. Couples and groups writhed in the darkened corners, a few even taking them on the benches for all to see. Another pair sat at the fountain's edge. This man had his hand up the woman's skirt as he drank from her—blood dripping along her bared skin.

Sparrow glanced back at her, her eyes gleaming with excitement. "This is amazing."

Amazing? Faye would have been shocked by such displays if Sparrow hadn't dragged her to several brothels, deeming it educational to watch when they reached eighteen and moved out on their own. "Drink it all in because you're about to lose in thirteen minutes."

Faye pulled her arm free from Sparrow when she got far too close to a woman being taken by two vampire men. "You don't have to be that close." Sparrow only fluttered her hand in response, and Faye rolled her eyes, stepping away from the trio.

Musk combined with the night-blooming flowers, scenting the air. It wasn't *entirely* unpleasant, though she could do without the overlapping sounds of bodies joining. Faye glanced over her surroundings, focusing on the more civilized vampires.

A large balcony overlooked the courtyard. Beneath it, dozens of vampires danced. Their gowns swayed with each sweeping step as they turned, circling the dance floor with their partners.

Faye watched, mesmerized.

A bell tolled, the single ring clear and crisp, reverberating through her chest. Faye swore under her breath, blinking her eyes as they began to burn.

"You okay?" Sparrow rubbed her back and led her away to a quieter area.

Faye rubbed her eyes. "I have a lash in my eye or something. We should go. It's one in the morning."

Sparrow snorted. "That wasn't the time." She tapped Faye's wrist. "Let me see."

Faye opened her eyes wide, meeting Sparrow's gaze. "What is it then?"

"Their sacred moon is at its apex. They're supposed to do a ritual." She scrunched her face, leaning closer. "Your eyes are shimmering."

"It's just the lights here." Faye rubbed her eyes, beginning to feel better. She blinked, testing her vision, then focused on her sister. "I'm so proud of you, doing research."

"I wouldn't have to if you had the balls to go the first time I asked." Sparrow's eyes grew wide at something behind her. "Bitch they have food here."

Faye let Sparrow drag her to a towering, intricate display of tiny plates arranged with fresh-cut flowers. "Do vampires even eat?"

Sparrow shrugged. "Maybe it's for the blood whores." She picked up a flaky square.

"What are you doing?"

"Sampling the High Queen's menu." Sparrow popped the pastry in her mouth and leaned back, closing her eyes. "That is the best shit I've ever tasted. You need to try this." She stood on her toes, looking around the courtyard. "Do you see any other food stations?"

"No!"

"Stop worrying. They can't see us. Here, try this." Sparrow thrusted a pastry near Faye's mouth.

"Hooker, get off me." Faye pulled her head back, taking a retreating step. Her heel caught on a stone, and Faye lost her balance, falling against a hard, male body.

Sparrow snatched her by her coat and yanked her away before she broke into a run, laughing.

Faye's heart raced. She expected Sparrow to be the one to do something stupid like this. She glanced over her shoulder as they fled.

The man she fell into was tall with long white-blonde hair that looked silvery under the courtyard lights. He wore a tailored black suit like every other male here. He turned in their direction, and Faye's steps faltered.

A crimson so deep it looked black covered the entirety of his eyes. Beneath his unnatural stare, shadows swayed, caressing the tops of his cheekbones, beckoning her. No, not shadows Faye realized, but the same mist that circled soul shards. The Darkness itself seemed to pour and dissipate beneath his dark gaze.

A wild sense of possession surged through her before leaving as quickly as it came. In those moments in between, she felt, *knew*, he belonged to her.

Faye mentally recoiled, unable to shake the lingering bone-deep instinct. She didn't want to own anyone. His dark gaze met hers, and Faye couldn't look away. Her lips parted as she exhaled a shaky breath, her skin heating in response to him.

He lifted his chin, taking a deep breath as his lids slid closed.

Faye remembered herself and turned away. What was wrong with her? "Sparrow, we need to leave."

Sparrow snorted, glancing back at her. "Fifteen minutes bitch."

"The guy I ran into is *sniffing*." They'd stopped at the opposite side of the courtyard near the ornate fountain, between two couples, feeding.

Sparrow's gaze bounced from the male, nuzzling a woman's throat to Faye. "But he's not *biting*, so we stay."

At her sister's words, Faye imagined she was seated on her vampire's lap. His long, elegant fingers traced circles on her thigh, inching higher with each rotation. Her nails scratched against the dark material of his jacket as his lips brushed the side of her neck.

"Figures, you would trip over the Shadow Prince." Sparrow glanced back at the man, who now walked to a more secluded corner of the courtyard.

He couldn't be. "How do you know who he is?"

"We're at the Hunter's Moon ball. Who else would dress like him.?"

"You think he's the only white-haired vampire?" Faye glanced back in his direction. She watched him, making sure he stayed on his side of the courtyard.

Sparrow hit Faye in the arm. "Look, it's the High Queen. Ritual time."

Faye followed Sparrow's gaze.

The High Queen stood at the center of the balcony, smiling at her guests. Her corseted gown tucked into every curve, accentuating her figure. Moonlight gleaming off the jeweled pins and combs in her shoulder-length rich brown hair tinged with bronze, she carried an effortlessly elegant air to herself.

The string quartet stopped playing as the guests silenced their chatter. Every attendee stood, focusing on their queen.

"Tonight, we give thanks to the Darkness," The High Queen's melodic voice carried through the courtyard.

Faye watched the High Queen raise a champagne flute. Her eyes darkened until they mirrored *his*. Faye's gaze snapped to the vampire she ran into earlier. The Shadow Prince. He watched the High Queen from a secluded alcove away from the crowd. A beautiful, dangerous male.

"For the wish granted that gave us life. Join me now as we cast our wishes to the Darkness." The High Queen continued.

Sparrow leaned closer to Faye. "This is not the vampire orgy I've dreamed of."

Faye glanced down at Sparrow and pouted her bottom lip. "Sad face."

"I'm stealing a plate of their food, and then we can go." Sparrow uncaringly walked around the vampires, who closed their eyes as they bowed their heads, making her way back to the food station.

The silence unnerved Faye. She crept around the solemn faces, her gaze wandering to the alcove. He bowed his head like the rest of them, clasping his wrist in front of him.

I wish for an equal.

Startled, Faye turned toward the voice, finding nothing. She heard a deep male voice; he spoke against her ear just behind her. Faye patted Sparrow's back. "Did you hear that?"

Sparrow turned, holding a plate piled with pastries. "Hear what?"

"Somebody wished for an equal."

Sparrow snorted. "Nope." She looked around at the motionless vampires. "I didn't spot any day-bloods. I would be upset about losing if they didn't get so boring. Let's go."

Faye followed Sparrow, taking one last look at the Hunter's Moon ball. At the rings housing their dark-blooded soul shards. They were all dark-bloods, Faye realized. She took a sweeping glance over the attendants. Not a day-blood among them.

Dark-bloods looked down on her kind. On anything weaker than them. They loved power, seeking out others they deemed equals.

Pain and anger whispered through her veins. She thought of all the times a dark-blood had dismissed her. Every dark-blood that wanted her, but only as a pet. She'd learned they couldn't hurt her if she rejected them first.

She thought of the deep male voice and willed all her seething frustration and hurt into a reply she cried in her mind. *I can hear you, but you're no equal to me.* A message to every dark-blood she'd met. Every dark-blood she had yet to meet. Her promise.

She would refuse them all.

Glad the night was over, Faye joined Sparrow on the street as they strolled away from the High Queen's estate back into the city.

"Did you have fun?" Sparrow linked arms with her and glanced in her direction, suddenly halting her steps. She leaned one way then the other, staring at her eyes. "Your eyes don't hurt?"

"What's wrong with them?"

"You're going to a healer." Sparrow grabbed her wrist and began leading her through the streets.

"I can't see a healer here." They were in Necromia, and she was wearing a fake dark-blooded soul shard.

The castes were more than just the soul shards. Dark-bloods didn't recognize her as a person. To them, she was nothing more than an animal. They refused to wait on her or let her purchase goods. The healers didn't waste their time on her kind.

"I'm dark-blooded, and I say they will." Being on the darker side of the spectrum among the dark-blooded, Sparrow always forced the issue.

"I feel fine. Let's just go home."

Sparrow pulled her up the stone stairs and pushed open a door. "Hello?"

The reception area of the clinic was small but well lit. The walls were painted in neutral earth tones. A middle-aged woman with a healer insignia on her chest came to the front desk. "How can we help you?"

"She needs to be seen. Her eyes are changing color."

Faye stiffened, apprehensive as the woman looked her up and down before she approached, pausing on her ring. She peered at her eyes, leaning closer. "That is peculiar."

Peculiar? What the hell did that mean? She smacked Sparrow, staring straight ahead so the healer could continue her inspection.

"What do you mean my eyes are changing color?"

The healer flattened her palm over Faye's eye, and warmth spread over the side of Faye's face.

Sparrow tried to bury her worry, but Faye could see it. "You have yellow streaks through your eyes."

"Well, the good news is I don't feel any damage." The healer flattened her palm over Faye's other eye.

The warmth covered the side of Faye's face and faded when the healer let her go.

"You should spend the night. If anything changes, we'll be here to heal you. I can recheck you in the morning." The healer motioned for them to follow her.

Faye glanced at Sparrow, who gave her a stern look and pointed after the healer. Defeated, Faye followed the healer to a small, furnished room with a single bed under a window.

As they entered, the healer asked, "Which court do you belong to?"

"Sparrow's Song," Sparrow answered.

The nurse nodded and closed the door.

"What are you doing?" Faye hissed, heading straight to the mirror over the dresser.

"Making sure you don't wake up blind."

Faye leaned closer, inspecting her eyes. Thin streaks of gold slashed through her black irises. She turned to face Sparrow. "You don't belong to a court." A fact the healer would find out in the morning when she invoiced a court that didn't exist. Or worse, it did, and Sparrow was sending them a bill.

"She doesn't know that." Sparrow settled in an overstuffed chair with her plate of stolen pastries. "If you don't get in that bed, I'm going to take it, and you can sleep in the chair."

"You can turn into a cat. We both fit on the bed." Neither of them knew their race, having grown up in an orphan home. Sparrow claimed Familiar, a race of secretive people who served the realm Chaos and worshiped fate, enabling them to see the future. Sparrow's chaotic nature and petite, voluptuous figure fit the race's characteristics. Her ability to turn into a small, fluffy, white cat when they were young girls was what convinced her. A trait only inherited by Familiar.

Sparrow rolled her eyes. "Last time I slept with you as a cat, you tried to suffocate me."

"We were seven."

"Which makes it worse now because I'm still the same size, and you have gotten much heavier."

Faye tucked into bed, glaring at Sparrow. "One time." She held the ring out at Sparrow. "Charge this."

"I'll do it in the morning before we leave."

Curling under the blankets, Faye debated on what worried her more—being dragged before the city's ruling court or the possibility of going blind.

Blindness won by a sliver.

Faye glanced out the window, looking up at the full moon that glowed blood red. She closed her eyes, enjoying the softness of the bed and how silky the sheets felt. Dark-bloods were spoiled things. Even the beds for their sick were fancy.

She took a last look at Sparrow, "Goodnight, hooker."

"Good night, bitch."

Two

Rune would never admit it aloud, but his existence was lonely. Leaning against the railing of the balcony, he glanced down at the masses who crowded the courtyard below him. The night garden was in full bloom, lending its sweet fragrance to the air. His gaze rose to the Hunter's Moon. It sang to a vampire's bloodlust, driving the desire to drink or for sex to a fever pitch.

Rune had never experienced such a pull. Not once in over three thousand years. He dreamt of reaching his twentieth year in his youth, wanting to feel it. He heard stories of how blood tasted richer. Vampires warned when he drank beneath the Hunter's Moon. It would ruin him, that he'd crave it until the following year when he could once again drink under the sway of the moon.

They described sex in the same way. That he should find an accommodating female vampire, so on edge, a brush of his fingers in the right place would bring her off.

"I brought you fresh blood since you're obviously not partaking," a woman said. But Rune knew that voice anywhere. Her scent of honey and citrus, covered with perfume deemed popular by the nobles for the time being, filled the space they stood in now.

"Ignoring your guests?"

The string quartet below played an eerie and sensuous melody.

It was a hypnotic trance lulling its prey to dance. Rune turned around, his eyes narrowing at her perfect appearance, taking the offered glass. He didn't participate in the showy preening for the houses and courts established in wealth or nobility. Lyssa seemingly thrived on it, relishing the opportunity to lord her status above others. From her silvery satin gown, tailored for this occasion, to her rich brown hair painstakingly pinned and styled. Despite her outward perfection, Lyssa's emotions tasted as they always did.

A lusting want soured with fear. He tasted a variation of this on every woman he'd come across. Some men as well.

Rune secretly longed for a woman who didn't fear him. But after century upon century of disappointment and embarrassment, he ceased looking. He was a Pure Blood, separated from the dancing fools below him as the turned vampires were from their originating species. They were vampires, turned who transitioned in death with vampiric blood in their system.

Pure Bloods were gifted with many abilities: strength, speed, heightened senses, and the ability to taste the emotions of those around them. But cursed with true bloodlust, far greater than the shadowed urges the turned felt.

The Ra'Voshnik was an entity separate from himself yet existing within him. The balance for his dark gifts tied him in a shared existence with a volatile creature he kept subdued.

"I think half of my guests only attend to catch a glimpse of you." Lyssa glanced in his direction momentarily before returning her attention to the masses.

He found crowds to be exhausting and lived a secluded, private life. When he was forced to attend a public gathering, the Ra'Voshnik picked up the scent of fear, fixating on what it considered prey. Which subsequently moved Rune to mentally hold its murderous urges at bay.

"I believe they are here in hopes of catching the attention of a darker court." Rune spared Lyssa a passing glance before teasing, "Or perhaps they wish to taste your wares." He could feel her glaring at him but continued to watch the vampires below. A bell tolled behind them, carrying across the courtyard.

"I should cut out your insolent tongue."

Rune knew he was undoubtedly a curiosity rarely seen in the flesh, but their presence at Lyssa's ball had nothing to do with him. This was a chance to see and be seen by other dark established courts.

Courts were a means of protection, typically forming around and led by a woman. Lyssa's mother, Belind, decreed a single law during her rule as High Queen of Necromia. Rape was punishable by death. The sentence was carried out by the ruler of the realm. Any other dispute, including murder, was to be resolved between the courts. Belonging to a strong court meant protection. Safety. Power.

The corner of his mouth lifted in a smirk. "You like my tongue when I care to use it."

He half expected another barb or a possible knife between his ribs. Lyssa quieted, folding her hands on the railing. "Will you see me tonight?"

Rune's gaze lifted to the Hunter's Moon. He took a deep breath and slowly exhaled. He'd been her consort once, over a dozen centuries ago. He tended to her now and again at her request, after he relinquished the title of consort.

More than a decade had passed since the last time he obliged her. She'd taken other lovers but always came back to him. His attempt to make light of their past prompted her to ask him to visit her bed.

"I think you should find a man who feels the same way toward you, that you feel toward him." He wasn't purposefully being unkind. This was for the best.

It didn't matter how well she masked her fear or schooled her expression. He could taste it on her. And with the taste of fear, his body refused to respond. The part of him she wanted most held no interest. He could service her with his hands and mouth, but she deserved more than that.

He deserved more than that.

"I am sorry." He brushed the back of his fingers over her arm.

"Thank you, Shadow Prince." She kept her eyes forward, standing tall. Regal. Dismissing him with his title.

Rune inclined his head. "High Queen."

Leaving the glass balanced on the railing, he phased away from Lyssa, materializing near the food station. This late in the evening, the blood whores would be engaged in—

Someone fell into him, elbowing him just under his ribs. His fangs lengthened with aggression as the Ra'Voshnik charged to the surface in a rush hungry for violence.

It bled through his eyes, coloring them a deep crimson as veined misted shadows crept from beneath his gaze, swaying over the tops of his cheekbones. A trait received when the original Pure Bloods drank the Darkness. It tore through their systems, transforming them.

Rune turned, seeing no one as a pair of footfalls retreated away from him. A scent carried to him, clean and subtle. A night breeze through plum blossoms. His fangs sharpened as an unfamiliar feeling settled over him.

Vsenia, the Ra'Voshnik purred deep in his mind.

His brows lowered in concern. Vsenia was High Tongue, loosely translated to *cherished beloved*. He'd grown used to the constant stream of aggression, the Ra'Voshnik whispering from the recesses of his mind he'd chained it to. Never in all his years had it behaved in this manner, thrashing wildly against his hold, urging him to find her. A loyal dog eager to get back to its master.

Rune leashed the Ra'Voshnik, cruelly tightening his hold until it fell silent. He listened, tracking the slowing footsteps until they stopped near the fountain he'd wager. He waited for the sight shields to drop, impatient for his first glance of the dark-blooded vampire who unwittingly brought the Ra'Voshnik's viciousness to heel.

He lifted his chin and inhaled as his lids slid shut. Her scent calmed his mind, sharpening his focus until she was all that remained. A long-forgotten feeling snaked through him. Rune opened his eyes, focusing on the place she stood, wrapped in a sight shield.

Movement caught his attention, and Rune cursed. Delilah stood within his line of sight, mere feet beyond his true interest. She raised her glass at him and smiled coyly. The dark-haired queen made his skin crawl. She ruled over the Court of Lace and Bone, a ruthless court that had a reputation for their sadistic appetites when they warred and captured rival courts.

Rune ignored her invitation, uncaring if he offended her. She could send her court for him if she wished. He would send them back to her. In pieces.

He turned, heading to a quiet, darkened alcove and Lyssa's voice pulled him from his musings.

He looked toward the balcony as she used a spell to carry her voice over the courtyard. She held up the glass he left on the railing in salute, reciting pretty words Belind once used. The festivities concluded with a wish to the Darkness, a tradition honoring the creation of the Pure Bloods.

He'd been a fledgling eager for his first centuries of life the last time he participated in this ancient ritual. Rune bowed his head and closed his eyes, his mind descending within himself.

Possessing a soul shard tied the mind to a great psychic ravine, allowing individuals to turn inward and descend to the depths of their power, to a space beneath the physical world—a private intangible place within themselves where it was stored and drawn. Within the ravine that cradled the Darkness were a few shared spaces. The Pure Blood's birthplace being one of them.

His shoes sank into the fine white sand as he materialized in the small cove. A steep cliffside rose out of sight to his back, and before him, the Darkness ascended in a towering wall.

It raged and coiled in on itself. Black, pulsating mist. The outer wisps and tendrils lined in a deep glowing purple. Rune listened to the low roar as it coiled onto itself and took the subtle mental shift to stand at the depth of his power.

I wish for an equal.

Rune mentally projected the words as he did each year during his first few centuries, hoping to be answered by a dark-blooded vampire who would match him in strength. He ran his hand over his mouth, feeling the accumulation of his many years.

He'd made a choice long ago during his first century. As he matured into what he was and the power he wielded, he saw two clearly defined paths before him: embrace the lessons and training that forged him into a terrifying weapon for his court's arsenal or squander his gift and strength to prove he wasn't a threat. Live as every other man, building a life with a partner he would trust and be devoted to.

He'd chosen the former, becoming the deadliest soul to walk the realms.

He thought of the life he had forsaken from time to time. Envied people who'd found their partners. Useless thoughts that pained him when he let his mind dwell. Knowing if he had to choose again, his choice would remain the same.

His mind wandered to his night breeze and he found himself full of questions. What had she wished for? What court did she belong to? Would his interest fade as the Hunter's Moon set? Rune couldn't decide if he wanted the feelings she stirred in him to stay or fade with the night.

He ascended, returning to his physical body, and opened his eyes.

The balcony was empty, and the night concluded. Guests would linger for another hour or so before returning to their courts and estates. Rune scented the air for his night breeze.

A mental sending struck his mind hard enough to make him flinch.

I can hear you, but you're no equal to me.

The Ra'Voshnik tore from his hold the moment her voice filled his mind, urging him to find her.

The corners of his mouth curled of their own accord as black bled through his gaze. His night breeze had steel to her backbone. Perhaps this would carry past the night. She held a shard of Darkness if she heard his wish. Strong enough not to fear him. A young vampiress who could accept his nature and darker urges.

He purred through the mental communication tether she established to his mind. *Good evening, my Lady.*

Courting was a delicate dance among the dark-blooded. One the woman controlled. Rune needed to meet her and learn what court she belonged to. He would send a letter of intent, seeking permission to pursue her romantically, accompanied by a talisman connected to his mind. If she accepted his advances, she would use it to speak to him.

Rune waited for her reply as he strolled through Lyssa's private gardens away from the lingering crowd. He walked past manicured rose bushes, the blooming black roses' sweet scent carrying to him.

He debated taking a flower for his night breeze. Who had yet to answer him.

She hadn't withdrawn her tether but remained silent. Rune slipped his power down the connection between them. The lick of force he used as a mental nudge touched an impressive mental shield. Withdrawing, Rune brushed his fingertips over an open bloom.

Rune was nothing if not patient. He bowed in the direction of the public courtyard to his unseen Lady and phased to his home in Hell.

The dark stone walls of his bedroom came into sharp focus.

Hell's ever-twilight sky streamed into his room through tall narrow windows evenly spaced along the exterior wall. A simple desk was arranged beneath the windows, and a four-post bed made of dark wood dominated the opposite wall. Dark silk draped over the posts, matching his sheets.

The Ra'Voshnik stirred, growing restless as it realized the object of its affection was no longer in its proximity. The creature's urgings were easy enough to control. The twinge in his chest was another matter. Rune rubbed his thumb over his sternum at the strange sensation. Not pain, but something akin to sadness. He unfastened his cuffs, deciding to reevaluate himself after the night passed.

He stripped, showered, and retired to his bed. Tucking a hand behind his head and gazing at the vaulted ceiling. He would find out which court she belonged to tomorrow and write his letter of intent. His mind drifted, leading him to thoughts of her. Her scent captivated him. He wanted to hold her close, purring in contentment. Rune closed his eyes. His breathing became deep and even as he drifted to sleep.

He wasn't sure how much time passed when soft images surfaced in his mind.

A woman held his hand. His vision cleared enough to see her while everything else remained blurred and dark. She walked ahead of him. Her arm outstretched and fingers twined with his as he followed her lead. Her long black hair fell between a pair of delicately boned reptilian wings. The iridescent scales glimmered in the soft light.

Rune glanced upward as their surroundings took shape. He followed her through a meadow in the moonlight. "Where are we headed this evening?" he asked, brushing his thumb over the back of her hand.

She turned her head slightly as she led him through the field. Not enough to glimpse her face, merely an acknowledgment she heard him. "You'll see."

The images faded as her words echoed, sounding far away. Rune's consciousness slipped once more, and he drifted back to sleep.

Hours later, Rune's lids fluttered as another dream softly drifted over his mind. He recognized the location through his slow, hazy awareness. Tall, dark wood bookshelves lined the walls, containing a number of tomes he studied out of in his youth. He comfortably sat lengthwise with his night breeze in his study on a settee before the fireplace. She curled against him between his legs, reading a book with her back to the fire. Its light danced over her smooth tanned skin.

"Good evening, my Lady."

She didn't respond. Rune couldn't see her face from this angle, only the tip of her nose and a teasing glimpse of her dark lips as she muttered to herself while she read.

"Are you enjoying your book?"

"I was."

Rune smiled at her teasing tone. She was warm. Having her in his arms felt so right. He ran his fingers through her hair, and she sighed, tilting her head to rest on his chest.

"Grant me your name."

He felt her shoulders slump. "You're ruining the mood, big guy." Rune conceded to silence and let her read, content to be in her company. He parted his lips, taking a shallow breath, and tasted nothing. Not a hint of her emotions. Perhaps it was for the best. She already commanded too much of the Ra'Voshnik's attention. If it had her emotions to fixate on, he might never subdue it.

She turned her page, reading against him like he was a favorite chair. He was patient and would see her in the flesh soon enough. He ran the back of his fingers over her wing and was rewarded with her giggle.

"Stop that." She laughed; her wing snapped open, pushing his hand away before tucking it back into place.

Rune chuckled and resumed stroking her hair. The scene darkened and faded as sleep settled over Rune's mind.

A low roaring filled his ears as images that felt like memories floated through his mind. Rune sat with his back against something hard. He glanced at his surroundings, waiting for the puzzle pieces to arrange themselves.

Rune recognized his bed, but this wasn't his room. He was in the center of a circular hollow the size of a large room. The Darkness surrounding him, a mass of swirling dark mist making up the walls of this place. The mist constantly churned, curling and twisting onto itself. Tendrils curled through the swirling fog, edged in a sharp glowing purple.

Fine white sand covered the ground in this strange place. Next to him, his night breeze stirred, rustling his sheets. She slept in a plain white nightgown tucked under his sheets. Her dark hair fanned over her pillow.

At first glance, Rune thought he dreamt of Sadi, the Familiar King's daughter. While their similarities were uncanny, they also possessed glaring differences. His night breeze had wings, while Sadi did not.

The twinge he'd felt in his chest earlier in the night eased as he gazed at the woman sleeping beside him. Her presence comforted him. Easing down, Rune lied on his side, watching her.

She blinked after a few moments, gazing back at him. "Hi."

He'd never seen eyes like hers. Midnight streaked with gold, framed by thick black lashes. Her high cheekbones tapered to her narrow chin.

"Evening."

Her full dark lips turned up in a lazy smile as her sharp nails grazed over his side. She was gentle, careful not to break his skin, but her nails felt more like claws.

She scooted closer to him, ducking her head under his chin and muttered, "You smell nice."

Rune didn't have time to ponder her words as she curled up to him. Her lips pressed to the base of his throat, and Rune froze. He spoke several languages but couldn't think of a single word.

She began to fade along with his surroundings, dissipating to reveal the gray stone walls of his room. Rune sat up to find himself in his room. Rested from a night's sleep.

Alone.

Acknowledgments

To my wonderful Muses: Phyllica and Kellbell. You mean more to me than I could ever express.

To @bookodinnyc: I can't thank you enough for beta reading. Your thoughts and reactions helped me shape Astrid and Dimitri's story. Soul Obsession would have taken so much longer without you.

To my Chaos Demon: I worship the very ground you walk on, Holy Father.

To the Raven King: Thank you for answering every intrusive thought Astrid and Dimitri had.

To my wildly talented narrators Corvin King and Autumn Ivy: Thank you for adding dimension and life into my words with your exceptional vocal talents. I can't wait for our next project.

To Erin, Angie, Rainer and the entire crew at Barnes & Noble Tempe Market Place - Tempe, AZ: You will always be my second home and I adore the ground you walk on. I could not ask for a better partnership and look forward to the years to come – your stray cat author.

To Allison Buehner with Golden Editorial: I cannot express my gratitude for the care you've shown to Astrid and Dimitri's story. Your ability to layer in nuance, emotional turmoil, and the polish you bring to my words without changing my voice is astounding. I appreciate your absolute mastery of our craft and can't wait for our next project.

To Brandi: Thanks for beta reading, you fucking cunt. lol. Ilysm.

To J.R.Hermes: Thank you for the Russian translations and recordings for my narrators.

To my readers: You are the reason I get to live my wildest stray cat author dreams. All my love from the bottom of my black heart.

And finally to my war horse: I would not be able to build this castle of my dreams without the foundation of your heart. Til death, baby.

About the Author

Kalista Neith
Where enemies go to fall in love...

Kalista Neith is an Amazon and Barnes & Noble best-selling dark fantasy romance author. She lives in the Phoenix area with her partner and several four-legged creatures. When she's not wrapping plot and filth in gorgeous art, Kalista can typically be found gazing at Sesshomaru art, or playing her favorite games.

Kalista Neith can be found online at:

www.KalistaNeith.com

www.Linktr.ee/KalistaNeith

www.patreon.com/Kalista_Neith